THE STORIES
THAT SHOULD HAVE WON!

In 1960, "The Lost Kafoozalum": To prevent war on the planet Incognita, a group of students attempts to intercept a spaceship which crashed 300 years ago. . . .

In 1963, "Stand-by": Unicephalon 40-D had taken over the mammoth job of governing the United States with a human standing by in the unlikely event of malfunction. But now a hostile flotilla has penetrated the Sol System, knocked out Unicephalon and a union drone has the most powerful position in history. . . .

In 1964, "Now Is Forever": In an age when the Reprostat supplies everything that one can need, a bank president and some wild-eyed teenagers find a new way of chasing thrills. . . .

These Outstanding Stories Represent the Best in the Extensive Field of Science Fiction. Hand-picked by Richard A. Lupoff, They Will Astound and Delight You—and Make You Wonder . . .

What If?

D0038780

Books edited by Richard A. Lupoff

What If? Volume 1
What If? Volume 2

Forthcoming

What If? Volume 3
What If? Volume 4

Published by POCKET BOOKS

WHAT IF?

IF

Volume
2

Stories
That Should
Have Won
the Hugo

Edited by
Richard A. Lupoff

PUBLISHED BY POCKET BOOKS NEW YORK

Another *Original* publication of POCKET BOOKS

POCKET BOOKS, a Simon & Schuster division of
GULF & WESTERN CORPORATION
1230 Avenue of the Americas, New York, N.Y. 10020

ISBN: 0-671-83190-9

First Pocket Books printing February, 1981

10 9 8 7 6 5 4 3 2 1

POCKET and colophon are trademarks of Simon & Schuster.

Printed in the U.S.A.

Acknowledgments

"The Pi Man" by Alfred Bester copyright © 1959 by Fantasy House,
Inc. Originally published in *The Magazine of Fantasy and Science
Fiction* for October 1959. Reprinted by permission of the author
and his agent, Kirby McCauley, Ltd.
"The Lost Kafoozalum" by Pauline Ashwell copyright © 1960 by
Street & Smith Publications. Originally published in *Analog Science
Fact & Fiction* for October 1960. Reprinted by permission of the
author.
"The Sources of the Nile" by Avram Davidson copyright © 1960
by Mercury Press, Inc. Originally published in *The Magazine of
Fantasy and Science Fiction* for January 1961. Reprinted by per-
mission of the author and the author's agent, Kirby McCauley, Ltd.
"Where Is the Bird of Fire?" by Thomas Burnett Swann copyright
© 1962 by Nova Publications, Ltd. Originally published in *Science-
Fantasy* for April 1962. Reprinted by permission of the author's estate.
"Stand-by" by Philip K. Dick copyright © 1963 by Ziff-Davis Pub-
lishing Company. Originally published in *Amazing Stories* for
October 1963. Reprinted by permission of the author and the
author's agents, Scott Meredith Literary Agency, Inc., 845 Third
Avenue, New York, N.Y. 10022.
"Now Is Forever" by Thomas M. Disch copyright © 1964 by Ziff-
Davis Publishing Company. Originally published in *Amazing Stories*
for March 1964. Reprinted by permission of the author.
"All the King's Men" by Barrington J. Bayley copyright © 1965.
Originally published in *New Worlds* for March 1965. Reprinted by
permission of the author and the author's agents, Scott Meredith
Literary Agency, Inc., 845 Third Avenue, New York, N.Y. 10022.

Contents

My Aunt Cora

AN INTRODUCTION BY
RICHARD A. LUPOFF

ALL RIGHT, so I've got a few silver hairs in my head (that's better than none at all!), and when I attend a science fiction convention I can't party all night, shower-and-change, and arrive, fresh as a daisy, for a panel discussion at nine o'clock the next morning. Twenty or thirty years ago I could. Today I can't.

But I'm not old enough to remember the events of 1903. I'm not *that* old.

My Aunt Cora is.

Cora, bless her ancient heart, was born in Dayton, Ohio, during the presidency of Benjamin Harrison, and has lived in that city ever since. As a child she was a precocious and an omnivorous reader, but her favorite reading matter was what we would call, today, *science fiction*. The term didn't exist back then—Hugo Gernsback invented it in 1929. But Cora had the heart of a devoted fan.

Her favorite authors were H. Rider Haggard, H. G. Wells, William H. Rhodes, Garrett P. Serviss, and in later years Edgar Rice Burroughs.

When I was a child in the 1940s I was sent, several times, to spend summer vacations in Dayton. My Aunt Cora would take me to hear band concerts in the park (and isn't *that* a piece of sadly lost Americana!), and on such occasions she would tell me of being taken to hear

7

just such concerts in her own childhood, nearly forty years earlier.

One of her most vivid memories, she told me, dated from the Sunday afternoon she had sat half-listening to the band while she devoured her brand-new, red-covered copy of *A Trip to Mars* by Fenton Ash. She still had her copy of the book, and showed it to me in, I believe, 1943. I read it and loved it and it was one of the first science fiction books I ever read.

She still has it, I believe.

She also showed me a torn and yellowed copy of the Dayton *Evening Herald* for Friday, December 18, 1903. Price, one cent. The *Herald* featured a somewhat sensationalistic four-deck headline, as follows:

DAYTON BOYS
FLY AIRSHIP

Machine Makes High Speed in the
Teeth of a Gale and Lands at
the Point Selected.

PROBLEM OF AERIAL NAVIGATION SOLVED
Ascent Made at Isolated Spot on Caro-
lina Coast, Where Wrights Experimented
for Three Years.

My Aunt Cora told me that when that headline appeared, her mother took her firmly by the hand and shook the *Herald* under her nose and said, approximately, "Now that men can fly in machines, I guess them crazy writers kin stop their nonsense and start writing about some sensible things for a change. And *you* can do something useful with yourself instead of sticking your nose in books all the time reading!"

If all of this seems strangely familiar, it *should*. The little scene was the prototype of one that has been replayed ever since, with "the death of science fiction" the predicted outcome each time. Happily, those predictions have proved consistently inaccurate, although there has been a surprising dip in the popularity of science fiction following a number of spectacular advances in science or technology in our century.

Certainly the year 1927 was an important one for technology. Transoceanic telephone service was initiated, the first successful television transmission took place (featuring Secretary of Commerce Herbert Hoover, live-from-Washington, D.C.), and Charles Lindbergh's famous flight in the *Spirit of St. Louis* created a world-wide aviation mania. I should also mention, at least in passing, the release of *The Jazz Singer,* opening the era of talking motion pictures.

Before long the fledgling science fiction industry (Gernsback had founded *Amazing Stories* in 1926) was on the rocks. Gernsback was in bankruptcy court and *Amazing* was in the hands of receivers. And this took place well *before* the infamous Crash of '29, so it can't be blamed on the Great Depression!

Science fiction was shaken again by the spectacular events of 1945 and '46: the explosion of the first atomic bombs and the successful testing of ENIAC, the world's first all-electronic computer.

We recovered both times.

In '29, Gernsback bounced back with a new string of magazines headed by *Science Wonder Stories;* a year later *Astounding* was founded with Harry Bates as its editor, and the ball game was really on! In the late 1940s and early '50s, a whole span of new science fiction magazines appeared, among them *F&SF, Galaxy, Fantastic Universe* and *Other Worlds.*

The next grossly exaggerated "death" of science fiction came in the late 1950s and early '60. Let's look at some chronology:

October 4, 1957: Soviet Union fires *Sputnik I* into space. It orbits earth successfully at a speed of 18,000 miles per hour.

November 3, 1957: Soviets orbit *Sputnik II* weighing 1,120 pounds. On board is Laika the dog, first known space traveler (and first space casualty—*Sputnik II* had no return mechanism).

January 2, 1959: *Lunik I,* weighing over 3,000 pounds, passes within approximately 2,000 miles of the moon.

September 12, 1959: *Lunik II,* weighing 858 pounds, impacts on moon—first known lunar "landing."

October 4, 1959: *Lunik III* circles moon and returns first photographs of "dark" side to earth.

April 12, 1961: *Vostok I,* carrying test-pilot Yuri Gagarin, successfully orbits earth and soft-lands upon return. Gagarin becomes the "first spaceman" in history.

Now you may have noticed a few things about this series of events. For one thing, they mark humanity's first wobbly steps into space, the realization of the dreams of every science fiction enthusiast of the past century or longer. (And certainly of my Aunt Cora.) For another, and without meaning to become excessively political about the matter, they were *all* achieved by the Soviet Union. The western world, the United States in particular, was forced to play catch-up ball, and the fact that we did, ultimately, win the contest to land safely on the moon seems to have been more of a blip on the screen of history than it was evidence of a long-term commitment on our part.

And thirdly, and of immediate interest to us, the period 1957-1961, which these events bracket, centers on the opening year of the period covered in this second volume of *What If?—Stories That Should Have Won the Hugo.*

Yes, in those days we were hearing the same old refrain. "Well, science has finally outstripped science fiction. Satellites in space. Spaceships to the moon. People traveling in space. What will the science fiction writers have left to write about? This is the end of science fiction!"

Of course it was *not* the end of science fiction. No more than was Armstrong, Aldrin and Collins' historic trip to the moon a decade later. And no more than the cloning, cyborging, gene-splicing, interplanetary probes, fusion-power experiments, superminiaturized computers and other advances of the 1980s spell the death of science fiction, now.

What the literary doom-criers simply fail to realize is this:

Each new advance of science does not *close* possible areas of exploration. Each advance *opens* new areas of exploration. I mean this in terms of scientific exploration, out there in the physical universe. I mean it equally in terms of the imagination, the conceptual exploration of possibilities and implications here in the literary universe.

Quasars, pulsars, black holes, quarks, tachyons, clones, recombinant DNA chains, gravity waves . . . These are just a handful of the topics that science fiction writers will be exploring over the next decade. These, and I'm sure a hundred more concepts that are unknown in 1980, will be introduced and will be startling by 1985, and will be commonplace by 1990.

And in *that* decade new concepts will flower forth that are utterly undreamable here at the start of the 1980s.

For science is itself an ongoing and endless process of exploration, conceptualization, experimentation; and as long as science continues to explore new realms and concepts, science fiction will have new nourishment. We should never forget that science is the great and inexhaustible wellspring of ideas for science fiction. When I was a fan I heard science fiction writers asked, uncounted times, "Where do you get your ideas?" (Of course, the very question has become a kind of running joke.)

The answer that I heard most often, especially from the *good* writers, was, "The journals. The scientific periodicals."

And in the fifteen years that I have been writing science fiction, I have found that answer to be absolutely true. Reading in the sciences, whether something as "soft" as sociology or psychology, or as "hard" as physics or math, is the best way to "get" ideas for science fiction stories.

I don't mean just so-called "hard science" stories either, although there has always been an audience for "hard science" stories and I expect there always will be. But even the "literary" science fiction writers—all the way from Wells to Bradbury to Delany to Ursula LeGuin to Gene Wolfe—have gone to the sciences for the solid underpinning of their stories, however much their literary focus has been on the humanistic implications of scientific advancement rather than on science itself.

The "hard science" ideas will pass through the hands of writers like Charles Sheffield, Robert Forward, James P. Hogan—and will be assimilated into the works of "softer" (*i.e.*, more humanistic) writers.

Science fiction dying?

Bosh!

Science fiction is just beginning to live.

If you don't believe me, just ask my Aunt Cora in Dayton.

—RICHARD A. LUPOFF

11

1959

BY 1959 THE World Science Fiction Convention had finally laid to rest the problem of defining a year. It had taken the better part of a decade to do it, and when it was finally worked out the solution was based on elementary common sense: "last year" means precisely that, *last year*. Thus, the 1959 convention awarded Hugos for stories published in 1958. Thus, for the 1960 World Convention, the Hugos to be awarded were for stories published in 1959.

It seems amazingly obvious, doesn't it? I guess you just had to be there to see how much struggle it took.

The category problem stayed around for a long time after the year problem was resolved. Basically, it amounts to this: a good long story will whip a good short story almost every time. The author simply has more room in which to develop characters, build up background, draw the reader's mind into the created reality of the work. It's the old story of the sledgehammer versus the tackhammer: the tackhammer can deliver a good sharp blow to a point target but it simply can't compare for heavy-duty wallop.

The first Hugos, following the pattern of the old International Fantasy Awards, had been for book-length works only. That avoided the unfair competition of setting a short story against a novel, but it did so by ruling the short story out of competition *prima facie*. That wasn't very fair either and it drew a *lot* of fire in the science fiction field, where the short story has always been a highly favored form.

So conventions started giving awards in categories by length. Some years the categories were *novel* and *short fiction*. Sometimes they were *novel, novelette* and *short story*. Or *novel* and *novelette-or-short-story*. The first time

12

around, in that weird, double set of awards for 1958,* the committee set up the unique arrangement of *novelette-or-novel* and *short story*.

(Not surprisingly, the *novel-or-novelette* Hugo was won by a serial, *The Big Time*, by Fritz Leiber. Good long story whup a good short story 'most every time.)

The 1960 convention, held in Pittsburgh, went back to *best novel, best short fiction*.

The winning novel was *Starship Troopers* by Heinlein, topping *Dorsai!* by Gordon R. Dickson, *The Pirates of Ersatz* by Murray Leinster, *That Sweet Little Old Lady* by "Mark Phillips" (Randall Garrett and Larry M. Harris), and *The Sirens of Titan* by Kurt Vonnegut.

Not a bad spread of nominees, ranging from amusing light reading to quite excellent work. The Heinlein was a fine, bang-up adventure novel despite certain political overtones that drew objections from a number of quarters. And in all honesty, the Heinlein *was* a better book than the Dickson, the Leinster or the Phillips.

But—better than *The Sirens of Titan?*

A violent dispute broke out over *The Sirens of Titan* in one of the prominent fan journals of the time. Bob Tucker the fan (who is also Wilson Tucker the author) liked the book very much. Another prominent fan of the day (and later a worthy professional writer and editor himself, so I won't embarrass him by mentioning his name) attacked the book violently. A travesty, a disgrace, an insult to science fiction!

How could this intelligent and perceptive man be so far off?

Well, he was young, his reading experience was heavily tilted toward traditional science fiction, and he read *The Sirens of Titan* as a traditional science fiction novel. Seen in that context, of course, it was—and is—a very poor book. If the fan had recognized the satirical content and the stylistic individuality of Vonnegut, he would surely have thought more highly of the book.

But I think this fellow's reaction—let's call him Fan X—I think Fan X's reaction to the book was fairly common among the science-fiction-reading, Hugo-ballot-casting population.

Still, to paraphrase Dr. Johnson, it is more remarkable

---

* See *What If?—Stories That Should Have Won the Hugo*, Volume I.

13

that *The Sirens of Titan* got onto the Hugo ballot at all than it is that it fared poorly once there. Especially against Heinlein.

In the *best short fiction* category, the nominees were works by Philip Jose Farmer, Ralph Williams, Daniel Keyes, Theodore Sturgeon, and Alfred Bester. Chances are, you know all those authors except Ralph Williams.

Who was this person?

First of all, not to be confused with Robert Moore Williams, the prolific individual who turned out literally hundreds of pieces in the 1930s, '40s, '50s and '60s.

Ralph Williams was a commercial fisherman from the Pacific Northwest. He also loved science fiction. He turned up with a short story, "The Head Hunters," in *Astounding* for October 1951. Over the next few years he published a total of eleven stories in *Astounding, If, Fantastic Universe* and a little horror-fantasy magazine called *Tales of the Frightened*.

One day he took his fishing boat out in squally weather. No one knows the details of what followed, and no body was ever recovered, but Williams never returned to port.

"Cat and Mouse" (*Astounding,* June 1950) was his final story and sole award nominee.

It was a fine story, but it fell among very strong contenders. The winner was Daniel Keyes' classic "Flowers for Algernon." That story went on, in expanded form, to win a Nebula for best novel, a Hugo nomination for best novel (beaten by another Heinlein) and to become a highly successful television production and motion picture.

It was a novelette in its original incarnation and (good long story whup a good short story 'most every time) it easily topped all the others, including Alfred Bester's admirable "The Pi Man."

I'm really glad that "Flowers for Algernon" won its Hugo. It is a story of power, of beauty and of amazing sensitivity.

But I wish there had been a separate category for short stories, because I think it *was* a case of unfair competition. I think "The Pi Man" deserved a Hugo, too.

As for Alfred Bester—here is the proverbial mystery wrapped in an enigma wrapped in a puzzle. Bester has had several careers as a science fiction writer interspersed with other careers writing for radio and television, for slick travel magazines and other posh journals and even for off-the-wall outlets like comic books.

His *first* career as a science fiction writer, back in the late 1930s and early '40s, produced works like the classic "Adam and No Eve."

Next time around, in the 1950s, Bester blew us all away with *The Demolished Man* and *The Stars My Destination*. The same era yielded astonishing stories like "Fondly Fahrenheit," "The Men Who Murdered Mohammed," "Time Is the Traitor," "5,271,009" and "The Pi Man."

Then he went away again and came back again with *The Computer Connection* in 1975. And then he went away still again and came back to open the 1980s with *Golem*[100].

How many Alfie Besters are there? Which of the many incarnations of this man represents the *real* Alfred Bester? Nobody knows for sure (except maybe Bester himself, and he isn't telling), but I think that "The Pi Man" gives us a good, if elliptical, clue!

(Some years later, Bester rewrote "The Pi Man," and the revised version was used in a volume of his collected fiction. Bester stated recently that both versions were acceptable to him, and agreed that—for historical purposes—the original version of the story was suitable for the present anthology.)

The Pi Man

ALFRED BESTER

How to say? How to write? When sometimes I can be
fluent, even polished, and then, *reculer pour mieux sauter,*
it takes hold of me. Push. Force. Compel. Sometimes

I
must
go
back
but
not
to

jump; no, not even to jump better. I have no control over
self, speech, love, fate. I must compensate. Always.

But I try anyway.

Quae nocent docent. Translation follows: Things that
injure, teach. I am injured and have hurt many. What have
we learned? However. I wake up the morning of the biggest hurt of all wondering which house. Wealth, you understand. Damme! Mews cottage in London, villa in Rome,
penthouse in New York, rancho in California. I awake. I
look. Ah! Layout is familiar. Thus:

```
        Bedroom          Foyer
                                      T
              Bath
                                      e
              Bath
                                      r
                  Living Room
                                      r
              Bedroom
                                      a
              Kitchen
                                      c
          T e r r a c e
                                      e
```

Oh-oh! I am in penthouse in New York; but that bath-bath back-to-back. Pfui. All rhythm wrong. Balance off. Pattern painful. I telephone downstairs to janitor-mans. At that moment I lose my English. (You must understand I speak in all tongues. A goulash. I am compelled. Why? Ah!)

"Pronto. Ecco mi, Signore Storm. No. Forced to *parlato Italiano.* Wait. I call back in *cinque minuti."*

Re infecta. Latin. The business being unfinished, I shower body, teeth, hairs, shave face, dry everything and try again. *Voilà!* The English, she come. Back to invention of A. G. Bell ("Mr. Watson, come here, I need you"). On telephone I speak to janitor. Nice chap. Gets a job of work done in two twos.

"Hallo? Abraham Storm here, again. Yes. Right. Chap in the penthouse. Mr. Lundgren, be my personal rabbi and get some workmen up here this morning. I want those two baths converted into one. Yes. I'll leave five thousand dollars on top of the refrigerator. Thanks, Mr. Lundgren."

Wanted to wear gray flannel this morning, but had to put on the sharkskin. Damnation! African nationalism has queer side-effects. Went to the back bedroom (see diagram) and unlocked the door which was installed by National Safe Co., Inc., I went in.

Everything broadcasting beautifully. Up and down the electromagnetic spectrum. Visual off from ultraviolet and jamming toward the infrared. Ultra shortwave screaming. Alpha, beta, and gamma radiation hearty. And the interruptors innn tt errrrr up ppp tttinggggg at random and

17

comfortably. I am at peace. Christ Jesus! To know even a moment of peace!

I take subway to office in Wall Street. Chauffeur too dangerous; might become friendly. I don't dare have friends. Best of all, morning subway jam-packed, mass-packed; no patterns to adjust, no shiftings and compensatings required. Peace! I buy all morning papers; because of the patterns, you understand. Too many *Timeses* being read; I must read *Tribune* to balance pattern. Too many *Newses;* I read *Mirror*. Etc.

In subway car I catch a glimpse of an eye; narrow, bleak, gray-blue, the possession of an anonymous man who conveys the conviction that you've never seen him before and will never again. But I picked up that glance and it rang a bell in the back of my mind. He knew it. He saw the flash in my eye before I could conceal it. So I was being tailed again? But by whom? U.S.A.? U.S.S.R.? Matoids?

I blasted out of the subway at City Hall and gave them a false trail to the Woolworth Building, in case they were operating double-tails. The whole theory of the hunters and the hunted is not to avoid being spotted . . . no one can escape that . . . but to lay so many trails for them to follow that they become overextended. Then they're forced to abandon you. They have so many men for so many operations. It's a question of diminishing returns.

City Hall traffic was out of sync (as it always is) and I had to walk on the hot side of the street to compensate. Took elevator up to tenth floor of bldg. There I was suddenly seized by something from sss ome wwwhh ere, SS ommme tth inggg b addd. I began to cry, but no help. An elderly clerk emerge from the office wearing alpaca coat, carry papers, gold spectacles.

"Not him," I plead with nowhere. "Nice mans. Not him. Please."

But I am force. Approach. Two blows; neck and gut. Down he go, writhing. I trample spectacles. Remove watch from pocket and smash. Shatter pens. Tear papers. Then I am permitted to get back into elevator and go downstairs again. It was 10:30. I was late. Damned inconvenient. Took taxi to 99 Wall Street. Tipped driver ten dollars. Sealed one thousand in envelope (secretly) and sent driver back to bldg to find and give to clerk.

Routine morning's work in office. Market jumpy; big board hectic; hell to balance and compensate, even though

18

I know the patterns of money. I am behind by the sum of $109,872.43 by eleven-thirty; but, *à pas de géant* the patterns put me ahead $57,075.94 by half-past 12:00 noon, Daylight Saving Time, which my father used to call Woodrow Wilson Time.

57075 makes a nice pattern, but that 94¢. Pfui. Made the whole balance sheet look lopsided, ugly. Symmetry above all else. Only 24¢ in my pocket. Called secretary, borrowed 70¢ from her and threw sum total out window. Felt better as I watched it chime down to the street, but then I caught her looking at me with surprise and delight. Very bad. Very dangerous. Fired girl on the spot.

"But why, Mr. Storm? Why?" she asked, trying not to cry. Darling little thing. Freckled face and saucy, but not so saucy now.

"Because you're beginning to like me."

"What's the harm in that?"

"When I hired you I warned you not to like me."

"I thought you were kidding."

"I wasn't. Out you go. Beat it."

"But why?"

"I'm afraid I might start liking you."

"Is this a new kind of pass?" she asked.

"God forbid."

"Well, you don't have to fire me," she flared. "I hate you."

"Good. Then I can go to bed with you."

She turned crimson and opened her mouth to denounce me, the while her eyes twinkled at the corners. A darling girl. I could not endanger her. I put her into her hat and coat, gave her a year's salary for a bonus, and threw her out. *Punkt*. Made memo: Hire nothing but men, preferably married, misanthropic, and murderous. Men who could hate me.

So, lunch. Went to nicely balanced restaurant. Tables attached to floor. No moving them. All chairs filled by patrons. Nice pattern. No need for me to compensate and adjust. Ordered nicely patterned luncheon for self:

Martini   Martini
Martini
Croque M'sieur Roquefort
Salad
Coffee

But so much sugar being consumed in restaurant, I had to take my coffee black, which I dislike. However, still a nice pattern. Balanced.

$X^2 + X + 41 =$ prime number. Excuse, please. Sometimes I'm in control and see what compensating must be done. Other times it's forced on me from God only knows where or why. Then I must do what I'm compelled to do, blindly, like speaking the gibberish I speak; sometimes hating it, like the clerk in the Woolworth Building. Anyway, the equation breaks down when $x=40$.

The afternoon was quiet. For a moment I thought I might be forced to leave for Rome (Italy), but something adjusted without needing me. The A.S.P.C.A. finally caught up with me for beating my dog to death, but I'd contributed $10,000 to their Shelter. Got off with a shaking of heads. I penciled moustaches on posters, rescued a drowning kitten, saved a woman from a mugging, and had my head shaved. Normal day.

In the evening to the ballet to relax with all the beautiful patterns, balanced, peaceful, soothing. Then I take deep breath, quash my nausea, and force myself to go to *Le Bitnique,* the beatnik joint. I hate *Le Bitnique,* but I need a woman and I must go where I hate. That freckled girl I fire . . . so slender and full of delicious mischief, and making eyes at me. *So, poisson d'avril,* I advance myself to *Le Bitnique.*

Chaos. Blackness. Sounds and smells a cacophony. One twenty-five watt bulb in ceiling. One maladroit pianist play Progressive. Against L. wall sit beatnik boys, wearing berets, black glasses, and pubic beards, playing chess. Against R. wall is bar and beatnik girls with brown paper bags under arms containing toilet articles. They are shuffling and maneuvering for a pad for the night.

Those beatnik girls! All skinny . . . exciting to me tonight because too many American men dream about overstuffed women, and I must compensate. (In England I like overstuff because England like women skinny.) All wear tight slack, loose sweater, Brigitte Bardot hair, Italian make-up . . . black eye, white lip . . . and when they walk they make with the gait that flipped that Herrick cat three centuries ago when he split and wrote:

> *Next, when I lift mine eyes and see*
> *That brave vibration each way free;*
> *Oh how that glittering taketh me!*

I pick one who glitter. I talk. She insult. I insult back and buy drinks. She drink and insult.[2] I hope she is lesbian and insult.[3] She snarl and hate, but helpless. No pad for tonight. The pathetic brown paper bag under her arm. I quell sympathy and hate back. She does not bathe. Her thinking patterns are jangles. Safe. No harm can come to her. I take her home to seduce by mutual contempt. And in living room (see diagram) sits slender little freckly-face secretary, recently fired, now waiting for me.

```
          !
          I
        now
       write
      part of
   s              P
   t              a
   o              r
   r              i
   y      in      s
     Capital of France
```

Address: 49 bis Avenue Hoche. Paris, 8ème, France.

Forced to go there by what happened in Singapore, you understand. It needed extreme compensation and adjustment. Almost, for a moment, I thought I would have to attack the conductor of the *Opéra Comique,* but fate was kind and let me off with nothing worse than indecent exposure under the *Petite Carousel.* And I was able to found a scholarship at the Sorbonne before I was taken away.

Anyway, she sat there, my little one, in my penthouse now with one (1) bathroom, and $1,997.00 change on top of the refrigerator. Ugh! Throw $6.00 out window and am soothed by lovely 1991 remaining. She sat there, wearing a basic black cocktail dress with tight skirt, sheer black stockings, black opera pumps. The freckly skin gleamed reddish rose from embarrassment. Also red for danger. Her saucy face was very tight from the daring thing she thought she was doing. Damme! I like that.

I also like the nice even curve of the legs, and the bosom. Balanced, you understand? * * Like so; but not too thrusting. Tactful. Also her cleavage. Like so; and just as rosy as her face, despite desperate powdering to make

21

her skin milky. That powder; a nuisance. I go to kitchen and rub burnt cork on shirt-front to compensate.

"Oh-so," I say. "Me-fella be ve'y happy ask why you-fella chop-chop invade along my apa'tment. Excep' mus' now speak pidgin-English. Ve'y much embarrass along me. Excuse please, until change come."

"I bribed Mr. Lundgren," she blurted. "I told him you needed important papers from your office."

"*Entschuldigen Sie, bitte. Meine pidgin haben sich geaendert. Sprachen Sie Deutsch?*"

"No."

"*Dann warte ich.*"

The beatnik turned on her heel and bounced out, her brave vibration each way free. I caught up with her in front of the elevator, put 101 (perfect pattern) into her hand and said good night in Spanish. She hated me. I did a naughty thing to her * * (no excuse) and returned to the apartment when my American-English returned to me.

"What's she got?" the Freckle ask.

"What's your name?" I indict.

"My God! I've been working in your office for three months. You don't know my name? You really don't?"

"No, and I don't want to know it now."

"I'm Lizzie Chalmers."

"Go away, Lizzie Chalmers."

"So that's why you always called me 'Miss'. Why did you shave your head?"

"Trouble in Vienna."

"It's chic," she said judgmatically, "but I don't know. You remind me of a movie star I loathe. What do you mean, trouble in Vienna?"

"None of your business. What are you doing here? What do you want from me?"

"You," she said, blushing fiery.

"Will you, for God's sake, go away!"

"What did she have that I don't?" Lizzie Chalmers demanded. Then her face crinkled. "Don't? Is that right? What. Did. She. Have. That. I. Do. Not. Yes, right. I'm going to Bennington. They're strong on aggression, but weak on grammar."

"What do you mean, you're going to Bennington?"

"Why, it's a college. I thought everybody knew."

"But *going?*"

22

"I'm in my junior year. They drive you out with whips to acquire practical experience in your field."

"What's your field?"

"It used to be economics. Now it's you. How old are you?"

"One hundred and nine thousand eight hundred and seventy-two."

"Oh, come on! Forty?"

"Thirty."

"No! Really?" She nodded contentedly. "That makes ten years difference between us. Just right."

"Are you in love with me, Lizzie?"

"Well, I'm trying to get something going."

"Does it have to be me?"

"I know it sounds like a notion." She lowered her eyes. "And I suppose women are always throwing themselves at you."

"Not always."

"What are you, blasé, or something? I mean . . . I know I'm not staggering, but I'm not exactly repulsive."

"You're lovely."

"Then why don't you touch me?"

"I'm trying to protect you."

"I can protect myself when the time comes."

"The time is now, Lizzie."

"The least you could do is offend me the way you did that girl in front of the elevator."

"You snooped?"

"Sure I snooped. You didn't expect me to sit here on my hands, did you? I've got my man to take care of."

"*Your* man?"

"It happens," she said in a low voice. "I never believed it, but it happens. You fall in and out of love, and each time you think it's for real and forever. And then you meet somebody and it isn't a question of love any more. You just know he's your man, and you're stuck. I'm stuck."

She raised her eyes and looked at me . . . violet eyes, full of youth and determination and tenderness, and yet older than twenty years . . . much older. And I knew how lonely I was, never daring to love, always compelled to live with those I hated. I could fall into those violet eyes and never come up.

"I'm going to shock you," I said. I looked at the clock. 1:30 A.M. A quiet time. Please God the American tongue would stay with me a while longer. I took off my jacket

23

and shirt and showed her my back, cross-hatched with scars. Lizzie gasped.

"Self-inflicted," I told her. "Because I permitted myself to like a man and become friendly with him. This is the price I paid, and I was lucky. Now wait here."

I went into the master bedroom where my heart's shame was embalmed in a silver case hidden in the right-hand drawer of my desk. I brought it to the living room. Lizzie watched me with great eyes.

"Five years ago a girl fell in love with me," I told her. "A girl like you. I was lonely then, as always. Instead of protecting her from myself, I indulged myself. Now I want to show you the price *she* paid. You'll loathe me for this but I must show you . . ."

A flash caught my eye. Lights in a building down the street going on. I leaped to the window and stared. The lights in the building three down from me went off . . . five seconds eclipse . . . then on. It happened to the building two down, and then to the one next door. The girl came to my side and took my arm. She trembled slightly.

"What is it?" she asked. "What's the matter?"

"Wait," I said.

The lights in my apartment went out for five seconds and then came on again.

"They've located me," I told her.

"They? Located?"

"They've spotted my broadcasts by d/f."

"What's d/f?"

"Direction-finder. Then they turned off the current in each building in the neighborhood for five seconds . . . building by building . . . until the broadcast stopped. Now they know I'm in this house, but they don't know which apartment." I put on my shirt and jacket. "Good night, Lizzie. I wish I could kiss you."

She clamped her arms around my neck and gave me a smacking kiss; all warmth, all velvet, all giving. I tried to push her away.

"You're a spy," she said. "I'll go to the chair with you."

"I wish to Heaven I were a spy," I said. "Goodbye, my dearest love. Remember me."

Soyez ferme. A great mistake letting that slip. It happen, I think, because my American slip, too. Suddenly talk jumble again. As I run out, the little devil kick off opera pumps and rip slit in cocktail skirt up to thigh so she can run. She is alongside me going down the fire stairs to the

24

garage in basement. I hit her to stop, and swear at her. She hit back and swear worse, all the time laughing and crying. I love her for it. Damnation! She is doomed.

We get into car, Aston-Martin, but with left-hand drive, and speed west on Fifty-third Street, east on Fifty-fourth Street, and north on First Avenue. I am making for Fifty-ninth Street bridge to get off Manhattan island. I own plane in Babylon, Long Island, which is always ready for this sort of awkwardness.

"*J'y suis, J'y reste* is not my motto," I tell Elizabeth Chalmers. Whose French is as uncertain as her grammar . . . an endearing weakness. "Once they trapped me in London at post office. I received mail at General Delivery. They sent me a blank letter in a red envelope, and that's how they followed me to 139 Piccadilly, London W.1. Telephone Mayfair 7211. Red for danger. Is your skin red all over?"

"It's not red!" she said indignantly.

"I mean rosy."

"Only where the freckles merge," she said. "What is all this escape? Why do you talk so funny, and act so peculiar? Are you sure you're not a spy?"

"Only positive."

"Are you a being from another world who came on an Unidentified Flying Object?"

"Would that horrify you?"

"Yes, if it meant we couldn't make love."

"What about conquering earth?"

"I'm only interested in conquering you."

"I am not and have never been a being from another world who came on an Unidentified Flying Object."

"Then what are you?"

"A compensator."

"What's that?"

"Do you know dictionary of Misters Funk & Wagnalls? Edited by Frank H. Vizetelly, Litt.D., LL.D.? I quote: One who or that which compensates, as a device for neutralizing the influence of local attraction upon a compass-needle or an automatic apparatus for equalizing the pressure of gas in the—Damn!"

Litt.D. Frank H. Vizetelly does not use that bad word. Is my own because roadblock now faces me on Fifty-ninth Street bridge. Should have anticipated. Should have felt patterns, but too swept up with this darling girl. Probably there are roadblocks on all bridges and tunnels

25

leading out of this $24.00 island. Could drive off bridge but might harm my angelic Elizabeth Chalmers which would make me a *brute figura* as well as sadden me beyond redemption. So. Stop car. Surrender.

"Kammerade," I pronounce, and ask: "Who you? Ku Klux Klan?"

Hard-faced mans say no.

"White Supremacists of the World, Inc.?"

No agains. I feel better. Always nasty when captured by lunatic fringes looking for figureheads.

"U.S.S.R.?"

He stare, then speak. "Special Agent Krimms from the FBI," and show his badge. I enthuse and embrace him in gratitude. FBI is salvation. He recoil and wonder if I am fairy. I don't care. I kiss Elizabeth Chalmers and she open mouth under mine to mutter: "Admit nothing: deny everything. I've got a lawyer."

Brilliant lights in the office in Foley Square. The chairs are placed just so; the shadows arranged just so. I have been through this so often before. The anonymous man with the bleak eyes from the subway this morning is questioning me. His name is S. I. Dolan. We exchange a glance. His says: I goofed this morning. Mine says: So did I. We respect each other, and then the grilling starts.

"Your name is Abraham Mason Storm?"

"The nickname is 'Base.' "

"Born December 25?"

"I was a Christmas baby."

"1929?"

"I was a Depression baby."

"You seem pretty jaunty."

"Gallows humor, S. I. Dolan. Despair. I know you'll never convict me of anything, and I'm desperate."

"Very funny."

"Very tragic. I want to be convicted . . . but it's hopeless."

"Hometown San Francisco?"

"Yes."

"Grand High School. Two years at Berkeley. Four years in the Navy. Finished at Berkeley. Majored in statistics."

"Yes. Hundred percent American boy."

"Present occupation, financier?"

"Yes."

"Offices in New York, Rome, Paris, London?"

"Also Rio."

26

"Known assets from bank deposits, stock and bond holdings, three million dollars?"

"No, no, no!" I was agonized. "Three million, three hundred and thirty-three thousand, three hundred and thirty-three dollars and thirty-three cents."

"Three million dollars," Dolan insisted. "In round numbers."

"There are no round numbers; there are only patterns."

"Storm, what the hell are you up to?"

"Convict me," I pleaded. "I want to go to the chair and get this over with."

"What are you talking about?"

"You ask and I'll explain."

"What are you broadcasting from your apartment?"

"Which apartment? I broadcast from all of them."

"In New York. We can't break the code."

"There is no code; only randomness."

"Only what?"

"Only peace, Dolan."

"Peace!"

"I've been through this so often before. In Geneva, Berlin, London, Rio. Will you let me explain it my own way, and for God's sake trap me if you can?"

"Go ahead."

I took a breath. It's always so difficult. You have to do it with metaphor. But it was 3:00 A.M. and my American would hold for a while. "Do you like to dance?"

"What the hell . . . ?"

"Be patient. I'm explaining. Do you like to dance?"

"Yes."

"What's the pleasure of dancing? It's a man and woman making rhythms together . . . patterns. Balancing, anticipating, following, leading, cooperating. Yes?"

"So?"

"And parades. Do you like parades? Masses of men and women cooperating to make patterns. Why is war a time of joy for a country, although nobody admits it? Because it's an entire people cooperating, balancing and sacrificing to make a big pattern. Yes?"

"Now wait a minute, Storm . . ."

"Just listen, Dolan. I'm sensitive to patterns . . . more than dancing or parades or war; far more. More than the 2/4 pattern of day and night, or the 4/4 pattern of the seasons . . . far, far more. I'm sensitive to the patterns of the whole spectrum of the universe . . . sight and sound, gamma rays, groupings of peoples, acts of hostility and benign charity, cruelties and kindnesses, the music of the spheres . . . and I'm forced to compensate. Always."

"Compensate?"

"Yes. If a child falls and hurts itself, the mother kisses it. Agreed? That's compensation. It restores a pattern. If a man beats a horse, you beat him. Yes? Pattern again. If a beggar wrings too much sympathy from you, you want to kick him, don't you? More compensation. The husband unfaithful to the wife is never more kind to her. All wives know the pattern, and dread it. What is sportsmanship but a compensating pattern to off-set the embarrassment of winning or losing? Do not the murderer and murderee seek each other to fulfill their patterns?

"Multiply that by infinity and you have me. I have to kiss and kick. I'm driven. Compelled. I don't know how to name my compulsion. They call Extra Sensory Perception, Psi. What do you call Extra Pattern Perception? Pi?"

"Pie? What pie?"

"Sixteenth letter of the Greek alphabet. It designates the relation of the circumference of a circle to its diameter. $3.14159+$. The series goes on endlessly. It is transcendental and can never be resolved into a finite pattern; and it's agony to me . . . like pi in printing, which means jumbled and confused type, without order or pattern."

"What the hell are you talking about?"

"I'm talking about patterns; order in the universe. I'm compelled to keep it and restore it. Sometimes I'm compelled to do wonderful and generous things; other times I'm forced to do insane things . . . talk garbage languages, go to stranges places, perform abominable acts . . . because patterns which I can't perceive demand adjustment."

"What abominable acts?"

"You can pry and I can confess, but it won't do any good. The patterns won't permit me to be convicted. They won't let me end. People refuse to testify. Facts will not give evidence. What is done becomes undone. Harm is transformed into good."

"Storm, I swear you're crazy."

"Maybe, but you won't be able to get me committed to an asylum. It's been tried before. I even tried committing myself. It didn't work."

"What about those broadcasts?"

"We're flooded with wave emissions, quanta, particles, and I'm sensitive to them, too; but they're too garbled to

28

shape into patterns. They have to be neutralized. So I broadcast an anti-pattern to jam them and get a little peace."

"Are you claiming to be a superman?"

"No. Never. I'm just the man *Simple Simon* met."

"Don't clown."

"I'm not clowning. Don't you remember the jingle? *Simple Simon met a pieman, going to the fair . . .* ? For Pee-eye-ee-man, read Pee-eye-man. I'm the Pi Man."

Dolan scowled. At last he said: "My full name is Simon Ignatius Dolan."

"I'm sorry. I didn't know. Nothing personal implied."

He glared at me, then threw my dossier down. He sighed and slumped into a chair. That made the pattern wrong and I had to shift. He cocked an eye at me.

"Pi Man," I explained.

"All right," he said. "We can't hold you."

"They all try," I said, "but they never can."

"Who try?"

"Governments, thinking I'm in espionage; police, wanting to know why I'm involved with so many people in such cockeyed ways; politicos in exile hoping I'll finance a counterrevolution; fanatics, dreaming I'm their rich messiah; lunatic fringes; religious sects; flat-worlders; Forteans . . . They all track me down, hoping they can use me. Nobody can. I'm part of something much bigger. I think maybe we all are, only I'm the first to be aware of it."

"Off the record, what's this about abominable acts?"

I took a breath. "That's why I can't have friends. Or a girl. Sometimes things get so bad somewhere that I have to make frightful sacrifices to restore the pattern. I must destroy something I love. I— There was a dog I loved. A Labrador retriever . . . I don't like to think about him. I had a girl once. She loved me. And I— And a guy in the Navy with me. He— I don't want to talk about it."

"Chicken, all of a sudden?"

"No, damn you; I'm accursed! Because some of the patterns I must adjust to are out-world rhythms . . . like nothing you ever felt on earth. 29/51 . . . 108/303 . . . tempi like that. What are you staring at? You don't think that can be terrifying? Beat a 7/5 tempo for me."

"I don't know music."

"This has nothing to do with music. Try to beat five with one hand and seven with the other, and make them come out even. Then you'll understand the complexity and

29

terror of those strange patterns that are coming to me. From where? I don't know. It's an unknown universe, too big to comprehend; but I have to beat the tempi of its patterns and make them come out even . . . with my actions, reactions, emotions, senses, while those giant pressures   push

and reverse me

back

and turn me

forth   inside

and   out

back . . ."

"The other arm now," Elizabeth said firmly. "Lift."

I am on my bed, me. Thinking upheaved again. Half (½) into pajamas; other half (½) being wrestled by freckly girl. I lift. She yank. Pajama now on, and it's my turn to blush. They raise me prudish in San Francisco.

"Om mani padme hum," I said. "Translation follows: Oh, the jewel in the lotus. Meaning you. What happened?"

"You passed out," she said. "Keeled over. Mr. Dolan had to let you go. Mr. Lundgren helped carry you into the apartment. How much should I give him?"

"Cinque lire. No. Parla Italiano, gentile Signorina?"

"Mr. Dolan told me what you told him. Is that your patterns again?"

"Si." I nod and wait. After stop-overs in Greece and Portugal, American-English finally returns to me. "Why don't you get the hell out of here while the getting's good, Lizzie Chalmers?"

"I'm still stuck," she said. "Get into bed . . . and make room for me."

"No."

"Yes. You can marry me later."

"Where's the silver case?"

"Down the incinerator."

"Do you know what was in it?"

"I know what was in it."

"And you're still here?"

"It was monstrous, what you did. Monstrous!" The saucy little face was streaked with mascara. She had been crying. "Where is she now?"

"I don't know. The checks go out every quarter to a number-account in Switzerland. I don't want to know. How much can the heart endure?"

"I think I'm going to find out," she said. She put out

30

the lights. In the darkness came the sound of rustling clothes. Never before have I heard the music of one I love undressing for me . . . for me. I made one last attempt to save this beloved.

"I love you," I said, "and you know what that means. When the patterns demand a sacrifice, I may be even crueler to you, more monstrous. . . ."

"No," she said. "You never were in love before. Love creates patterns, too." She kissed me. Her lips were parched, her skin was icy. She was afraid, but her heart beat hot and strong. "Nothing can hurt us now. Believe me."

"I don't know what to believe any more. We're part of a universe that's big beyond knowledge. What if it turns out to be too gigantic for love?"

"All right," she said composedly. "We won't be dogs in the manger. If love is a little thing and has to end, then let it end. Let all the little things like love and honor and mercy and laughter end . . . if there's something bigger beyond."

"But what can be bigger? What can be beyond?"

"If we're too small to survive, how can we know?"

She crept close to me, the tips of her body like frost. And so we huddled together, breast to breast, warming ourselves with our love, frightened creatures in a wondrous world beyond knowing . . . fearful, and yet an tic ccip ppat inggg.

1960

THE SEATTLE CONVENTION in 1961 continued the pattern set in Pittsburgh, i.e., that of giving one Hugo for the best novel of the year and another for the best shorter work. The writers thus faced a situation in which the briefest of short stories stood in competition with lengthy tales that came in just under the line that separates novellas from novels.

Nonetheless, this pattern persisted through another six years; it was not until 1967 that *novelette* was separated from *short story* and not until 1968 that the *novella* category was established. This was done in obvious response to the Nebula awards, established by the Science Fiction Writers of America in 1965. And as for confusion, how about this: in 1966 Jack Vance's "The Last Castle" won the Nebula as best novella, and in 1967 the same story won the Hugo (for 1966) as best novelette!

As for the awards given in Seattle, the winning novel was *A Canticle for Leibowitz* by Walter M. Miller, Jr. The wisdom of the choice is manifest; 20 years later the book is a recognized classic. The quasi-legalistic aspect of the award is interesting. The novel is episodic in structure, and the episodes had appeared as separate stories in *Fantasy and Science Fiction* between 1955 and 1957.

The Lippincott edition of 1960 contained little new material, but it was nonetheless the first appearance of the book as such, and no loud protest was heard over its eligibility.

Two of the other nominees were amusing but lightweight adventure yarns: *Deathworld* by Harry Harrison and *The High Crusade* by Poul Anderson. Another, *Venus Plus X* by Theodore Sturgeon, was a utopian novel of obvious sincerity and substance. It shared the common fault of utopian novels, however, in being so heavily weighted in favor of exposition over action that it stood little chance of winning.

The strongest challenge to Miller came from Algis Budrys's *Rogue Moon*. The Budrys was an outstanding effort, a tense puzzle novel of great force. But it had the misfortune of coming up against *A Canticle for Leibowitz*. In another year, *Rogue Moon* might have had a better chance.

Contention for the short fiction Hugo was strong. Philip Jose Farmer gained a nomination for "Open to Me, My Sister," in *F&SF*. This story was another sexual shocker of the sort for which Farmer was known. By no stretch of the imagination pornographic, it was a valid and wrenching examination of a problem that might, conceivably, arise someday, that of the mating of human and humanoid. This, of course, was the theme of Farmer's first story, "The Lovers," but in "Open to Me" he handled it in a wholly new manner.

"Need" by Theodore Sturgeon had the disadvantage of appearing in a British magazine, *Science Fantasy*, rather than an American one. I have previously mentioned this as a handicap in Hugo competition. There was no question that appearance in *Science Fantasy* rendered the story ineligible for the award, merely that most of the voters resided on *this* side of the Atlantic and most of the copies of *Science Fantasy* were circulated on the *other* side of the Atlantic.

There was a problem over the date of publication of "Need." The issue of *Science Fantasy* carrying the story was dated April 1961. Under the old Hugo "year" rules, "Need" would have been eligible for the 1961 award. Under the newer rules, it should have been held over for the awards given in 1962. Somehow it made the ballot, anyway, but it didn't win, so the question of eligibility was moot.

The final losing nominee was "The Lost Kafoozalum" by Pauline Ashwell. Ashwell was the author of only one earlier story, "Unwillingly to School," in the January 1958 *Astounding*. The story had been popular in its time, had gained a Hugo nomination, and had won for its author a nomination as best new author of 1958. (That prize, incidentally, went to "no award.")

Ashwell returned with "The Lost Kafoozalum" in the October 1960 issue of *Analog* (the old *Astounding* under a new name). Again the story was highly popular, again it gained a Hugo nomination . . . and again the author submerged. This time, never to re-emerge.

Who was this talented, enigmatic person? Was Pauline Ashwell the same individual as Paul Ash, another popular writer of the late '50s and early '60s? Were they both pseudonyms of some third individual, say, Poul Anderson, for example?

That would fit. Anderson was a prolific and popular author then, as he is now. He was known to use pseudonyms on occasion. And there would have been a certain aptness to the fact, as well as a certain irony, as it was Anderson's own story "The Longest Voyage" (in the December *Analog*) that won the Hugo from Ashwell.

But Anderson stoutly denies that he was either Ashwell or Ash.

Bob Silverberg claims that he met Pauline Ashwell— or someone claiming to be Pauline Ashwell—in London, at the World Convention of 1957. But that's a trail that quickly goes cold.

For what it's worth, a careful search of the records of *Analog* magazine has revealed the following, after all these years. Yes, Pauline Ashwell is a real person, not Poul Anderson or anyone else known to the science fiction world, under a clever disguise. Her name is not Pauline Ashwell, and I have not been able to obtain her permission to reveal her real name. She does, indeed, live in Britain. And no, I have not been able to learn why she stopped writing, so abruptly and permanently, after so brilliant a beginning as "Unwillingly to School" and "The Lost Kafoozalum" had made.

For what it's worth, I think "The Lost Kafoozalum"— which has never been reprinted from *Analog* until now —is the most egregiously overlooked of all the overlooked stories in the present anthology. If you are like me, you will suspect at the outset of the story that it is marred by a bizarre string of typographical errors.

Not so!

The author was writing in a futuristic jargon, just one of the many fine touches of craft present in the story.

If you have never before read a Pauline Ashwell story, I think you will become an instant fan when you have read "The Lost Kafoozalum." When I think of a person

34

whose career was as brief—I might say, as needlessly brief—as Pauline Ashwell's was, I don't know whether to weep for loss of the stories she never wrote, or to sigh with pleasure at the very few she did write.

Probably a combination of the two would be most appropriate.

The Lost Kafoozalum

PAULINE ASHWELL

I REMEMBER SOME bad times, most of them back home on Excenus 23; the worst was when Dad fell under the reaping machine but there was also the one when I got lost twenty miles from home with a dud radio, at the age of twelve; and the one when Uncle Charlie caught me practicing emergency turns in a helicar round the main weather-maker; and the one on Figuerra being chased by a cyber-crane; and the time when Dad decided to send me to Earth to do my Education.

This time is bad in a different way, with no sharp edges but kind of a desolation.

Most people I know are feeling bad just now, because at Russett College we finished our Final Examination five days ago and Results are not due for two weeks.

My friend B Laydon says this is yet another Test anyone still sane at the end being proved tough enough to break a molar on; she says also The worst part is in bed remembering all the things she could have written and did not; The second worst is also in bed picturing how to explain to her parents when they get back to Earth that *someone* has to come bottom and in a group as brilliant as Russett College Cultural Engineering Class this is really no disgrace.

I am not worried that way so much, I cannot remember what I wrote anyway and I can think of one or two peo-

36

ple I am pretty sure will come bottomer than me—or B either.

I would prefer to think it is just Finals cause me to feel miserable but it is not.

In Psychology they taught us The mind has the faculty of concealing any motive it is ashamed of, especially from itself; seems unfortunately mine does not have this gadget supplied.

I never wanted to come to Earth, I was sent to Russett against my will and counting the days till I could get back to Home, Father and Excenus 23, but the sad truth is that now the longed-for moment is nearly on top of me I do not want to go.

Dad's farm was a fine place to grow up, but now I had four years on Earth the thought of going back there makes me feel like a three-weeks' chicken got to get back in its shell.

B and I are on an island in the Pacific. Her parents are on Caratacus researching on local art forms, so she and I came here to be miserable in company and away from the rest.

It took me years on Earth to get used to all this water around, it seemed unnatural and dangerous to have it all lying loose that way, but now I shall miss even the Sea.

The reason we have this long suspense over Finals is that they will not use Reading Machines to mark the papers for fear of cutting down critical judgment; so each paper has to be read word by word by three Examiners and there are forty-three of us and we wrote six papers each.

What I think is I am sorry for the Examiners, but B says they were the ones who set the papers and it serves them perfectly right.

I express surprise because D. J. M'Clare our Professor is one of them, but B says He is one of the greatest men in the galaxy, of course, but she gave up thinking him perfect *years* ago.

One of the main attractions on this Island is swimming under water, especially by moonlight. Dad sent me a fish-boat as a birthday present two years back, but I never used it yet on account of my above-mentioned attitude to water. Now I got this feeling of Carpe Diem, make the most of Earth while I am on it because probably I shall not pass this way again.

The fourth day on the Island it is full moon at ten

o'clock, so I pluck up courage to wriggle into the boat and go out under the Sea. B says Fish parading in and out of reefs just remind her of Cultural Engineering—crowd behavior—so she prefers to turn in early and find out what nightmare her subconscious will throw up *this* time.

The reefs by moonlight are everything they are supposed to be, why did I not do this often when I had the chance? I stay till my oxygen is nearly gone, then come out and sadly press the button that collapses the boat into a thirty-pound package of plastic hoops and oxygen cans. I sling it on my back and head for the chalet B and I hired among the coconut trees.

I am crossing an open space maybe fifty yards from it when a Thing drops on me out of the air.

I do not see the Thing because part of it covers my face, the rest is grabbed round my arms and my waist and my hips and whatever, I cannot see and I cannot scream and I cannot find anything to kick. The Thing is strong and rubbery and many-armed and warmish, and less than a second after I first feel it I am being hauled up into the air.

I do not care for this at all.

I am at least fifty feet up before it occurs to me to bite the hand that gags me and then I discover it is plastic, not alive at all. Then I feel self and encumberance scraping through some kind of aperture; there is a sharp click as of a door closing and the Thing goes limp all around me.

I spit out the bit I am biting and it drops away so that I can see.

Well!

I am in a kind of cup-shaped space maybe ten feet across but not higher than I am; there is a trap door in the ceiling; the Thing is lying all around me in a mess of plastic arms, with an extensible stalk connecting it to the wall. I kick free and it turns over exposing the label FRAGILE CARGO right across the back.

The next thing I notice is two holdalls, B's and mine, clamped against the wall, and the next after that is the opening of a trap door in the ceiling and B's head silhouetted in it remarking Oh there you are Liz.

I confirm this statement and ask for explanations.

B says She doesn't understand all of it but it is all right. It is not all right I reply, if she has joined some Society
38

such as for the Realization of Fictitious Improbabilities that is her privilege but no reason to involve me.

B says Why do I not stop talking and come up and see for myself?

There is a slight hitch when I jam in the trap door, then B helps me get the boat off my back and I drop it on the Fragile Cargo and emerge into the cabin of a Hopper, drop-shaped, cargo-carrying; I have been in its hold till now.

There are one or two peculiar points about it, or maybe one or two hundred, such as the rate at which we are ascending which seems to be bringing us right into the Stratosphere; but the main thing I notice is the pilot. He has his back to us but is recognizably Ram Gopal who graduated in Cultural Engineering last year, Rumor says next to top of his class.

I ask him what kind of a melodramatic shenanigan is this?

B says We had to leave quietly in a hurry without attracting attention so she booked us out at the Hotel *hours* ago and she and Ram have been hanging around waiting for me ever since.

I point out that the scope-trace of an Unidentified Flying Object will occasion a lot more remark than a normal departure even at midnight.

At this Ram smiles in an inscrutable Oriental manner and B gets nearly as cross as I do, seems she has mentioned this point before.

We have not gone into it properly when the cabin suddenly shifts through a right angle. B and I go sliding down the vertical floor and end sitting on a window There is a jolt and a shudder and Ram mutters things in Hindi and then suddenly Up is nowhere at all.

B and I scramble off the window and grab fixtures so as to stay put. The stars have gone and we can see nothing except the dim glow over the instruments; then suddenly lights go on outside.

We look out into the hold of a ship.

Out ten-foot teardrop is sitting next to another one, like two eggs in a rack. On the other side is a bulkhead; behind, the curve of the hull; and directly ahead an empty space, then another bulkhead and an open door, through which after a few seconds a head pokes cautiously.

The head is then followed by a body which kicks off against the wall and sails slowly towards us. Ram presses a stud and a door slides open in the hopper; but the new arrival stops himself with a hand on either side of the frame, his legs trailing any old how behind him. It is Peter Yeng Sen who graduated the year I did my Field Work.

He says, Gopal, dear fellow, there was no need for the knocking, we heard the bell all right.

Ram grumbles something about the guide beam being miss-set, and slides out of his chair. Peter announces that we have only just made it as the deadline is in seven minutes time; he waves B and me out of the hopper, through the door and into a corridor where a certain irregular vibration is coming from the walls.

Ram asks what is that tapping? And Peter sighs and says The present generation of students has no discipline at all.

At this B brakes with one hand against the wall and cocks her head to listen; next moment she laughs and starts banging with her fist on the wall.

Peter exclaims in Mandarin and tows her away by one wrist like a reluctant kite. The rapping starts again on the far side of the wall and I suddenly recognize a primitive signaling system called Regret or something, I guess because it was used by people in situations they did not like such as Sinking ships or solitary confinement; it is done by tapping water pipes and such.

Someone found it in a book and the more childish element in College learned it up for signaling during compulsory lectures. Interest waning abruptly when the lecturers started to learn it, too.

I never paid much attention not expecting to be in Solitary confinement much; this just shows you; next moment Ram opens a door and pushes me through it, the door clicks behind me and Solitary confinement is what I am in.

I remember this code is really called Remorse which is what I feel for not learning when I had the chance.

However I do not have long for it, a speaker in the wall requests everyone to lie down as acceleration is about to begin. I strap down on the couch which fills half the compartment, countdown begins and at zero the floor is suddenly *down* once more.

I wait till my stomach settles, then rise to explore.

I am in an oblong room about eight by twelve, it looks as though it had been hastily partitioned off from a larger space. The walls are prefab plastic sheet, the rest is standard fittings slung in and bolted down with the fastenings showing.

How many of my classmates are on this ship? *Remorse* again as tapping starts on either side of me.

Discarding such Hypotheses as that Ram and Peter are going to hold us to ransom—which might work for me, since my Dad somehow got to be a millionaire, but not for B because her parents think money is vulgar—or that we are being carried off to found an ideal Colony somewhere —any first-year student can tell you why that won't work—only one idea seems plausible.

This is that Finals were not final and we are in for a Test of some sort.

After ten minutes I get some evidence; a Reading Machine is trundled in, the door immediately slamming shut so I do not see who trundles it.

I prowl round it looking for tricks but it seems standard; I take a seat in it, put on the headset and turn the switch.

Hypothesis confirmed, I suppose.

There is a reel in place and it contains background information on a problem in Cultural Engineering all set out the way we are taught to do it in Class. The Problem concerns developments on a planet got settled by two groups during the Exodus and been isolated ever since.

Well while a Reading Machine is running there is no time to think, it crams in data at full speed and evaluation has to wait. However my subconscious goes into action and when the reel stops it produces a Suspicion full grown.

The thing is too tidy.

When we were First Year we dreamed up situations like this and argued like mad over them, but they were a lot too neat for real life and too dramatic as well.

However one thing M'Clare said to us, and every other lecturer too, just before the Finals, was Do not spend time trying to figure what the examiner was after but answer the question as set; I am more than halfway decided this is some mysterious Oriental idea of a joke but I get busy thinking in case it is not.

The Problem goes like this:

The planet is called Incognita in the reel and it is right on the edge of the known volume of space, it got settled by two groups somewhere between three and three and a

41

half centuries ago. The rest of the human race never heard of it till maybe three years back.

(Well it happens that way, inhabited planets are still turning up eight or ten a century, on account of during the Exodus some folk were willing to travel a year or more so as to get away from the rest.)

The ship that spotted the planet as inhabited did not land, but reported to Central Government, Earth, who shipped observers out to take a look.

(There was a rumor circulating at Russett that the Terry Government might employ some of us on that kind of job, but it never got official. I do not know whether to believe this bit or not.)

It is stated the observers landed secretly and mingled with the natives unobserved.

(This is not physically impossible but sounds too like a Field Trip to be true.)

The observers are not named but stated to be graduates of the Cultural Engineering Class.

They put in a few months' work and sent home unanimous Crash Priority reports the situation is *bad*, getting worse and the prognosis is War.

Brother.

I know people had wars, I know one reason we do not have them now is just that with so many planets and cheap transportation, pressure has other outlets; these people scrapped their ships for factories and never built more.

But.

There are only about ten million of them and surely to goodness a whole planet gives room enough to keep out of each other's hair?

Well this is not Reasoning but a Reaction, I go back to the data for another look.

The root trouble is stated to be that two groups landed on the planet without knowing the others were there, when they met thirty years later they got a disagreeable shock.

I cannot see there was any basic difference between them, they were very similar, especially in that neither lot wanted anything to do with people they had not picked themselves.

So they divided the planet along a Great Circle which left two of the main land-masses in one hemisphere and two in another.

They agree each to keep to its own section and leave the other alone.

Twenty years later, trading like mad; each has certain minerals the other lacks; each has certain agricultural products the other finds it difficult to grow.

You think this leads to Co-operation Friendship and ultimate Federation?

I will not go into the incidents that make each side feel it is being gypped, it is enough that from time to time each has a scarcity or hold-up on deliveries that upsets the other's economy; and they start experimenting to become self-sufficient: and the exporter's economy is upset in turn. And each thinks the other did it on purpose.

This sort of situation reacts internally leading to Politics.

There are troubles about a medium-sized island on the dividing line, and the profits from interhemispherical transport, and the laws of interhemispherical trade.

It takes maybe two hundred years, but finally each has expanded the Police into an army with a whole spectrum of weapons not to be used on any account except for Defense.

This situation lasts seventy years getting worse all the time, now Rumors have started on each side that the other is developing an Ultimate Weapon, and the political parties not in power are agitating to move first before the thing is complete.

The observers report War not maybe this year or the next but within ten, and if neither side was looking for an Ultimate Weapon to begin with they certainly are now.

Taking all this at face value there seems an obvious solution.

I am thinking this over in an academic sort of way when an itchy trickle of sweat starts down my vertebrae.

Who is going to apply this solution? Because if this is anything but another Test, or the output of a diseased sense of humor, I would be sorry for somebody.

I dial black coffee on the wall servitor and wish B were here so we could prove to each other the thing is just an exercise; I do not do so well at spotting proofs on my own.

Most of our class exercises have concerned something that happened, once.

After about ninety minutes the speaker requests me to write not more than one thousand words on any scheme to improve the situation and the equipment required for it.

I spent ten minutes verbalizing the basic idea and an hour or so on "equipment"; the longer I go on the more

43

unlikely it all seems. In the end I have maybe two hundred words which acting on instructions I post through a slit in the door.

Five minutes later I realize I have forgotten the Time Factor.

If the original ship took a year to reach Incognita, it will take at least four months now; therefore it is more than four months since that report was written and will be more than a year before anyone arrives and War may have started already.

I sit back and by transition of ideas start to wonder where this ship is heading? We are still at one gee and even on Mass-Time you cannot juggle apparent acceleration and spatial transition outside certain limits; we are not just orbiting but must be well outside the Solar System by now.

The speaker announces Everyone will now get some rest; I smell sleep-gas for one moment and have just time to lie down.

I guess I was tired, at that.

When I wake I feel more cheerful than I have for weeks; analysis indicates I am glad something is *happening* even if it is another Exam.

I dial breakfast but am too restless to eat; I wonder how long this goes on or whether I am supposed to show Initiative and break out; I am examining things with this in mind when the speaker comes to life again.

It says, "Ladies and gentlemen. You have not been told whether the problem that you studied yesterday concerned a real situation or an imaginary one. You have all outlined measures which you think would improve the situation described. Please consider, seriously, whether you would be prepared to take part yourself in the application of your plan."

Brother.

There is no way to tell whether those who say No will be counted cowardly or those who say Yes rash idiots or what, the owner of that voice has his inflections too well trained to give anything away except intentionally.

D. J. M'Clare.

Not in person but a recording, anyway M'Clare is on Earth surrounded by exam papers.

I sit back and try to think, honestly, if that crack-brained notion I wrote out last night were going to be tried in dead earnest, would I take a hand in it?

The trouble is, hearing M'Clare's voice has convinced me it is a Test, I don't know whether it is testing my courage or my prudence in fact I might as well toss for it.

Heads I am crazy, Tails a defaulter; Tails is what it is.

I seize my styler and write the decision down.

There is the slit in the door.

I twiddle the note and think Well nobody asked for it yet.

Suppose it is real, after all?

I remember the itchy, sweaty feeling I got yesterday and try to picture really embarking on a thing like this, but I cannot work up any lather today.

I begin to picture M'Clare reading my decision not to back up my own idea.

I pick up the coin and juggle it around.

The speaker remarks When I am quite ready will I please make a note of my decision and post it through the door.

I go on flipping the coin up and presently it drops on the floor, it is Heads this time.

Tossing coins is a pretty feeble way to decide.

I drop the note on the floor and take another sheet and write "YES. Lysistrata Lee."

Using that name seems to make it more legal.

I slip the paper in the slit and poke till it falls through on the other side of the door.

I am suddenly immensely hungry and dial breakfast all over again.

Just as I finish M'Clare's voice starts once more.

"It's always the minor matters that cause the most difficulty. The timing of this announcement has cost me as much thought as any aspect of the arrangements. The trouble is that however honest you are—and your honesty has been tested repeatedly—and however strong your imagination—about half of your training has been devoted to developing it—you can't possibly be sure, answering a hypothetical question, that you are giving the answer you would choose if you knew it was asked in dead earnest.

"Those of you who answered the question in the negative are out of this. They have been told that it was a test, of an experimental nature, and have been asked to keep the whole thing a secret. They will be returning to Earth in a few hours' time. I ask the rest of you to think it over once again. Your decision is still private. Only the two people who gathered you together know which members of the class are in this ship. The list of possible helpers was compiled by a computer. I haven't seen it myself.

"You have a further half hour in which to make up your minds finally. Please remember that if you have any private reservations on the matter, or if you are secretly afraid, you may endanger us all. You all know enough psychology to realize this.

"If you still decide in favor of the project, write your name on a slip of paper and post it as before. If you are not absolutely certain about it, do nothing. Please think it over for half an hour."

Me, I had enough thinking. I write my name—just L. Lee—and post it straight away.

However I cannot stop thinking altogether. I guess I think very hard, in fact. My Subconscious insists afterwards that it did register the plop as something came through the slit, but my Conscious failed to notice it at all.

Hours later—my watch says twenty-five minutes but I guess the Mass-Time has affected it—anyway I had three times too much solitary confinement—when will they let me *out* of here?—there is a knock at the door and a second later it slides apart.

I am expecting Ram or Peter so it takes me an appreciable fraction of a moment to realize I am seeing D. J. M'Clare.

Then I remember he is back on Earth buried in Exam papers and conclude I am having a hallucination.

This figment of my imagination says politely, "Do you mind if I sit down?"

He collapses on the couch as though thoroughly glad of it.

It is a strange thing, every time I see M'Clare I am startled all over again at how good-looking he is; seems I forget it between times which is maybe why I never fell for him as most female students do.

However what strikes me this time is that he looks tired, three-days-sleepless tired with worries on top.

I guess he is real, at that.

He says, "Don't look so accusing, Lizzie, I only just got on this ship myself."

This does not make sense; you cannot just arrive on a ship twenty-four hours after it goes on Mass-Time; or can you?

M'Clare leans back and closes his eyes and inquires whether I am one of the Morse enthusiasts?

So that is the name; I say when we get back I will learn it first thing.

"Well," says he, "I did my best to arrange privacy for all of you; with so many ingenious idiots on board I'm not really surprised that they managed to circumvent me. I had to cheat and check that you really were on the list; and I knew that whoever backed out you'd still be on board."

So I should hope he might: Horrors there is my first answer screwed up on the floor and Writing side topmost.

However he has not noticed it, he goes on "Anyway you of all people won't be thought to have dropped out because you were afraid."

I have just managed to hook my heel over the note and get it out of sight, M'Clare has paused for an answer and I have to dredge my Subthreshold memories for—

WHAT?

M'Clare opens his eyes and says like I am enacting Last Straw, "Have some sense, Lizzie." Then in a different tone, "Ram says he gave you the letter half an hour ago."

What letter?

My brain suddenly registers a small pale patch been occupying a corner of my retina for the last half hour; it turns out to be a letter postmarked Excenus 23.

I disembowel it with one jerk. It is from my Dad and runs like this:

My dear Liz,

Thank you for your last letter, glad you are keeping fit and so am I.

I just got a letter from your College saying you will get a degree conferred on you on September 12th and parents if on Earth will be welcome.

Well Liz this I got to see and Charlie says the same, but the letter says too Terran Authority will not give a permit to visit Earth just for this, so I wangled on to a Delegation is coming to discuss trade with the Department of Commerce. Charlie and I will be arriving on Earth on August 24th.

Liz it is good to think I shall be seeing you again after four years. There are some things about your future I meant to write to Professor M'Clare about,

47

but now I shall be able to talk it over direct. Please give him my regards.

Be seeing you Lizzie girl, your affectionate Dad.

J. X. Lee.

Dear old Dad, after all these years farming with a weather-maker on a drydust planet I want to see his face the first time he sees real rain.

Hell's fires and shades of darkness, I shan't be there!

M'Clare says, "Your father wrote to me saying that he will be arriving on Earth on 24th August. I take it your letter says the same. I came on a dispatch boat; you can go back on it."

Now what is he talking about? Then I get the drift.

I say, "Look. So Dad will be on Earth before we get back. What difference does that make?"

"You can't let him arrive and find you missing."

Well I admit to a qualm at the thought of Dad let loose on Earth without me, but after all Uncle Charlie is a born Terrie and can keep him in line; Hell he is old enough to look after himself anyway.

"You met my Dad," I point out. "You think J. X. Lee would want any daughter of his backing out on a job so as to hold his hand? I can send him a letter saying I am off on a job or a Test or whatever I please and hold everything till I get back; what are you doing about people's families on Earth already?"

M'Clare says we were all selected as having families *not* on Earth at present, and I must go back.

I say like Hell I will.

He says he is my official guardian and responsible for me.

I say he is just as responsible for everyone else on this ship.

I spent years and years trying to think up a remark would really get home to M'Clare; well I have done it now.

I say, "Look. You are tired and worried and maybe not thinking so well just now.

"I know this is a very risky job, don't think I missed that at all. I tried hard to imagine it like you said over the speaker. I cannot quite imagine dying but I know how Dad will feel if I do.

"I did my level best to scare myself sick, then I decided it is just plain worth the risk anyway.

"To work out a thing like this you have to have a kind

48

of arithmetic, you add in everybody's feelings with the other factors, then if you get a plus answer you forget everything else and go right ahead.

"I am not going to think about it any more, because I added up the sum and got the answer and upsetting my nerves won't help. I guess you worked out the sum, too. You decided four million people were worth risking twenty, even if they do have parents. Even if they are your students. So they are, too, and you gave us all a chance to say No.

"Well nothing has altered that, only now the values look different to you because you are tired and worried and probably missed breakfast, too."

Brother some speech, I wonder what got into me? M'Clare is wondering, too, or maybe gone to sleep sitting, it is some time before he answers me.

"Miss Lee, you are deplorably right on one thing at least. I don't know whether I was fit to make such a decision when I made it, but I'm not fit now. As far as you personally are concerned . . ." He trails off looking tireder than ever, then picks up again suddenly. "You are again quite right, I am every bit as responsible for the other people on board as I am for you."

He climbs slowly to his feet and walks out without another word.

The door is left open and I take this as an invitation to freedom and shoot through in case it was a mistake.

No because Ram is opening doors all along the corridor and ten of Russett's brightest come pouring out like mercury finding its own level and coalesce in the middle of the floor.

The effect of release is such that after four minutes Peter Yeng Sen's head appears at the top of a stairway and he says the row is lifting the desk plates, will we for Time's sake go along to the Conference Room which is soundproof.

The Conference Room is on the next deck and like our cabins shows signs of hasty construction; the soundproofing is there but the acoustics are kind of muffled and the generator is not boxed in but has cables trailing all over, and the fastenings have a strong but temporary look.

Otherwise there is a big table and a lot of chairs and a small projection box in front of each with a note-taker beside.

It is maybe this very functional setup or maybe the dead flatness of our voices in the damped room, but we do not have so much to talk about any more. We automatically take places at the table, all at one end, leaving seven vacant chairs near the door.

Looking round, I wonder what principle we were selected on.

Of my special friends Eru Te Whangoa and Kirsty Lammergaw are present but Lily Chen and Likofo Komom'baratse and Jean LeBrun are not; we have Cray Patterson who is one of my special enemies but not Blazer Weigh or the Astral Cad; the rest are P. Zapotec, Nick Howard, Aro Mestah, Dillie Dixie, Pavel Christianovitch, Lennie DiMaggio and Shootright Crow.

Eru is at the end of the table, opposite the door, and maybe feels this position puts it up to him to start the discussion; he opens by remarking "So nobody took the opportunity to withdraw."

Cray Patterson lifts his eyebrows ceilingwards and drawls out that the decision was supposed to be a private one.

B says Maybe but it did not work out that way, everyone who learned Morse knows who was on the ship, anyway they are all still here so what does it matter? And M'Clare would not have picked people who were going to funk it, after all.

My chair gets a kick on the ankle which I suppose was meant for B; Eru is six foot five but even his legs do not quite reach; he is the only one of us facing the door.

M'Clare has somehow shed his weariness; he looks stern but fresh as a daisy. There are four with him; Ram and Peter looking serious, one stranger in Evercleans looking determined to enjoy the party and another in uniform looking as though nothing would make him.

M'Clare introduces the strangers as Colonel Delano-Smith and Mr. Yardo. They all sit down at the other end of the table; then he frowns at us and begins like this:

"Miss Laydon is mistaken. You were not selected on any such grounds as she suggests. I may say that I was astonished at the readiness with which you all engaged yourselves to take part in such a desperate gamble; and, seeing that for the last four years I have been trying to persuade you that it is worth while, before making a decision of any importance, to spend a certain amount of thought on it, I was discouraged as well."

Oh.

"The criterion upon which you were selected was a very simple one. As I told you, you were picked not by me but by a computer; the one in the College Office which registers such information as your home addresses and present whereabouts. You are simply that section of the class which could be picked up without attracting attention, because you all happened to be on holiday by yourselves or with other members of the class; and because your nearest relatives are not on Earth at present."

Oh, well.

All of us can see M'Clare is doing a job of deflation on us for reasons of his own, but it works for all that.

He now seems to feel the job is complete and relaxes a bit.

"I was interested to see that you all, without exception, hit on variations of the same idea. It is of course the obvious way to deal with the problem." He smiles at us suddenly and I get mad at myself because I know he is following the rules for inducing a desired state of mind, but I am responding as meant. "I'll read you the most succinct expression of it; you may be able to guess the author."

Business with bits of paper.

"Here it is. I quote: 'Drag in some outsider looks like he is going for both sides; they will gang up on him.' "

Yells of laughter and shouts of "Lizzie Lee!" even the two strangers produce sympathetic' grins; I do not find it so funny as all that myself.

"Ideas as to the form the 'outsider' should take were more varied. This is a matter I propose to leave you to work out together, with the assistance of Colonel Delano-Smith and Mr. Yardo. Te Whangoa, you take the chair."

Exit M'Clare.

This leaves the two halves of the table eying one another. Ram and Peter have been through this kind of session in their time; now they are leaning back preparing to watch us work. It is plain we are supposed to impress the abilities of Russett near-graduates on the two strangers, and for some moments we are all occupied taking them in. Colonel Delano-Smith is a small, neat guy with a face that has all the muscular machinery for producing an expression; he just doesn't care to use it. Mr. Yardo is taller than any of us except Eru and flesh is spread very thin on his bones, including his face which splits now and then in a grin like an affable skeleton. Where the colonel fits is guessable enough, Mr. Yardo is presumably Expert at something but no data on *what*.

Eru rests his hands on the table and says we had better start; will somebody kindly outline an idea for making the Incognitans "gang up"? The simpler the better and it does not matter whether it is workable or not; pulling it to pieces will give us a start.

We all wait to see who will rush in; then I catch Eru's eye and see I am elected Clown again, I say "Send them a letter postmarked Outer Space signed BEM saying we lost our own planet in a nova and will take over theirs two weeks from Tuesday."

Mr. Yardo utters a sharp "Ha! Ha!" but it is not seconded: the colonel having been expressionless all along becomes more so; Eru says, "Thank you, Lizzie." He looks across at Cray who is opposite me; Cray says there are many points on which he might comment; to take only one, two weeks from Tuesday leaves little time for "ganging up" and what happens when the BEMs fail to come?

We are suddenly back in the atmosphere of a seminar; Eru's glance moves to P. Zapotec sitting next to Cray, and he says, "These BEMs who lost their home planet in a nova, how many ships have they? Without a base they cannot be very dangerous unless their fleet is very large."

It goes round the table.

Pavel: "How would BEMs learn to write?"

Nick: "How are they supposed to know that Incognita is inhabited? How do they address the letter?"

The Crow: "Huh. Why write letters? Invaders just invade."

Kirsty: "We don't want to inflame these people against alien races. We might *find* one some day. It seems to me this idea might have all sorts of undesirable by-products. Suppose each side regards it as a ruse on the part of the other. We might touch off a war instead of preventing it. Suppose they turn over to preparations for repelling the invaders, to an extent that cripples their economy? Suppose a panic starts?"

Dilly: "Say, Mr. Chairman, is there any of this idea left at all? How about an interim summary?"

Eru coughs to get a moment for thought, then says: "In brief, the problem is to provide a menace against which the two groups will be forced to unite. It must have certain characteristics.

"It must be sufficiently far off in time for the threat to last several years, long enough to force them into a real combination.

"It must obviously be a plausible danger and they must get to know of it in a plausible manner. Invasion from outside is the only threat so far suggested.

"It must be a limited threat. That is, it must appear to come from one well-defined group. The rest of the Universe should appear benevolent or neutral."

He just stops, rather as though there is something else to come; while the rest of us are waiting B sticks her oar in to the following effect.

"Yes but look, suppose this goes wrong; it's all very well to make plans but suppose we do get some of Kirsty's side-effects just the same, well what I mean is suppose it makes the mess worse instead of better we want some way we can sort of switch it off again.

"Look this is just an illustration, but suppose the Menace was pirates, if it went wrong we could have an Earth ship making official contact and they could just happen to say By the way have you seen anything of some pirates, Earth fleet wiped them up in this sector about six months ago.

"That would mean the whole crew conniving, so it won't do, but you see what I mean."

There is a bit of silence, then Aro says, "I think we should start fresh. We have had criticisms of Lizzie's suggestion, which was not perhaps wholly serious, and as Dilly says there is little of it left, except the idea of a threat of invasion. The idea of an alien intelligent race has objections and would be very difficult to fake. The invaders must be men from another planet. Another unknown one. But how do the people of Incognita come to know that they exist?"

More silence, then I hear my own voice speaking although it was my intention to keep quiet for once: it sounds kind of creaky and it says: "A ship. A crashed ship from Outside."

Whereupon another voice says, "Really! Am I expected to swallow this?"

We had just about forgotten the colonel, not to mention Mr. Yardo who contributes another "Ha! Ha!" so this

53

reminder comes as a slight shock, nor do we see what he is talking about but this he proceeds to explain.

"I don't know why M'Clare thought it necessary to stage this discussion. I am already acquainted with his plan and have had orders to co-operate. I have expressed my opinion on using undergraduates on a job like this and have been overruled. If he, or you, imagine that priming you to bring out his ideas like this is going to reconcile me to the whole business you are mistaken. He might have chosen a more suitable mouthpiece than that child with the curly hair——"

Here everybody wishes to reply at once; the resulting jam produces a moment of silence and I get in first.

"As for curly hair I am rising twenty-four and I was only saying what we all thought, if we have the same ideas as M'Clare that is because he taught us for four years. How else would you set about it anyway?"

My fellow students pick up their stylers and tap solemnly three times on the table; this is the Russett equivalent of "Hear! Hear!" and the colonel is surprised.

Eru says coldly, "This discussion has not been rehearsed. As Lizzie . . . as Miss Lee says, we have been working and thinking together for four years and have been taught by the same people."

"Very well," says Delano-Smith testily. "Tell me this, please: Do you regard this idea as practicable?"

Cray tilts his chair back and remarks to the ceiling, "This is rather a farce. I suppose we had to go through our paces for the colonel's benefit—and Mr. Yardo's of course—but can't we be briefed properly now?"

"What do you mean by that?" snaps the colonel.

"It's been obvious right along," says Cray, balancing his styler on one forefinger, "so obvious none of us has bothered to mention it, that accepting the normal limitations of Mass-Time, the idea of interfering in Incognita was doomed before it began. No conventional ship would have much hope of arriving before war broke out; and if it did arrive it couldn't do anything effective. Therefore I assume that this is *not* a conventional ship. I might accept that the Government has sent us out in a futile attempt to do the impossible, but I wouldn't believe that of M'Clare."

Cray is the only Terry I know acts like an Outsider's idea of one; many find this difficult to take and the colonel is plainly one of them. Eru intervenes quickly.

"I imagine we all realized that. Anyway this ship is obviously *not* a conventional model. If you accept the usual Mass-Time relationship between the rate of transition and the fifth power of the apparent acceleration, we must have reached about four times the maximum already."

"Ram!" says B suddenly, "What did you do to stop the Hotel scope registering the little ship you picked up me and Lizzie in?"

Everybody cuts in with something they have noticed about the capabilities of this ship or the hoppers, and Lenny starts hammering on the table and chanting! "Brief! Brief!Brief!" and others are just starting to join in when Eru bangs on the table and glares us all down.

Having got silence, he says very quietly, "Colonel Delano-Smith, I doubt whether this discussion can usefully proceed without a good deal more information; will you take over?"

The colonel looks round at all the eager earnest interested maps hastily put on for his benefit and decides to take the plunge.

"Very well. I suppose it is . . . very well. The decision to use students from Russett was made at a very high level, and I suppose—" Instead of saying "Very well" again he shrugs his shoulders and gets down to it.

"The report from the planet we decided to call 'Incognita' was received thirty-one days ago. The Department of Spatial Affairs has certain resources which are not generally known. This ship is one of them. She works on a modified version of Mass-Time which enables her to use about a thousand channels instead of the normal limit of two hundred; for good and sufficient reasons this has not been generally released."

Pause while we are silently dared to doubt the Virtue and sufficiency of these reasons which personally I do not.

"To travel to Incognita direct would take about fifteen days by the shortest route. We shall take eighteen days as we shall have to make a detour."

But presumably we shall take only fifteen days back. Hurrah we can spend a week round the planet and still be back in time for Commemoration. We shall skip maybe a million awkward questions and I shall not disappoint Dad.

It is plain the colonel is not filled with joy; far from it, he did not enjoy revealing a Departmental secret however obvious, but he likes the next item even less.

"We shall detour to an uninhabited system twelve days'

transit time from here and make contact with another ship, the *Gilgamesh*."

At which Lennie DiMaggio who has been silent till now brings his fist down on the table and exclaims, "You *can't!*"

Lennie is much upset for some reason; Delano-Smith gives him a peculiar look and says what does he know about it? and Lennie starts to stutter.

Cray remarks that Lennie's childhood hobby appears to have been spaceships and he suffers from arrested development.

B says it is well known Lennie is mad about the Space Force and why not? It seems to have uses Go on and tell us Lennie.

Lennie says *"G-Gilgamesh* was lost three hundred years ago!"

"The flaw in that statement," says Cray after a pause, "is that this may be another ship of the same name."

"No," says the colonel. "Explorer Class cruiser. They went out of service two hundred eighty years back."

The Space Force, I remember, does not re-use names of lost ships: some say Very Proper Feeling some say Superstitious Rot.

B says, "When was she found again?"

Lennie says it was j-just thirty-seven revolutions of his native planet which means f-f-fifty-three Terrestrial years ago, she was found by an Interplanetary scout called *Crusoe*.

Judging by the colonel's expression this data is Classified; he does not know that Lennie's family come from one of the oldest settled planets and are space-goers to a man, woman and juvenile; they pick up ship gossip the way others hear about the relations of people next door.

Lennie goes on to say that the Explorer Class were the first official exploration ships sent out from Earth when the Terries decided to find out what happened to the colonies formed during the Exodus. *Gilgamesh* was the first to re-make contact with Garuda, Legba, Lister, Corbis and Antelope; she vanished on her third voyage.

"Where was she found?" asks Eru.

"Near the p-p-pole of an uninhabited planet—maybe I shouldn't say where because that may be secret, but the rest's History if you know where to look."

Maybe the colonel approves this discretion; anyway his face thaws very slightly unless I am Imagining it.

56

"Gilgamesh crashed," he says. "Near as we can make out from the log, she visited Seleucis system. That's a swarmer sun. Fifty-seven planets, three settled; and any number of fragments. The navigator calculated that after a few more revolutions one of the fragments was going to crash on an inhabited planet. Might have done a lot of damage. They decided to tow it out of the way.

"Grappling-beams hadn't been invented. They thought they could use Mass-Time on it a kind of reverse thrust—throw it off course.

"Mass-Time wasn't so well understood then. Bit off more than they could chew. Set up a topological relation that drained all the free energy out of the system. Drive, heating system—everything.

"She had emergency circuits. When the engines came on again they took over—landed the ship, more or less, on the nearest planet. Too late, of course. Heating system never came on—there was a safety switch that had to be thrown by hand. She was embedded in ice when she was found. Hull breached at one point—no other serious damage."

"And the . . . the crew?"

Dillie ought to know better than that.

"Lost with all hands," says the colonel.

"How about weapons?"

We are all startled. Cray is looking whitish like the rest of us but maintains his normal manner, *i.e.*, offensive affection while pointing out that *Gilgamesh* can hardly be taken for a Menace unless she has some means of aggression about her.

Lennie says The Explorer Class were all armed—

Fine, says Cray, presumably the weapons will be thoroughly obsolete and recognizable only to a Historian—

Lennie says that the construction of no weapon developed by the Space Department has ever been released; making it plain that anyone but a Nitwit knows that already.

Eru and Kirsty have been busy for some time writing notes to each other and she now gives a small sharp cough and having collected our attention utters the following Address.

"There is a point we seem to have missed. If I may recapitulate, the idea is to take this ship *Gilgamesh* to Incognita and make it appear as though she had crashed there while attempting to land. I understand that the ship

57

has been buried in the polar cap; though she must have been melted out if the people on *Crusoe* examined the engines. Of course the cold— All the same there may have been . . . well . . . changes. Or when . . . when we thaw the ship out again—"

I find I am swallowing good and hard, and several of the others look sick, especially Lennie. Lennie has his eyes fixed on the colonel; it is not prescience but a slight sideways movement of the colonel's eye causes him to blurt out, "What is *he* doing here?"

Meaning Mr. Yardo who seems to have been asleep for some time, with his eyes open and grinning like the spikes on a dog collar. The colonel gives him another sideways look and says. "Mr. Yardo is an expert on the rehabilitation of space-packed materials."

This is stuff transported in unpowered hulls towed by grappling-beams; the hulls are open to space hence no need for refrigeration, and the contents are transferred to specially equipped orbital stations before being taken down to the planet. But—

Mr. Yardo comes to life at the sound of his name and his grin widens alarmingly.

"Especially meat," he says.

It is maybe two hours afterwards, Eru having adjourned the meeting abruptly so that we can . . . er . . . take in the implications of the new data. Lennie has gone off somewhere by himself; Kirsty has gone after him with a view to Mothering him; Eru, I suspect, is looking for Kirsty; Pavel and Aro and Dillie and the Crow are in a cabin arguing in whispers; Nick and P. Zapotec are exploring one of the Hoppers, cargo-carrying, drop-shaped, and I only hope they don't hop through the hull in it.

B and I having done a tour of the ship and ascertained all this have withdrawn to the Conference Room because we are tired of our cabins and this seems to be the only other place to sit.

B breaks a long silence with the remark that However often you see it M'Clare's technique is something to watch, like choosing my statement to open with, it broke the ice beautifully.

I say, "Shall I tell you something?"

B says Yes if it's interesting.

"My statement," I inform her, "ran something like this: 'The best hope of inducing a suspension of the aggressive
58

attitude of both parties, long enough to offer hope of ultimate reconciliation, lies in the intrusion of a new factor in the shape of an outside force seen to be impartially hostile to both."

B says: "Gosh. Come to think of it Liz you have not written like that in years, you have gone all pompous like everyone else; well that makes it even *more* clever of M'Clare."

Enter Cray Patterson and drapes himself sideways on a chair, announcing that his own thoughts begin to weary him.

I say this does not surprise me, at all.

"Lizzie my love," says he, "you are twice blessed being not only witty yourself but a cause of wit in others; was that bit of Primitive Lee with which M'Clare regaled us really not from the hand of the mistress, or was it a mere pastiche?"

I say Whoever wrote that it was not me anyway.

"It seemed to me pale and lukewarm compared with the real thing," says Cray languidly, "which brings me to a point that, to quote dear Kirsty, seems to have been missed."

I say, "Yep. Like what language it was that these people wrote their log in that we can be *certain* the Incognitans won't know."

"More than that," says B, "we didn't decide who they are or where they were coming from or how they came to crash or anything."

"Come to think of it, though," I point out, "the language and a good many other things must have been decided already because of getting the right hypnotapes and translators on board."

B suddenly lights up.

"Yes, but look, I bet that's what we're here for, I mean that's why they picked us instead of Space Department people—the ship's got to have a past history, it has to come from a planet somewhere only no one must ever find out *where* it's supposed to be. Someone will have to fake a log, only I don't see how—"

"The first reel with data showing the planet of origin got damaged during the crash," says Cray impatiently.

"Yes, of course—but we have to find a reason why they were in that part of Space and it has to be a *nice* one, I mean so that the Incognitans when they finally read the log won't hate them any more—"

"Maybe they were bravely defending their own planet by hunting down an interplanetary raider," I suggest.

Cray says it will take only the briefest contact with other planets to convince the Incognitans that interplanetary raiders can't and don't exist, modern planetary alarm and defense systems put them out of the question.

"That's all he knows," says B, "some interplanetary pirates raided Lizzie's father's farm once Didn't they Liz?"

"Yes in a manner of speaking, but they were bums who pinched a spaceship from a planet not many parsecs away, a sparsely inhabited mining world like my own which had no real call for an alarm system; so that hardly alters the argument."

"Well," says B, "the alarm system on Incognita can't be so hot or the observation ships could not have got in, or out for that matter; unless of course they have some other gadget we don't know about.

"On the other hand," she considers, "to mention Interplanetary raiders raises the idea of Menace in an Unfriendly Universe again, and this is what we want to cancel out.

"These people," she says at last with a visionary look in her eye, "come from a planet which went isolationist and abandoned space travel; now they have built up their civilization to a point where they can build ships of their own again, and the ones on *Gilgamesh* have cut loose from the ideas of their ancestors that led to their going so far afield—"

"How far afield?" says Cray.

"No one will ever know," I point out to him. "Don't interrupt."

"Anyway," says B, "they set out to rejoin the rest of the Human Race just like the people on *Gilgamesh really* did, in fact a lot of this is the truth only kind of backwards—they were looking for the Cradle of the Race, that's what. Then there was some sort of disaster that threw them off course to land on an uninhabited section of a planet that couldn't understand their signals. And when Incognita finally does take to space flight again I bet the first thing the people do is to try and follow back to where *Gilgamesh* came from and make contact with *them*. It'll become a legend on Incognita—the Lost People . . . the Lost . . . Lost—"

"The Lost Kafoozalum," says Cray. "In other words we switch these people off a war only to send them on a wild goose chase."

At which a strange voice chimes in, "No, no, no, son, you've got it all *wrong.*"

Mr. Yardo is with us like a well-meaning skeleton.

During the next twenty-five minutes we learn a lot about Mr. Yardo including material for a good guess at how he came to be picked for this expedition; doubtless there are many experts on Reversal Of Vacuum-Induced Changes in Organic Tissues but maybe only one of them a Romantic at heart.

Mr. Yardo thinks chasing the Wild Goose will do the Incognitans all the good in the galaxy, it will take their minds off controversies over interhemispherical trade and put them on to the quest of the Unobtainable; they will get to know something of the Universe outside their own little speck. Mr. Yardo has seen a good deal of the Universe in the course of advising on how to recondition space-packed meat and he found it an Uplifting Experience.

We gather he finds this desperate bit of damfoolery we are on now pretty Uplifting altogether.

Cray keeps surprisingly quiet but it is as well that the rest of the party start to trickle in about twenty minutes later the first arrivals remarking Oh *that's* where you've got to!

Presently we are all congregated at one end of the table as before, except that Mr. Yardo is now sitting between B and me; when M'Clare and the colonel come in he firmly stays where he is evidently considering himself One of Us now.

"The proposition," says M'Clare, "is that we intend to take *Gilgamesh* to Incognita and land her there in such a way as to suggest that she crashed. In the absence of evidence to the contrary the Incognitans are bound to assume that that was her intended destination, and the presence of weapons, even disarmed, will suggest that her mission was aggressive. Firstly, can anyone suggest a better course of action? or does anyone object to this one?"

We all look at Lennie who sticks his hands in his pockets and mutters "No."

Kirsty gives her little cough and says there is a point which has not been mentioned.

If a heavily-armed ship crashes on Incognita, will not the government of the hemisphere in which it crashes be presented with new ideas for offensive weapons? And won't this make it more likely that they will start aggression?

61

And won't the fear of this make the other hemisphere even *more* likely to try and get in first before the new weapons are complete?

Hell, I ought to have thought of that.

From the glance of unwilling respect which the colonel bestows on M'Clare it is plain these points have been dealt with.

"The weapons on *Gilgamesh* were disarmed when she was rediscovered," he says. "Essential sections were removed. The Incognitans won't be able to reconstruct how they worked."

Another fact for which we shall have to provide an explanation. Well how about this: The early explorers sent out by these people—the people in *Gilgamesh* . . . oh, use Cray's word and call them Lost Kafoozalum anyway their ships were armed, but they never found any enemies and the Idealists of B's story refused even to carry arms any more.

(Which is just about what happened when the Terries set out to rediscover the colonies, after all.)

So the Lost Kafoozalum could not get rid of their weapons completely because it would have meant rebuilding the ship; so they just partially dismantled them.

Mr. Yardo suddenly chips in, "About that other point, girlie, surely there must be some neutral ground left on a half-occupied planet like that?" He beams round, pleased at being able to contribute.

B says, "The thing is," and stops.

We wait.

We have about given up hope when she resumes, "The thing is, it will have to be neutral ground of course, only that might easily become a thingummy . . . I mean a, a *casus belli* in itself. So the *other* thing is it ought to be a place which is very hard to get at, so difficult that neither side can really get to it first, they'll have to reach an agreement and co-operate."

"Yeah," says Dillie, "that sounds fine, but what sort of place is that?"

I am sorting out in my head the relative merits of mountains deserts, gorges, et cetera, when I am seized with inspiration at the same time as half the group; we say the same thing in different words and for a time there is Babel, then the idea emerges:

"Drop her into the sea!"

The colonel nods resignedly.

"Yes," he says, "that's what we're going to do."

He presses a button and our projection-screens light up, first with a map of one pole of Incognita, expanding in scale till finally we are looking down on one little bit of coast on one of the polar islands. A glacier descends on to it from mountains inland and there is a bay between cliffs. Then we get a stereo scene of approximately the least hospitable of scenery I ever did see—except maybe when Parvati Lal Dutt's brother made me climb up what he swore was the smallest peak in the Himalayas.

It is a small bay backed by tumbled cliffs. A shelving beach can be deduced from contour and occasional boulders big enough to stick through the snow that smothers it all. A sort of mess of rocks and mud at the back may be the glacial moraine. Over the sea the ice is split in all directions by jagged rifts and channels; the whole thing is a bit like Antractica but nothing is high enough or white enough to uplift the spirit, it looks not only chilly but kind of mean.

"This place," says the colonel, "is the only one, about which we have any topographical information, that seems to meet the requirements. Got to know about it through an elementary planetography. One of the observers had the sense to see we might need something of the sort. This place"—the stereo jigs as he taps his projector—"seems it's the center of a rising movement in the crust . . . that's not to the point. Neither side has bothered to claim the land at the poles . . ."

I see their point if it's all like this—

". . . And a ship trying to land on those cliffs might very well pitch over into the sea. That is, if she were trying to land on emergency rockets."

Rockets—that brings home the ancientness of this ship *Gilgamesh*—but after all the ships that settled Incognita probably carried emergency rockets, too.

This settled, the meeting turns into a briefing session and merges imperceptibly with the beginning of the job.

The job of course is Faking the background of the crash; working out the past history and present aims of the Lost Kafoozalum. We have to invent a planet and what's more difficult convey all the essential information about it by the sort of sideways hints you gather among peoples' personal possessions; diaries, letters et cetera; and what is even *more* difficult we have to leave out anything

63

that could lead to definite identification of our unknown world with any known one.

We never gave that world a name; it might be dangerous. Who speaks of their world by name, except to strangers? They call it "home"—or "Earth," as often as not.

Some things have been decided for us. Language, for instance—one of two thousand or so Earth tongues that went out of use late enough to be plausible as the main language of a colonized planet. The settlers on Incognita were not the sort to take along dictionaries of the lesser-known tongues, so the computers at Russett had a fairly wide choice.

We had to take a hypnocourse in that language. Ditto the script, one of several forgotten phonetic shorthands. (Designed to enable the tongues of Aliens to be written down; but the Aliens have never been met. It is plausible enough that some colony might have kept the script alive; after all Thasia uses something of the sort to this day.)

The final result of our work looks pretty small. Twenty-three "Personal Background Sets"—a few letters, a diary in some, an assortment of artifacts. Whoever stocked this ship we are on supplied wood, of the half-dozen kinds that have been taken wherever men have gone; stocks of a few plastics—known at the time of the Exodus, or easily developed from those known, and not associated with any particular planet. Also books on Design, a Formwriter for translating drawings into materials, and so on. Someone put in a lot of work before this voyage began.

Most of the time it is like being back on Russett doing a group Project. What we are working on has no more and no less reality than that. Our work is all read into a computer and checked against everybody else's. At first we keep clashing. Gradually a consistent picture builds up and gets translated finally into the Personal Background Sets. The Lost Kafoozalum start to exist like people in a History book.

Fifteen days hard work and we have just about finished; then we reach—call it Planet Gilgamesh.

I wake in my bunk to hear that there will be a brief cessation of weight; strap down, please.

We are coming off Mass-Time to go on planetary drive.

Colonel Delano-Smith is in charge of operations on the planet, with Ram and Peter to assist. None of the rest of us see the melting out of fifty years' accumulation of ice, the pumping away of the water, the fitting and testing of the holds for the grappling-beams. We stay inside the ship, on five-eights gee which we do not have time to get used to, and try to work, and discard the results before the computer can do so. There is hardly any work left to do, anyway.

It takes nearly twelve hours to get the ship free, and caulked, and ready to lift. (Her hull has to be patched because of Mr. Yardo's operations which make use of several sorts of vapors.) Then there is a queer blind period with Up now one way, now another, and sudden jerks and tugs that upset everything not in gimbals or tied down; interspersed with periods when weightlessness supervenes with no warning at all. After an hour or two of this it would be hard to say whether Mental or physical discomfort is more acute; B consulted, however, says my autonomic system must be quite something, after five minutes *her* thoughts were with her viscera entirely.

Then, suddenly, we are back on Mass-Time again.

Two days to go.

At first being on Mass-Time makes everything seem normal again. By sleep time there is a strain, and next day it is everywhere. I know as well as any that on Mass-Time the greater the mass the faster the shift; all the same I cannot help feeling we are being slowed, dragged back by the dead ship coupled to our live one.

When you stand by the hull *Gilgamesh* is only ten feet away.

I should have kept something to work on like B and Kirsty who have not done their Letters for Home in Case of Accidents; mine is signed and sealed long ago. I am making a good start on a Neurosis when Delano-Smith announces a Meeting for one hour ahead.

Hurrah! now there is a time-mark fixed I think of all sorts of things I should have done before; for instance taking a look at the controls of the Hoppers.

I have been in one of them half an hour and figured out most of the dials—Up down and sideways are controlled much as in a helicar, but here a big viewscreen has been hooked in to the autopilot—when across the hold I see the air lock start to move.

Gilgamesh is on the other side.

It takes forever to open. When at last it swings wide

on the dark tunnel what comes through is a storage rack, empty, floating on antigrav.

What follows is a figure in a spacesuit; modern type, but the windows of the hopper are semipolarized and I cannot make out the face inside the bubble top.

He slings the rack up on the bulkhead, takes off the helmet and hangs that up, too. Then he just stands. I am beginning to muster enough sense to wonder why when he comes slowly across the hold.

Reaching the doorway he says: "Oh, it's you, Lizzie. You'll have to help me out of this. I'm stuck."

M'Clare.

The outside of the suit is still freezing cold; maybe this is what has jammed the fastening. After a few minutes tugging it suddenly gives away. M'Clare climbs out of the suit, leaving it standing, and says, "Help me count these, will you?"

These are a series of transparent containers from a pouch slung at one side of the suit. I recognize them as the envelopes in which we put what are referred to as Personal Background Sets.

I say, "There ought to be twenty-three."

"No," says M'Clare dreamily, "twenty-two, we're saving one of them."

What on earth is the use of an extra set of faked documents and oddments—

He seems to wake up suddenly and says: "What are you doing here, Lizzie?"

I explain and he wanders over to the hopper and starts to explain the controls.

There is something odd about all this. M'Clare is obviously dead tired, but kind of relaxed; seeing that the hour of Danger is only thirty-six hours off I don't understand it. Probably several of his students are going to have to risk their lives—

I am on the point of seeing something important when the speaker announces in the colonel's voice that Professor M'Clare and Miss Lee will report to the Conference Room at once please.

M'Clare looks at me and grins. "Come along, Lizzie. Here's where we take orders for once, you and I."

It is the colonel's Hour. I suppose that having to work with Undergraduates is something he could never quite forget, but from the way he looks at us we might almost be Space Force personnel—low-grade, of course, but respectable.

Everything is at last worked out and he has it on paper in front of him; he puts the paper four square on the table, gazes into the middle distance and proceeds to recite.

"One. This ship will go off Mass-Time on 2nd August at 11.27 hours ship's time . . ."

Thirty-six hours from now.

". . . At a point one thousand miles vertically above Coordinates 165OE, 7320S, on Planet Incognita, approximately one hour before midnight local time."

Going on planetary drive as close as that will indicate that something is pretty badly wrong to begin with.

"Two. This ship will descend, coupled to *Gilgamesh* as at present, to a point seventy miles above the planetary surface. It will then uncouple, discharge one hopper, and go back on Mass-Time. Estimated time for this stage of descent forty minutes.

"Three. The hopper will then descend on its own engines at the maximum speed allowed by the heat-disposal system; estimated at thirty-seven minutes. *Gilgamesh* will complete descent in thirty-three minutes. Engines of *Gilgamesh* will not be used except for the heat-disposal and gyro auxiliaries. The following installations have been made to allow for the control of the descent; a ring of eight rockets in peltathene mounts around the tail end, and one outsize antigrav unit inside the nose. 'Sympathizer' controls hooked up with a visiscreen and a computer have also been installed in the nose.

"Four. *Gilgamesh* will carry one man only. The hopper will carry a crew of three. The pilot of *Gilgamesh* will establish the ship on the edge of the cliff, supported on antigrav a foot or so above the ground and leaning towards the sea at an angle of approximately 20° with the vertical. Except for this landing will be automatic.

"Five."

The colonel's voice has lulled us into passive acceptance; now we are jerked into sharper attention by the faintest possible check in it.

"The greatest danger attaching to the expedition is that the Incognitans may discover that the crash has been faked. This would be inevitable if they were to capture (a) the hopper; (b) any of the new installations in *Gilgamesh*, especially the antigrav; (c) any member of the crew.

"The function of the hopper is to pick up the pilot of *Gilgamesh* and also to check that ground appearances are consistent. If not, they will produce a landslip on the cliff edge, using power tools and explosives carried for the purpose. That is why the hopper has a crew of three; but the chance of their having to do this is slight."

So I should think; ground appearances are supposed to show that *Gilgamesh* landed using emergency rockets and then toppled over the cliff and this will be exactly what happened.

"The pilot will carry a one-frequency low-power transmitter activated by the change in magnetic field on leaving the ship. The hopper will remain at five hundred feet until this signal is received. It will then pick up the pilot, check ground appearances, and rendezvous with this ship at two hundred miles up at 18.27 hours."

The ship and the hopper both being radar-absorbent will not register on alarm systems, and by keeping to planetary nighttime they should be safe from being seen.

"Danger (b) will be dealt with as follows. The rocket-mounts being of peltathene will be destroyed by half an hour's immersion in water. The installations in the nose will be destroyed with Andite."

Andite produces complete molecular disruption in a very short range, hardly any damage outside it; the effect will be as though the nose broke off on impact; I suppose the Incognitans will waste a lot of time looking for it on the bed of the sea.

"Four ten-centimeter cartridges will be inserted within the nose installations. The fuse will have two alternative settings. The first will be timed to act at 12.50 hours, seven minutes after the estimated time of landing. It will not be possible to deactivate it before 12.45 hours. This takes care of the possibility of the pilot's becoming incapacitated during the descent.

"Having switched off the first fuse the pilot will get the ship into position and then activate a second, timed to blow in ten minutes. He will then leave the ship. When the antigrav is destroyed the ship will, of course, fall into the sea.

"Six. The pilot of *Gilgamesh* will wear a spacesuit of the pattern used by the original crew and will carry Personal Brackground Set number 23. Should he fail to escape from the ship the crew of the hopper will on no account attempt to rescue him."

The colonel takes up the paper, folds it in half and puts it down one inch further away.

"The hopper's crew" he says, "will give the whole game away should one of them fall into Incognitan hands, alive or dead. Therefore they don't take any risks of it."

He lifts his gaze ceilingwards. "I'm asking for three volunteers:"

Silence. Manning the hopper is definitely second best. Then light suddenly bursts on me and I lift my hand and hack B on the ankle.

"I volunteer," I say.

B gives me a most dubious glance and then lifts her hand, too.

Cray on the other side of the table is slowly opening his mouth when there is an outburst of waving on the far side of B.

"Me too, colonel! I volunteer!"

Mr. Yardo proceeds to explain that his special job is over and done, he can be more easily spared than anybody, he may be too old to take charge of *Gilgamesh* but will back himself as a hopper pilot against anybody.

The colonel cuts this short by accepting all three. He then unfolds his paper again.

"Piloting *Gilgamesh*," he says, "I'm not asking for volunteers now. You'll go to your cabins in four hours' time and those who want to will volunteer, secretly. To a computer hookup. Computer will select on a random basis and notify the one chosen. Give him his final instructions, too. No one need know who it was till it's all over. He can tell anyone he likes, of course."

A very slight note of triumph creeps into the next remark. "One point. Only men need volunteer."

Instant outcry from Kirsty and Dilly: B turns to me with a look of awe.

"Nothing to do with prejudice," says the colonel testily. "Just facts. The crew of *Gilgamesh* were all men. Can't risk one solitary woman being found on board. Besides —spacesuits, personal background sets—all designed for men."

Kirsty and Dilly turn on me looks designed to shrivel and B whispers Lizzie how wonderful you are.

The session dissolves. We three get an intensive session course of instruction on our duties and are ordered off to sleep. After breakfast next morning I run into Cray who says Before I continue about what is evidently pressing business would I care to kick him, hard?

Not right now I reply, what for anyway?

"Miss Lee," says Cray, dragging it out longer than ever, "although I have long realized that your brain functions in a way much superior to logic I had not sense enough yesterday to follow my own instinct and do what you do as soon as you did it; therefore that desiccated meat handler got in first."

I say: "So you weren't picked for pilot? It was only one chance in ten."

"Oh," says Cray, "did you really think so?" He gives me a long look and goes away.

I suppose he noticed that when the colonel came out with his remarks about No women in *Gilgamesh* I was as surprised as any.

Presently the three of us are issued with protective clothing; we just might have to venture out on the planet's surface and therefore we get white one-piece suits to protect against Cold, heat, moisture, desiccation, radioactivity and mosquitoes, and they are quite becoming, really.

B and I drag out dressing for thirty minutes; then we just sit while Time crawls asymptotically towards the hour.

Then the speaker calls us to go.

We are out of the cabin before it says two words and racing for the hold; so that we are just in time to see a figure out of an Historical movie—padded, jointed, tin bowl for head and blank reflecting glass where the face should be—stepping through the air lock.

The colonel and Mr. Yardo are there already. The colonel packs us into the hopper and personally closes the door, and for once I know what he is thinking; he is wishing he were *not* the only pilot in this ship who could possibly rely on bringing the ship off and on Mass-Time at one particular defined spot of Space.

Then he leaves us; half an hour to go.

The light in the hold begins to alter. Instead of being softly diffused it separates into sharp-edged beams, reflecting and crisscrossing but leaving cones of shadow between. The air is being pumped into store.

Fifteen minutes.

The hull vibrates and a hatch slides open in the floor so that the black of Space looks through; it closes again.

70

Mr. Yardo lifts the hopper gently off its mounts and lets it back again.

Testing; five minutes to go.

I am hypnotized by my chronometer; the hands are crawling through glue; I am still staring at it when, at the exact second, we go off Mass-Time.

No weight. I hook my heels under the seat and persuade my esophagus back into place. A new period of waiting has begun. Every so often comes the impression we are falling head-first; the colonel using ship's drive to decelerate the whole system. Then more free fall.

The hopper drifts very slowly out into the hold and hovers over the hatch, and the lights go. There is only the glow from the visiscreen and the instrument board.

One minute thirty seconds to go.

The hatch slides open again. I take a deep breath.

I am still holding it when the colonel's voice comes over the speaker: "Calling *Gilgamesh*. Calling the hopper. Goodby and Good luck. You're on your own."

The ship is gone.

Yet another stretch of time has been marked off for us. Thirty-seven minutes, the least time allowable if we are not to get overheated by friction with the air. Mr. Yardo is a good pilot; he is concentrating wholly on the visiscreen and the thermomcter. B and I are free to look around.

I see nothing and say so.

I did not know or have forgotten that Incognita has many small satellites; from here there are four in sight.

I am still looking at them when B seizes my arm painfully and points below us.

I see nothing and say so.

B whispers it was there a moment ago, it is pretty cloudy down there— Yes Lizzie there it is *look*.

And I see it. Over to the left, very faint and far below, a pin-prick of light.

Light in the polar wastes of a sparsely inhabited planet, and since we are still five miles up it is a very powerful light too.

No doubt about it, as we descend farther; about fifty miles from our objective there are men, quite a lot of them.

I think it is just then that I understand, *really* understand, the hazard of what we are doing. This is not an exercise. This is in dead earnest, and if we have missed an essential factor or calculated something wrong the result will be not a bad mark or a failed exam, or even our personal deaths, but incalculable harm and misery to millions of people we never even heard of.

Dead earnest. How in Space did we ever have cheek enough for this?

The lights might be the essential factor we have missed, but there is nothing we can do about them now.

Mr. Yardo suddenly chuckles and points to the screen. "There you are, girlies! He's down!"

There, grayly dim, is the map the colonel showed us; and right on the faint line of the cliff edge is a small brilliant dot.

The map is expanding rapidly, great lengths of coastline shooting out of sight at the edge of the screen. Mr. Yardo has the cross-hairs centered on the dot which is *Gilgamesh*. The dot is changing shape; it is turning into a short ellipse, a longer one. The gyros are leaning her out over the sea.

I look at my chronometer; 12.50 hours exactly. B looks, too, and grips my hand.

Thirty seconds later the Andite has not blown; first fuse safety turned off. Surely she is leaning far enough out by now?

We are hovering at five hundred feet. I can actually see the white edge of the sea beating at the cliff. Mr. Yardo keeps making small corrections; there is a wind out there trying to blow us away. It is cloudy here: I can see neither moons nor stars.

Mr. Yardo checks the radio. Nothing yet.

I stare downwards and fancy I can see a metallic gleam.

Then there is a wordless shout from Mr. Yardo; a bright dot hurtles across the screen and at the same time I see a streak of blue flame tearing diagonally downwards a hundred feet away.

The hopper shudders to a flat concussion in the air, we are all thrown off balance, and when I claw my way back to the screen the moving dot is gone.

So is *Gilgamesh*.

B says numbly, "But it wasn't a meteor. It can't have been."

"It doesn't matter what it was," I say. "It was some sort of missile, I think. They must be even nearer to war than we thought."

We wait. What for, I don't know. Another missile, perhaps. No more come.

At last Mr. Yardo stirs. His voice sounds creaky.

"I guess," he says, then clears his throat, and tries again. "I guess we have to go back up."

B says, "Lizzie, who was it? Do you know?"

Of course I do. "Do you think M'Clare was going to risk one of us on that job? The volunteering was a fake. He went himself."

B whispers, "You're just guessing."

"Maybe," says Mr. Yardo, "but I happened to see through that face plate of his. It was the professor all right."

He has his hand on the controls when my brain starts working again. I utter a strangled noise and dive for the hatch into the cargo hold. B tries to grab me but I get it open and switch on the light.

Fifty-fifty chance—I've lost.

No, this is the one we came in and the people who put in the new cargo did not clear out my fish-boat, they just clamped it neatly to the wall.

I dive in and start to pass up the package. B shakes her head.

"No, Lizzie. We can't. Don't you remember? If we got caught, it would give everything away. Besides . . . there isn't any chance—"

"Take a look at the screen," I tell her.

Sharp exclamation from Mr. Yardo. B turns to look, then takes the package and helps me back.

Mr. Yardo maneuvers out over the sea till the thing is in the middle of the screen; then drops to a hundred feet. It is sticking out of the water at a fantastic angle and the waves are hardly moving it. The nose of a ship.

"The antigrav," whispers B. "The Andite hasn't blown yet."

"Ten minutes," says Mr. Yardo thoughtfully. He turns to me with sudden briskness. "What's that, Lizzie girl? A fish-boat? Good. We may need it. Let's have a look."

"It's mine," I tell him.

"Now look—"

"Tailor made," I say. "You might get into it, though I doubt it. You couldn't work the controls."

It takes him fifteen seconds to realize there is no way

73

round it; he is six foot three and I am five foot one. Even B would find it hard.

His face goes grayish and he stares at me helplessly. Finally he nods.

"All right, Lizzie. I guess we have to try it. Things certainly can't be much worse than they are. We'll go over to the beach there."

On the beach there is wind and spray and breakers but nothing unmanageable; the cliffs on either side keep off the worst of the force. It is queer to feel moving air after eighteen days in a ship. It takes six minutes to unpack and expand the boat and by that time it is ten minutes since the missile hit and the Andite has not blown.

I crawl into the boat. In my protective clothing it is a fairly tight fit. We agree that I will return to this same point and they will start looking for me in fifty minutes' time and will give up if I have not returned in two hours. I take two Andite cartridges to deal with all eventualities and snap the nose of the boat into place. At first I am very conscious of the two little white cigars in the pouch of my suit, but presently I have other things to think about.

I use the "limbs" to crawl the last few yards of shingle into the water and on across the sea bottom till I am beyond the line of breakers; then I turn on the motor. I have already set the controls to "home" on *Gilgamesh* and the radar will steer me off any obstructions. This journey in the dark is as safe as my trip around the reefs before all this started—though it doesn't feel that way.

It takes twelve minutes to reach *Gilgamesh*, or rather the fragment that antigrav is supporting; it is about half a mile from the beach.

The radar stops me six feet from her and I switch it off and turn to Manual and inch closer in.

Lights, a very small close beam. The missile struck her about one third of her length behind the nose. I know, because I can see the whole of that length. It is hanging just above the water, sloping at about 30° to the horizontal. The ragged edge where it was torn from the rest is just dipping into the sea.

If anyone sees this, I don't know what they will make of it but no one could possibly think an ordinary spaceship suffered an ordinary crash, and very little investigation would show up the truth.

I reach up with the forward set of "limbs" and grapple

on to the break. I now have somehow to get the hind set of "limbs" up without losing my grip. I can't.

It takes several minutes to realize that I can just open the nose and crawl out.

Immediately a wave hits me in the face and does its best to drag me into the sea. However the interior of the ship is relatively sheltered and presently I am inside and dragging the boat up out of reach.

I need light. Presently I manage to detach one of the two from the boat. I turn it down to minimum close beam and hang it round my neck; then I start up the black jag-edged tunnel of the ship.

I have to get to the nose, find the fuse, change the setting to twenty minutes—maximum possible—and get out before it blows—out of the water I mean. The fish-boat is not constructed to take explosions even half a mile away. But the first thing is to find the fuse and I cannot make out how *Gilgamesh* is lying and therefore cannot find the door through this bulkhead; everything is ripped and twisted. In the end I find a gap between the bulkhead itself and the hull, and squeeze through that.

In the next compartment things are more recognizable and I eventually find the door. Fortunately ships are designed so that you can get through doors even when they are in the ceiling; actually here I have to climb up an overhang, but the surface is provided with rungs which make it not too bad. Finally I reach the door. I shall have to use antigrav to get down . . . why didn't I just turn it on and jump? I forgot I had it.

The door was a little way open when the missile struck; it buckled in its grooves and is jammed fast. I can get an arm through. No more. I switch on antigrav and hang there directing the light round the compartment. No rents anywhere, just buckling. This compartment is divided by a partition and the door through that is open. There will be another door into the nose on the other side.

I bring back my feet ready to kick off on a dive through that doorway.

Behind me, something stirs.

My muscles go into a spasm like the one that causes a falling dream, my hold tears loose and I go tumbling through the air, rebound from a wall, twist, and manage to hook one foot in the frame of the door I was aiming

75

for. I pull myself down and turn off the antigrav; then I just shake for a bit.

The sound was—

This is stupid, with everything torn to pieces in this ship there is no wonder if bits shake loose and drop around—

But it was not a metallic noise, it was a kind of soft dragging, very soft, that ended in a little thump.

Like a—

Like a loose piece of plastic dislodged from its angle of rest and slithering down, pull yourself together Lizzie Lee.

I look through the door into the other half of this level. Shambles. Smashed machinery every which way, blocking the door, blocking everything. No way through at all.

Suddenly I remember the tools. Mr. Yardo loaded the fish-boat with all it would take. I crawl back and return with a fifteen-inch expanding beam-lever, and overuse it; the jammed trap door does not slide back in its grooves but flips right out of them, bent double; it flies off into the dark and clangs its way to rest.

I am halfway through the opening when I hear the sound again. A soft slithering; a faint defeated thump.

I freeze where I am, and then I hear the sigh; a long, long weary sound, almost musical.

An air leak somewhere in the hull and wind or waves altering the air pressure below.

All the same I do not seem able to come any farther through this door.

Light might help; I turn the beam up and play it cautiously around. This is the last compartment, right in the nose; a sawn-off cone-shape. No breaks here, though the hull is buckled to my left and the "floor"—the partition horizontal when the ship is in the normal operating position, which holds my trap door—is torn up; some large heavy object was welded to a thin surface skin which has ripped away leaving jagged edges and a pattern of girders below.

There is no dust here; it has all been sucked out when the ship was open to space; nothing to show the beam except the sliding yellow ellipse where it touches the wall. It glides and turns, spiraling down, deformed every so often where it crosses a projection or a dent, till it halts suddenly on a spoked disk, four feet across and standing nearly eighteen inches out from the wall. The antigrav.

I never saw one this size, it is like the little personal affairs as a giant is like a pigmy, not only bigger but a

76

bit different in proportion. I can see an Andite cartridge fastened among the spokes.

The fuse is a "sympathizer" but it is probably somewhere close. The ellipse moves again. There is no feeling that I control it; it is hunting on its own. To and fro around the giant wheel. Lower. It halts on a small flat box, also bolted to the wall, a little way below. This is it, I can see the dial.

The ellipse stands still, surrounding the fuse. There is something at the very edge of it.

When *Gilgamesh* was right way up the antigrav was bolted to one wall, about three feet above the floor. Now the lowest point is the place where this wall joins what used to be the floor. Something has fallen down to that point and is huddled there in the dark.

The beam jerks suddenly up and the breath whoops out of me; a round thing sticking out of the wall—then I realize it is an archaic space-helmet, clamped to the wall for safety when the wearer took it off.

I take charge of the ellipse of light and move it slowly down, past the fuse, to the thing below. A little dark scalloping of the edge of the light. The tips of fingers. A hand.

I turn up the light.

When the missile struck the big computer was wrenched loose from the floor. It careened down as the floor tilted, taking with it anything that stood in its way.

M'Clare was just stooping to the fuse, I think. The computer smashed against his legs and pinned him down in the angle between the wall and the floor. His legs are hidden by it.

Because of the spacesuit he does not look crushed; the thick clumsy joints have kept their roundness, so far as they are visible; only his hands and head are bare and vulnerable looking.

I am halfway down, floating on minimum gravity, before it really occurs to me that he may be still alive.

I switch to half and drop beside him. His face is colorless but he is breathing all right.

First-aid kit. I will never make fun of Space Force thoroughness again. Rows and rows of small plastic ampoules. Needles.

Pain-killer, first. I read the directions twice, sweating. Emergencies only—this is. One dose *only* to be given and if patient is not in good health use—never mind that. I

77

fit on the longest needle and jab it through the suit, at the back of the thigh, as far towards the knee-joint as I can get because the suit is thinner. Half one side, half the other.

Now to get the computer off. At a guess it weighs about five hundred pounds. The beam-lever would do it but it would probably fall back.

Antigrav; the personal size is supposed to take up to three times the weight of the average man. I take mine off and buckle the straps through a convenient gap. I have my hands under the thing when M'Clare sighs again.

He is lying on his belly but his head is turned to one side, towards me. Slowly his eyelids open. He catches sight of my hand; his head moves a little, and he says, "Lizzie. Golden Liz."

I say not to worry, we will soon be out of here.

His body jumps convulsively and he cries out. His hand reaches my sleeve and feels. He says, "Liz! Oh, God, I thought . . . what—"

I say things are under control and just keep quiet a bit.

His eyes close. After a moment he whispers, "Something hit the ship."

"A homing missile, I think."

I ought not to have said that; but it seems to make no particular impression, maybe he guessed as much.

I was wrong in wanting to shift the computer straight away, the release of pressure might start a hemorrhage; I dig out ampoules of blood-seal and inject them into the space between the suit and the flesh, as close to the damage as I can.

M'Clare asks how the ship is lying and I explain, also how I got here. I dig out the six-by-two-inch packet of expanding stretcher and read the directions. He is quiet for a minute or two, gathering strength; then he says sharply: "Lizzie. Stop that and listen.

"The fuse for the Andite is just under the antigrav. Go and find it. Go *now*. There's a dial with twenty divisions. Marked in black—you see it. Turn the pointer to the last division. Is that done?

"Now you see the switch under the pointer? Is your boat ready? I beg your pardon, of course you left it that way. Then turn the switch and get out."

I come back and see by my chrono that the blood-seal

should be set; I get my hands under the computer. M'Clare bangs his hand on the floor.

"Lizzie, you little idiot, don't you realize that even if you get me out of this ship, which is next to impossible, you'll be delayed all the way—and if the Incognitans find either of us the whole plan's ruined? Much worse than ruined, once they see it's a hoax—"

I tell him I have two Andite sticks and they won't find us and on a night like this any story of explosions will be put down to sudden gusts or to lightning.

He is silent for a moment while I start lifting the computer, carefully; its effective weight with the antigrav full on is only about twenty pounds but it has all its inertia. Then he says quietly, "Please, Lizzie—can't you understand that the worst nightmare in the whole affair has been the fear that one of you might get injured? Or even killed? When I realized that only one person was needed to pilot *Gilgamesh*—it was the greatest relief I ever experienced. Now you say . . ." His voice picks up suddenly. "Lizzie, you're beaten anyway. The . . . I'm losing all feeling. Even pain. I can't feel anything behind my shoulders . . . it's creeping up—"

I say that means the pain-killer I shot him with is acting as advertised, and he makes a sound as much like an explosive chuckle as anything and is quiet again.

The curvature between floor and wall is not helpful, I am trying to find a place to wedge the computer so it cannot fall back when I take off the antigrav. Presently I get it pushed on to a sort of ledge formed by a dent in the floor, which I think will hold it. I ease off the antigrav and the computer stays put, I don't like the looks of it so let's get out of here.

I push the packaged stretcher under his middle and pull the tape before I turn the light on to his legs to see the damage. I cannot make out very much; the joints of the suit are smashed some, but as far as I can see the inner lining is not broken which means it is still air-and-water-tight.

I put a hand under his chest to feel how the stretcher is going; it is now expanded to eighteen inches by six and I can feel it pushing out, but it is *slow,* what else have I to do—oh yes, get the helmet.

I am standing up to reach for it when M'Clare says, "What are you doing? Yes . . . well, don't put it on for a minute. There's something I would like to tell you, and

79

with all respect for your obstinacy I doubt very much whether I shall have another chance. Keep that light off me, will you? It hurt my eyes.

"You know, Lizzie, I dislike risking the lives of any of the students for whom I am responsible, but as it happens I find the idea of you—blowing yourself to atoms particularly objectionable because . . . I happen to be in love with you. You're also one of my best students, I used to think that . . . was why I'd been so insistent on your coming to Russett, but I rather think . . . my motives were mixed even then. I meant to tell you this after you graduated, and to ask you to marry me, not that . . . I thought you would, I know quite well . . . you never quite forgave me, but I don't-want-to-have to remember . . . I didn't . . . have the guts to—"

His voice trails off, I get a belated rush of sense to the head and turn the light on his face. His head is turned sideways and his fist is clenched against the side of his neck. When I touch it his hand falls open and five discharged ampoules fall out.

Pain-killer.

Maximum dose, one ampoule.

All that talk was just to hold my attention while he fixed the needles and—

I left the kit spread out right next to him.

While I am taking this in some small cold corner of my mind is remembering the instructions that are on the pain-killer ampoule; it does not say, outright, that it is the last refuge for men in the extremity of pain and 'despair; therefore it cannot say, outright, that they sometimes despair too soon; but it does tell you the name of the antidote.

There are only three ampoules of this and they also say, maximum dose one ampoule. I try to work it out but lacking all other information the best I can do is inject two and keep one till later. I put that one in my pocket.

The stretcher is all expanded now; a very thin but quite rigid grid, six feet by two; I lash him on it without changing his position and fasten the helmet over his head.

Antigrav; the straps just go round him and the stretcher.

I point the thing up towards the trap door and give it a gentle push; then I scramble up the rungs and get there just in time to guide it through. It takes a knock then and some more while I am getting it down to the next partition, but he can't feel it.

This time I find the door, because the roar of noise behind it acts as a guide. The sea is getting up and is dashing halfway to the door as I crawl through. My boat is awash, pivoting to and fro on the grips of the front "limbs."

I grab it, release the limbs and pull it as far back as the door. I maneuver the stretcher on top and realize there is nothing to fasten it with . . . except the antigrav, I get that undone, holding the stretcher in balance, and manage to put it under the stretcher and pass the straps between the bars of the grid . . . then round the little boat, and the buckle just grips the last inch. It will hold, though.

I set the boat to face the broken end of the ship, but I daren't put it farther back than the doorway; I turn the antigrav to half, fasten the limb-grips and rush back towards the nose of the ship. Silver knob under the dial. I turn it down, hear the thing begin a fast, steady ticking, and turn and run.

Twenty minutes.

One and a half to get back to the boat, four to get inside it without overturning. Nearly two to get down to the sea—balance difficult. One and a half to lower myself in.

Thirty seconds' tossing before I sink below the wave layer; then I turn the motor as high as I dare and head for the shore.

In a minute I have to turn it down; at this speed the radar is bothered by water currents and keeps steering me away from them as though they were rocks; I finally find the maximum safe speed but it is achingly slow. What happens if you are in water when Andite blows half a mile away? A moment's panic as I find the ship being forced up, then I realize I have reached the point where the beach starts to shelve, turn off radar and motor and start crawling. Eternal slow reach out, grab, shove, haul, with my heart in my mouth; then suddenly the nose breaks water and I am hauling myself out with a last wave doing its best to overbalance me.

I am halfway out of the boat when the Andite blows behind me. There is a flat slapping sound; then an instant roar of wind as the air receives the binding energies of several tons of matter; then a long wave comes pelting up the beach and snatches at the boat.

I huddle into the shingle and hold the boat; I have just got the antigrav turned off, otherwise I think it would have been carried away. There are two or three more big waves and a patter of spray; then it is over.

The outlet valve of the helmet is working, so M'Clare is still breathing; very deep, very slow.

I unfasten the belt of the antigrav, having turned it on again, and pull the belt through the buckle. No time to take it off and rearrange it; anyway it will work as well under the stretcher as on top of it. I drag the boat down to the water, put in an Andite cartridge with the longest fuse I have, set the controls to take it straight out to sea at maximum depth the radar control will allow—six feet above bottom—and push it off. The other Andite cartridge starts burning a hole in my pocket; I would have liked to put that in too, but I must keep it, in case.

I look at my chrono and see that in five minutes the hopper will come.

Five minutes.

I am halfway back to the stretcher when I hear a noise further up the beach. Unmistakable. Shingle under a booted foot.

I stand frozen in mid-stride. I turned the light out after launching the boat but my eyes have not recovered yet; it is murkily black. Even my white suit is only the faintest degree paler than my surroundings.

Silence for a couple of minutes. I stand still. But it can't have gone away. What happens when the hopper comes? They will see whoever it is on the infrared vision screen. They won't come—

Footsteps again. Several.

Then the clouds part and one of those superfluous little moons shines straight through the gap.

The bay is not like the stereo the colonel showed because that was taken in winter; now the snow is melted, leaving bare shingle and mud and a tumble of rocks; more desolate than the snow. Fifty feet off is a man.

He is huddled up in a mass of garments but his head is bare, rising out of a hood which he has pushed back, maybe so as to listen better; he looks young, hardly older than me. He is holding a long thin object which I never saw before, but it must be a weapon of some sort.

This is the end of it. All the evidence of faking is destroyed; except M'Clare and me. Even if I use the Andite he has seen me—and that leaves M'Clare.

I am standing here on one foot like a dancer in a jammed

movie, waiting for Time to start again or the world to end—

Like the little figure in the dance-instruction kit Dad got when I was seven, when you switched her off in the middle.

Like a dancer—

My weight shifts on to the forward foot. My arms swing up, forwards, back. I take one step, another.

Swing. Turn. Kick. Sideways.

Like the silly little dancer who could not get out of the plastic block; but I am moving forward little by little, even if I have to take three steps roundabout for every one in advance.

Arms, up. Turn, round. Leg, up. Straighten, out. Step.

Called the Dance of the Little Robot, for about three months Dad thought it was no end cute, till he caught on I was thinking so, too.

It is just about the only kind of dance you could do on shingle, I guess.

When this started I thought I might be going crazy, but I just had not had time to work it out. In terms of Psychology it goes like this; to shoot off a weapon a man needs a certain type of Stimulus like the sight of an enemy over the end of it. So if I do my best not to look like an enemy he will not get the Stimulus. Or put it another way most men think twice before shooting a girl in the middle of a dance. If I should happen to get away with this, nobody will believe his story, he won't believe it himself.

As for the chance of getting away with it, i.e., getting close enough to grab the gun or hit him with a rock or something, I know I would become a Stimulus to shooting before I did that but there are always the clouds, if one will only come back over the moon again.

I have covered half the distance.

Twenty feet from him, and he takes a quick step back. Turn, kick, out, step. I am swinging round away from him, let's hope he finds it reassuring. I dare not look up but I think the light is dimming. Turn, kick, out, step. Boxing the compass. Coming round again.

And the cloud is coming over the moon, out of the corner of my eye I see darkness sweeping towards us—and I see his face of sheer horror as he sees it, too; he jumps back, swings up the weapon, and fires straight in my face.

And it is dark. So much for Psychology.

There is a clatter and other sounds—

Well, quite a lot for Psychology maybe, because at twenty feet he seems to have missed me.

I pick myself up and touch something which apparently is his weapon, gun or whatever. I leave it and hare back to the strecher, next to fall over it but stop just in time, and switch on the antigrav. Up; level it; now where to? The cliffs enclosing the bay are about thirty yards off to my left and they offer the only cover.

The shingle is relatively level; I make good time till I stumble against a rock and nearly lose the stretcher. I step up on to the rock and see the cliff as a blacker mass in the general darkness, only a yard away. I edge the stretcher round it.

It is almost snatched out of my hand by a gust of wind. I pull it back and realize that in the bay I have been sheltered; there is pretty near half a gale blowing across the face of the cliff.

Voices and footsteps, away back among the rocks where the man came from.

If the clouds part again they will see me, sure as shooting.

I take a hard grip on the stretcher and scramble round the edge of the cliff.

After the first gust the wind is not so bad; for the most part it is trying to press me back into the cliff. The trouble is that I can't see. I have to shuffle my foot forward, rubbing one shoulder against the cliff to feel where it is because I have no hand free.

After a few yards I come to an impasse; something more than knee high; boulder, ridge, I can't tell.

I weigh on the edge of the stretcher and tilt it up to get it over the obstacle. With the antigrav full on it keeps its momentum and goes on moving up. I try to check it, but the wind gets underneath.

It is tugging to get away; I step blindly upwards in the effort to keep up with it. One foot goes on a narrow ledge, barely a toe hold. I am being hauled upwards. I bring the other foot up and find the top of a boulder, just within reach. Now the first foot—

And now I am on top of the boulder, but I have lost touch with the cliff and the full force of the wind is pulling the stretcher upwards. I get one arm over it and fumble underneath for the control of the antigrav; I must give it weight and put it down on this boulder and wait for the wind to drop.

Suddenly I realize that my weight is going; bending over the stretcher puts me in the field of the antigrav. A moment later another gust comes, and I realize I am rising into the air.

Gripping the edge of the stretcher with one hand I reach out the other, trying to grasp some projection on the face of the cliff. Not being able to see I simply push farther away till it is out of reach.

We are still rising.

I pull myself up on the stretcher; there is just room for my toes on either side of M'Clare's legs. The wind roaring in my ears makes it difficult to think.

Rods of light slash down at me from the edge of the cliff. For a moment all I can do is duck; then I realize we are still below them, but rising every moment. The cliff face is about six feet away; the wind reflecting from it keeps us from being blown closer.

I must get the antigrav off. I let myself over the side of the stretcher, hanging by one hand, and fumble for the controls. I can just reach. Then I realize this is no use. Antigrav controls are not meant to go off with a click of the finger; they might get switched off accidentally. To work the switch and the safety you must have two hands, or one hand in the optimum position. My position is about as bad as it could be. I can stroke the switch with one finger; no more.

I haul myself back on to the stretcher and realize we are only about six feet under the beam of light. Only one thing left. I feel in my pocket for the Andite. Stupidly, I am still also bending over the outlet valve of the helmet, trying to see whether M'Clare is still breathing or not.

The little white cigar is not fused. I have to hold on with one hand. In the end I manage to stick the Andite between thumb and finger-roots of that hand while I use the other to find the fuse and stick it over the Andite. The shortest; three minutes.

I think the valve is still moving—

Then something drops round me: I am hauled tight against the stretcher; we are pulled strongly downwards with the wind buffeting and snatching, banged against the edge of something, and pulled through into silence and the dark.

For a moment I do not understand; then I recognize the feel of Fragile Cargo, still clamping me to the stretcher, and I open my mouth and scream and scream.

Clatter of feet. Hatch opens. Fragile Cargo goes limp.

I stagger to my feet. Faint light through the hatch; B's head. I hold out the Andite stick and she turns and shouts; and a panel slides open in the wall so that the wind comes roaring in.

I push the stick through and the wind snatches it away and it is gone.

After that—

After that, for a while, nothing, I suppose, though I have no recollection of losing consciousness; only without any sense of break I find I am flat on my back on one of the seats in the cabin of the hopper.

I sit up and say "How—"

B who is sitting on the floor beside me says that when the broadcaster was activated of course they came at once, only while they were waiting for the boat to reach land whole squads of land cars arrived and started combing the area, and some came up on top of the cliff and shone their headlights out over the sea so Mr. Yardo had to lurk against the cliff face and wait till I got into a position where he could pick me up and it was *frightfully* clever of me to think of floating up on antigrav—

I forgot about the broadcaster.

I forgot about the hopper come to that, there seemed to be nothing in the world except me and the stretcher and the enemy.

Stretcher.

I say, "Is M'Clare—"

At which moment Mr. Yardo turns from the controls with a wide smile of triumph and says "Eighteen twenty-seven, girls!" and the world goes weightless and swings upside down.

Then still with no sense of any time-lapse I am lying in the big lighted hold, with the sound of trampling all round: it is somehow filtered and far off and despite the lights there seems to be a globe of darkness around my head. I hear my own voice repeating, "M'Clare? How's M'Clare?"

A voice says distantly, without emphasis, "M'Clare? He's dead."

The next time I come round it is dark. I am vaguely aware of having been unconscious for quite a while.

There is a single thread of knowledge connecting this moment with the last: M'Clare's dead.

This is the central factor: I seem to have been debating it with myself for a very long time.

I suppose the truth is simply that the Universe never guarantees anything; life, or permanence, or that your best will be good enough.

The rule is that you have to pick yourself up and go on; and lying here in the dark is not doing it.

I turn on my side and see a cluster of self-luminous objects including a light switch. I reach for it.

How did I get into a hospital?

On second thoughts it is a cabin in the ship, or rather two of them with the partition torn out, I can see the ragged edge of it. There is a lot of paraphernalia around; I climb out to have a look.

Holy horrors what's happened? Someone borrowed my legs and put them back wrong; my eyes also are not functioning well, the light is set at Minimum and I am still dazzled. I see a door and make for it to get Explanations from somebody.

Arrived, I miss my footing and stumble against the door and on the other side someone says "Hello, Lizzie. Awake at last?"

I think my heart stops for a moment. I can't find the latch. I am vaguely aware of beating something with my fists, and then the door gives, sticks, gives again and I stumble through and land on all fours the other side of it.

Someone is calling: "Lizzie! Are you hurt? Where the devil have they all got to? Liz!"

I sit up and say, "They said you were *dead!*"

"*Who* did?"

"I . . . I . . . someone in the hold. I said How's M'Clare? and they said you were dead."

M'Clare frowns and says gently, "Come over here and sit down quietly for a bit. You've been dreaming."

Have I? Maybe the whole thing was a dream—but if so how far does it go? Going down in the heli? The missile? The boat? crawling through the black tunnel of a broken ship?

No, because he is sitting in a sort of improvised chaise longue and his legs are evidently strapped in place under

87

the blanket; he is fumbling with the fastenings or something.

I say "Hey! Cut that out!"
He straightens up irritably.
"Don't *you* start that, Lysistrata. I've been suffering the attentions of the damnedest collection of amateur nurses who ever handled a thermocouple, for over a week. I don't deny they've been very efficient, but when it comes to—"

Over a *week?*

He nods. "My dear Lizzie, we left Incognita ten days ago. Amateur nursing again! They have some unholy book of rules which says that for Exposure, Exhaustion and Shock the best therapy is sleep. I don't doubt it, but it goes on to say that in extreme cases the patient has been known to benefit by as much as two weeks of it. I didn't find out that they were trying it on you until about thirty-six hours ago when I began inquiring why you weren't around. They kept *me* under for three days—in fact until their infernal Handbook said it was time for my leg muscles to have some exercise. Miss Lammergaw was the ringleader."

No wonder my legs feel as though someone exchanged the muscles for cotton wool, just wait till I get hold of Kirsty.

If it hadn't been for her, I shouldn't have spent ten days remembering, even in my sleep, that—

I say, "Hell's feathers, it was *you!*"

M'Clare makes motions as though to start getting out of his chair, looking seriously alarmed. I say, "It was your voice! When I asked—"

M'Clare, quite definitely, starts to blush. Not much, but some.

"Lizzie, I believe you're right. I have a sort of vague memory of someone asking how I was—and I gave what I took to be a truthful answer. I remember it seemed quite inconceivable that I could be alive. In fact I still don't understand it. Neither Yardo nor Miss Laydon could tell me. How *did* you get me out of that ship?"

Well, I do my best to explain, glossing over one or two points; at the finish he closes his eyes and says nothing for a while.

Then he says, "So except for this one man who saw you, you left no traces at all?"

Not that I know of, but—

"Do you know, five minutes later there were at least twenty men in that bay, most of them scientists? They don't seem to have found anything suspicious. Visibility was bad, of course, and you can't leave footprints in shingle—"

Hold on, what *is* all this?

M'Clare says, "We've had two couriers while you were asleep. Yes, I know it's not ordinarily possible for a ship on Mass-Time to get news. One of these days someone will have an interesting problem in Cultural Engineering, working out how to integrate some of these Space Force secrets into our economic and social structure without upsetting the whole of the known volume. Though courier boats make their crews so infernally sick I doubt whether the present type will ever come into common use. Anyway, we've had transcripts of a good many broadcasts from Incognita, the last dated four days ago; and as far as we can tell they're interpreting *Gilgamesh* just as we meant them to.

"The missile, by the way, was experimental, waiting to be test-fired the next day. The man in charge saw *Gilgamesh* on the alarm screens and got trigger-happy. The newscasters were divided as to whether he should be blamed or praised; they all seem to feel he averted a menace, at least temporarily, but some of them think the invaders could have been captured alive.

"The first people on the scene came from a scientific camp; you and Miss Laydon saw their lights on the way down. You remember that area is geophysically interesting? Well, by extraordinary good luck an international group was there studying it. They rushed straight off to the site of the landing—they actually saw *Gilgamesh,* and she registered on some of their astronomical instruments, too. They must be a reckless lot. What's more, they started trying to locate her on the sea bottom the next day. Found both pieces; they're still trying to locate the nose. They were all set to try raising the smaller piece when their governments both announced in some haste that they were sending a properly equipped expedition. Jointly.

"There's been no mention in any newscast of anyone seeing fairies or sea maidens—I expect the poor devil thinks you were an hallucination."

So we brought it off.

*   *   *
89

I am very thankful in a distant sort of way, but right now the Incognitans have no more reality for me than the Lost Kafoozalum.

M'Clare came through alive.

I could spend a good deal of time just getting used to that fact, but there is something I ought to say and I don't know how.

I inquire after his injuries and learn they are healing nicely.

I look at him and he is frowning.

He says, "Lizzie. Just before my well-meant but ineffective attempt at suicide—"

Here it comes.

I say quick If he is worrying about all that nonsense he talked in order to distract my attention, forget it; I have.

Silence, then he says wearily, "I talked nonsense, did I?"

I say there is no need to worry, under the circumstances anyone would have a perfect right to be raving off his Nut.

I then find I cannot bear this conversation any longer so I get up saying I expect he is tired and I will call someone.

I get nearly to the door when

"No, Lizzie! you can't let that crew loose on me just in order to change the conversation. Come back here. I appreciate your wish to spare my feelings, but it's wasted. We'll have this out here and now.

"I remember quite well what I said, and so do you: I said that I loved you. I also said that I had intended to ask you to marry me as soon as you ceased to be one of my pupils. Well, the results of Finals were officially announced three days ago.

"Oh, I suppose I always knew what the answer would be, but I didn't want to spend the rest of my life wondering, because I never had the guts to ask you.

"You don't dislike me as you used to—you've forgiven me for making you come to Russett—but you still think I'm a cold-blooded manipulator of other people's minds and emotions. So I am; it's part of the job.

"You're quite right to distrust me for that, though. It is the danger of this profession, that we end up by looking on everybody and everything as a subject for manipulation. Even in our personal lives. I always knew that: I didn't begin to be afraid of it until I realized I was in love with you.

"I could have made you love me, Lizzie. I could! I didn't try. Not that I didn't want love on those terms, or any terms. But to use professional . . . tricks . . . in private life, ends by destroying all reality. I always treated you exactly as I treated my other students—I think. But I could have made you think you loved me . . . even if I am twice your age—"

This I cannot let pass, I say "Hi! According to College rumor you cannot be more than thirty-six; I'm twenty-three."

M'Clare says in a bemused sort of way He will be thirty-seven in a couple of months.

I say, "I will be twenty-four next week and your arithmetic is still screwy; and here is another datum you got wrong. I do love you. Very much."

He says, "Golden Liz."

Then other things which I remember all right, I shall keep them to remember any time I am tired, sick, cold, hungry Hundred-and-ninety—; but they are not for writing down.

Then I suppose at some point we agreed it is time for me to go, because I find myself outside the cabin and there is Colonel Delano-Smith.

He makes me a small speech about various matters ending that he hears he has to congratulate me.

Huh?

Oh Space and Time did one of those unmitigated so-and-sos, my dear classmates, leave M'Clare's communicator on?

The colonel says he heard I did very well in my Examinations.

Sweet splitting photons I forgot all about Finals.

It is just as well my Education has come to an honorable end, because . . . well, shades of . . . well, Goodness gracious and likewise Dear me, I am going to marry a *Professor*.

Better just stick to it I am going to marry M'Clare, it makes better sense that way.

But Gosh we are going to have to do some re-adjusting to a changed Environment. Both of us.

Oh, well, M'Clare is Professor of Cultural Engineering and I just passed my Final Exams in same; surely if anyone can we should be able to work out how you live Happily Ever After?

1961

MORE CONTROVERSY AROSE over the Hugos presented in Chicago in 1962. The lineup of nominees for best novel was the weakest that had appeared in some years. The losers were *Dark Universe* by Daniel F. Galouye, *The Fisherman* (also known as *Time Is the Simplest Thing*) by Clifford Simak, *Sense of Obligation (Planet of the Damned)* by Harry Harrison, and *Second Ending* by James White.

I don't mean to suggest that these were terrible novels, merely that they were rather routine. If only *Rogue Moon* had come along a year later than it did. . . .

Even the winner was a disappointment. It was *Stranger in a Strange Land* by Heinlein. Started 20 years earlier as a tightly constructed, traditional-type science fiction novel, it had been abandoned by its author. Picked up again and completed, the book had turned into a rambling, discursive exposition of vapid philosophical platitudes. A few years later *Stranger* developed a cult following among certain elements of the Flower Generation—much to the dismay of its author, an old Annapolis man whose values were anything but those of the neo-tribalistic hippies.

Still, he *was* Heinlein, and the byline, if not the book, was able to draw votes in a rather sparse field of nominees.

In the category of short fiction, there was still more controversy. The British author Brian Aldiss had written an episodic novel, rather in the pattern of Miller's *Canticle for Leibowitz*. The episodes had run in five issues of *The Magazine of Fantasy and Science Fiction* in 1961, and as a Signet book, *The Long Afternoon of Earth* in 1962.

Under the precedent of *A Canticle for Leibowitz*, the Aldiss material should probably have been considered a novel and held over for consideration a year later. But many fans voted for one or another of the five episodes as separate stories. And the convention committee, under the leadership of its chairman, Earl Kemp, elected to total these votes, regardless of which of the five stories the voter had named, and apply them *all* to "The Hothouse Series."

Not too surprisingly, Aldiss won.

I do not suggest any impropriety on the part of the convention committee—only poor judgment. Nor do I think the Aldiss stories poor stuff. On the contrary, I read them in 1961 and enjoyed them greatly. I may even have been one of the fans who voted for one of them in the Hugo balloting. Time dims one's memory.

The losing nominees were "Lion Loose" by James Schmitz, "Monument" by Lloyd Biggle, "Scylla's Daughter" by Fritz Leiber, and "Status Quo" by Mack Reynolds. All admirable works. There was also a very long list of "honorable mentions" in the convention's program book, and I think that one of these, Avram Davidson's "The Sources of the Nile," must stand high among the stories of 1961.

It's one of those sneaky little paranoia-inspired (or paranoia-inspiring) notions that most of us entertain from time to time. Of all the stories in *What If?*, I think it most resembles those by Shirley Jackson and Alfred Bester. All take place against the commonplace background of the ordinary world of the here and the now.

There are no tentacled aliens, no mighty spacecraft or world-altering plagues. The strangeness—the *otherness*—that is so much a part of science fiction's appeal is merely insinuated into the ordinary world of offices and homes, supermarkets and schools, the advertising agencies of mid-town Manhattan, the clothing manufactures of the garment district, the urban and suburban and exurban homes of the smart, on-the-make executives who work for them and the slick, on-the-make women who work for (and on) *them*.

Oh, I suppose that last comment is objectionably sexist. Well, I'm writing this note almost 20 years after Avram Davidson wrote his story, "The Sources of the Nile."

Nothing like that goes on anymore.

I should mention that after the "Hothouse" incident the fans did change the Hugo rules. They made the rules read that a series of short stories was *not* eligible for a short fiction award. Any one story in the series could be nominated and might win a Hugo, or (as with *A Canticle for Leibowitz*) the series might be stitched together and run as a novel. But there would not again be the kind of cumulative voting that had taken place in 1962.

The Sources of the Nile

AVRAM DAVIDSON

It was in the Rutherford office on Lexington that Bob Rosen met Peter ("Old Pete"—"Sneaky Pete"—"Poor Pete": take your pick) Martens for the first and almost last time. One of those tall, cool buildings on Lexington with the tall, cool office girls it was; and because Bob felt quite sure he wasn't and damned well never was going to be tall or cool enough for him to mean anything to them, he was able to sit back and just enjoy the scenery. Even the magazines on the table were cool: *Spectator, Botteghe Oscuro,* and *Journal of the New York State Geographical Society*. He picked up the last and began to leaf through "Demographic Study of The Jackson Whites."

He was trying to make some sense out of a mass of statistics relating to albinism among that curious tribe (descended from Tuscarora Indians, Hessian deserters, London street women, and fugitive slaves), when one of the girls—delightfully tall, deliciously cool—came to usher him in to Tressling's office. He laid the magazine face down on the low table and followed her. The old man with the portfolio, who was the only other person waiting, got up just then, and Bob noticed the spot of blood in his eye as he passed by. They were prominent eyes, yellowed, reticulated with tiny red veins, and in the corner of one of them was a bright red blot. For a moment it made Rosen feel uneasy, but he had no time then to think about it.

95

"Delightful story," said Joe Tressling, referring to the piece which had gotten Rosen the interview, through his agent. The story had won first prize in a contest, and the agent had thought that Tressling . . . if Tressling . . . maybe Tressling . . .

"Of course, we can't touch it because of the theme," said Tressling.

"Why, what's wrong with the Civil War as a theme?" Rosen said.

Tressling smiled. "As far as Aunt Carrie's Country Cheese is concerned," he said, "the South *won* the Civil War. At least, it's not up to Us to tell Them differently. It might annoy Them. The North doesn't *care*. But write another story for us. The Aunt Carrie Hour is always on the lookout for new dramatic material."

"Like for instance?" Bob Rosen asked.

"What the great cheese-eating American public wants is a story of resolved conflict, concerning young contemporary American couples earning over ten thousand dollars a year. But nothing sordid, controversial, outré, or passé."

Rosen was pleased to be able to see Joseph Tressling, who was the J. Oscar Rutherford Company's man in charge of scripts for the Aunt Carrie Hour. The *Mené Mené* of the short story was said that year to be on the wall, the magazines were dying like mayflies, and the sensible thing for anyone to do who hoped to make a living writing (he told himself) was to get into television. But he really didn't expect he was going to make the transition, and the realization that he didn't really know any contemporary Americans—young, old, married, single— who were earning over ten thousand dollars a year seemed to prophesy that he was never going to earn it himself.

"And nothing avant-garde," said Tressling.

The young woman returned and smiled a tall, cool smile at them. Tressling got up. So did Bob. "Mr. Martens is still outside," she murmured.

"Oh, I'm afraid I won't be able to see him today," said Joe Tressling. "Mr. Rosen has been so fascinating that the time seems to have run over, and then some. . . . Great old boy," he said, smiling at Bob and shaking his hand. "Really one of the veterans of advertising, you know. Used to write copy for Mrs. Winslow's Soothing Syrup. Tells some fascinating yarns. Too bad I haven't the time to listen. I expect to see you back here soon, Mr. Rosen," he said, still holding Bob's hand as they walked to the door, "with another one of your lovely stories. One that we can feel delighted to buy. No costume dramas, no foreign settings, nothing outré, or passé, or avant-garde, and above all—nothing controversial or sordid. You're not going to be one of those *hungry* writers, are you?"

Even before he answered, Rosen observed Tressling's eyes dismiss him; and he resolved to start work immediately on an outré, controversial, sordid costume drama with a foreign setting, etc., if it killed him.

He made the wrong turn for the elevator and on coming back he came face to face with the old man. " 'Demography of the Jackson Whites'," the old man said, feigning amazement. "What do you care about those poor suckers for? They don't buy, they don't sell, they don't start fashion, they don't follow fashion. Just poach, fornicate, and produce oh-point-four hydrocephalic albinoes per hundred. Or something."

The elevator came and they got in together. The old man stared at him, his yellow-bloody eye like a fertilized egg. "Not that I blame them," he went on. "If I'd had any sense I'd've become a Jackson White instead of an advertising man. The least you can do," he said, without any transition, "is to buy me a drink. Since Truthful Tressling blames it onto you that he can't see me, the lying bugger. Why, for crying out loud!" he cried. "What I've got here in this little old portfolio—why, it's worth more to those men on Madison, Lexington, Park—if they only—"

"Let me buy you a drink," said Rosen, resignedly. The streets were hot, and he hoped the bar would be cool.

"A ball of Bushmill," said old Peter Martens.

The bar *was* cool. Bob had stopped listening to his guest's monologue about what he had in his little old portfolio (something about spotting fashion trends way in advance) and had begun talking about his own concerns. By and by the old man, who was experienced beyond the norm in not being listened to, had begun to listen to *him*.

"This was when everybody was reading *Aku-Aku*," Bob said. "So I thought for sure that mine would go over good because it was about Rapa Nui—Easter Island—and Peruvian blackbirders and hints of great legends of the past and all that."

"And?"

"And it didn't. The publisher, the only one who showed any interest at all, I mean, *that* publisher, he said *he* liked the writing but the public wouldn't buy it. He advised me to study carefully the other paperbacks on the stands. See what they're like, go thou and do likewise. So I did. You know the stuff. On even-numbered pages the heroine gets her brassiere ripped off while she cries, *'Yes! Yes! Now! Oh!'* "

He was not aware of signaling, but from time to time a hand appeared and renewed their glasses. Old Martens asked, "Does she cry 'rapturously'—or 'joyously'?"

"Rapturously *and* joyously. What's the matter, you think she's frigid?"

Martens perished the thought. At a nearby table a large blonde said lugubriously, "You know, Harold, it's a lucky thing the Good Lord didn't give me any children or I would of wasted my life on them like I did on my rotten step-children." Martens asked what happened on the odd-numbered children.

"I mean, 'pages'," he corrected himself, after a moment.

The right side of Bob Rosen's face was going numb. The left side started tingling. He interrupted a little tune he was humming and said, "Oh, the equation is invariable: On odd-numbered pages the hero either clonks some bastard bloodily on the noggin with a roscoe, or kicks him in the collions and *then* clonks him, or else he's engaged —with his shirt off, you're not allowed to say what gives with the pants, which are so much more important: presumably they melt or something—he's engaged, shirtless, in arching his lean and muscular flanks over some bimbo, *not* the heroine, because these aren't her pages, some other female in whose pelvis he reads strange mysteries . . ." He was silent for a moment, brooding.

"How could it fail, then?" asked the old man, in his husky voice. "I've seen the public taste change, let me tell you, my boy, from *A Girl of the Limberlost* [which was so pure that nuns could read it] to stuff which makes stevedores blench: so I am moved to inquire, How could the work you are describing to me fail?"

The young man shrugged. "The nuns were making a come-back. Movies about nuns, books about nuns, nuns on TV, westerns. . . . So the publisher said public taste had changed, and could I maybe do him a life of St. Teresa?"

"Coo."

"So I spent three months doing a life of St. Teresa at a furious pace, and when I finished it turned out I'd done the wrong saint. The simple slob had no idea there was any more than one of the name, and I never thought to ask did he mean the Spanish St. Teresa or the French one? D'Avila or The Little Flower?"

"Saints preserve us. . . . Say, do you know that wonderful old Irish toast? 'Here's to the Council of Trent, that put the fasting on the meat and not on the drink'?"

Bob gestured to the barkeeper. "But I didn't understand why if one St. Teresa could be sold, the other one couldn't. So I tried another publisher, and all *he* said was, public taste had changed, and could I do him anything with a background of juvenile delinquency? After that I took a job for a while selling frozen custard in a penny arcade and all my friends said, BOB! You with *your talent?* How COULD you?"

The large blonde put down a jungle-green drink and looked at her companion. "What you mean, they love me? If they love me why are they going to Connecticut? You don't go to Connecticut if you love a person," she pointed out.

Old Martens cleared his throat. "My suggestion would be that you combine all three of your mysteriously unsalable novels. The hero sails on a Peruvian blackbirder to raid Easter Island, the inhabitants whereof he kicks in the collions, if male, or arches his loins over, if female; until he gets converted by a vision of both St. Teresas who tell him their life stories—as a result of which he takes a job selling frozen custard in a penny arcade in order to help the juvenile delinquents who frequent the place."

Bob grunted. "Depend on it, with my luck I would get it down just in time to see public taste change again. The publishers would want a pocket treasury of the McGuffey Readers, or else the memoirs of Constantine Porphyrogenetus. I could freeze my arse climbing the Himalayas only to descend, manuscript in hand, to find everybody on Publishers' Row vicariously donning goggles and spearing fish on the bottom of the Erythrean Sea. . . . Only thing is, I never was sure to what degree public taste changed by itself or how big a part the publishers play in changing it. . . ."

The air, cool though he knew it was, seemed to shimmer in front of him, and through the shimmer he saw Peter Martens sitting up straight and leaning over at him, his seamed and ancient face suddenly eager and alive. "And would you like to be sure?" old Martens asked. "Would you like to be able to know, really to *know?*"

"What? How?" Bob was startled. The old man's eye looked almost all blood by now.

"Because," Martens said, "*I* can tell you what. *I* can tell you how. Nobody else. Only *me*. And not just about books, about everything. Because——"

There was an odd sort of noise, like the distant sussuration of wind in dry grass, and Rosen looked around and he saw that a man was standing by them and laughing. This man wore a pale brown suit and had a pale brown complexion, he was very tall and very thin and had a very small head and slouched somewhat. He looked like a mantis, and a mustache like an inverted V was cropped out of the broad blue surface of his upper lip.

"Still dreaming your dreams, Martens?" this man asked, still wheezing his dry whispery laugh. "Gates of Horn, or Gates of Ivory?"

"Get the hell away from me, Shadwell," said Martens.

Shadwell turned his tiny little head to Rosen and grinned. "He been telling you about how he worked on old Mrs. Winslow's Soothing Syrup Account? Too bad the Harrison Narcotics Act killed that business! He tell you how he worked on the old Sapolio account? The old Stanley Steamer account?" ["Shove off, Shadwell," Martens ordered, planting his elbow on the table and opening his mouth at Bob again.] "Or has he been muttering away like an old Zambezi hand who claims to know the location of the Elephants' Graveyard? Tell me, where is fashion bred?" he intoned. "In the bottle—or in Martens' head?"

Martens' head, thinly covered with yellowish-white hair, jerked in the direction of the new arrival. "This, my boy, is T. Pettys Shadwell, the most despicable of living men. He runs—out of his pocket, because no one will sell him a hat on credit—he runs a so-called market research business. Though who in blazes would hire him since Polly Adler went respectable beats the hell out of me. I'm warning you, Shadwell," he said, "take off. I've had my fill of you. I'm not giving you any more information." And with a further graphic description of what else he would *not* give T. Pettys Shadwell if the latter was dying of thirst, he folded his arms and fell silent.

The most despicable of living men chuckled, poked a bone-thin hand into a pocket, plucked out a packet of white flaps of cardboard, one of which he tore along a perforated line and handed to Bob. "My card, sir. My operation, true, is not large, but it is Ever Growing. Don't take Mr.

Martens too seriously. And don't buy him too many drinks. His health is not as good as it used to be—but then, it never was." And with a final laugh, like the rustling of dried corn-shucks, he angled away.

Martens sighed, lapped the last few dewy drops of Bush-mill's off a molten ice-cube. "I live in mortal fear that some day I'll have the money to buy all the booze I want and wake up finding I have spilled the beans to that cockatrice who just walked out. Can you imagine anyone having business cards printed to be torn off of perforated pads? Keeps them from getting loose and wrinkled, is his reason. Such a man has no right, under natural or civil law, to live."

In the buzzing coolness of the barroom Bob Rosen tried to catch hold of a thought which was coyly hiding behind a corner in his mind. His mind otherwise, he felt, was lucid as never before. But somehow he lost the thought, found he was telling himself a funny story in French and —although he had never got more than an 80 in the course, back in high school—marvelled at the purity of his accent and then chuckled at the punch-line.

" 'Never mind about black neglijays,' " the stout blonde was saying. " 'If you want to keep your husband's affections,' I said to her, 'then listen to me—' "

The errant thought came trotting back for reasons of its own, and jumped into Bob's lap. " 'Spill the beans'?" he quoted, questioningly. "Spill *what* beans? To Shadwell, I mean."

"Most despicable of living men," said old Martens, me-chanically. Then a most curious expression washed over his antique countenance: proud, cunning, fearful . . .

"Would you like to know the sources of the Nile?" he asked. "Would you?"

" 'Let him *go* to Maine,' I said. 'Let him paint rocks all day,' I said. 'Only for heaven's sake, keep him the hell off of Fire Island,' I said. And was I right, Harold?" de-manded the large blonde.

Pete Martens was whispering something, Bob realized. By the look on his face it must have been important, so the young man tried to hear the words over the buzzing, and thought to himself in a fuddled fashion that they ought to be taken down on a steno pad, or something of that sort . . . *want to know, really know, where it begins and how, and how often?* But no; what do I know? For years

101

I've been Clara the rotten step-mother, and now I'm Clara the rotten mother-in-law. *Are there such in every generation? Must be . . . known for years . . . known for years . . . only, Who? —and Where?—searched and sought, like Livingston and all the others searching and seeking, enduring privation, looking for the sources of the Nile . . .*

Someone, it must have been Clara, gave a long, shuddering cry; and then for a while there was nothing but the buzzing, buzzing, buzzing, in Bob Rosen's head; while old Martens lolled back in the chair, regarding him silently and sardonically with his blood-red eye, over which the lid slowly, slowly drooped: but old Martens never said a word more.

It was one genuine horror of a hangover, subsiding slowly under (or perhaps despite) every remedy Bob's aching brain could think of: black coffee, strong tea, chocolate milk, raw-egg-red-pepper-worcestershire sauce. At least, he thought gratefully after a while, he was spared the dry heaves. At least he had all the fixings in his apartment and didn't have to go out. It was a pivotal neighborhood, and he lived right in the pivot, a block where lox and bagels beat a slow retreat before the advance of hog maw and chitterlings on the one hand and *bodegas, comidas criollas,* on the other; swarms of noisy kids running between the trucks and buses, the jackhammers forever wounding the streets.

It took him a moment to realize that the noise he was hearing now was not the muffled echo of the drills, but a tapping on his door. Unsteadily, he tottered over and opened it. He would have been not in the least surprised to find a raven there, but instead it was a tall man, rather stooping, with a tiny head, hands folded mantis-like at his bosom.

After a few dry, futile clickings, Bob's throat essayed the name "Shadburn?"

"Shadwell," he was corrected, softly. "T. Pettys Shadwell . . . I'm afraid you're not well, Mr. Rosen . . ."

Bob clutched the doorpost, moaned softly. Shadwell's hands unfolded, revealed—not a smaller man at whom he'd been nibbling, but a paper bag, soon opened.

". . . so I thought I'd take the liberty of bringing you some hot chicken broth."

It was gratefully warm, had both body and savor. Bob lapped at it, croaked his thanks. "Not at all, not-a-tall," Shadwell waved. "Glad to be of some small help." A

102

silence fell, relieved only by weak, gulping noises. "Too bad about old Martens. Of course, he *was* old. Still, a shocking thing to happen to you. A stroke, I'm told. I, uh, trust the police gave you no trouble?"

A wave of mild strength seemed to flow into Bob from the hot broth. "No, they were very nice," he said. "The sergeant called me 'son.' They brought me back here."

"Ah." Shadwell was reflective. "He had no family. I know that for a fact."

"Mmm."

"But—assume he left a few dollars. Unlikely, but— And assume he'd willed the few dollars to someone or some charity, perhaps. Never mind. Doesn't concern us. He wouldn't bother to will his papers . . . scrapbooks of old copy he'd written, so forth. That's of no interest to people in general. Just be thrown out or burned. But it would be of interest to *me*. I mean, I've been in advertising all my life, you know. Oh, yes. Used to distribute handbills when I was a boy. Fact."

Bob tried to visualize T. Pettys Shadwell as a boy, failed, drank soup. "Good soup," he said. "Thanks. Very kind of you."

Shadwell urged him strongly not to mention it. He chuckled. "Old Pete used to lug around some of the darndest stuff in that portfolio of his," he said. "In fact, some of it referred to a scheme we were once trying to work out together. Nothing came of it, however, and the old fellow was inclined to be a bit testy about that, still— I believe you'd find it interesting. May I show you?"

Bob still felt rotten, but the death wish had departed. "Sure," he said. Shadwell looked around the room, then at Bob, expectantly. After a minute he said, "Where is it?" "Where is what?" "The portfolio. Old Martens'."

They stared at each other. The phone rang. With a wince and a groan, Bob answered. It was Noreen, a girl with pretensions to stagecraft and literature, with whom he had been furtively lecherous on an off-and-on basis, the off periods' commencements being signaled by the presence in Noreen's apartment of Noreen's mother (knitting, middle-class morality and all), when Bob came, intent on venery.

"I've got a terrible hangover," he said, answering her first (guarded and conventional) question; "and the place is a mess."

"See what happens if I turn my back on you for a minute?" Noreen clucked, happily. "Luckily, I have neither work nor social obligations planned for the day, so I'll be right over."

Bob said, "Crazy!", hung up, and turned to face Shadwell, who had been nibbling the tips of his prehensile fingers. "Thanks for the soup," he said, in tones of some finality.

"But the portfolio?" "I haven't got it." "It was leaning against the old man's chair when I saw the two of you in the bar." "Then maybe it's still *in* the bar. Or in the hospital. Or maybe the cops have it. But—" "It isn't. They don't." "But *I* haven't got it. Honest, Mr. Shadwell, I appreciate the soup, but I don't know where the hell—"

Shadwell rubbed his tiny, sharp mustache, like a ∧-mark pointing to his tiny, sharp nose. He rose. "This is really too bad. Those papers referring to the business old Peter and I had been mutually engaged in—really, I have as much right to them as . . . But look here. Perhaps he may have spoken to you about it. He always did when he'd been drinking and usually did even when he wasn't. What he liked to refer to as, 'The sources of the Nile'? Hmm?" The phrase climbed the belfry and rang bells audible, or at least apparent, to Shadwell. He seemed to leap forward, long fingers resting on Bob's shoulders.

"You do know what I mean. Look. You: Are a writer. The old man's ideas aren't in your line. I: Am an advertising man. They are in my line. For the contents of his portfolio—as I've explained, they are rightfully mine—I will give: One thousand: Dollars. In fact: For the opportunity of merely *looking* through it: I will give: One *hundred*. Dollars."

As Bob reflected that his last check had been for $17.72 (Monegasque rights to a detective story), and as he heard these vasty sums bandied about, his eyes grew large, and he strove hard to recall what the hell *had* happened to the portfolio—but in vain.

Shadwell's dry, whispery voice took on a pleading note. "I'm even willing to pay you for the privilege of discussing your conversation with the old f— the old gentleman. Here—" And he reached into his pocket. Bob wavered. Then he recalled that Noreen was even now on her way uptown and crosstown, doubtless bearing with her, as usual, in addition to her own taut charms, various tokens of exotic victualry to which she—turning her back on the veal chops and green peas of childhood and suburbia—was given: such as Shashlik makings, *lokoumi*, wines of the warm south, *baklava, provolone,* and other living witnesses to the glory that was Greece and the grandeur that was Rome.

Various hungers, thus stimulated, began to rise and clamor, and he steeled himself against Shadwell's possibly unethical and certainly inconveniently timed offers.

"Not now," he said. Then, throwing delicacy to the winds, "I'm expecting a girl friend. Beat it. Another time."

Annoyance and chagrin on Shadwell's small face, succeeded by an exceedingly disgusting leer. "Why, of *course,*" he said. "Another time? Cer-tain-ly. My card—" He hauled out the perforated pack. "I already got one," Bob said. "Goodbye."

He made haste to throw off the noisome clothes in which he had been first hot, then drunk, then comatose; to take a shower, comb his mouse-colored hair, shave the pink bristles whose odious tint alone prevented him from growing a beard, to spray and anoint himself with various nostra which T. Pettys Shadwell's more successful colleagues in advertising had convinced him (by a thousand ways, both blunt and subtle) were essential to his acceptance by good society; then to dress and await with unconcealed anticipation the advent of the unchaste Noreen.

She came, she kissed him, she prepared food for him; ancient duties of women, any neglect of which is a sure and certain sign of cultural decadence and retrogression. Then she read everything he had written since their last juncture, and here she had some fault to find.

"You waste too much time at the beginning, in description," she said, with the certainty possible to those who have never sold a single manuscript. "You've got to make your characters come *alive*—in the very first sentence."

" 'Marley was dead, to begin with,' " muttered Bob.

"What?" murmured Noreen, vaguely, feigning not to hear. Her eye, avoiding lover boy, lit on something else. "What's this?" she asked. "You have so much money you just leave it lying around? I thought you said you were broke." And Bob followed her pointing and encarnadined fingertip to where lay two crisp twenty-dollar bills, folded lengthwise, on the table next the door.

"Shadwell!" he said, instantly. And, in response to her arched brows (which would have looked much better unplucked, but who can hold what will away?), he said, "A real rat of a guy—a louse, a boor—who had some crumby proposal."

105

"And who also has," said Noreen, going straight to the heart of the matter, "money." Bob resolved never to introduce the two of them, if he could help it. "Anyway," she continued, laying aside Bob's manuscript, "now you can take me out somewhere." Feebly he argued the food then cooking; she turned off the gas and thrust the pots incontinently into the icebox, rose, and indicated she was now ready to leave. He had other objections to leaving just then, which it would have been impolitic to mention, for in Noreen's scheme of morality each episode of passion was a sealed incident once it was over, and constituted no promise of any other yet to come.

With resignation tempered by the reflection that Shadwell's four sawbucks couldn't last forever, and that there was never so long-drawn-out an evening but would wind up eventually back in his apartment, Bob accompanied her out the door.

And so it was. The next day, following Noreen's departure in mid-morning, found Bob in excellent spirit but flat-broke. He was reviewing the possibilities of getting an advance from his agent, Stuart Emmanuel, a tiny, dapper man whose eyes behind double lenses were like great black shoe-buttons, when the phone rang. ESP or no ESP, it was Stuart himself, with an invitation to lunch.

"I'm glad *some* of your clients are making money," said Bob, most ungraciously.

"Oh, it's not my money," said Stuart. "It's J. Oscar Rutherford's. One of his top men—no, it's not Joe Tressling, I know you saw him the day before yesterday, yes, I know nothing came of it, this is a different fellow altogether. Phillips Anhalt. I want you to come."

So Bob left yesterday's half-cooked chow in the icebox and, very little loath, set out to meet Stuart and Phillips Anhalt, of whom he had never heard before. The first rendezvous was for a drink at a bar whose name also meant nothing to him, though as soon as he walked in he recognized it as the one where he had been the day before yesterday, and this made him uneasy—doubly so, for he had callously almost forgotten what had happened there. The bartender, it was at once evident, had not. His wary glance at the three of them must have convinced him that they were reasonably good insurance risks, however, for he made no comment.

Anhalt was a middle-sized man with a rather sweet and slightly baffled face and iron-grey haircut *en brosse*. "I enjoyed your story very much," he told Bob—thus breaking in at once upon the shallow slumber of the little scold who boarded in Bob's Writer's Consciousness. Of *course* (it shrilled) I know *exactly* the one you mean, after all, I've written only *one* story in my entire *life* so *"your story"* is the only identification it needs. I liked your *novel,* Mr. Hemingway. I enjoyed your *play,* Mr. Kaufman.

Stuart Emmanuel, who knew the labyrinthine ways of writers' minds as he knew the figures in his bank statement, said smoothly, "I expect Mr. Anhalt refers to *Unvexed to the Sea.*"

With firm politeness Mr. Anhalt disappointed this expectation. "I know that's the prize-winner," he said, "and I mean to read it, but the one I referred to was *The Green Wall.*" Now, as it happened, this very short little story had been bounced thirteen times before its purchase for a negligible sum by a low-grade salvage market of a magazine; but it was one of Bob's favorites. He smiled at Phillips Anhalt, Anhalt smiled at him, Stuart beamed and ordered drinks.

The waiter passed a folded slip of paper to Bob Rosen when he came with the popskull. "The lady left it," he said. "What lady?" "The blonde lady." Agent and ad man smiled, made appropriate remarks while Bob scanned the note, recognized it as being in his own handwriting, failed to make it out, crammed it in his pocket.

"Mr. Anhalt," said Stuart, turning dark, large-pupiled eyes on his client, "is a very important man at Rutherford's: he has a corner office." A gentle, somewhat tired smile from Anhalt, who gave the conversation a turn and talked about his home in Darien, and the work he was doing on it, by himself. Thus they got through the round of drinks, then walked a few blocks to the restaurant.

Here Bob was infinitely relieved that Anhalt did not order poached egg on creamed spinach, corned beef hash, or something equally simple, wholesome, and disgusting, and tending to inhibit Bob's own wide-ranging tastes: Anhalt ordered duckling, Stuart had mutton chops, and Bob chose tripe and onions.

"Joe Tressling tells me that you're going to write something for the cheese show," said Anhalt, as they disarranged the pickle plate. Bob half-lifted his eyebrows, smiled. Stuart gazed broodingly into the innards of a sour tomato as if he might be saying to himself, "Ten percent of $17.72, Monegasque rights to a detective story."

107

"More cheese is being eaten today in the United States than twenty-five years ago," Anhalt continued. "Much, much more. . . . Is it the result of advertising? Such as the Aunt Carrie Hour? Has that changed public taste? Or—has public taste changed for, say, other reasons, and are we just riding the wave?"

"The man who could have answered that question," Bob said, "died the day before yesterday."

Anhalt let out his breath. "How do you know he could have?"

"He said so."

Anhalt, who'd had a half-eaten dilled cucumber in his hand, carefully laid it in the ash-tray, and leaned forward. "What else did he say? Old Martens, I mean. You *do* mean Old Martens, don't you?"

Bob said that was right, and added, with unintentional untruthfulness, that he'd been offered a thousand dollars for that information, and had turned it down. Before he could correct himself, Anhalt, customary faint pink face gone almost red, and Stuart Emmanuel, eyes glittering hugely, said with one voice, *"Who* offered—?"

"What comes out of a chimney?"

Stuart, recovering first (Anhalt continued to stare, said nothing, while the color receded), said, "Bob, this is not a joke. That is the reason we have this appointment. An awful lot of money is involved—for you, for me, for Phil Anhalt, for, well, for everybody. For just everybody. So—"

It slipped out. "For T. Pettys Shadwell?" Bob asked.

The effect, as they used to say in pre-atomic days, was electrical. Stuart made a noise, between a moan and a hiss, rather like a man who, having trustingly lowered his breeches, sits all unawares upon an icicle. He clutched Bob's hand. "You didn't godforbid *sign* anything?" he wailed. Anhalt, who had gone red before, went white this time around, but still retained diffidence enough to place his hand merely upon Bob's jacket-cuff.

"He's a cad!" he said, in trembling tones. "A swine, Mr. Rosen!"

" 'The most despicable of living men'," quoted Mr. Rosen. ["Exactly," said Anhalt.]

"Bob, you didn't *sign* anything, godforbid?"

"No. No. No. But I feel as if I've had all the mystery I intend to have. And unless I get Information, why, gents, I shan't undo one button." The waiter arrived with the food and, according to the rules and customs of the Waiters' Union, gave everybody the wrong orders. When this was straightened out, Stuart said, confidently, "Why, of course, Bob: Information: Why, certainly. There is nothing to conceal. Not from *you*," he said, chuckling. "Go ahead, start eating. I'll eat and talk, you just eat and listen."

And so, as he tucked away the tripe and onions, Bob heard Stuart recount, through a slight barrier of masticated mutton-chop, a most astonishing tale. In every generation (Stuart said) there were leaders of fashion, arbiters of style. At Nero's court, Petronius. In Regency England, Beau Brummel. At present and for some time past, everyone knew about the Paris designers and their influence. And in the literary field ["Ahah!" muttered Bob, staring darkly at his forkful of stewed ox-paunch]—in the literary field, said Stuart, swallowing in haste for greater clarity, they all knew what effect a review by any one of A Certain Few Names, on the front page of the Sunday Times book section, could have upon the work of even an absolute unknown.

"It will sky-rocket it to Fame and Fortune with the speed of light," said Stuart.

"Come to the point." But Stuart, now grinding away on a chunk of grilled sheep, could only gurgle, wave his fork, and raise his eyebrows. Anhalt stopped his moody task of reducing the duckling to a mass of orange-flavored fibres, and turned to take the words, as it were, from Stuart's mutton-filled mouth.

"The point, Mr. Rosen, is that poor old Martens went up and down Madison Avenue for years claiming he had found a way of predicting fashions and styles, and nobody believed him. Frankly, *I* didn't. But I do now. What caused me to change my mind was this: When I heard, day before yesterday, that he had died so suddenly, I had a feeling that I *had* something of his, something that he'd left for me to look at once, something I'd taken just to get rid of him. And, oh, perhaps I was feeling a bit guilty, certainly a bit sorry, so I asked my secretary to get it for me. Well, you know, with the J. Oscar Rutherford people, as with Nature, nothing is ever lost"—Phillips Anhalt smiled his rather shy, rather sweet and slightly baffled smile— "so she got it for me and I took a look at it. . . . I was . . . " he paused, hesitated for the *mot juste*.

Stuart, with a masterful swallow, leaped into the breach, claymore in hand. "He was flabbergasted!"

Astounded, amended Anhalt. He was astounded.

109

There, in an envelope addressed to Peter Martens, and postmarked November 10, 1945, was a color snapshot of a young man wearing a fancy weskit.

"Now, you know, Mr. Rosen, no one in 1945 was wearing fancy weskits. They didn't come in till some years later. How did Marten *know* they were going to come in? And there was another snapshot of a young man in a charcoal suit and a pink shirt. Nobody was wearing that outfit in '45 . . . I checked the records, you see, and the old gentleman had left the things for me in December of that year. I'm ashamed to say that I had the receptionist put him off when he called again . . . But just think of it: fancy weskits, charcoal suits, pink shirts, in 1945." He brooded. Bob asked if there was anything about grey flannel suits in the envelope, and Anhalt smiled a faint and fleeting smile.

"Ah, Bob, now, Bob," Stuart pursed his mouth in mild (and greasy) reproof. "You still don't seem to realize that this is S*E*R*I*O*U*S*."

"Indeed it is," said P. Anhalt. "As soon as I told Mac about it, do you know what he said, Stu? He said, 'Phil, don't spare the horses.' " And they nodded soberly, as those who have received wisdom from on high.

"Who," Bob asked, "is Mac?"

Shocked looks. Mac, he was told, the older men speaking both tandem and *au pair*, was Robert R. Mac Ian, head of the happy J. Oscar Rutherford corporate family.

"Of course, Phil," Stuart observed, picking slyly at his baked potato, "I won't ask why it took you till this morning to get in touch with me. With some other outfit, I might maybe suspect that they were trying to see what they could locate for themselves without having to cut our boy, here, in for a slice of the pie. He being the old man's confidante and moral heir, anyway, so to speak." [Bob stared at this description, said nothing. Let the thing develop as far as it would by itself, he reflected.] "But not the Rutherford outfit. It's too big, too ethical, for things like that." Anhalt didn't answer.

After a second, Stuart went on, "Yes, Bob, this is really something big. If the late old Mr. Martens' ideas can be successfully developed—and I'm sure Phil, here will not expect you to divulge until we are ready to talk Terms—they will be really invaluable to people like manufacturers, fashion editors, designers, merchants, and, last but not least—advertising men. Fortunes can literally

110

be made, and saved. No wonder that a dirty dog like this guy Shadwell is trying to horn in on it. Why listen—but I'm afraid we'll have to terminate this enchanting conversation. Bob has to go home and get the material in order"— [What material? Bob wondered. Oh, well, so far: $40 from Shadwell and a free lunch from Anhalt]— "and you and I, Phil, will discuss those horses Mac said not to spare."

Anhalt nodded. It seemed obvious to Rosen that the ad man was unhappy, unhappy about having given Peter Martens the brushoff while he was alive, unhappy about being numbered among the vultures now that he was dead. And so, thinking, Bob realized with more than a touch of shame, that he himself was now numbered among the vultures; and he asked about funeral arrangements. But it seemed that the Masonic order was taking care of that: the late Peters Martens was already on his way back to his native town of Marietta, Ohio, where his lodge brothers would give him a formal farewell: aprons, sprigs of acacia, and all the ritual appurtenances. And Bob thought, why not? And was feeling somehow, very much relieved.

On the uptown bus which he had chosen over the swifter, hotter, dingier subway, he tried to collect his thoughts. What on earth could he ever hope to remember about a drunken conversation, which would make any sense to anybody, let alone be worth money? "The Sources of the Nile," the old man had said, glaring at him with bloody eye. Well, Shadwell knew the phrase, too. Maybe Shadwell knew what it meant, exactly what it meant, because he, Bob Rosen, sure as hell didn't. But the phrase did catch at the imagination. Martens had spent years —who knew how many?—seeking the sources of his particular Nile, the great river of fashion, as Mungo Park, Livingstone, Speke, and other half-forgotten explorers, had spent years in search of theirs. They had all endured privation, anguish, rebuffs, hostility . . . and in the end, just as the quest had killed Mungo Park, Livingstone, Speke, the other quest had killed old Peter Martens.

But, aside from insisting that there *was* a source or sources, and that he knew *where*, what had Pete said? Why hadn't Bob stayed sober? Probably the fat blonde at the next table, she of the poisonously green drink and the rotten step-children, probably she retained more of the old man's tale, picked up by intertable osmosis, than did Bob himself.

And with that he heard the voice of the waiter at the bar that noon: *The lady left it . . . What lady . . . ? The blonde lady . . .* Bob scrabbled in his pocket and came up with the note. On the sweaty, crumpled bit of paper, scrawled in his own writing, or a cruel semblance of it, he read: *Ditx sags su Bimsoh oh—*

"What the hell!" he muttered, and fell to, with furrowed face, to make out what evidently owed more to Bushmill's than to Eberhard Faber. At length he decided that the note read, *Peter says, see Bensons on Purchase Place, the Bronx, if I don't believe him. Peter says, write it down.*

"It must mean something," he said, half-aloud, staring absently from Fifth Avenue to Central Park, as the bus roared and rattled between opulence and greenery. "It has to mean something."

"Well, what a shame," said Mr. Benson. "But how nice it was of you to come and tell us." His wavy gray hair was cut evenly around in soupbowl style, and as there was no white skin at the back of his neck, had evidently been so cut for some time. "Would you like some iced tea?"

"Still, he Went Quickly," said Mrs. Benson, who, at the business of being a woman, was in rather a large way of business. "I don't think there's any iced tea, Daddy. When I have to go, that's the way I want to go. Lemonade, maybe?"

"There isn't any lemonade if what Kitty was drinking was the last of the lemonade. The Masons give you a nice funeral. A real nice funeral. I used to think about joining up, but I never seem to get around to it. I think there's some gin. Isn't there some gin, Mommy? How about a nice cool glass of gin-and-cider, Bob? Kit will make us some, by and by."

Bob said, softly, that that sounded nice. He sat half-sunken in a canvas chair in the large, cool living-room. A quarter of an hour ago, having found out with little difficulty *which* house on Purchase Place was the Bensons', he had approached with something close to fear and trembling. Certainly, he had been sweating in profusion. The not-too-recently painted wooden house was just a blind, he told himself. Inside there would be banks of noiseless machines into which cards were fed and from which tapes rolled in smooth continuity. And a large broad-shouldered young man whose hair was cut so close to the skull that the scars underneath were plain to see, this young man would bar Bob's way and, with cold, calm, confidence, say, "Yes?"

"Er, um, Mr. Martens told me to see Mr. Benson."

"There is no Mr. Martens connected with our organization and Mr. Benson has gone to Washington. I'm afraid you can't come in: everything here is Classified."

And Bob would slink away, feeling Shoulders' scornful glance in the small of his shrinking, sweaty back.

But it hadn't been like that at all. Not anything like that at all.

Mr. Benson waved an envelope at Bob. "Here's a connivo, if you like," he said. "Fooled I don't know how many honest collectors, and dealers, too: Prince Abu-Somebody flies over here from Pseudo-Arabia without an expense account. Gets in with some crooked dealers, *I* could name them, but I won't, prints off this *en—tire* issue of airmails, pre-cancelled. Made a mint. Flies back to Pseudo-Arabia, *whomp!* They cut off his head!" And he chuckled richly at the thought of this prompt and summary vengeance. Plainly, in Mr. Benson's eyes, it had been done in the name of philatelic ethics; no considerations of dynastic intrigues among the petrol pashas entered his mind.

"Kitty, are you going to make us some cold drinks?" Mrs. B. inquired. "Poor old Pete, he used to be here for Sunday dinner on and off, oh, for just years. Is that Bentley coming?"

Bob just sat and sucked in the coolness and the calm and stared at Kitty. Kitty had a tiny stencil cut in the design of a star and she was carefully lacquering her toenails with it. He could hardly believe she was for real. "Ethereal" was the word for her beauty, and "ethereal" was the only word for it. Long, long hair of an indescribable gold fell over her heart-shaped face as she bent forward towards each perfectly formed toe. And she was wearing a dress like that of a child in a Kate Greenaway book.

"Oh, Bentley," said B., Senior. "What do you think has happened? Uncle Peter Martens passed away, all of a sudden, day before yesterday, and this gentleman is a friend of his and came to tell us about it; isn't that thoughtful?"

Bentley said, "Ahhh." Bentley was a mid-teener who wore jeans cut off at the knees and sneakers with the toes, insteps, and heels removed. He was naked to the

113

waist and across his suntanned and hairless chest, a neat curve commencing just above his left nipple and terminating just under his right nipple, was the word *VIPERS* stenciled in red paint.

"*Ahhh*," said Bentley Benson. "And Pepsies?"

"Well, I'd asked you to bring some," his mother said, mildly. "Make a nice, big pitcher of gin-and-cider, Bentley, please, but only a *little* gin for yourself, in a separate glass, remember, now." Bentley said, "Ahhh," and departed, scratching on his chest right over the bright, red S.

Bob's relaxed gaze took in, one by one, the pictures on the mantelpiece. He sat up a bit, pointed. "Who is that?" he asked. The young man looked something like Bentley and something like Bentley's father.

"That's my oldest boy, Barton, Junior," said Mother B. "You see that nice vest he's wearing? Well, right after the War, Bart, he was in the Navy then, picked up a piece of lovely brocade over in Japan, and he sent it back home. I thought of making a nice bed-jacket out of it, but there wasn't enough material. So I made it into a nice vest, instead. Poor old Uncle Peter, he liked that vest, took a picture of Bart in it. Well, what do you know, a few years later fancy vests became quite popular, and, of course, by that time Bart was tired of his ["Of course," Bob murmured], so he sold it to a college boy who had a summer job at Little and Harpey's. Got $25 for it, and we all went out to dinner down town that night."

Kitty delicately stenciled another star on her toenails.

"I see," Bob said. After a moment, "Little and Harpey's?" he repeated.

Yes, that same. The publishers. Bart, and his younger brother, Alton, were publishers' readers. Alt had been with Little and Harpey but was now with Scribbley's Sons; Bart had worked for Scribbley's at one time, too. "They've been with *all* the biggest publishing houses," their mother said, proudly. "Oh, *they* aren't any of your stick-in-the-muds, no sirree." Her hands had been fiddling with a piece of bright cloth, and then, suddenly, cloth and hands went up to her head, her fingers flashed, and—complete, perfect—she was wearing an intricately folded turban.

Bentley came in carrying a pitcher of drink in one hand and five glasses—one to each finger—in the other. "I told you to mix yours separately, I think," his mother said. Taking no notice of her youngest's *Ahhh,* she turned to Bob. "I have a whole basket of these pieces of madras," she said, "some silk, some cotton . . . and it's been on my mind all day. Now, if I just remember the way those old women from the West Indies used to tie them on their heads when I was a girl . . . and now, sure enough, it just came back to me! How does it look?" she asked.

"Looks very nice, Mommy," said Bart, Sr. And added, "I bet it would cover up the curlers better than those babushkas the women wear, you know?"

Bob Rosen bet it would, too.

So here it was and this was it. The sources of the Nile. How old Peter Martens had discovered it, Bob did not know. By and by, he supposed, he would find out. How did they *do* it, was it that they had a *panache*—? or was it a "wild talent," like telepathy, second sight, and calling dice or balls? He did not know.

"Bart said he was reading a real nice manuscript that came in just the other day," observed Mrs. Benson, dreamily, over her glass. "About South America. He says he thinks that South America has been neglected, and that there is going to be a revival of interest in nonfiction about South America."

"No more Bushmen?" Barton, Sr., asked.

"No, Bart says he thinks the public is getting tired of Bushmen. He says he only gives Bushmen another three months and then—poo—you won't be able to *give* the books away." Bob asked what Alton thought. "Well, Alton is reading fiction now, you know. He thinks the public is getting tired of novels about murder and sex and funny war experiences. Alt thinks they're about ready for some novels about ministers. He said to one of the writers that Scribbley's publishes, 'Why don't you do a novel about a minister?' he said. And the man said he thought it was a good idea."

There was a long, comfortable silence.

There was no doubt about it. *How* the Bensons did it, Bob still didn't know. But they did do it. With absolute unconsciousness and with absolute accuracy, they were able to predict future trends in fashion. It was marvelous. It was uncanny. It —

Kitty lifted her lovely head and looked at Bob through the long, silken skein of hair, then brushed it aside. "Do you ever have any money?" she asked. It was like the sound of small silver bells, her voice. Where, compared to this, were the flat Long Island vocables of, say, Noreen? Nowhere at all.

"Why, Kitty Benson, what a question," her mother said, reaching out her glass for Bentley to refill. "Poor Peter Martens, just to think—a little more, Bentley, don't think you're going to drink what's left, young man."

"Because if you ever have any money," said the voice like the Horns of Elfland, "we could go out somewhere together. Some boys don't ever have any money," it concluded, with infinitely loving melancholy.

"I'm going to have some money," Bob said at once. "Absolutely. Uh—when could—"

She smiled an absolute enchantment of a smile. "Not tonight," she said, "because I have a date. And not tomorrow night, because I have a date. But the day after tomorrow night, because then I don't have a date."

A little voice in one corner of Bob's mind said, "This girl has a brain about the size of a small split pea; you know that, don't you?" And another voice, much less little, in the opposite corner, shrieked, "Who *cares?* Who *cares?*" Furthermore, Noreen had made a faint but definite beginning on an extra chin, and her bosom tended (unless artfully and 'artificially supported) to droop. Neither was true of Kitty at all, at all.

"The day after tomorrow night, then," he said. "It's a date."

All that night he wrestled with his angel. "You can't expose these people to the sordid glare of modern commerce," the angel said, throwing him with a half-nelson. "They'd wither and die. Look at the dodo—look at the buffalo. Will you *look?*" "*You* look," growled Bob, breaking the hold, and seizing the angel in a scissors-lock. "I'm not going to let any damned account executives get their chicken-plucking hands on the Bensons. It'll all be done through me, see? Through *me!*" And with that he pinned the angel's shoulders to the mat. "And besides," he said, clenching his teeth, "I need the money . . ."

Next morning he called up his agent. "Here's just a few samples to toss Mr. Phillips Anhalt's way," he said grandiosely. "Write 'em down. Soupbowl haircuts for men. *That's* what I said. They can get a sunlamp treatment for the backs of their necks in the barber-shops. Listen. Women will stencil stars on their toenails with nail polish Kate Greenaway style dresses for women are going to

116

come in. Huh? Well, you bet your butt that Anhalt will know what Kate Greenaway means. Also, what smart women will wear will be madras kerchiefs tied up in the old West Indian way. This is very complicated, so I guess they'll have to be pre-folded and pre-stitched. Silks and cottons. . . . You writing this down? Okay.

"Teen-agers will wear, summer-time, I mean, they'll wear shorts made out of cut-down blue jeans. And sandals made out of cut-down sneakers. No shirts or undershirts—barechested, and— What? *NO*, for cry-sake, just the *boys!*"

And he gave Stuart the rest of it, books and all, and he demanded and got an advance. Next day Stuart reported that Anhalt reported that Mac Ian was quite excited. Mac had said—did Bob know what Phil said Mac said? Well, Mac said, "Let's not spoil the ship for a penny's worth of tar, Phil."

Bob demanded and received another advance. When Noreen called, he was brusque.

The late morning of his date-day he called to confirm it. That is, he tried to. The operator said that she was sorry, but that number had been disconnected. He made it up to the Bronx by taxi. The house was empty. It was not only empty of people, it was empty of everything. The wallpaper had been left, but that was all.

Many years earlier, about the time of his first cigarette, Bob had been led by a friend in the dead of night (say, half-past ten) along a quiet suburban street, pledged to confidence by the most frightful vows. Propped against the wall of a garage was a ladder—it did not go all the way to the roof: Bob and friend had pulled themselves up with effort which, in another context, would have won the full approval of their gym teacher. The roof made an excellent post to observe the going-to-bed preparations of a young woman who had seemingly never learned that window shades could be pulled down. Suddenly lights went on in another house, illuminating the roof of the garage; the young woman had seen the two and yelled; and Bob, holding onto the parapet with sweating hands and reaching for the ladder with sweating feet, had discovered that the ladder was no longer there. . . .

He felt the same way now.

Besides feeling stunned, incredulous, and panicky, he also felt annoyed. This was because he acutely realized that he was acting out an old moving picture scene. The scene would have been closer to the (film) realities had

117

he been wearing a tattered uniform, and in a way he wanted to giggle, and in a way he wanted to cry. Only through obligation to the script did he carry the farce farther: wandering in and out of empty rooms, calling out names, asking if anyone was there.

No one was. And there were no notes or messages, not even *Croatan* carved on a doorpost. Once, in the gathering shadows, he thought he heard a noise, and he whirled around, half-expecting to see an enfeebled Mr. Benson with a bacon-fat lamp in one hand, or an elderly Negro, perhaps, who would say, tearfully, "Marse Bob, dem Yankees done burn all de cotton . . ." But there was nothing.

He trod the stairs to the next house and addressed inquiries to an old lady in a rocking-chair. "Well, I'm sure that *I* don't know," she said, in a paper-thin and fretful voice. "I saw them, all dressed up, getting to the car, and I said, 'Why, where are you all *going,* Hazel?' ["Hazel?" "Hazel Benson. I thought you said you *knew* them, young man?" "Oh, yes. Yes, of course. Please go on."] Well, I said, 'Where are you all *going,* Hazel?' And she said, 'It's time for a change, Mrs. Machen.' And they all laughed and they waved and they drove away. And then some men came and packed everything up and took it away in trucks. Well! 'Where did they all *go?*' I asked them. 'Where did they all *go?*' But do you think they'd have the common decency to *tell* me, after I've lived here for fifty-four years? Not-a-word. Oh—"

Feeling himself infinitely cunning, Bob said, offhandedly, "Yes, I know just the outfit you mean. O'Brien Movers."

"I do *not* mean O'Brien Movers. Whatever gave you such an idea? It was the Seven Sebastian Sisters."

And this was the most that Bob Rosen could learn. Inquiries at other houses either drew blanks or produced such probably significant items as, "Kitty said, 'Here are your curlers, because I won't need them anymore,'"; "Yes, just the other day I was talking to Bart, Senior, and he said, 'You know, you don't realize that you're in a rut until you have to look up to see the sky.' Well, those Bensons always talked a little crazy, and so I thought nothing of it, until—"; and, "I said to Bentley, 'Vipe, how about tomorrow we go over to Williamsbridge and pass the chicks there in review?' and he said, 'No, Vipe, I can't make that scene tomorrow, my ancients put another poster on the billboard.' So I said, 'Ay-las,' and next thing I knew—"

"His who did what?"

"Fellow, you don't wot this Viper talk one note, do you? His *family*, see, they had made other plans. They really cut loose, didn't they?"

They really did. So there Bob was, neat and trim and sweet-smelling, and nowhere to go, and with a pocketful of money. He looked around the tree-lined street and two blocks away, on the corner, he saw a neon sign. *Harry's*, it flashed (green). *Bar and Grill* (red).

"Where's Harry?" he asked the middle-aged woman behind the bar.

"Lodge meeting," she said. "He'll be back soon. They aren't doing any labor tonight, just business. Waddle ya have?"

"A ball of Bushmill," he said. He wondered where he had heard that, last. It was cool in the bar. And then he remembered, and then he shuddered.

"Oh, that's bad," Stuart Emmanuel moaned. "That sounds very bad . . . And you shouldn't've gone to the moving van people yourself. Now you probably muddied the waters."

Bob hung his head. His efforts to extract information from the Seven Sebastian Sisters—apparently they were septuplets, and all had grey mustaches—had certainly failed wretchedly. And he kept seeing Kitty Benson's face, framed in her golden hair like a sun-lit nimbus, kept hearing Kitty Benson's golden voice.

"Well," Stuart said, "I'll do my damndest." And so doubt he did, but it wasn't enough. He was forced to come clean with Anhalt. And Anhalt, after puttering around, his sweet smile more baffled than ever, told Mac everything. Mac put the entire *force majeure* of the T. Oscar Rutherford organization behind the search. And they came up with two items.

Item. The Seven Sebastian Sisters had no other address than the one on Purchase Place, and all the furniture was in their fireproof warehouse, with two years' storage paid in advance.

Item. The owner of the house on Purchase Place said, "I told them I'd had an offer to buy the house, but I wouldn't, if they'd agree to a rent increase. And the next thing I knew, the keys came in the mail."

Little and Harpey, as well as Scribbley's Sons, reported only that Alt and Bart, Junior, had said they were leaving, but hadn't said where they were going.

119

"Maybe they've gone on a trip somewhere," Stuart suggested. "Maybe they'll come back before long. Anhalt has ears in the publishing houses, maybe he'll hear something."

But before Anhalt heard anything, Mac decided that there was no longer anything to hear. "I wash my hands of it all," he declared. "It's a wild goose chase. Where did you ever pick up this crackpot idea in the first place?" And Phillips Anhalt's smile faded away. Weeks passed, and months.

But Bob Rosen has never abandoned hope. He has checked with the Board of Education about Bentley's records, to see if they know anything about a transcript or transfer. He has haunted Nassau Street, bothering—in particular—dealers specializing in Pseudo-Arabian airmail issues, in hopes that Mr. Benson has made his whereabouts known to them. He has hocked his watch to buy hamburgers and pizzas for the Vipers, and innumerable Scotches on innumerable rocks for the trim young men and the girls fresh out of Bennington who staff the offices of our leading publishers. He—

In short, he has taken up the search of Peter Martens (Old Pete, Sneaky Pete). He is looking for the sources of the Nile. Has he *ever* found *anything?* Well, yes, as a matter of fact, he has.

The strange nature of cyclical coincidences has been summed up, somewhere, in the classical remark that one can go for years without seeing a one-legged man wearing a baseball cap; and then, in a single afternoon, one will see three of them. So it happened with Bob Rosen.

One day, feeling dull and heavy, and finding that the elfin notes of Kitty Benson's voice seemed to be growing fainter in his mind, Bob called up her old landlord.

"No," said the old landlord, "I never heard another word from them. And I'll tell you who else I never heard from, either. The fellow who offered to buy the house. He never came around and when I called his office, he just laughed at me. Fine way to do business."

"What's his name?" Bob asked, listlessly.

"Funny name," said the old landlord. "E. Peters Shadwall? Something like that. The hell with him, anyway."

Bob tore his rooms apart looking for the card with the perforated top edge which Shadwell had—it seemed so very long ago—torn off his little book and given him. Also, it struck him, neither could he find the piece of paper on which he had scribbled Old Martens' last message, with

120

the Bensons' name and street on it. He fumbled through the Yellow Book, but couldn't seem to locate the proper category for the mantis-man's business. And he gave up on the regular directory, what with Shad, Shadd, -wel, -well, -welle, etc.

He would, he decided, go and ask Stuart Emmanuel. The dapper little agent had taken the loss of the Bensons so hard ["It was a beauty of a deal," he'd all but wept] that he might also advance a small sum of money for the sake of the Quest. Bob was in the upper East 40s when he passed a bar where he had once taken Noreen for cocktails —a mistake, for it had advanced her already expensive tastes another notch—and this reminded him that he had not heard from her in some time. He was trying to calculate just how much time, and if he ought to do something about it, when he saw the third one-legged man in the baseball cap.

That is to say, speaking non-metaphorically, he had turned to cross a street in the middle of a block, and was halted by the absence of any gap between the two vehicles (part of a traffic jam caused by a long-unclosed incision in the street) directly in front of him. Reading from right to left, the vehicles consisted of an Eleanor-blue truck reading *Grandma Goldberg's Yum-Yum Borsht,* and an obscene-pink Jaguar containing T. Pettys Shadwell and Noreen.

It was the Moment of the Shock of Recognition. He understood everything.

Without his making a sound, they turned together and saw him, mouth open, everything written on his face. And they knew that he knew.

"Why, Bob," said Noreen. "Ah, Rosen," said Shadwell.

"I'm sorry that we weren't able to have you at the *wedding,*" she said. "But everything happened so *quickly.* Peter just swept me off my feet."

Bob said, "I'll bet."

She said, "Don't be bitter"—seeing that he was, and enjoying it. Horns sounded, voices cursed, but the line of cars didn't move.

"You did it," Bob said, coming close. Shadwell's hands left the wheel and came together at his chest, fingers down. "*You* saw that crisp green money he left and you saw his card and got in touch with him and *you* came in and took the note and—*Where are they?*" he shouted, taking hold of the small car and shaking it. "I don't give a damn about

121

the money, just tell me where they are! Just let me see the girl!"

But T. Pettys Shadwell just laughed and laughed, his voice like the whisper of the wind in the dry leaves. "Why *Bob*," said Noreen, bugging her eyes and flashing her large, coarse gems, and giving the scene all she had, "why, Bob, was there a *girl?* You never told *me*."

Bob abandoned his anger, disclaimed all interest in the commercial aspect of the Bensons, offered to execute bonds and sign paper in blood, if only he were allowed to see Kitty. Shadwell, fingering his tiny caret of a mustache, shrugged. "Write the girl a letter," he said, smirking. "I assure you, all mail will be forwarded." And then the traffic jam broke and the Jag zoomed off, Noreen's scarlet lips pursed in blowing a kiss.

"Write?" Why, bless you, of course Bob wrote. Every day and often twice a day for weeks. But never a reply did he get. And on realizing that his letters probably went no farther than Noreen (Mrs. T. Pettys) Shadwell, who doubtless gloated and sneered in the midst of her luxury, he fell into despair, and ceased. Where is Kitty of the heart-shaped face, Kitty of the light-gold hair, Kitty of the elfin voice? Where are her mother and father and her three brothers? Where now are the sources of the Nile? Ah, where?

So there you are. One can hardly suppose that Shadwell has perforce kidnapped the entire Benson family, but the fact is that they have disappeared almost entirely without trace, and the slight trace which remains leads directly to and only to the door of T. Pettys Shadwell Associates, Market Research Advisors. Has he whisked them all away to some sylvan retreat in the remote recesses of the Great Smoky Mountains? Are they even now pursuing their prophetic ways in one of the ever-burgeoning, endlessly proliferating suburbs of the City of the Angels? Or has he, with genius diabolical, located them so near to hand that far-sighted vision must needs forever miss them?

In deepest Brooklyn, perhaps, amongst whose labyrinthine ways an army of surveyors could scarce find their own stakes?—or in fathomless Queens, red brick and yellow brick, world without end, where the questing heart grows sick and faint?

Rosen does not know, but he has not ceased to care. He writes to live, but he lives to look, now selling, now searching, famine succeeding feast, but hope never failing.

Phillips Anhalt, however, has not continued so success-fully. He has not Bob's hopes. Anhalt continues, it is true, with the T. Oscar Rutherford people, but no longer has his corner office, or any private office at all. Anhalt failed: Anhalt now has a desk in the bullpen with the other failures and the new apprentices.

And while Bob ceaselessly searches the streets—for who knows in which place he may find the springs bubbling and welling?—and while Anhalt drinks bitter tea and toils like a slave in a salt mine, that swine, that cad, that most de-spicable of living men, T. Pettys Shadwell, has three full floors in a new building of steel, aluminum, and blue-green glass a block from the Cathedral; he has a box at the Met, a house in Bucks County, a place on the Vineyard, an apartment in Beekman Place, a Caddy, a Bentley, *two* Jaguars, a yacht that sleeps ten, and one of the choicest small (but ever-growing) collections of Renoirs in private hands today. . . .

1962

The year 1962 was a good one for science fiction. It had been almost a decade since the great crash of the pulp magazines, the remaining—perhaps I should say, *surviving* —magazines had established some equilibrium, and book publishers had apparently decided that this science fiction stuff wasn't just a nutty fad bu was going to be here to stay.

Of course they were right.

This is not to say that there were to be no further ups and downs, overexpansions followed by abrupt shrinkages in the amount of science fiction being published. But from here on out, even at its periodic low ebbs, science fiction would remain a commercially and artistically viable field for publishers. And at its peaks, it would eventually prove itself capable of producing true best sellers, books that would hit the six-figure mark in hardcover sales, and (given enough time and steady support from publishers) the seven-figure mark in paperback.

The Hugos for 1962 were presented at the 1963 World Science Fiction Convention in Washington, D.C. For the first time, I had a personal stake in their outcome. Along with my wife, Patricia, and our friend Bob (or, as he spelled it in those funny long-ago days, "bhob") Stewart, I had been publishing a fanzine, *Xero*. When it came time for the climactic banquet and awards ceremony of the convention, others might have been interested in Murray Leinster's guest-of-honor speech or in the question of whose work would be named best novel of the year, best short fiction of the year, which science fiction magazine would be honored as best of the year, or which illustrator.

But I had ears only for *best fanzine.*

In all honesty, though, I suppose that the world—even the science fiction world—more noticed the identities of the Hugo winners for best novel and best short fiction than that of the publisher of the best fanzine.

The nominated novels were *A Fall of Moondust* by Arthur C. Clarke, *Little Fuzzy* by H. Beam Piper, *The Man in the High Castle* by Philip K. Dick, and *Sylva* by Vercors (Jean Bruller). It's interesting to note that not one of the nominees was a magazine story. The magazines did serialize some novels, and some pretty good ones. *Analog* ran *Anything You Can Do* by Darrel T. Langart (Randall Garrett), *Border, Breed, Nor Birth* by Mack Reynolds, *A Life for the Stars* by James Blish, and *Space Viking* by H. Beam Piper—an amazing performance for a single year.

Amazing Stories serialized one old-style potboiler, *Pawn of the Black Fleet* by Mark Clifton, and one more significant novel, *A Trace of Memory* by Keith Laumer.

Galaxy ran only one serial in 1962, but it was a good one—Frederik Pohl's *A Plague of Pythons*. And *If* presented the voters with a pair of puzzles: two serials that split the years. *Masters of Space* by E. E. Smith and E. E. Evans started in 1961 and ended in '62; *Podkayne of Mars* by Heinlein started in 1962 and carried over to '63. And the last of the "majors," *F&SF*, had *The Journey of Joenes* by Robert Sheckley.

It was unfortunate that the British magazines received little U.S. distribution. The best of them, *New Worlds*, had even tried out an American edition for a few issues in 1960, but that didn't quite work, either. In 1962, *New Worlds* ran serials by James White, John Rackham, Brian Aldiss, and Keith Woodcott.

All to no avail. The readers were thoroughly hooked on *books* now—or so it seemed. In later years, a number of successful novels had both magazine and book editions, but the day when a novel could triumph on the basis of magazine serialization alone was over.

The winner for 1962 was *The Man in the High Castle*, and it won on the basis of its original (Putnam) and book club (Science Fiction Book Club) editions. There wasn't even a paperback until 1964!

In the short fiction realm, of course the magazines remained dominant. Patterns were changing, however, and for the first time since records had been kept of runners-up as well as winners, there was not a single nominee from *Analog*. The nominees were "The Dragon Masters" by Jack Vance *(Galaxy)*, "Myrrha" by Gary Jennings *(F&SF)*, "The Unholy Grail" by Fritz Leiber *(Fantastic)*, "When You Care, When You Love" by Theodore Sturgeon *(F&SF)*, and "Where Is the Bird of Fire?" by Thomas Burnett Swann *(Science Fantasy)*.

The winner was "The Dragon Masters." It was a worthy winner, without a doubt. It was further enhanced by appearing in *Galaxy* accompanied by a stunning cover painting and portfolio of original illustrations by Jack Gaughan.

But I cannot help wondering if "Where Is the Bird of Fire?" wouldn't have given "The Dragon Masters" a run for the money—perhaps even have won a victory in a *very* tight race—save for two disadvantages. For one, it appeared in *Science Fantasy*. Again, that old bugbear of publication in Britain, when most of the voters resided in America. How many voting fans even *saw* the story before they cast their ballots? And for another, the fact that "Where Is the Bird of Fire?" is a fantasy, one of those sensitive, pastel fantasies of the classical Mediterranean world that Swann made his own until his tragic death in 1976.

It had been well established that fantasy was considered within the purview of the Science Fiction Achievement Awards, despite the name of the awards. And Bloch, with "That Hell-Bound Train," had proved as early as 1959 that fantasy could not only compete for the Hugo, but could win it.

Still, the emphasis has always been on science fiction, or at least on borderline material, and any "pure" fantasy in the Hugo competition has competed under a severe handicap.

Between its unfortunate place of publication and its pure fantasy aspect, "Where Is the Bird of Fire?" never had a chance. It is more remarkable that Swann made the ballot, than that he failed to win. And several times more—with a novel and a novelette published in 1966, and with *two* novels in 1972—Swann was nominated for either the Hugo or Nebula awards.

He never won either.

Oh, and about that Hugo for having published the best fanzine of 1962. The other nominees were Jack Chalker for *Mirage,* the team of Patten, Lewis, Trimble, and Trimble for *Shangri-L'Affaires,* Richard Bergeron for

Warhoon, and Robert and Juanita Coulson for *Yandro.* Chalker, both Coulsons, and I went on to become science fiction writers. I wonder if the others, who managed somehow to preserve their relatively amateur status, aren't the more fortunate ones among us.

But in any case, *Xero* did win.

Where Is the Bird of Fire?

THOMAS BURNETT SWANN

I

I AM VERY old by the counting of my people, the Fauns—
ten full years. Hardly a boyhood, men would say, but we
are the race with cloven hooves and pointed, furry ears,
descendants of the great god Faunus who roamed with
Saturn in the Golden Age. Like the goats, our cousins, we
count ten years a lifetime.

And in my years, I have seen the beginning of Rome,
a city on the Palatine which Romulus says will straddle
the orange Tiber and spread west to the Tyrrhenian Sea,
south through the new Greek settlement at Cumae to
the tip of Italy, and north through Etruria to the land of
the Gauls. Romulus, the Wolf, says these things, and I
believe him, because with one exception he has never
failed. Now, however, I do not wish to speak of Romulus,
but of his twin brother, Remus, who was also part of the
beginning. Remus, the bird of fire. With a reed pen, I will
write his story on papyrus and trust it to the coffers of
time which, cool in the earth, endure and preserve.

My people have wandered the hills and forests of Central
Italy since the reign of Saturn: the blue-rocked Apennines
where the Tiber springs, and the forests of beech and oak
where Dryads comb green hair in the sun-dappled branches.
When invaders arrived from Africa and from the tall Alps

'to the north, Saturn withdrew to a land where the Fauns could not follow him. Forsaken, they remained in Italy, together with the Dryads in their leafy houses.

A Faun's life has always been brief and simple. We wear no clothes to encumber our movements except, in the winter months which have no name, a covering of wolf skin. Our only weapon is a simple sling with a hempen cord. We have no females of our own and must propagate by enticing maidens from the walled towns. I was born to an Alba Longan who had come to draw water from the Numicus River, outside her city.

Because the city was bowed under King Amulius, a tyrant who some years before had stolen the throne from his kindly brother Numitor and imprisoned him in the palace, she was willing to stay, for a little, with my father in the woods. But when she gave birth to me and saw my cloven hooves and pointed ears, she cried, "I would rather nurse a goat!" and hurried back to her town and its tyrannical king. I was left to be reared by a band of Fauns, who had built a small encampment in the woods, with branches raised on stakes to shelter them from the rains of Jupiter, and a low palisade to guard against marauding wolves or unfriendly shepherds.

It was night and we had built a fire, not only to cook our supper but to comfort ourselves in the loneliness of the black woods. Evil forces had come with the flight of Saturn, Lemures or ghosts and blood-sucking Striges. My father, holding nine black beans in his mouth, made the circuit of our camp and spat them out one by one, mumbling each time, "With this I ransom me and mine." The Lemures, it was said by the shepherds who had taught him the custom, followed and ate the beans and were appeased.

This done, he bathed his hands in a clay vessel of water, clanged together two copper cooking pots left by my mother, and said, "Good Folks, get you gone." At six months old—five years or so in human terms—I was much impressed with my father's ritual. He had never shown me the least affection, but neither had anyone else, and a Faun's place, I judged, was to be brave and clever, not affectionate.

My father looked very gallant confronting the ghosts and very wise since, even while facing them bravely, he spoke with discretion. The other Fauns, eight of them, gnarled, brown, hairy creatures as old, one would think, as the oaks of the forest, squatted on their hooves and

129

watched with admiration and also impatience, since they had not yet enjoyed their supper of roasted hares and myrtle berries.

But scarcely had my father uttered "Good Folks" than a tree trunk crashed through the thin palisade and figures ran through the opening and thrashed among us with wooden staves. Lemures, I thought at first, but their staves and goatskin loin cloths marked them as shepherds. I heard the names "Romulus" and "Wolf" applied to the same man and guessed him to be their leader, the brawniest and the youngest.

The first thing they did was to stamp out our fire. I scrambled to shelter in a thicket of witch grass and watched with round-eyed terror and with ears quivering above my head. By the light of smoldering embers, I saw my father struck to the ground by Romulus himself. I roused myself and scurried to his side, but Romulus's brawny arms scooped me into the air. He raised me above his head, opened his mouth, and gave the high thin wail of a hunting she-wolf. Then with the camp in shambles and the Fauns either fallen or staggering, he leaped through the broken fence with me in his arms, and his shepherds followed him, hugging roasted hares.

I gave my captor a sharp kick with my hoof, but he squeezed me so hard that I gasped for breath, and I thought it best to lie still.

Through the woods we raced; through oak trees older than Saturn, and feathery cypresses like Etruscan maidens dancing to soundless flutes. At last the earth became marshy and Romulus's sandals squished in the sodden grass. I had heard my father speak of this malarial country near the Tiber, and I held my breath to avoid the poisonous vapors. Finally I grew faint and gulped in breaths, expecting the air to burn as it entered my lungs. Throughout the journey, Romulus never seemed short of breath, never stumbled, never rested.

We began to climb and soon reached the summit of what I guessed to be that hill of shepherds, the Palatine. On a broad plateau, hearth fires flickered through the doorways of circular huts. The jogging motion of my captor made the fires seem to dance and sway, and I blinked my eyes to make sure that they were real and not some feverish dream implanted by the swamp. From their pens of stone, pigs grunted and cattle lowed in resentment at being awakened.

One of the huts, the largest, seemed to belong to Romulus. We entered through a low door—though Romulus stooped, he brushed my ears against the lintel—and I found myself in a windowless, goat-smelling room with an earthen floor baked hard by the central fire. Romulus thrust me against a wall where a goat was nibbling a pile of straw. A hole in the roof allowed some smoke to escape, but some remained, and I waited for my eyes to stop watering before I could get a clear look at my captor.

I saw that the powerful arms which had held me belonged to one little more than a boy (at the time, of course, he looked overpoweringly adult, but still the youngest in the hut). Yet he was tall, broad, with muscular legs and with muscles tight across the bare abdomen above his loin cloth. A thin adolescent down darkened his chin, but the furrow between his eyebrows suggested ambitions beyond his years. His crow-black hair, unevenly cropped about an inch from his scalp, rioted in curls.

He stood in the firelight and laughed, and I dimly understood even then why men twice his age could follow and call him Wolf. His handsome face held a wolf's cruelty, together with its preternatural strength. Had I been older, I might have seen also a wolf's fierce tenderness toward those it loves; for this boy, though he loved rarely, could love with great tenacity. As it was, I thought him cruel and powerful, nothing more, and I cowered in terror.

An aged shepherd, his long white hair bound in a fillet behind his head, rose from the fire when Romulus entered with his five men. The five immediately began to laugh and boast about their victory over my people. But when Romulus spoke, the others were silent.

"The Fauns were driving out spirits, Faustulus," he explained to the old man. "Their leader said, 'Good Folks, get you gone,' and in we come! See, I have captured a baby."

"In a year he will be full grown," said Faustulus, whose face, though wrinkled like a brick shattered in a kiln, held an ageless dignity. He was no mere shepherd, I later found, but a man of learning from Carthage. Shipwrecked near the mouth of the Tiber, he had wandered inland to take shelter with herdsmen and married a girl named Larentia. When his rustic bride hesitated to return with him to Carthage, he remained with her people and learned their trade.

"What will you do with him then? Your nocturnal games are childish, Romulus. They bring you no closer to the throne of Alba Longa."

Romulus frowned. "Everything I do, Faustulus, brings me closer to the throne. Tonight we wrestle with Fauns. Tomorrow, soldiers. My men need practice."

His ominous tone and the thought of what he had done to my father made me tremble. I burrowed into the hay where the goat seemed unlikely to eat (a foul-smelling beast, cousin though he was!) and peered out between wisps of straw.

Romulus saw my terror. To Faustulus he said, "You ask me what I will do with our captive. Eat him, before he grows up! Goat flesh cooked on a spit." When Faustulus seemed ill-disposed to the joke (or serious intention, I was not sure which), Romulus addressed a young shepherd with the stupid, flattened eyes of a ram. "Faustulus, it seems, is not hungry. What about you, Celer?"

Winking at Romulus, Celer felt my arms and muttered, "Too thin, too thin. Fatten him first, eh?" His speech was thick and slow, as if he were speaking with a mouthful of wine.

Romulus seemed to debate. "No," he said finally. "He may be thin, but I am hungry. And I want to make a belt of his ears." With that he hoisted me from the ground and lowered me toward the fire by the stump of my tail! I lay very still until I felt the flames singe my ears. Then I began to bleat, and Romulus and the ram-eyed Celer threw back their heads in merriment.

A voice spoke from the doorway, low but forceful. "Put him down, Romulus."

Romulus turned and, recognizing the speaker, tossed me back into the straw. With one tremendous bound he reached the door and embraced his brother.

"Remus," he cried, "I thought they had kept you in Veii!"

Remus returned his brother's embrace with enthusiasm, though his slight frame was almost engulfed by Romulus's massive hug. Like the others, he wore a loin cloth, but of wool, not goatskin, and dyed to the green of the woodpecker which haunts the forests of Latium. Over his shoulder hung a bow, and at his side, a quiver of arrows, their bronze nocks enwreathed with feathers to match his loin cloth. When I saw his hair, bound with a fillet but spilling in silken fire behind his head, I caught my breath.

Picus, the woodpecker god, I thought. Who except gods and Gauls, in this part of Italy, had yellow hair (and Etruscan ladies, with the help of their famous cosmetics)?

He released himself from Romulus's hug and walked over to my nest of straw. I squirmed away from him. A god he might be, but after all I had been kidnapped and almost cooked by his brother. I need not have feared him, however. He lifted me in his arms as my mother might if she had not disliked my ears. He cradled me against his smooth bronze chest—fragrant with clover as if he had slept in a meadow—and stroked the fur of my ears, smoothing it toward the tips.

"Little Faun," he said. "Don't be afraid. Tomorrow I will take you back to your people."

"Take him back!" protested Romulus. "I caught him myself."

"Fauns are not animals," said Remus. "At least, not entirely. They have lived in this forest for centuries, and we have no right to capture their children." He pointed to Romulus's bloody stave. "Or fight their fathers."

"They enjoy a fight as much as we do," shrugged Romulus. "We knocked them about a bit, nothing more. If I don't train my shepherds, how can they capture a city?" He grinned broadly, his sharp white teeth glittering in the firelight. "If we don't take the city, what will we do for women?" Celer and the others—except Faustulus —whooped their approval. I was later to learn that these young shepherds, driven from Alba Longa and other towns of Latium for minor crimes, were womanless, and that Romulus had promised a house in the city and a wife for every man. Romulus winked at Celer. "My brother knows much of animals, but nothing of women. We will find him a girl when we take Alba Longa—a saucy wench with breasts like ripe pomegranates."

"Brother," said Remus, a slow smile curving his lips. "What do you know of pomegranates? You must have been gardening beyond the Palatine!"

"I know!" cried Celer. "I know about them! The girls I remember—"

"And the girls I imagine," sighed Remus.

"Remember, imagine," said Romulus. "One is as bad as the other. But once we take the city—! Now, brother, tell us about your journey to Veii."

Romulus and the others seated themselves around the fire, while Remus remained standing. Clearly there had

133

been an urgent purpose behind his visit to Veii, the Etruscan city twelve miles to the north. Even at my age, I sensed that purpose and, crouching at his feet, awaited his words more eagerly than those of my father when he told me stories of Dryads and river goddesses. What I failed to understand at the time was later clarified for me by Remus.

The brothers, it seemed, claimed to be sons of the war god Mars and a Vestal princess, Rhea, daughter of that same King Numitor whom Amulius had deposed and imprisoned in the palace. As Remus spoke, I learned how these royal twins in exile longed, above everything, to seize the throne of Alba Longa and restore their grandfather or rule in his place. Remus had gone to Veii to ask the *lucomo* or king to back their cause. It was a brazen thing for a young Latin shepherd, even a deposed prince, to seek audience with an Etruscan king and ask him to make war against a Latin city. But Romulus and Remus, after all, were very young.

I passed into the city (said Remus) with farmers taking shelter for the night. The palace astonished me. Its walls were of purple stucco, and terra cotta sphinxes flanked the entrance. I told the guards that I wished to see their king; that I could speak only with him. Would they tell him that Remus, exiled prince of Alba Longa, sought an audience.

"Yellow Hair," one of them said. "Our king is a jolly man. I will take him word. Your boldness will make him laugh."

After a long time, the guard returned and said that the king would see me now—in his banquet hall. In the great hall, the ceiling was painted with winged monsters and strange enormous cats. The king was lying on a couch with a young woman at his side. She was almost unrobed. He motioned me to a couch next to him and laid his arm, heavy with amber and gold, on my shoulder.

"Remus," he said, "I have heard your story from shepherds who once served Amulius but now serve me. They told me how your mother, the Vestal Rhea, bore you to the God Mars and was buried alive for breaking her vow of chastity. How her uncle, King Amulius, ordered the shepherd Faustulus to drown you in the Tiber, but the shepherd set you adrift in a hollow log. How the log came ashore and a she-wolf suckled you in her cave and a woodpecker brought you berries, until Faustulus found and reared you as his own children.

"The story, it seems, is widely known in the country, though Amulius himself believes you long dead—for tyrants are rarely told the truth. I greet you as the prince you are. But we of Veii want peace with Rome, our closest neighbor. Lead your shepherds against Amulius, if you must, and pray to Mars that the townspeople rise to help you. When you have captured the city, come to me again and we shall sign treaties of amity. Until then, let us be friends but not allies."

I looked closely into his face, the short pointed beard, black as a vulture, the arched eyebrows, the almond eyes, and saw that he would not change his mind. I took my leave and followed the basalt road through the great arched gate and returned to you.

Romulus sprang to his feet, narrowly avoiding my ears. "No help from Veii then. And we are not yet strong enough alone. Thirty shepherds at most, even if we scour the countryside." He fingered the stubble on his chin, as if craving the ample beard—and the years—of a man. "We shall have to wait at least a year before we attack," he continued, with the heavy weariness of one who was not used to waiting—who, at seventeen, was something of a leader already and covetous of wider leadership. "Gather more shepherds around us. Send scouts to the city and feel out the mood of the crowd." Neither Romulus nor Remus had visited Alba Longa: their royal blood made it difficult to pass as herdsmen. "Father Mars, let it not be long!"

He strode to the corner of the hut where a wreathed bronze spear, green with age, lay apart like a holy relic. Mars, as everyone knows, manifests himself in spears and shields. "One day soon, Great Father, let me say to you: 'Mars, awaken!' "

"But even if we take the city," asked Remus, "will our grandfather let us rule? The throne is rightfully his."

"He is very old," said Romulus. "When he steps aside— and he will, very soon—we will build a temple to Mars and train an army even the Etruscans will fear."

"And offer asylum to slaves, and even to birds and animals."

"Oh, Remus," chided his brother. "This is a *city* we will rule, not a menagerie! For once, forget your animals."

"But the city can learn from the forest! Remember

when I cured your fever with berries last year? A bear showed them to me, growing beside the Tiber."

Romulus shook his head. "Remus," he smiled, "we shall have our problems ruling together. I sometimes wish that I had no brother or that I did not love him above all men. But let us capture the city—then we shall plan our government. Now it is late. Almost Cockcrow time."

With a warm goodnight to Romulus and Faustulus, Remus gathered me in his arms and left the hut. Of course I could walk quite by myself, but rather than lose my ride I said nothing. Stumbling a bit with his burden, he descended the bank of the Palatine toward the Tiber, which looped like an adder in the starlight and swelled in places as if digesting a meal. Near the foot of the hill we entered the mouth of a cave where a small fire burned on a raised clay hearth. Remus stirred the fire.

"I hate the dark," he said. "It is sad with spirits. People who died like my mother, without proper rites."

Sleepily I looked around me and saw that the earthen floor had been covered with rushes and clover, that a pallet of clean white wool lay in the corner, and that earthen pots lined the opposite wall. There was no one in the cave, but a large dog lay asleep beyond the fire. As we entered, the animal awoke and opened its eyes. A dog indeed! An immense wolf, its yellow-gray fur matted with age, rose on its haunches and faced us. Whether it snarled or grinned, I could not be sure. When Remus bent to deposit me on the pallet, I refused at first to let go of his neck.

"Lie still, little Faun," he laughed. "This is Luperca, my foster mother. It was she who found Romulus and me on the bank of the Tiber and brought us to this very cave. She is very old now. Sometimes she walks in the woods, but at night she shares my cave and my supper." He knelt beside her and stroked her black-rimmed ears. In looking back, I can see the nobility of the scene, this boy with slender hands and hair as yellow as sunflowers, the aged wolf that had suckled him in this very cave. But at six months old, I saw only a flea-bitten animal which monopolized my friend's attention.

"My name is Sylvan," I said haughtily. They were the first words I had spoken since my capture.

"I did not know you could talk," he laughed, rising from my rival and coming to lie beside me.

"Nobody asked me," I said, less haughty now that he

136

had answered my summons. As the firelight dwindled, he talked of Alba Longa and how, when he ruled the city with Romulus, Fauns would be as welcome as men.

"You have surely seen the city," he said, and before I could tell him yes, that my father had carried me once to see the walls and pointed, "That is where your mother ran off to," he continued. "It is a very small city, really just a town. But its houses are white and clean, and its temple to Vesta is as pure as the goddess's flame. It is now an unhappy city. Amulius is a harsh ruler. He killed my mother, Sylvan. He laughed when she told him that Mars was my father: 'You have broken your vow,' he said, and buried her alive in the earth. Faustulus saw her before she died. Just a girl, really. Bewildered but proud. She looked at Amulius with her large black eyes and said: 'Mars is my husband and he will look after my sons.'

"Everyone believed her except Amulius. You see why I hate him. And I have other reasons. He taxes the vintners a third of their wine and the shepherds a fourth of their sheep. What do they get in return? The protection of his soldiers—when they are not stealing wine and sheep! But Sylvan, forgive me. I am keeping you awake with problems beyond your months. Sleep little Faun. Tomorrow I will take you home."

But I already knew that I did not wish to return to my people.

II

Twelve months had passed. Growing two inches a month, I had reached a Faun's full height of five feet. Sometimes I looked in the stream that flowed near our cave and admired my reflection, for Fauns are vain as long as they resemble young saplings, and until they begin to grow gnarled—alas, too quickly—like the oaks of Saturn. My skin was the bronze of Etruscan shields. I wore my ears proudly, waving their silken fur above my head. I combed my tail with a hazel branch and kept it free from thistles and burrs. Remus was eighteen now but soon I would overtake him. Together with Luperca, I still shared his cave and we often hunted together, I with a sling, he with a bow and arrow. But at his insistence we hunted only the lower animals, and then from necessity—the hare and the wild pig. Bears and deer and even wolves had nothing to fear from us. Sometimes on these hunts I saw my father and called to him in passing. The first time he stopped to speak with me. I saw the scar which Romulus's staff had left between his ears. He looked much older than I remembered and a little stooped.

"Is it well with you?" he asked, ignoring Remus.

"Yes, Father," I answered, half expecting him to embrace me. For I had grown used to Remus's affection.

But family ties among Fauns are usually shallow; we live such a little time. "Good," he said. "I thought they might have killed you." He galloped into the forest.

On the Palatine Hill, new huts had risen near that of Romulus and Faustulus. Sabine shepherds had moved there from a neighboring hill, the Quirinal (named for their spear god, Quirinus), and also thieves and murderers from the forest, whom Romulus welcomed too readily into his group. When Remus objected, Romulus argued that thieves, much more than shepherds, could help to capture a town. They could move with stealth and strike with sudden fury.

As shepherds, of course, the brothers must care for a large herd of cattle and sheep, leading them from pasture to pasture both on and below the Palatine, guarding them from wolves and bears, and making sacrifice to the deities called the Pales. The herds they tended belonged to an Alba Longan named Tullius, who often sent an overseer from the city to count or examine his animals; hence, our source of news about Amulius and his increasing tyrannies.

One day the overseer complained that the king had doubled taxes, the next, that his soldiers had insulted a Vestal or executed a boy for petty theft. The soldiers numbered a thousand—all the able bodied men in town were subject to duty at one time or another—and by no means the whole number approved of Amulius or victimized civilians. But a hard core, rewarded with land, cattle, or armor (there was no coinage yet in Latium), served Amulius willingly.

Inflamed by word from the city, Romulus left his herds in the care of sheep dogs and drilled his men; he taught them how to climb rocky cliffs like city walls or move with the swiftness of wolves. On the hill called Aventine, Remus taught them to whittle bows from hickory limbs and feather their arrows for deadly accuracy.

One day, when Remus was resting from both the herds and the training of archers, we had an adventure

138

which seemed at the time unrelated to war and conquest, though it later proved vastly important. I found Remus standing under the fig tree near the mouth of his cave. He called it the Fig-Tree of Rumina, the goddess who protected suckling infants, because he felt that she had watched over him and Romulus while they fed from the she-wolf.

Finding him preoccupied, I crept up silently, seized his waist, and rolled him to the grass. My disadvantage in such matches was my tail, which he liked to take hold of and jerk until I begged for mercy. This morning, however, I had caught him by surprise, and soon I was sitting on his chest, triumphant. Already I had grown to outweigh him, with my hooves and my slim but sinewy body.

"Enough," he gasped. "Let me up!" I rose and we fell against each other, laughing and catching our breath.

"The next time you turn your back," he swore, "I will pull out your tail by the roots!" Suddenly he became serious. "Sylvan, my bees are dying."

He had found the bees in a poorly concealed log, stunned them with smoke, and removed them to a hollow in the fig tree, safe from hungry bears and shepherds. For awhile they had seemed to thrive and Remus had been delighted, taking their honey only when they had enough to spare. But now—

"Look," he said, drawing me to the tree which lifted its broad rough leaves to a remarkable forty feet. "The bees are very ill."

I stood beside him, my hand on his shoulder, and peered up into the tree. The bees were carrying off their dead in great numbers. Two of them, overwhelmed by the weight of a third, fell to the ground at my feet.

"They look beyond our help," I said. "But there are other hives, Remus. There will be no lack of honey."

"But I am fond of *these*," he protested, turning to face me. "They are my friends, Sylvan. Not once have they stung me, even when I took their honey." He looked so troubled, so young and vulnerable, that I was speechless. In the year I had known him he had hardly changed. His face was still beardless, his hair like woven sunlight. Who could explain how this blond, green-eyed boy, so different from Romulus, had been born to a dark Latin Mother? Only Mars knew the answer. Yet Rhea, the gentle Vestal, and not the warlike Mars, seemed more truly his parent.

"Wait," I said. "Fauns love honey and sometimes keep bees. My father will know what to do."

139

We went to find him in the forest south of the Aventine. Though a Faun without clothes and with only a slingshot to encumber me, I could barely keep pace with Remus, who raced through the woods as if he wore wings. As a matter of fact, he had sewn his loin cloth with those same woodpecker feathers he used to wreathe his arrows.

"Remus, take pity," I gasped. "I expect you to rise through the treetops!"

Remus laughed. "They say a woodpecker fed me when I was small."

"And gave you his wings."

In the deepest part of the forest, the trees were tall as hills and older than Saturn. What they had seen had left them weary—bent, twisted, and sagging—but still powerful. Oaks were the oldest, but ilex trees, too, and gray-barked beeches mixed sunlight and shadows in a venerable mist of limbs. Blue-eyed owls hooted among the leaves and magpies, birds of good omen, chattered in hidden recesses. A woodpecker burned his small green flame against the greater fire of the forest, and Remus pointed to him excitedly. "It was one like that who fed me berries."

Remus might have wandered for days without finding my father, but Fauns have an instinct in the woods and I led him straight to our camp.

Outside the palisade, I bleated like a goat to signify kinship with those behind the barrier. A section was lifted aside and a Faun, knotty and mottled like the underside of a rock, filled the entrance. His ears quivered with suspicion.

"It is Sylvan," I said. "Will you tell Nemus, my father, I wish to see him?"

The Faun vanished without a word. Another took his place. To human eyes—to Remus, as he later confessed—there was nothing to distinguish this Faun from the first. But I knew my father by the scar on his head and by the length of his ears—they were very long, even for a Faun.

"Sylvan," he said without emotion. "You want me?"

"Yes, Father. This is Remus, my friend."

"I have seen you together."

"We need your help. Remus's bees are dying. We hoped you could help us save them. The hive is well placed. But a sickness has taken them. They are carrying off their dead."

140

Nemus thought a moment. "Ah," he said. "You must find a Dryad."

"A Dryad, Father?"

"Yes. They speak to the bees. They know all cures."

"But Dryads are rare. I have never seen one."

"I have," said Nemus proudly. "Her hair was the color of oak leaves, and her skin, like milk—" He broke off, as if embarrassed by his own enthusiasm. "But I will tell you where to look. Two miles to the south of this camp, there is a circle of oaks. Some say Saturn planted them. At any rate, one is inhabited by a Dryad. Which one I cannot say. I saw her dipping water from a spring and followed her to a ruined altar among the oaks. There she escaped me. You must hide in the bushes and watch the bees for an hour or more. In the tree where the most of them light will be your Dryad. Taking her nectar, you know. But tell me, Sylvan, why are these bees so important? Let them die. There are others."

Remus answered for me. "They are friends. We like to hear them work outside our cave. Now they are almost quiet."

"Friends, you call them? You are one of the Old Ones, aren't you, boy? Your hair is ripe barley, but your heart might have lived with Saturn. In the old time, there was love in the forest. So the records of my people say. A scrawl on a stone, a picture, an image of clay—always they tell of love. Fauns, men and animals living in harmony." He turned to his son.

"Look after him, Sylvan. Help him to find his Dryad. Help him always. He is one who is marked to be hurt."

I reached out and touched my father on the shoulder, as I often touched Remus. He seemed surprised, whether pleased or offended I could not say. When he turned his back, we went to find our Dryad.

There was the ring of oaks, just as he had said. Not the most ancient trees, if planted by Saturn, but old nonetheless. In their midst rose a pile of crumbling stones which had once formed an altar. Fingertips of sun touched the stones and live plants overrunning them, white narcissi with red-rimmed coronas, spiny-leafed acanthuses, and jonquils yellow as if the sunlight had flowered into the petals. We did not explore the altar however, and risk discovery by the Dryad, but crouched in some bushes beyond the oaks and watched for bees.

141

Soon a faint buzzing tingled my ears. I cocked them toward the sound and nudged Remus. A swarm of bees was approaching the ring of oaks. We watched them circle and vanish in the oak tree nearest the altar, a large tree with a trunk perhaps twenty feet wide at the base, and a welter of greenery high in the air. Yes, it could easily house a Dryad. I started to rise, but Remus grasped my tail.

"No," he whispered. "Your father said to watch where the *most* bees go."

We waited, I fretfully, since a minute to a man seems like ten to a Faun. Soon I grew sleepy and, using Remus's back for a pillow, slept until he shook me.

"Three swarms have entered that tree and left again," he said. "No other tree has attracted so many. That must be the one."

We rose and walked to the tree in question. "We forgot to ask your father how to get inside," Remus said, staring at the great trunk. Apparently the bees had entered through a hole invisible to us and far above our heads. The trunk was much too rough and broad to climb, and there were no branches within reach of our hands. We circled the base, prodding among the roots for an entrance, but succeeded only in dislodging a turquoise lizard that ran over Remus's sandal and flickered toward the altar.

Thoughtful, Remus stared after him. "Your father lost sight of the Dryad near the altar." We followed the lizard to the crumbling stones and began to kick among the rubble, careful, however, not to crush the jonquils or narcissi. A field mouse, poised for escape, stared at us from the tallest stone. A honey bee surged from a shaken jonquil.

"Sylvan," Remus cried at last. "I think we have found it!" Eagerly he brushed aside bushes and, head first, squirmed into an opening just large enough for one body at a time. I followed him without enthusiasm. Such holes concealed poisonous adders as well as harmless lizards and mice.

The walls were smooth; neither roots nor rocks tore at our bodies. But the journey seemed long and the blackness grew oppressive. I imagined an adder with every bend of the tunnel.

Suddenly Remus stood up and pulled me beside him. We had entered the trunk of a tree, the Dryad's tree, I hoped. Far above our heads, a light shone roundly through an opening. Climbing toward the light, wooden rungs had been carved in the side of the trunk.

"We have found it," he cried, joyfully pulling my tail. "We have found her house!"

"I hope she is more accessible than her house," I muttered.

We started to climb and at once I felt dizzy, since the tree was very tall. I consoled myself that our Dryad would perhaps be beautiful. I had heard that they remained young until they died with their trees. Remus and I saw no women on the Palatine, and imagination was a poor substitute. I had seen him scratching pictures on the walls of our cave, Rumina and other goddesses. He invariably drew them young, beautiful, radiant, the image of Woman in his own young heart. Did such a woman await us now?

Through the circular opening, we drew ourselves into a room which roughly followed the shape of the trunk. Small round windows cut in the walls admitted sunshine. A couch stood across the room, with feet like a lion's and a silken coverlet prancing with warriors. The air smelled of living wood, and white narcissus petals carpeted the floor. Somewhat hesitantly we advanced into the room. At once I collided with a table and almost upset a lamp like a twisted dragon. Remus, meanwhile, had settled in a backless chair.

"It is citrus wood from Carthage," he said. "I saw one like it in Veii. But where is the Dryad?"

"The ladder continues," I noted, hastily ridding myself of the dragon lamp. "There must be a second room over our head."

Remus walked to the ladder. "I will call her. She must not think we are robbers."

But he did not have to call, for we heard footsteps descending the ladder. I lifted the sling from my neck in case the Dryad should be armed. Aeneas, after all, had found a race of fierce Amazons in Italy. Dryads who lived alone, Amazons or not, must know how to fight for their trees.

The Dryad paused at the foot of the ladder and faced us. She was diminutive even to a five-foot Faun—no taller than four herself. Her hair fell long and loosely over her shoulders, green hair, a dark leaf-green that in the shadows looked black, but where the sunlight struck it smoldered like jade that travelers bring from the East. Her mouth was pink and small; her skin, the pure fresh white of goat's milk. A brown linen robe, bordered with tiny acorns, rippled to sandaled feet.

She waited for us to speak and explain ourselves. When we said nothing—what could we say? our invasion was evident—she spoke herself, slowly as if out of practice, but with great precision.

"You have violated my house. I was sleeping above when your clumsy sandals woke me. May Janus, the door-god, curse you with evil spirits!"

"I am sorry we woke you," said Remus. "As for violating your house, we were not sure it *was* a house until we found this room. Then we forgot ourselves in its beauty." He paused. "We have come to ask a favor."

"A favor?" she cried. "I can guess the favor you mean." She fixed her glare on me. "You are the worst, you Fauns. Did it never occur to you to cover your loins, as your friend does?"

"If you notice my nakedness," I said proudly, "perhaps it is because you admire it. Dryads need men, and Fauns need women. Why should they not be friends?"

"I have banqueted kings," she spat. "Shall I frolic with strangers who blunder in from the woods—a Faun and a shepherd?"

"We only want to ask you about our bees." Remus blinked, a small hurt child scolded for a deed he has not committed. He stepped toward her and she did not move. "Our bees are dying and we want you to heal them." They stared at each other. Then, incredibly, unpredictably even to me, he took her in his arms. Like the scolded child who does the very thing of which he has been accused, he kissed her small pink lips. Quick as an adder her hand rose—for the first time I saw the dagger—and raked down his side.

With a cry he withdrew, staring not at his blood-streaked side but at her, and not with anger but shame at his own affront. I seized the knife before she could use it again and caught her, struggling in my arms. Furious because she had hurt my friend, I pressed her wrists cruelly until she lay still. I felt her breasts against my flesh, and then, before I could want her too much myself, said, "Remus, she is yours. Kiss her again!"

"Let her go," he said.

"But Remus, she attacked you. She deserves what she feared."

"Sylvan, let her go," he said, a small boy, baffled, defeated, but not to be disobeyed. I released her. She stared at the streak down his side.

"Please," he said to her. "My bees are dying. Tell me what to do for them."

She drew him into the clear light of a window and dabbed the blood with a corner of her robe. "Burn galbanum under the hive and carry them clusters of raisins in leaves of thyme. They will heal and grow strong again." Then she took a long, unhurried look at him, and I might have been in another oak, for all they noticed me. "You are very young. At first you were hidden in the shadows. When you kissed me, I was sure you were like the rest."

"I am," he said. "I came to ask you about my bees, but I forgot them. I wanted your body. You made me think of grass and flowers in the hot sun. I am like the rest."

"But you told your friend to release me. Why weren't you angry when I hurt you?"

"I was. With myself."

She held his face between her hands. "You are fragrant from the forest. You have lain in clover, I think. Like Aeneas, the Trojan. I loved him, you know. He came to me just as you have. All Latium rang with his triumphs —Turnus defeated, Camilla's Amazons put to rout! He sat on my couch and said, 'Mellonia, I am tired. Since the sack of Troy I have wandered and fought. I have lost my wife and my father and forsaken a queen of Carthage. And I am tired.'

"I took his head between my hands and kissed him, my prince, my warrior. In the years that followed, I watched him grow old. He married the princess Lavinia to found a royal line here in Latium. But he died in my arms, an old man with hair like a white waterfall. And I cursed this tree which kept me young. I wanted to die with Aeneas. The years passed and I did not give myself, even in loneliness. I have waited for another Aeneas."

She turned away from him and stared through a window at a swarm of bees approaching the tree. "They are bringing me honey. My little friends. Your friends too." She faced him again.

"Why are you young? Aeneas was gray when he came to me, older than I in wars and loves, though younger in years. Now I am ancient. But you are young. You cannot have waited for anything very long. Your eyes are naked, a child's. You have not learned to hide your thoughts. You

145

want me and fear me. I could stab you with words more sharply than with this dagger. Why do you come here young and virginal? I will make you old. My face is a girl's, but my eyes are tired with waiting."

Like round-built merchant ships laden with precious oils, the bees invaded the room and unloaded their nectar in a cup of agate. She held out her hand and some of them lit in her palm. "To me, Remus, you are like the bees. Their life is six weeks."

"Then help me to be like Aeneas!"

She reached up to him and loosened the fillet which bound his hair. "It spills like sunflowers. I am cold, so cold. Give me your sunflowers, Remus. Prince of Alba Longa!"

"You know me?"

"Not at first. Only when I had hurt you. I knew you by your yellow hair and your gentleness. The forest speaks of you, Remus. With love."

Their voices blended with the whirr of bees, and the scent of nectar throbbed in my nostrils like a sweet intoxicant. I had lingered too long. I backed down the ladder and returned to the pile of stones.

Much later, when Remus stepped from the tunnel, he said, "Sylvan, you are crying!"

"I am *not* crying," I protested. "Fauns don't cry. We take things as they come and make light of everything. A bramble bush scratched my eyes and made them water."

He looked doubtful but did not press me. In fact, he said little even after we left the circle of oaks and plunged into the forest.

"The Dryad," I asked. "Was she hospitable?" I pressed him with the hope that he would speak of her lightly, as a woman possessed and forgotten. I wanted him to reassure me that I was not replaced in his heart by a bad-tempered Dryad older than Aeneas!

"Yes."

"Remus," I chided. "Your spirits seem mildewed. Have you nothing to tell me about Mellonia?"

It was almost as if the aged Faustulus were speaking. "What is there to say about love? It isn't happiness, altogether; it is sadness too. It is simply possession."

"I should think you would feel like wrestling," I said. "Or drawing one of your goddesses. Or swimming the Tiber. You don't look possessed to me, you look vacant."

"I am thinking of many things," he said. "Yesterday,

146

I wanted to punish the man who had killed my mother, and I wanted to be king for the sake of Fauns and wolves and runaway slaves. Now I want to be king for her sake also."

We were nearing the Palatine. At the mouth of our cave, he stopped and faced me and placed his hands on my shoulders.

"Sylvan, why were you crying back there?"

"I told you," I snapped.

"Did you think she had driven you out of my heart, little Faun?"

He had not called me "little Faun" since that night a year—ten years—ago, when Romulus stole me from my camp. "Yes," I said, losing control of my tears. "And not to a girl but a witch! Or squirrel, I should say, the way she lives in a tree. Remus, she will bite you yet." Being half goat, I always saw people as animals.

He did not laugh at me and try to make light of my tears, but touched his fingers, lightly as butterflies, to my ear. "In the circle of oaks," he said, "there were jonquils and narcissi growing together. There was room for both. Do you understand what I am saying, Sylvan?"

Just then the ram-eyed Celer hurried toward us down the hill. If anything, his eyes had grown flatter and more stupid with the passing year.

"Remus," he called in his thick slurred way. "News from the city! Romulus wants you in his hut."

III

In the early dusk, the hill lay shadowed and strange, and the hut of Romulus seemed misted to stone. Solemn and dignified, sheep roamed the paths and, pausing, were hardly separable from the low rocks which Vulcan, it was said, had thrust from his caverns in a fiery temper. Shepherds and those who had recently joined them, Romulus's latest recruits, loitered in small groups talking about the day's work or tomorrow's drill. The newcomers held apart from the original shepherds. Their garb was the same simple loin cloth, but their faces, though mostly young, were scared and sullen. One, I knew, was a murderer who had fled from Lavinium after killing his wife; another, a parricide from the new Greek colony at Cumae. It was men like these whom Remus wished to bar from the Palatine, and Romulus welcomed because they knew how to fight.

When the wife-killer saw me, he bleated like a goat. Remus wheeled in anger but I shoved him toward Romulus's hut. He must not fight on my account.

"You sound like a frog," I called good-naturedly. "Do it like this." And I bleated so convincingly that she-goats answered from every direction.

A figure loomed toward us, a tall ship scudding in a sea of mist. It was Romulus. To me he nodded, to Remus he smiled.

"Brother," he said. "Gaius is here from the city. He has brought us news." We walked into his hut, where a small, bearded man who reminded me of a water bug, so freely did he skip about the room, was telling a story he seemed to have told several times and would no doubt tell again. His eyes sparkled when he saw Remus and me, a new audience.

"Remus," he said. "And Sylvan, is it not? Listen to what I have seen! I met Numitor in the market yesterday with two attendants. Lately Amulius has allowed him considerable freedom. To appease the people, I expect, and keep them from growling about taxes. Anyway, a half-grown sheep dog was barking at one of Amulius's soldiers. A friendly dog, wanting to play. But the soldier did not. He raised his spear and drove it through the animal's heart. Numitor cried out in anger and raised his staff to strike the man. The soldier, far from cowed, drew his sword, but a barber and a vintner intervened while Numitor's attendants hurried him back to the palace.

"As the old man disappeared, I heard him shout, 'If my grandsons had lived, there would be no soldiers!' Everyone who had watched the scene—myself included—was stirred by Numitor's courage. And everyone wished that there were truly grandsons to drive the soldiers from the street."

With a vigorous skip, he ended his story and smote Remus's shoulder for emphasis. Remus's emotion was evident. His eyes, wide and troubled, mirrored the flames from the hearth: mournful lights in a green, sad forest. As far as I knew, no one had told the overseer the boy's real identity. But Gaius watched him with unusual interest. Perhaps he had overheard the shepherds.

Sparing Gaius the temptation to repeat his story, Romulus led him to the door. "It is bad news you bring us,

148

Gaius. Thank Jove we are kingless here! Do you wonder we stay in the country?"

Gaius smiled ironically. Doubtless he guessed that most of Romulus's men and Romulus himself avoided the city for reasons that had nothing to do with a fondness for the countryside.

"When I think of Amulius," he sighed, "I am tempted to stay here with you. They call him The Toad, you know, though he calls himself The Bear. But Tullius, my master, depends on me. His herds have multiplied, Romulus. I shall take him good news." With a backward wave, he bobbed down the Palatine.

In Romulus's hut, Faustulus, Celer, the twins, and I gathered by the fire to evaluate Gaius's news. On such occasions, Remus always included me, though the first time both Romulus and Celer had objected to the presence of a Faun.

"We have waited with patience," Romulus said with unsuppressed excitement. "Now the mood of the city seems right. They will flock to our side the minute they know us! But they have to be told who we are, and our grandfather is the one to tell them. First we must identify ourselves to him. I will go to Alba Longa tomorrow and get an audience."

"But he lives in Amulius's palace," cried the aged Faustulus bent like a hickory bow but taut, like the rest of us, with the spirit of revolt. "How can you get an audience?"

"He is right," said Remus. "You can't simply walk to the palace as I did in Veii and ask to see Numitor. Amulius's guards are much too suspicious. Your height and bearing set you apart at once. I should be the one to go."

"You, Remus? What about your hair? Blond men in Latium are as rare as virgins in Etruria. They will take you for a spy from the Gauls! Even if they don't, how will you gain an audience with Numitor?"

"I have thought what I would do for some time. First I will dye my hair dark brown. You know the umber that's dug from the banks of the Tiber? I will rub some in my hair and disguise the color. Then I will steal one of Numitor's cows. His shepherds will catch me and take me to Numitor. In the theft of cows, the owner and not the king has the right to pass judgment. Amulius will have no hand in this unless Numitor turns me over to him. I don't believe he will."

149

"No," said Romulus, "it is much too dangerous. I won't let you take the risk."

Usually I wanted to kick him with both my hooves. Now I wanted to embrace him.

"Remus is right," said that idiot, Celer, mouthing his usual monosyllables. "Old men love him. He's soft and polite. Let him go, Romulus. I have a stake in this too."

Yes, I thought, cattle, women, and a house in town. That's all you want. What do you know about government? Remus, my friend, even if you win the city, you will not have won your justice.

"It is settled then," said Remus with a finality that ended argument.

"And I will help you," I said.

"No, I will do it alone. Fauns are not popular in Latium. The shepherds might kill you right off."

Romulus looked troubled. He stroked his beginning beard and furrowed his brow. This fierce, ambitious young man, who feared neither wolves nor warriors, was unashamedly afraid for his brother. At last, like a father sending his son to fight the Gauls, he placed his hands on Remus's shoulders and said, "Go then, Brother. But while you are gone, I will gather the shepherds. We will be ready to attack the city when you return with word from Numitor. If you don't return within three days, we will attack anyway. The gate is strong, but the walls aren't high to shepherds who live on hills."

"Or to shepherds led by princes," said Faustulus proudly, drawing the twins to his side. "For eighteen years I have called you my sons. In fact, since I found you in the cave at the breast of Luperca. After you had fed, she let me take you—she, your second mother, knew that the time had come for a third. And I carried you back to this very hut and to Larentia, my wife. When Larentia died a year later, I brought you up myself. Now, like the wolf, I must step aside and return you to your grandfather. You will not shame him."

In our cave the next morning, Remus veiled his head in a cloak and addressed a prayer to the god Bonus Eventus, whose image he had scratched on the wall. No one knew the god's true appearance, but Remus had made him young and round-cheeked, with a spray of barley in his hand. Holding out his arms and quite oblivious to Luperca and me, Remus prayed:

150

"Bonus Eventus, god who brings luck to the farmer with his barley and his olive trees, bring me luck too; send me safely to my grandfather!"

After the prayer, he set a cup of milk before the image, for everyone knows that the gods, whether human as Remus and the Etruscans supposed, or bodiless powers in the wind, the rock, the tree, demand offerings of food. (Luperca eyed the milk, and I hoped that the god drank quickly!) Then he attended to his bees, burning galbanum under the hive and carrying them raisins in thyme.

"Look after them, will you?" he asked. "And Luperca too. You may have to feed her from your hands. She is very feeble." (Not too feeble to drink that milk, I thought.) "And Sylvan. Will you tell Mellonia where I have gone? I had meant to visit her today."

I stamped my hoof in protest. "The squirrel lady?"

"Goddess," he corrected.

"Goddess? She will live no longer than her tree!"

"But her tree has lived hundreds of years, and will live hundreds more. Till Saturn returns. Then he will find her another."

"Is that what she told you? What about lightning? And floods? And woodcutters?"

"Your ears are quivering," he grinned. "They always do when you are angry." And he began to stroke them with his irresistible fingers. "You will see Mellonia? Promise me, Sylvan."

"Don't do that," I cried. "You know how it tickles."

"But you like to be tickled."

"That's my point. You can make me promise anything."

"Would you rather I yanked your tail?"

"All right, all right. I will see Mellonia. Now go and steal your cow."

Of course I had meant all along to help him. My problem was how to remain hidden until he had begun his theft, then run out and implicate myself and share his capture. I followed his tracks at a safe distance. In the marshes, I was careful not to let my hooves squish noisily, and among the Sabine burial mounds, some fresh, some covered with grass, I steeled myself not to take fright at the presence of spirits and break into a gallop. I was careful to keep a tree or a hill between us. He moved rapidly, as always, but his tracks and my keen sense of hearing kept me on his trail.

151

Numitor's shepherds lay asleep in the shade, three gnarled men as ancient as their master, who, it was said, hired only the old to work for him because the young reminded him of his lost daughter and grandsons. At the feet of the shepherds lay an aged sheep dog who also seemed to be sleeping. I hid behind an ilex tree and waited for developments.

Remus advanced into the herd and singled out a thin, black cow with a shrunken udder. The dog stared at him sleepily as the three shepherds continued to drowse.

"Ho there, cow, off with you!" Remus cried, scuffing through the bushes with a great racket. Like a child chasing geese, he seemed to enjoy himself.

The dog made no move until he saw the shepherds open their eyes. Then he hobbled forward and warily circled the intruder. The men rubbed their eyes and began to shout, "Thief, thief!" Remus pretended to be bewildered by their cries and ran in circles around the cow. I sprang from my ilex tree and joined him.

"I told you not to come," he whispered, as angry as I had ever seen him.

"Two of them," croaked a shepherd. "And one a Faun. They might have made off with the herd!"

They cautiously approached the spot where we circled the cow, who, unperturbed by our sallies, continued her breakfast of grass, while the dog, preening himself on his vigilance, barked from a bed of lupine.

"Brave dog, brave Balbus," the shepherds muttered, stroking the animal on its flea-bitten head. One of them fetched some leathern thongs from a lean-to beside the pasture.

"Now," said the least infirm of the three, who seemed their leader. "Tie their hands."

Without resistance, we offered our hands. While a shepherd bound them, the leader waved his staff threateningly and the dog rushed in and out barking, then withdrew to catch his breath.

"They are just boys," said our binder, craning his neck and squinting for a clear look. "Need we take them to Numitor in town? It's such a long walk, Julius. A good thrashing may be all they need."

Remus hurried to speak. "My father thrashed me once. That is why I ran away. It made me rebellious. No, I am afraid you must take us to Numitor, unless you want every cow stolen and sold to the Etruscans across the river." He looked very fierce and tilted his head as if to look down in scorn on these men who dared call him just a boy. "And my friend here, the Faun. Would you believe it! Young as he is, he has already carried off six maidens." He added wickedly, "I have carried off seven. But then, I am older."

"Boys they may be," sighed the leader, "but dangerous ones. Numitor will have to judge. Can the two of you get them to town while Balbus and I watch the herds?"

The old men looked at each other and then toward town, as if weighing the effect of twenty-four miles on their weathered ankles. One of them prodded Remus with his staff, the other me. We lurched forward obligingly. "We will try," they sighed.

"Give them a whack if they talk," advised the leader, and off we went to find Numitor.

Alba Longa, the city of Romulus's and Remus's dream, which I myself had seen only from the woods at the foot of its plateau, was in truth a modest walled town of five thousand people. Its rock walls, though tall, were starting to crumble, and its streets grew grass between their cobblestones. Nevertheless the houses glittered whitely with plaster and looked to us both like little palaces.

"And their roofs," Remus whispered, "They are covered with *baked clay shingles*." We were used, of course, to the thatched roofs of shepherd huts. "No danger of fire, no rain soaking through."

"Ho there, thieves, get on with you," our captors shouted, and prodded us with their staves. Everywhere the people stared at our advance, to the obvious pleasure of the shepherds, who cried the more loudly, "Ho there!" A vestal with a black Etruscan vase almost spilled her water. A vintner dropped his pig-skin of wine and a thin red stream trickled among the cobblestones. There were barbers in stalls by the road, and sellers of vegetables holding great melons in their hands; children, sheep dogs, and asses; and, brash and numerous, the soldiers of Amulius. In most Latin cities, I knew, there was no standing army, no soldiers except in wartime. But Amulius's men, brandishing spears tipped with bronze, marched through the city as if to say, "We march on the king's business, and it is not for civilians to inquire its nature."

"Ho there," shouted our captors once too often, and a soldier swatted them both on the head with the shaft of

153

his spear. "Be quiet, old men. You are near the palace."
Chastened, the shepherds fell silent and ceased to prod us.

To the left lay the temple of Vesta, raised by Etruscan
architects on a stone platform, with four square pillars
across the front. Its pediment twinkled with orange terra
cotta but not with the images beloved by the Etruscans,
for the Latin goddess Vesta lived in the flame of her hearth
and had no physical semblance. Opposite the temple
crouched the palace of Amulius, a low white rectangle
distinguished only by size from the houses we had passed.
It was whispered that one day Amulius hoped to build a
true Etruscan palace, multi-colored instead of white, with
frescoes and colonnades, from the cattle he took in taxes;
he would trade them to the Etruscans for architects and
stone.

As a start, at least, he had flanked his gate with bronze
Etruscan lions, slender and lithe-legged, their tails looped
over to touch their backs, their eyes almond-shaped like
those of the men who had made them. In front of the
lions stood a pair of human guards, only less lordly than
the animals.

"Have you business in the king's palace?" one of them
demanded. His jerkin was leather, his crested helmet,
bronze.

Our captors had not recovered their composure since
the scene with the soldier. They stammered awkwardly
and Remus had to speak for them.

"They caught us stealing Numitor's cattle. They want
to receive his judgment."

At mention of Numitor, the guards softened. One of
them leaned into the gate and called, and a withered attendant appeared from the interior. Guard and attendant
whispered together; attendant disappeared and shortly returned. He led us down a hallway supported by wooden
timbers and into a garden behind the palace, enclosed on
three sides by a brick wall. Roses rioted in vermilion chaos
and crocuses spilled like golden goblets. It was the first
flower garden I had ever seen. I wanted to roll in the blos-
soms, thorns and all, and kick my hooves in the air. Then
I saw the king of the garden and forgot to dream. He sat
in a backless chair and stared into a milky pool. His white
curving hair was hardly distinguishable from his robes,
which billowed around his feet and hid his sandals.

He seemed unaware of us. The attendant drew his attention. "Prince, your shepherds have brought two thieves to receive justice."

He raised his head and looked at us without expression. His face was as yellow and cracked as papyrus, laid in a tomb by pharaohs older than Saturn; god-men ruling the Nile before the Etruscans had passed through Egypt and brought her lore to Italy. A face like papyrus whose writing had been erased by time; inscrutable.

"Bring them forward," he said. We knelt and Remus took his hand.

"My king," he said, nothing more, but with infinite sincerity.

Numitor withdrew his hand and motioned the boy to rise. "I am not your king," he said stiffly. "I never was. You are much too young—the age of my grandsons, had they lived. And they were born after I had lost my throne. Tell me, boy, why did you steal my cattle?"

"Because I wanted to see you."

"To see me? I don't understand."

"As a thief, I knew they would bring me to receive your judgment."

"You were right. Before I deliver judgment, what favor do you ask? I warn you, I have few to give."

"Your blessing. Your love."

"An old man loves his children. I have none. His grandchildren. I have none. My heart has rid itself of love. A nest without swallows. But what is your name? Something about you stirs me to remember—"

"A shepherd named me Remus, and my brother, Romulus. We are twins."

The names, of course, were meaningless to him, but he caught at Remus's last word. "Twins, you say?"

"Soon after we were born, our mother was buried in a pit and we were taken to be drowned in the Tiber. But Faustulus saved us and made us his sons."

Numitor groaned and surged to his feet, like the geysers of Vulcan, white with borax, which roar from the earth and shudder in the air.

"What are you saying?" he thundered. "You lie as well as steal. I saw my grandsons when Amulius took them from my daughter. One had dark hair, darker than yours. One had gold, gold like this flower." He crushed a crocus under his sandal. "A gift from the god, his father. Which are you?"

"The gold-haired." Remus fell to his knees and ducked

155

his head in the pool, which began to run rivulets of brown. He rose and shook out his hair. Though streaked with umber, it glittered yellowly like gold among veins of iron.

I watched the papyrus mask. The worn and time-veined surface trembled and softened, the forgotten language of love spoke in misting eyes. He ran his hand through Remus's hair and felt the molten umber between his fingers.

"Time," he said. "Give me time. I am not used to tears. They burn like wine." An old man sightless with tears, he took the boy in his arms. "Rhea," he whispered, "your son has come back to me."

"You are a senile old fool," a voice croaked from the door. "This boy has played a trick on you. He should be taught a lesson."

I recognized Amulius though I had never seen him. I knew him from the veined toad eyes which never blinked, the hunched and dwarfish shape. Amulius the Toad.

"Guards!" he called.

"Go to Romulus," Remus whispered. "I will hold them off."

Behind me a prince and a tyrant grappled in roses and thorns. With a single thrust of my hooves, I clutched the top of the wall and drew myself up the bricks. "Bonus Eventus," I prayed, "help me to bring him help!"

IV

I landed in a narrow street behind the palace and my hooves clattered on the cobblestones. An old woman, carrying melons from market, paused in surprise, then trudged down the street with a shrug that seemed to say: "Let Amulius protect his own palace. If Fauns can rob it, good for them." There was no one else in sight, but an ass, tethered to a stake, watched me vacantly. His master, it seemed, had business in the shop of a dyer, which reeked with decaying trumpet shells, much prized for their purple dye.

Remus had given me seconds. As soon as the guards overpowered him, they would follow me or send their friends. I must reach the gate quickly; I must run. But a running Faun, in a city of soldiers, would look suspicious. They would take me for a thief. Nibbling grass between the stones, the tethered ass browsed in the sun. I loosed his rope and kicked him with the full force of my hoof. He galloped down the street.

"Whoa, whoa," I shouted, galloping after him as if to recover my own escaping property. Round a bend he sped and into the central street and straight toward the towers of the gate. When he slowed, I slowed. When he quickened, I quickened and yelled "Whoa!" A hand reached out to stop him; I caught my breath; but he burst free and charged for the gate. The guards laughed and spurred him on with a slap to his flank and a cry of "Giddyap!" Upsetting a potter's cart, laden with orange clay lamps, I hurried after him.

"May thieves crack your skull," cried the potter. I waved without looking back and raced down the hill toward the forest. To the left of me, Lake Albanus glittered in the afternoon sun, and skiffs of hollowed alder poised like dragonflies on its molten turquoise. Ahead of me dusky cypresses signaled the path to the Palatine.

I found Romulus with Celer and the herd at the foot of the Palatine. When I told him what had happened, he turned very pale and drove his staff into the ground.

"I *knew* I should have gone."

"Never mind," I consoled. "Who can say no to Remus?"

"If they harm him, I will burn the city! Celer, watch the cattle." He hurried me up the hill, making plans as he went. "We will attack tonight. In the dark, we may be able to climb the walls before we are seen."

"But the people won't know us. Remus had no chance to tell Numitor about our plan."

"No matter. We can't delay. Once in the city, we will shout his name—'Long live Numitor!'—and hope to rally support."

Romulus was right, we could not delay. But what could we do against walls and soldiers? If we battered down the gate with a tree, soldiers would surely be waiting. If we climbed the walls, they might see us and still be waiting. Since Alba Longa stands on a ridge, it is difficult to reach the walls without detection, even at night. I said nothing; Romulus knew the dangers. But I could not risk Remus's life with such a puny effort.

I descended the Palatine and headed for the cave. I wanted to think. On the way I passed Celer with the herd. He leaned against a rock, staff in hand and a straw between his teeth. Complacent oaf, I thought. Calm as a sheep when Remus's life is in danger.

"So they shut the Woodpecker in a cage," he grinned. "Big games tonight, eh?" Before I could hoof him, he changed the subject. "Sylvan, I hear you found a Dryad. Where's her tree?"

"She is Remus's Dryad," I said indignantly.

"And yours," he smirked. "And mine, if you show me her tree."

"North of the Quirinal," I lied. "An ilex tree with a lightning mark on the trunk." I lowered my ears to muffle his answer and hurried to the cave. Inside, I threw myself on a pallet of clover, but the fragrance reminded me of Remus and clouded my thoughts. I paced the floor. Luperca crept from the rear of the cave and pressed against my leg. I knelt and took her head in my hands.

"Luperca," I said. "Remus has gone to the city. They have taken him captive. What shall I do?" She looked at me with such intelligence that I felt she understood my words; she began to whine and I wished that I understood hers.

Then I heard a swarming of bees outside the cave. I walked out and looked at the hive in the fig tree. Mellonia's remedy had worked. The bees were recovering their health. Mellonia! She was the one to help Remus. She had cured his bees. Might she not have secrets to release him from prison? After all, she had loved Aeneas, the incomparable warrior. I galloped for the circle of oaks. Behind me a conch shell boomed from the Palatine, and I knew that Romulus was summoning his men.

I stood at the foot of her oak and called: "Mellonia, I have come from Remus." No answer.

Again I called. A voice, muffled by branches, answered. "I am coming down. Wait for me by the altar."

In a surprisingly short time, she emerged from the tunnel. She was not the Mellonia I remembered, hard and queenly, but a pale tree child blinking in the alien sun. She raised a hand to shelter her eyes.

"He is hurt?"

"No. But Amulius has taken him prisoner." I told her about his capture.

"What does Romulus mean to do?"

I explained his plan—as much as I knew.

"Romulus's shepherds," she sighed. "I have seen them drilling in the woods. They are brave but they have no armor. They have no spears. Only their staves and bows.

What good are bows against walls, or in fighting hand to hand through the streets? They will cost Remus his life."

"Mellonia," I cried desperately. "You can save him, I know you can."

She touched my cheek with the tips of her fingers, like little blades of grass. "You are a good friend to him, Sylvan. You and I and the forest, we are his friends. Perhaps we can save him. Go back to Romulus now. Say that when Arcturus shines directly over the temple of Vesta, I will come to him in the woods below the city gate. Let him do nothing till I come, but have his men in readiness."

I pressed her hand; it was warm and small like a swallow. "Mellonia, I have not been kind to you."

"Nor I to you. But Remus has made us friends. You are his brother, Sylvan. Far more than Romulus, the Wolf. Trust me."

I turned to go and she called after me. "Sylvan, wait. In truth I am afraid for him. The forest is restless. The cranes have been flying all day, as they do before a storm. But there has been no storm. And all last night, owls cried in my tree. I have looked for vultures, birds of good omen. Especially for woodpeckers. There are none to be seen."

"Good omens?" I cried. "You are Remus's good omen!"

Tall above Alba Longa, the temple of Vesta burned in the moonlight, and orange Arcturus, the star of spring, climbed above the stone pediment. Fifty shepherds crouched in the forest below the gate: Romulus with his ancient spear consecrated to Mars; several with bows and arrows, the use of which Remus had taught them; but most armed only with knives, staves, or slingshots. The bodies of all were bare except for loin cloths—no greaves on their legs nor metal corselets to hide their chests and backs from the plunge of an arrow or the bite of a sword.

Their battering ram was an elm tree cut in the forest; their ladders looked as frail as saplings untested by storms. How many shepherds, I wondered, would survive the night? I was glad that the bent Faustulus, at Romulus's insistence, had remained on the Palatine. A momentary pity possessed me. Who could blame them, rough though they were, for wanting houses in town and women to tend their hearths?

"We can wait no longer," said Romulus. It fretted him following orders from a Dryad he had never seen. Nothing but concern for Remus, I think, and knowledge of his own inadequacy, could have made him listen at all.

"But Arcturus has just now risen above the temple," I protested. "Before, it was still climbing. I know she will come!"

"What can she do if she does? We are fools to try the gate, which seems to be her intention. We should scale the wall on the far side."

Then I heard the bees. "Hush," I said. "She is coming."

My ears quivered. The droning grew louder; curiously the men peered into the forest. I felt like a traveler approaching a waterfall. At first he hears just a murmur, faint and distant. Then the trees fall away and the murmur roars in his ears.

Now they surrounded us, bees beyond counting. Kindled by the moonlight, they curved like a Milky Way above our heads and wove a shield from the darkness. Mellonia led them. She seemed to be made out of leaves and mist and moonlight. She walked in a cloud of bees, and I had to look closely to see that her feet touched the ground. The men gaped at her; Romulus too, and that stupid Celer most of all.

"Is that your Dryad?" he whispered. "She looks like a goddess!"

I gaped too, but less at her beauty than at the dark stains on her face—were they blood?—and at her torn, disheveled robe.

"It is nothing," she whispered, passing me. "Part of my plan." She singled out Romulus. It was not hard for her to recognize him, the brawniest of all of the young men and the only one with a spear.

"Romulus," she said. "Brother of Remus, I salute you. When the gate is open, I will raise my arm. Enter with your men."

Before he could question her somewhat cryptic directions, she was gone, climbing the hill toward the gate. The bees swirled high above her; their droning died, their fires flickered out in the darkness.

"What does she mean to do?" Romulus gasped. "Sylvan, she is mad."

"Or a witch," cried Celer, staring after her.

The men shuddered and whispered among themselves. Something moved in the forest. Shapes inseparable from the trees, not to be seen, scarcely to be heard. Something breathed.

160

"Striges," went the whisper. "Vampires."

"Lemures. She sent to make us follow her!"

Now she was midway to the gate. "Guards," she called out, her voice broken as if with pain, yet strong enough to be heard in the towers that flanked the gate. "Help me. I am hurt." She fell to her knees. "Help me."

Silence. Then a voice, hesitant, testing. "Who are you?"

"I have come from Veii. Wolves attacked my escort in the forest."

Creaking, the gate swung inward on its massive stone pivot. A lamp flickered in one of the towers, vanished, reappeared on the ground. Its bearer paused in the gateway. Mellonia rose, staggered, fell again. "Help me." The guard walked toward her, sword in hand.

She raised her arm.

"They will shut the gate in our face," groaned Romulus. "We can never climb the hill in time!" But his hesitation was brief. Whatever his faults, he was not a coward. With a low cry to his men, he raced up the hill toward the gate. I ran beside him. The hill swelled above us, endless and black. I felt like a swimmer in the trough of a mountainous wave. Would we never make its crest?

Kneeling beside Mellonia, the guard raised his head and saw us. "Shut the gate!" he shouted. He scurried to safety; the gate swung inward, monstrous, implacable.

Then a shadow crossed the moon. I looked up; my ears stood on end. Mellonia's bees! In a deadly amber stream, they poured from the sky. A shout, a thrashing in the tower. The gate groaned slowly to silence, half open.

I dug my hooves in the turf, kicked aside stones, drove myself furiously forward. Romulus tripped and I heaved him back in the path. Through the half open gate, I saw the movement of men, the flash of a spear, the swirling of bees and bronze. Then we were in the city. The bees withdrew and left us to fight our battle.

A soldier charged me, leveling his spear and grinning like the demons of death in Etruscan tombs. I raised my sling and caught him in the teeth. He stopped, a round black hole where his teeth had been, and stared at me. Blood gushed out of the hole. Like a broken bow, he fell at my feet.

"We have them outnumbered," Romulus shouted. "They are falling back!" Spears wavered, shields swung aside. The street near the gate lay empty except for ourselves.

"Numitor! Numitor is king!" Romulus began the cry,

and the rest of us took it up. "Numitor is king!" Dazed with too easy a victory, we surged toward the heart of town, the temple, the palace, and Remus.

But the street was barred. A row of spears glittered across our path, like the oars of a galley raised from the sea in sparkling unison. A wall of spears to bar our advance, and behind them another, another, and finally a row of archers, grim as Etruscan bronzes. The soldiers we had routed were few. Now we must meet an army. Already our limbs were streaked with blood. We had spent our wind in the climb and the fight at the gate. We had lost some men—six I counted with a hasty glance in the street. We were tired, outnumbered, and armorless. How could we shake those fixed, immovable spears?

"Where are the bees?" I cried. "Mellonia, where are your bees?"

Then I saw the wolves, thudding through the gate and into the street. Muffled as raindrops, their feet padded on the stones. My nostrils quivered with the scent of fur, grassy and wet from the forest. I felt hot breath and smelled decaying flesh. We crouched against the walls to let them pass. The wolves ignored us. Straight toward the soldiers they went, the leveled spears and the tightening bows. Mellonia and Luperca followed them.

Mellonia spoke so softly that I could not make out her words, or should I say incantation. It is said that the Etruscan princes, when they hunt, bewitch the animals with the piping of flutes and lure them into their nets. Mellonia's voice, it seemed, had such a power over wolves. Sometimes, it is true, an animal balked or threatened to turn from the pack. But Luperca, surprisingly agile, snapped at his heels and hurried him back into line. The venerable wolf who had suckled my friend in a cave and the aged, ageless Dryad: both were queens.

The line trembled, the spears wavered, like oars engulfed by a wave. The long taut bows swayed in the archers' arms. And the wolves attacked. High above the wavering spears, a body spun in the air. Spears shot up to ward off its deadly fall. The line was broken. The archers never fired. Men and animals rolled in the street; armor clattered on stones and weighed men down; animals sprang on their chests and tore at their naked faces. Spears were useless, arrows worse. A few had time to draw daggers. Most used their hands.

Some of the men broke free and began to run. Wolves

loped after them. Wounded, in pain, the soldiers reeled against doorways and beat their fists for admittance. The doors remained shut.

The city had wakened. On the rooftops, torches flared, people crouched behind them and stared at the rout of the tyrants who, a few hours ago, had tyrannized Alba Longa. Now a weird procession formed: Mellonia and Luperca with the wolf pack, a cloud of returning bees above their heads: Romulus with his shepherds, raising their staves in token of victory.

But an army's march is slow, and Remus was still in the palace. Ignoring the wolves, I pushed to Mellonia's side.

"Come ahead with me," I urged.

She nodded. "Luperca can watch the wolves."

In a cloud of bees, we raced through the market of silent stalls, where tomorrow the vintner would hawk his wine and the farmer his gourds and grapes. A terrified soldier reeled from our path. A sheep dog snapped at our heels but, hearing the wolves, ducked in an alleyway.

The palace was almost dark. The temple of Vesta, across the road, lent a fitful light from its eternal hearth. The Etruscan lions growled in brazen impotence. They had no soldiers to guard them. The gate was unbarred. We entered the central corridor and, following a light, turned aside into a large hall.

"Amulius's audience room," Mellonia said. She pointed to a curule chair of gold and ivory raised on a stone platform. A tall candelabrum, hung with lamps, cast mournful flickerings on the tapestry behind the throne. Seeing that the room was empty, I turned to continue our search. Mellonia stopped me.

"We will lose minutes. Let my bees find him." She raised her arms and inscribed in the air a series of circles and lines, like the loopings of bees when they tell the location of flowers. The bees understood and swarmed from the room.

We looked at each other. Where was the powerful sorceress who had opened the gate of a city to admit the forest? Like a swallow after a storm, beaten and bruised, she sank to the floor. I motioned her to sit in the chair.

"No," she said. "Amulius sat there." She stared at the plum-colored hangings behind the chair. "Even his dye is false. Not Tyrian purple, the color of kings, but the dye of trumpet shells."

I sat beside her and rested her in my arms. "It will be all right," I said. "Soon we will have him back again."

"Now perhaps. But later? He will always be hurt, always be threatened."

"We will look after him."

"We are vulnerable too. Even now I am weary for my tall bark walls. I cannot leave them for long."

Abruptly the bees returned, circling in the doorway to catch our attention. In the dark corridor, we lost sight of them, but their droning guided us through several turnings and down a stairway redolent of rocks and moisture. We stepped into a cellar lit by a single torch, smoky and pungent with resin. The room opened through a barred door into a small cell. The door swung wide on its pivot and Amulius's body, clutching a dagger, hunched like a bloated toad across the sill. Remus stood in the cell beyond the body.

"He came to get me," he said, dazed.

"And you had to kill him?"

"No. They did." He pointed to the bees which had lit on the pallet in his cell. I knelt beside the body and saw the red welts, a hundred or more, and the closed swollen eyes.

"He unbolted the door and said that my friends were coming; he was going to make me his hostage. I stepped backward. He drew his dagger, and they hit him from the back like a hundred hundred slingshots. He scraped at his eyes, groaned, and fell to the floor. Then you came."

"The bees love you," Mellonia said proudly. "Some may have come from your own hive. They sensed your danger."

He buried his face in the fall of her hair and she held him with exquisite tenderness. For the first time, I loved him loving her. Two children they seemed, warm in each other's arms and forgetful that love, however strong, is also brief, because it is bound by the frailties of the flesh. I wanted to enfold them in the magic circle of my own love and blunt, like a ring of shields, all menacing arrows. But I was a Faun, briefer than men.

At last she drew apart from him. "How pale you have grown, shut up in the palace. In a single day, you wilt like a lotus."

"Come," I said. "We must find Romulus. He is much concerned." We climbed the stairs.

The palace thundered with men. Their shadows bristling

164

on tapestried walls, they stalked through the rooms with torches and gasped at treasures which, to the eyes of a shepherd (and mine as well), rivaled the riches of Carthage. A fan made of peacock feathers. Pearls as big as acorns. A mirror whose handle was the neck of a graceful swan! Guards and servants were nowhere in evidence. They must have fled with our arrival, and the palace lay temptingly accessible. The shepherds seemed to forget that they had come to liberate and not to loot.

We found Romulus in Amulius's audience room, and I must say for him that he was not himself looting, but, torch in hand, trying to organize a search for Remus. He was having trouble; his men were more concerned with found treasures than with lost brothers. When he saw us, he whooped like a Gaul on the warpath. Throwing his torch to me, he lifted his twin from the floor and hugged him with brotherly ardor. Often he seemed the crudest of warriors, a brash young wolf who, in spite of his tender years, had somehow missed youthfulness. But with Remus he was youthful as well as young, and only with Remus could I like him.

"We have taken the city," he cried, while I steadied his torch and shielded my eyes from its sputtering resin. "Brother, Alba Longa is ours!"

"And Numitor's," Remus reminded us. "Has anyone seen the king?"

In a room at the back of the palace, we found him on a couch, his white beard overflowing a crimson coverlet. He had slept through the fall of the city, and he thought himself still asleep when Remus explained what had happened and said, "This is your grandson, Romulus."

At last the sleep had cleared from his eyes. He held out his arms to Romulus, though clearly he was ill at ease with this great muscular grandson, smelling of wolves and blood, who came to him from the forest.

Romulus and Remus supported the king between them and, with Mellonia and me, headed for the gate. Along the way, in corridors and sleeping chambers, Romulus gathered his men, and a sizable procession emerged from the palace. Beyond the Etruscan lions, twenty or more shepherds lounged or sat in the street, placed there by Romulus and awaiting his signal to enter the palace. They stared at Numitor with mild curiosity.

On the roofs of the houses, the townspeople waited too. But Mellonia's wolves still prowled the streets, and the timorous Alba Longans, though visibly moved at the presence of Numitor, were not yet ready to risk descent.

Romulus stepped forward with Numitor and raised the aged king's arm into the air. "People of Alba Longa, your king is restored to you!"

With a slight motion, Numitor released himself from Romulus's support and stood alone. He straightened his bowed shoulders and lifted his weathered face. Forgetting their timidity, the people cheered as if they themselves had restored him to his throne. The shepherds were silent; it was not Numitor they wanted but Romulus. Had they fought to restore an old man to a throne he had lost before they were born? I watched Romulus's face and saw his impatience for Numitor to address the people and abdicate in favor of his grandsons. The Wolf had done the honorable thing; he had proclaimed his grandfather king. The next move was Numitor's.

Meanwhile, Mellonia had left us. I saw her in the street with Luperca, gathering her wolves and bees as a shepherd gathers sheep. Remus saw her too, but she shook her head: he was not to follow.

"She is tired," I whispered. "She wants her tree."

"People of Alba Longa," Numitor was saying in a clear, resonant voice. "Amulius is dead. My grandsons have come back to me. A staff in my old age, they will help me to live out my years—to rule wisely if only for a little while. As king of Alba Longa, I hereby declare an amnesty to all who supported Amulius. I will end my reign with peace, even as I began it. The years between are forgotten." He paused, I should say posed, and lifted his arms with the studied flourish of a mime. A king, it seemed, even in exile, never forgot the gestures of royalty.

The applause was vehement.

"Long live Numitor!"

"King of Alba Longa!"

The people clambered from the rooftops and thrust their way through Romulus's men to the feet of their restored king. Remus tightened his hand on my shoulder. Romulus paled. A mutter, lost in the general cheering, ran among the shepherds. We had rescued Remus; for me, that was enough. But the shepherds wanted more, and rightly, while Romulus and Remus had dreamed of a throne since childhood.

At last the old man's strength was failing. "Help me to bed, will you, my grandsons? Tell your men the largess of

166

the palace is theirs. The wines, the fruits, the venisons. Tomorrow I will rule—with your help. Now I will sleep."

When Numitor slept and Romulus's men roamed the palace, a sausage in one hand, a cluster of grapes in the other, Romulus, Remus, and I talked in the garden. The jonquils, beaten gold goblets by day, had paled with the moon into silver and seemed to be spilling moonlight into the pool.

For once, Celer was absent from our council. Romulus assured us that he had not been wounded, but no one had seen him since Numitor addressed his people.

"Chasing some wench," I muttered.

Our conversation turned to Numitor.

"Did you see his excitement?" Remus asked. "He will reign for years!"

"Then we will build our own city," Romulus announced. "Even if we reign with Numitor, we can't have our way in Alba Longa. What changes can we make while an old man holds the throne? His people will not accept changes as long as he lives. They have had a tyrant; now they want a venerable figurehead. Let them have what they want. We will build *our* city on the Palatine. Already we have a circle of huts. Next, add a wall, then a temple to Mars, then a place of government—"

"And a shrine to our mother," said Remus, kindling to the plan. "A temple to Rumina and a park for the birds and animals. I think, though, Romulus, that the Palatine is not the best hill. True, there are huts already. But some of the owners are thieves and cutthroats, as you well know. Let them keep their huts, but in our new city there will not be room for such men. Why not build on the Aventine? It is almost as high, and closer to the forest, to Mellonia and her friends, who won us our victory."

"Ask Father Mars who won our victory," Romulus snapped. "Mellonia helped, it is true. But my shepherds, Remus, took the city. The men you call thieves and cutthroats."

"Men like Celer make good warriors," Remus granted. "But not good citizens. I mean no disrespect to the man. But Romulus, can you see him worshiping in a temple or sitting in a senate house? Give him a woman and herds, but leave him on the Palatine. Build our city on the Aventine!"

"Ask for a sign from heaven," I interrupted. The gods, I thought, should favor Remus, who worshiped all of

167

them and not the war god only. "Consult a sheep's liver, as the Etruscan augurs do, or watch for birds of good omen."

"Very well," said Romulus reluctantly. "We shall ask for a sign. Early one morning—the best time for omens—we shall climb our respective hills and watch the sky for vultures, the luckiest of birds. Whoever sees the most shall choose his hill for our city. Now, my brother, let us sleep before we quarrel."

The palace abounded in couches; I chose one with feet like an eagle's and fell asleep, dreaming of vultures.

V

With less reluctance than the brothers anticipated, Numitor received their declaration that they wished to build a city on the Tiber. Doubtless realizing that such a city would stand as a safeguard between Alba Longa and the Etruscans—now friendly, but expanding—Numitor had promised to send workmen and materials, and he had already purchased the herds of Tullius and given them to the twins who had long been their shepherds.

But first a site must be chosen. At sunrise three days after the capture of Alba Longa, Remus and I stood atop the Aventine, watching for vultures. The day had been chosen because it was sacred to the Pales, deities of shepherds who had given their name to the Palatine. Before sunrise, Remus had fumigated his herds with sulphur to drive out evil spirits and scattered the stalls with arbute boughs, beloved by the goats, and wreaths of myrtle and laurel. Later the shepherds on the Palatine would leap through bonfires and, facing the east, pray to the Pales. A lucky day, one would think, for omens. But for whom?

"I wonder why the gods favor vultures," I said, wrinkling my nose as I pictured the birds at a feast. "Such an ugly creature."

Remus laughed. "Ugly, yes. But helpful. They rid the forest of carcasses. And they never kill."

"Which way will they come?"

"They may not come at all. They are very rare in this country. Mellonia says to watch the river, where the animals go to drink and die."

He had visited her daily since the fall of Alba Longa.

Her name had grown pleasant even to my long ears. Instead of his usual loin cloth, he was wearing a tunic, almost sleeveless and falling just below the thighs, which the Dryad had woven from rushes and leaves. Soon it would wilt, but Mellonia had promised him a leaf-colored garment of wool to take its place. "Now you are part of my tree," she had said. "Green leaves, green tunic. You carry the forest with you."

"But how will Romulus know if we *really* see the number we say?"

"He will take our word," said Remus, surprised.

"And you will take his?"

"Of course."

"It means a lot to him to build on the Palatine."

"I know. But he would never lie to us."

"Remus. Have you ever thought of building your own city—without Romulus. It won't be easy to rule with him. If you win your hill, it will be even harder. And men like Celer, how will you keep them out? Or make them behave if they enter?"

"I will build with Romulus or not at all. He is my brother. Do you realize, Sylvan, I shared the same womb with him? We have never been apart."

"You love him deeply, don't you?"

"He is one of three. You, Romulus, Mellonia. I love Mellonia as someone beyond me, a goddess or a queen. Green leaves in the uppermost branches of a tree. I love her with awe and a little sadness. I love you, Sylvan, as someone close and warm. A fire on a cold night. Barley loaves baking on the hearth. You never judge me. With you I am most myself. And Romulus? The stone pillars of a temple. The bronze of a shield. Hard things, yes. But strong and needed."

"You are very different from Romulus. He is not always a shield. He is"—I chose my words carefully, not wishing to offend him—"rash in some ways."

"I know," he said sadly. "And I try to temper his rashness. In return, he gives me courage."

"Courage, Remus? You have strength enough of your own. I never saw you hesitate when you knew what was right."

"You can't see my heart. It leaps like a grasshopper sometimes! Romulus, though, is fearless."

Then you are the braver, I thought. You conquer fear,

while Romulus's courage is thoughtless, instinctive. But I said nothing; he would only make light of himself.

And then we saw them: High above the orange turbulence of the Tiber, six vultures glided to the north. Clumsy birds, ugly—I had not changed my mind—but oh, how welcome.

"Remus, you have won!" I cried. "Even if Romulus sees them, we saw them first. They are flying *toward* and not away from him."

We raced down the hill and scrambled up the Palatine, a few hundred yards to the north.

"Slow down, Woodpecker," I shouted. "Your tunic has given you wings."

He laughed and tore me a leaf from his waist. "Catch my feathers and fly!"

In a flurry of leaves and dust, we burst through the circle of huts and found Romulus, waiting with a small band of men, on the highest part of the hill.

"Six of them," Remus cried. "Romulus, we saw six at once!"

Romulus looked surprised, but he spoke blandly. "So did we. Just before you came." His face at last showed the start of a beard, a small black V below his chin. The ambitious boy, impatient but waiting, had hardened into a man who, no less ambitious, had ceased to wait.

"It must have been the same six. They were flying this way."

"No matter. They still count."

"Then we are tied."

"No," put in Celer. "We have seen *twelve*." He twisted his mouth to the caricature of a smile, but his flat eyes were cold.

"Twelve? There have never been so many near these hills!"

Romulus started to speak, but Celer continued. "Today there were. The six that just passed, and before them, six more. Even larger—as big as eagles. They circled twice to be sure we saw them. Sent by the gods, eh, Romulus?"

"Is it true?" Remus asked his brother.

Romulus glowered. "Of course it is true. Celer has told you. And the city is mine to build where I choose."

Remus paled and spoke with an effort. "Build it then." It must have been clear to him that Celer had lied and that Romulus, though hesitant at first, had repeated the lie. "Sylvan," Remus said to me, "I am going to the cave."

170

We started down the hill. Behind us Romulus was giving orders. "Find me a bull and a heifer. We will plow the boundaries of our new city. But first we will celebrate the feast of the Pales. Celer, break out the wine. And the rest of you, build us some bonfires."

The men whooped approval and scuffled about their work. After the feast, Romulus would yoke the animals to a bronze-tipped plow and drive them around the base of the hill where he meant to build his walls, leaving a space for the gate. The area enclosed by the plow would be fortunate ground. Whoever crossed the furrow instead of entering by the designated gate would shatter the luck of the builders and allow the invasion of hostile spirits.

Remus was silent until we reached the cave. He threw himself on his pallet and Luperca, as if she sensed his trouble, crept beside him.

"You can build your own city," I suggested.

"No, I will help Romulus. But first I must understand him."

"I know how you feel. Your hill was the best."

He looked up at me. "The hill is not important. Romulus lied. That is important. He is building his city on a lie and the men know."

"No one objected. They like the Palatine."

"That is the harm. They knew and said nothing."

I left him alone all morning and waited under the fig tree. Once I looked in the cave. His eyes were open, but he did not appear to see me, nor to hear the merriment on top of the hill.

"Rumina," I said, more in conversation than in prayer. "You are the goddess of the suckling herds. But your tree stands right at our door. Neglect the lambs for awhile and help my friend."

In the afternoon, I climbed the fig tree and captured some honey in a round clay bowl. The bees, sensing perhaps for whom it was meant (or instructed by Rumina herself), made no objection. In the cave I knelt beside Remus.

"Eat it," I said crossly. "You have brooded enough."

He smiled, sat up, and took the bowl from my hands. He tilted it to his lips as if it were milk, for he relished the honey from his own bees, and drained the bowl.

"Now," he said, "I will help Romulus with his walls. But first I want to see Mellonia."

"I will wait for you here."

"No, come with me."

"You must have things to say in private. Who wants a Faun's big ears at such a time?"

"She has grown to love you. Besides—" His smile faded. "I want you with me. It is something I feel—a loneliness, a fear—I am not sure what. I want you with me."

In the woods beyond the Aventine, we encountered Celer and three of his friends, leaning on each other for support and thrashing through the undergrowth with such a racket that turquoise lizards flew in all directions. When they saw us they stopped, and Celer looked momentarily sobered. He forced a grin.

"Big Ears and Woodpecker," he said. "You missed our feast. The gods will be hurt."

"They are hurt already," said Remus, without slowing. "But not by Sylvan and me." The revelers made for the Palatine with surprising directness.

Suddenly I remembered that Celer had asked me the location of Mellonia's tree. I had not told him, but the night of the wolves he had vanished from Alba Longa. Had he followed her home, I wondered, and then today, emboldened with wine and friends, returned to invade her tree?

"Remus," I said. "Do you think he has found her tree?"

We began to run.

The branches of Mellonia's oak tree sprawled like a city which has grown without planning, its temples and archways mingled in artless beauty. From a distance, there was nothing to hint an invasion.

We approached the trunk.

"That lowermost branch," said Remus tensely. "I think it is starting to wilt."

"Too little sun," I said, but without conviction.

He began to call. "Mellonia! Mellonia!"

I searched the ground for traces of a fire or other means of assault, but the trunk was untouched. Around the altar, however, there were definite signs of Celer and his friends —jonquils in crushed profusion, rocks overturned, and, yes, they had entered the tunnel; it reeked of their wine.

Mellonia's room lay hushed and broken. We found her beside the couch, a white small body blackened with bruises and cradled, incongruously, in a bed of narcissus petals. Remus lifted her on to the couch and smoothed her tangled

172

green hair, in which petals had caught as if to take root in its venture. She opened her eyes.

"Little bird," she said. "Who will look after you?" That was all.

He covered her body with petals and kissed her on the mouth which could no longer feel bruises. "I had never meant to outlive you," he said.

I turned my head but I heard his tears. Or was it the column of bees that swayed through the open window, the forest grieving for its queen, and for the king who had loved her? The shepherds say that bees speak only what is in our hearts—our grief, our joy, not theirs. That their murmur is always the same, and it is we who darken or lighten it to our mood. Perhaps, then, I heard my own tears.

We left her in the tree with the bees. "She would not want to be moved," Remus said. "The oak is dying. They will go to earth together."

We stared at the tree and already, it seemed, the wilt was stealing upward to the green and sunny towers.

"Did you hear what she said?" he asked.

I pressed his hand. "Yes. Yes, little bird."

When we reached the Palatine, Romulus had driven his team around the foot of the hill. For one short space, the gate, he had left the earth unbroken. Stripped completely in the hot April sun, he leaned on the plow, his massive thighs diamonded with sweat. Drops rolled down his beard. He looked very tired—and very royal.

With mattocks and shovels, the shepherds were setting to work inside the circle. Romulus had captured the *numen* or magic of the gods. Now they must build strong walls and enclose the magic securely. They sang as they dug, Celer and his friends the loudest:

Romulus, son of the spear god Mars,
Nursed by the long gray wolf . . .

Celer looked up from his work and saw us. He dropped his shovel.

Pausing outside the circle, Remus cried: "Romulus, your walls are useless, the luck is gone. A murderer stands inside!" He jumped the furrow. The shepherds stared at him in horror. I myself, midway to the gate, gasped at his daring. He sprang at Celer. Celer recovered his shovel but

173

Remus parried, wrestled it from his hands, and felled him with a blow to his shoulder.

Romulus snatched a shovel from the shepherd nearest him. "Idiot!" he shouted to Remus. "It is you who have broken our luck. Fight me, not Celer."

"Keep away from me," Remus warned. But he made no move to defend himself from Romulus; he was waiting for Celer, dazed but conscious, to regain his feet.

Romulus struck him with the back of his shovel. I saw Remus's eyes. Surprise, that was all. Not fear, not anger. Then he fell. In the forest, once, I heard a she-wolf cry when a shepherd killed her cubs. All pain, all yearning. A cry from the vital organs of her body, as if their red swift pulsing could wrench her cubs from death. So Romulus cried and knelt beside his brother. In Remus's hair, the stains were of earth, not blood; the umber soil mingling with the sunflowers. But the stalk was broken.

I took Remus's shovel. "Stand up," I said to Romulus. "I am going to kill you."

He looked up at me through tears. "Sylvan, I wish you would."

I think it was Remus who held my hand. Born of one womb, he had said. Romulus, his brother, his pillar and shield of bronze. Instead of killing him, I knelt at his side.

Troubled and respectful, the shepherds surrounded us, and Faustulus laid his hand on Romulus's neck.

"My son, you meant him no harm. Let me prepare his body for burial."

Romulus shook his head. "I must make my peace with him first."

"And you, Sylvan?"

"I will stay with Remus."

The men climbed the hill. The sunlight thinned and shadows came to watch with us. Somewhere a cow lowed with quiet urgency. It is late, I thought. She is waiting for Remus to milk her.

"He must have a place for the night," I said. "He never liked the dark."

Romulus stirred. I think he had forgotten me. "The cave?"

"No. He would be alone there. We will take him to Mellonia's tree. Celer killed her, you know—he and his friends."

He looked at me with stunned comprehension. "Then

174

that was why Remus attacked him. They will die for this, Sylvan."

I kindled a torch in the cave with pieces of flint and returned to Romulus. Luperca followed me. Romulus stroked her head.

"Old mother," he said, "you loved him too." He lifted his brother and held him lightly, with Remus's hair against his cheek. "His hair smells of clover."

"I know."

We walked slowly—Luperca was very weak—and came at last to the tree. Trembling but quiet, she waited outside the cave.

We placed him on the couch beside Mellonia. I pressed my cheek to the shoulder where, as a child, I had clung to be warmed and loved. I crossed his arms as if I were folding wings.

"Little bird," I said. "You reproached Mellonia because you had to outlive her. But I am the one you punished. All of your life was loving—except for this. Where is your city, my friend?"

"In me," Romulus answered.

I turned on him angrily. "In you?" Then I was sorry. Tears ran out of his eyes. He made no effort to hide them. I thought that he was going to fall and held out my hand. He grasped it and steadied himself.

"You think I want walls and armies," he said, "and nothing more? At first I did. This morning I did, when I lied about the birds. But then I had Remus; it seemed I would always have him. Whatever I did, he would love me. He was all I needed of gentleness. Now he is gone —unless I capture him in my city. A great city, Sylvan. Men will call her Rome after me, and her legions will conquer the world—Carthage and Sardis, Karnak, Sidon, and Babylon. But her highways will carry laws as well as armies, learning as well as conquest. Sylvan, don't you see? Remus will live in us and the city we build. Come back with me, Little Faun!"

Where is the bird of fire? In the tall green flame of the cypress, I see his shadow, flickering with the swallows. In the city that crowds the Palatine, where Fauns walk with men and wolves are fed in temples, I hear the rush of his wings. But that is his shadow and sound. The bird himself is gone. Always his wings beat just beyond my hands, and

175

the wind possesses his cry. Where is the bird of fire? Look up, he burns in the sky, with Saturn and the Golden Age. I will go to find him.

ACKNOWLEDGMENTS

I wish to express a particular debt to Alan Lake Chidsey's *Romulus: Builder of Rome* and Carlo Maria Franzero's *The Life and Times of Tarquin the Etruscan.* T. B. S.

1963

THE 1964 CONVENTION committee—the convention was held in Oakland, California—did something that had never been done before regarding the Hugos. They published the number of nominating votes and the number of final-ballot votes received by each contender. You may be slightly shocked at the numbers. We do tend to think of science fiction conventions in terms of thousands of members, almost all of whom may be expected to nominate and vote for Hugo awards.

Well, that's wrong.

For one thing, the "giant" science fiction convention is a thing of relatively recent development. The early "World" conventions drew between 100 and 200 persons each. It was not until the tenth World Science Fiction Convention, in Chicago in 1952, that 1,000 people turned out. The following year attendance fell off again, and it did not surpass 1,000 a second time until 1967. Nowadays, attendance in the 4,000-to-6,000 range is usual, but *that* didn't happen until the mid-1970s.

For another thing, not anywhere *near* all the fans bother to vote; and still fewer, to nominate. In 1964, out of an estimated attendance of 525 persons, it took as few as *eleven* nominations to place a novel on the final ballot, and as few as *nine* to do the same for a shorter work. The *winning* novel received just 63 votes on the *final* ballot. The winning short fiction did better—it drew 93 votes.

There was another little flap over category and date of publication of nominated works, and it came about like this. At the time of his death in 1950, that old science fiction genius Edgar Rice Burroughs had published three interconnected novelettes in what was to have been the seventh book in his Pellucidar series.

Following Burroughs's death, most of his works went out of print and nobody even bothered to inventory his papers, thereby passing up a fascinating trove of unpublished stories—including the fourth and final segment of that Pellucidar book.

A dozen years later, amidst much hue and cry over copyright expirations, authorized versus pirated editions, and endless finger-pointing and blame-hurling, most of Burroughs came *back* into print. Canaveral Press, a publisher which had reissued a number of earlier Burroughs works, obtained rights to his manuscripts, and Canaveral's editor set to work reading, sorting, and trying to figure out what to do with the various fragments and oddments.

I know a good bit about that operation, as I was the editor assigned the task.

Among other publications, the new-old novelette "Savage Pellucidar" appeared in *Amazing Stories*. And the complete book, a pretty good novel cobbled together from the four novelettes, was published by Canaveral. The novel, too, was called *Savage Pellucidar*.

A lot of fans liked the new yarn and voted for it for the Hugo in 1964. How many of them really thought that much of *Savage Pellucidar*, how many voted for it because they were Burroughs fanatics and would vote for *anything* by the Master, and how many did so merely out of sentimental or nostalgic motivation—are moot points.

But in any case, *Savage Pellucidar* received enough nominations to place it on the ballot as both a novel (the Canaveral Press edition) and a work of short fiction (the *Amazing Stories* edition). The committee decided that three-quarters of the book was "old stuff" and threw out the novel nomination, leaving "Savage Pellucidar" on the ballot only as short fiction. In that category it finished last. Whether it would have done better competing as a novel, instead, is also a moot point.

The nominees that *did* stay on the ballot for best novel were *Cat's Cradle* by Kurt Vonnegut, *Dune World* by Frank Herbert, *Glory Road* by Robert A. Heinlein, *Here Gather the Stars* by Clifford Simak (since that time published as *Way Station*), and *Witch World* by Andre Norton.

That was a remarkable lineup of nominees; the degree to which they were remarkable may be measured by the fact that all five books have remained in print constantly for the past decade and a half. (For that matter, so has *Savage Pellucidar*.) Frankly, with my usual 20-20 hindsight, I think I'd have voted for *Cat's Cradle* were the balloting held this morning instead of back in 1964. I don't remember *which* book I voted for back then. But then I was Ed Burroughs's editor, and if *Savage Pellucidar* had stayed on the ballot, I'd probably have been duty-bound to vote for my own man.

Well, it was all a long time ago, wasn't it? And the actual winner, in case you weren't around at the time, was *Way Station*. Certainly a good novel, Simak near or at the top of his form; and it might make an interesting exercise to read (or re-read) all of the nominees and see which holds up the best.

As for short fiction—the fans were still bunching together everything from an anecdote to a novella as "short fiction"—there were only four stories on the ballot. These were "Code Three" by Rick Raphael, "No Truce with Kings" by Poul Anderson, "A Rose for Ecclesiastes" by Roger Zelazny (his first award nomination!), and the Burroughs piece.

The winner—which had originally appeared in *F&SF* —was "No Truce with Kings."

Meanwhile, Philip K. Dick had followed up his Hugo-winning *Man in the High Castle* with a serial, *All We Marsmen,* in *Worlds of Tomorrow;* an Ace novel, *The Game-Players of Titan;* and several short stories in *Amazing* and *Fantastic*. *Amazing* and *Fantastic* had been on a roller coaster for years. *Down* with the departure of Ray Palmer and protégé Bill Hamling, back *up* with their refurbishing under Howard Browne in the early 1950s, *down* again when the spiffy new versions failed to produce enough new customers to cover their increased budgets, and *up* again with the accession to their editorship of the brilliant Cele Goldsmith.

Goldsmith encouraged the early works of such talents as Roger Zelazny, R. A. Lafferty, Ursula K. LeGuin, David R. Bunch, Phyllis Gotlieb, Ben Bova, Kate Wilhelm, and Philip K. Dick—as well as countless veterans, and occasional surprising contributors like the Soviet writers Boris and Arkady Strugatsky.

Under the name "Stand-by," she featured this Phil Dick story in *Amazing* for October 1963. That it didn't win the Hugo is not especially shocking; that it failed even to make the ballot is.

Stand-by

PHILIP K. DICK

AN HOUR BEFORE his morning program on channel six, ranking news clown Jim Briskin sat in his private office with his production staff, conferring on the report of an unknown and possibly hostile flotilla detected at eight hundred astronomical units from the sun. It was big news, of course. But how should it be presented to his several-billion viewers scattered over three planets and seven moons?

Peggy Jones, his secretary, lit a cigarette and said, "Don't alarm them, Jim-Jam. Do it folksy-style." She leaned back, riffled the dispatches received by their commercial station from Unicephalon 40-D's teletypers.

It had been the homeostatic problem-solving structure Unicephalon 40-D at the White House in Washington, D.C., which had detected this possible external enemy; in its capacity as President of the United States it had at once dispatched ships of the line to stand picket duty. The flotilla appeared to be entering from another solar system entirely, but that fact of course would have to be determined by the picket ships.

"Folksy-style," Jim Briskin said glumly, "I grin and say, Hey look, comrades—it's happened at last, the thing we all feared, ha ha." He eyed her. "That'll get baskets full of laughs all over the Earth and Mars but just possibly not on the far-out moons." Because if there were some kind

180

of attack it would be the farther colonists who would be hit first.

"No, they won't be amused," his continuity advisor Ed Fineberg agreed. He, too, looked worried; he had a family on Ganymede.

"Is there any lighter piece of news?" Peggy asked. "By which you could open your program? The sponsor would like that." She passed the armload of news dispatches to Briskin. "See what you can do. Mutant cow obtains voting franchise in court case in Alabama . . . you know."

"I know," Briskin agreed as he began to inspect the dispatches. One such as his quaint account—it had touched the hearts of millions—of the mutant blue jay which learned, by great trial and effort, to sew. It had sewn itself and its progeny a nest, one April morning, in Bismarck, North Dakota, in front of the TV cameras of Briskin's network.

One piece of news stood out; he knew intuitively, as soon as he saw it, that here he had what he wanted to lighten the dire tone of the day's news. Seeing it, he relaxed. The worlds went on with business as usual, despite this great newsbreak from eight hundred a.u.'s out.

"Look," he said, grinning. "Old Gus Schatz is dead. Finally."

"Who's Gus Schatz?" Peggy asked, puzzled. "That name . . . it does sound familiar."

"The union man," Jim Briskin said. "You remember. The stand-by President, sent over to Washington by the union twenty-two years ago. He's dead, and the union—" He tossed her the dispatch; it was lucid and brief. "Now it's sending a new stand-by President over to take Schatz' place. I think I'll interview him. Assuming he can talk."

"That's right," Peggy said. "I keep forgetting. There still is a human stand-by in case Unicephalon fails. Has it ever failed?"

"No," Ed Fineberg said. "And it never will. So we have one more case of union featherbedding. The plague of our society."

"But still," Jim Briskin said, "people would be amused. The home life of the top stand-by in the country . . . why the union picked him, what his hobbies are. What this man, whoever he is, plans to do during his term to keep from going mad with boredom. Old Gus learned to bind books; he collected rare old motor magazines and bound them in vellum with gold-stamped lettering."

Both Ed and Peggy nodded in agreement. "Do that," Peggy urged him. "You can make it interesting, Jim-Jam; you can make anything interesting. I'll place a call to the White House, or is the new man there yet?"

"Probably still at union headquarters in Chicago," Ed said. "Try a line there. Government Civil Servants' Union, East Division."

Picking up the phone, Peggy quickly dialed.

At seven o'clock in the morning Maximilian Fischer sleepily heard noises; he lifted his head from the pillow, heard the confusion growing in the kitchen, the landlady's shrill voice, then men's voices which were unfamiliar to him. Groggily he managed to sit up, shifting his bulk with care. He did not hurry; the doc had said not to over-exert, because of the strain on his already-enlarged heart. So he took his time dressing.

Must be after a contribution to one of the funds, Max said to himself. *It sounds like some of the fellas. Pretty early, though.* He did not feel alarmed. *I'm in good standing,* he thought firmly. *Nuthin to fear.*

With care, he buttoned a fine pink and green-striped silk shirt, one of his favorites. *Gives me class,* he thought as with labored effort he managed to bend far enough to slip on his authentic simulated deerskin pumps. *Be ready to meet them on an equality level,* he thought as he smoothed his thinning hair before the mirror. *If they shake me down too much I'll squawk directly to Pat Noble at the Noo York hiring hall; I mean, I don't have to stand for any stuff, I been in the union too long.*

From the other room a voice bawled, "Fischer—get your clothes on and come out. We got a job for you and it begins today."

A *job,* Max thought with mixed feelings; he did not know whether to be glad or sorry. For over a year now he had been drawing from the union fund, as were most of his friends. Well what do you know. *Cripes,* he thought; *suppose it's a hard job, like maybe I got to bend over all the time or move around.* He felt anger. *What a dirty deal. I mean, who do they think they are?* Opening the door, he faced them. "Listen," he began, but one of the union officials cut him off.

"Pack your things, Fischer. Gus Schatz kicked the bucket and you got to go down to Washington, D.C., and take over the number one stand-by; we want you there before they abolish the position or something and we have to go out on strike or go to court. Mainly, we want to get someone right in clean and easy with no trouble; you understand? Make the transition so smooth that no one hardly takes notice."

At once, Max said, "What's it pay?"

Witheringly, the union official said, "You got no decision to make in this; *you're picked.* You want your freeloader fund-money cut off? You want to have to get out at your age and look for work?"

"Aw come on," Max protested. "I can pick up the phone and dial Pat Noble—"

The union officials were grabbing up objects here and there in the apartment. "We'll help you pack. Pat wants you in the White House by ten o'clock this morning."

"Pat!" Max echoed. He had been sold out.

The union officials, dragging suitcases from the closet, grinned.

Shortly, they were on their way across the flatlands of the Midwest by monorail. Moodily, Maximilian Fischer watched the countryside flash past; he said nothing to the officials flanking him, preferring to mull the matter over and over in his mind. What could he recall about the number one stand-by job? It began at 8:00 A.M.—he recalled reading that. And there always were a lot of tourists flocking through the White House to catch a glimpse of Unicephalon 40-D, especially the school kids . . . and he disliked kids because they always jeered at him due to his weight. Cripes, he'd have a million of them filing by, because he had to be on the premises. By law, he had to be within a hundred yards of Unicephalon 40-D at all times, day and night, or was it fifty yards? Anyhow it practically was right on top, so if the homeostatic problem-solving system failed— *Maybe I better bone up on this,* he decided. *Take a TV educational course on government administration, just in case.*

To the union official on his right, Max asked, "Listen, goodmember, do I have any powers in this job you guys got me? I mean, can I—"

"It's a union job like every other union job," the official answered wearily. "You sit. You stand by. Have you been out of work that long, you don't remember?" He laughed, nudging his companion. "Listen, Fischer here wants to know what authority the job entails." Now both men laughed. "I tell you what, Fischer," the official drawled.

183

"When you're all set up there in the White House, when you got your chair and bed and made all your arrangements for meals and laundry and TV viewing time, why don't you amble over to Unicephalon 40-D and just sort of whine around there, you know, scratch and whine, until it notices you."

"Lay off," Max muttered.

"And then," the official continued, "you sort of say, Hey Unicephalon, listen. I'm your buddy. How about a little 'I scratch your back, you scratch mine.' You pass an ordinance for me—"

"But what can he do in exchange?" the other union official asked.

"Amuse it. He can tell it the story of his life, how he rose out of poverty and obscurity and educated himself by watching TV seven days a week until finally, guess what, he rose all the way to the top; he got the job—" The official snickered. "Of stand-by President."

Maximilian, flushing, said nothing; he stared woodenly out of the monorail window.

When they reached Washington, D.C., and the White House, Maximilian Fischer was shown a little room. It had belonged to Gus, and although the faded old motor magazines had been cleared out, a few prints remained tacked on the walls: a 1963 Volvo S-122, a 1957 Peugeot 403 and other antique classics of a bygone age. And, on a bookcase, Max saw a hand-carved plastic model of a 1950 Studebaker Starlight coupe, with each detail perfect.

"He was making that when he croaked," one of the union officials said as he set down Max's suitcase. "He could tell you any fact there is about those old pre-turbine cars— any useless bit of car knowledge."

Max nodded.

"You got any idea what you're going to do?" the official asked him.

"Aw hell," Max said, "how could I decide so soon? Give me time." Moodily, he picked up the Studebaker Starlight coupe and examined its underside. The desire to smash the model car came to him; he put the car down, then, turning away.

"Make a rubber band ball," the official said.

"What?" Max said.

"The stand-by before Gus. Louis somebody-or-other . . . he collected rubber bands, made a huge ball, big as a house, by the time he died. I forget his name, but the rubber band ball is at the Smithsonian now."

There was a stir in the hallway. A White House receptionist, a middle-aged woman severely dressed, put her head in the room and said, "Mr. President, there's a TV news clown here to interview you. Please try to finish with him as quickly as possible because we have quite a few tours passing through the building today and some may want to look at you."

"Okay," Max said. He turned to face the TV news clown. It was Jim-Jam Briskin, he saw, the ranking clown just now. "You want to see me?" he asked Briskin haltingly. "I mean, you're sure it's *me* you want to interview?" He could not imagine what Briskin could find of interest about him. Holding out his hand he added, "This is my room, but these model cars and pics aren't mine; they were Gus'. I can't tell you nuthin about them."

On Briskin's head the familiar flaming-red clown wig glowed, giving him in real life the same bizarre cast that the TV cameras picked up so well. He was older, however, than the TV image indicated, but he had the friendly, natural smile that everyone looked for: it was his badge of informality, a really nice guy, even-tempered but with a caustic wit when occasion demanded. Briskin was the sort of man who . . . *well,* Max thought, *the sort of fella you'd like to see marry into your family.*

They shook hands. Briskin said, "You're on camera, Mr. Max Fischer. Or rather, Mr. President, I should say. This is Jim-Jam talking. For our literally billions of viewers located in every niche and corner of this far-flung solar system of ours, let me ask you this. How does it feel, sir, to know that if Unicephalon 40-D should fail, even momentarily, you would be catapulted into the most important post that has ever fallen onto the shoulders of a human being, that of actual, not merely stand-by, President of the United States? Does it worry you at night?" He smiled. Behind him the camera technicians swung their mobile lenses back and forth; lights burned Max's eyes and he felt the heat beginning to make him sweat under his arms and on his neck and upper lip. "What emotions grip you at this instant?" Briskin asked. "As you stand on the threshold of this new task for perhaps the balance of your life? What thoughts run through your mind, now that you're actually here in the White House?"

After a pause, Max said, "It's—a big responsibility." And then he realized, he saw, that Briskin was laughing at him, laughing silently as he stood there. Because it was all a gag Briskin was pulling. Out in the planets and moons his audiences knew it, too; they knew Jim-Jam's humor.

"You're a large man, Mr. Fischer," Briskin said. "If I may say so, a stout man. Do you get much exercise? I ask this because with your new job you pretty well will be confined to this room, and I wondered what change in your life this would bring about."

"Well," Max said, "I feel of course that a Government employee should always be at his post. Yes, what you say is true; I have to be right here day and night, but that doesn't bother me. I'm prepared for it."

"Tell me," Jim Briskin said, "do you—" And then he ceased. Turning to the video technicians behind him he said in an odd voice, "We're off the air."

A man wearing headphones squeezed forward past the cameras. "On the monitor, listen." He hurriedly handed the headphones to Briskin. "We've been pre-empted by Unicephalon; it's broadcasting a news bulletin."

Briskin held the phones to his ear. His face writhed and he said, "Those ships at eight hundred a.u.'s. They are hostile, it says." He glanced up sharply at his technicians, the red clown's wig sliding askew. "They've begun to attack."

Within the following twenty-four hours the aliens had managed not only to penetrate the Sol System but also to knock out Unicephalon 40-D.

News of this reached Maximilian Fischer in an indirect manner as he sat in the White House cafeteria having his supper.

"Mr. Maximilian Fischer?"

"Yeah," Max said, glancing up at the group of Secret Servicemen who had surrounded his table.

"You're President of the United States."

"Naw," Max said, "I'm the stand-by President; that's different."

The Secret Serviceman said, "Unicephalon 40-D is out of commission for perhaps as long as a month. So according to the amended Constitution, you're President and also Commander-in-Chief of the armed forces. We're here to guard you." The Secret Serviceman grinned ludicrously.

186

Max grinned back. "Do you understand?" the Secret Serviceman asked. "I mean, does it penetrate?"

"Sure," Max said. Now he understood the buzz of conversation he had overheard while waiting in the cafeteria line with his tray. It explained why White House personnel had looked at him strangely. He set down his coffee cup, wiped his mouth with his napkin, slowly and deliberately, pretended to be absorbed in solemn thought. But actually his mind was empty.

"We've been told," the Secret Serviceman said, "that you're needed at once at the National Security Council bunker. They want your participation in finalization of strategy deliberations."

They walked from the cafeteria to the elevator.

"Strategy policy," Max said, as they descended. "I got a few opinions about that. I guess it's time to deal harshly with these alien ships, don't you agree?" The Secret Serviceman nodded. "Yes, we got to show we're not afraid," Max said. "Sure, we'll get finalization; we'll blast the buggers."

The Secret Servicemen laughed good-naturedly.

Pleased, Max nudged the leader of the group. "I think we're pretty goddam strong; I mean, the U.S.A. has got teeth."

"You tell 'em, Max," one of the Secret Servicemen said, and they all laughed aloud, Max included.

As they stepped from the elevator they were stopped by a tall, well-dressed man who said urgently, "Mr. President, I'm Jonathan Kirk, White House press secretary; I think before you go in there to confer with the NSC people you should address the nation in this hour of gravest peril. The public wants to see what their new leader is like." He held out several sheets of paper. "Here's a statement drawn up by the Political Advisory Board; it codifies your—"

"Nits," Max said, handing it back without looking at it. "I'm the President, not you. I don't even know you. Kirk? Burke? Shirk? Never heard of you. Show me the microphone and I'll make my own speech. Or get me Pat Noble; maybe he's got some ideas." And then he remembered that Pat had sold him out in the first place; Pat had gotten him into this. "Not him either," Max said. "Just give me the microphone."

"This is a time of crisis," Kirk grated.

"Sure," Max said, "so leave me alone; you keep out of

my way and I'll keep out of yours. Ain't that right?" He slapped Kirk good-naturedly on the back. "And we'll both be better off."

A group of people with portable TV cameras and lighting appeared, and among them Max saw Jim-Jam Briskin, in the middle, with his staff.

"Hey, Jim-Jam," he yelled. "Look, I'm President now!"

Stolidly, Jim Briskin came toward him.

"I'm not going to be winding no ball of string," Max said. "Or making model boats, nuthin like that." He shook hands warmly with Briskin. "I thank you," Max said. "For your congratulations."

"Congratulations," Briskin said, then, in a low voice.

"Thanks," Max said, squeezing the man's hand until the knuckles creaked. "Of course, sooner or later they'll get that noise-box patched up and I'll just be stand-by again. But—" He grinned gleefully around at all of them; the corridor was full of people now, from TV to White House staff members to Army officers and Secret Servicemen, all kinds of people.

Briskin said, "You have a big task, Mr. Fischer."

"Yeah," Max agreed.

Something in Briskin's eyes said: *And I wonder if you can handle it. I wonder if you're the man to hold such power.*

"Sure I can do it," Max declared, into Briskin's microphone, for all the vast audience to hear.

"Possibly you can," Jim Briskin said, and on his face was dubiousness.

"Hey, you don't like me any more," Max said. "How come?"

Briskin said nothing, but his eyes flickered.

"Listen," Max said, "I'm President now; I can close down your silly network—I can send FBI men in any time I want. For your information I'm firing the Attorney General right now, whatever his name is, and putting in a man I know, a man I can trust."

Briskin said, "I see." And now he looked less dubious; conviction, of a sort which Max could not fathom, began to appear instead. "Yes," Jim Briskin said, "you have the authority to order that, don't you? *If* you're really President. . . ."

"Watch out," Max said. "You're nothing compared to me, Briskin, even if you do have that great big audience."

188

Then, turning his back on the cameras, he strode through the open door, into the NSC bunker.

Hours later, in the early morning, down in the National Security Council subsurface bunker, Maximilian Fischer listened sleepily to the TV set in the background as it yammered out the latest news. By now, intelligence sources had plotted the arrival of thirty more alien ships in the Sol System. It was believed that seventy in all had entered. Each was being continually tracked.

But that was not enough, Max knew. Sooner or later he would have to give the order to attack the alien ships. He hesitated. After all, who were they? Nobody at CIA knew. How strong were they? Not known either. And—would the attack be successful?

And then there were domestic problems. Unicephalon had continually tinkered with the economy, priming it when necessary, cutting taxes, lowering interest rates . . . that had ceased with the problem-solver's destruction. *Jeez,* Max thought dismally. *What do I know about unemployment? I mean, how can I tell what factories to reopen and where?*

He turned to General Tompkins, Chairman of the Joint Chiefs of Staff, who sat beside him examining a report on the scrambling of the tactical defensive ships protecting Earth. "They got all them ships distributed right?" he asked Tompkins.

"Yes, Mr. President," General Tompkins answered.

Max winced. But the general did not seem to have spoken ironically; his tone had been respectful. "Okay," Max murmured. "Glad to hear that. And you got all that missile cloud up so there're no leaks, like you let in that ship to blast Unicephalon. I don't want that to happen again."

"We're under Defcon one," General Tompkins said. "Full war footing, as of six o'clock, our time."

"How about those strategic ships?" That, he had learned, was the euphemism for their offensive strike-force.

"We can mount an attack at any time," General Tompkins said, glancing down the long table to obtain the assenting nods of his co-workers. "We can take care of each of the seventy invaders now within our system."

With a groan, Max said, "Anybody got any bicarb?" The whole business depressed him. *What a lot of work and sweat,* he thought. *All this goddam agitation—why don't*

189

*the buggers just leave our system? I mean, do we have to
get into a war? No telling what their home system will do
in retaliation; you never can tell about unhuman life forms
—they're unreliable.*

"That's what bothers me," he said aloud. "Retaliation."
He sighed.

General Tompkins said, "Negotiation with them evidently is impossible."

"Go ahead, then," Max said. "Go give it to them." He
looked about for the bicarb.

"I think you're making a wise choice," General Tompkins said, and, across the table, the civilian advisors nodded
in agreement.

"Here's an odd piece of news," one of the advisors said
to Max. He held out a teletype dispatch. "James Briskin
has just filed a writ of mandamus against you in a Federal
Court in California, claiming you're not legally President
because you didn't run for office."

"You mean because I didn't get *voted* in?" Max said.
"Just because of that?"

"Yes sir. Briskin is asking the Federal Courts to rule on
this, and meanwhile he has announced his own candidacy."

"WHAT?"

"Briskin claims not only that you must run for office
and be voted in, but you must run against him. And with
his popularity he evidently feels—"

"Aw nuts," Max said in despair. "How do you like
that."

There was silence in the bunker.

"Well anyhow," Max said, "it's all decided; you military
fellas go ahead and knock out those alien ships. And meanwhile—" He decided there and then. "We'll put economic
pressure on Jim-Jam's sponsors, that Reinlander beer and
Calbest Electronics, to get him not to run."

The men at the long table nodded. Papers rattled as
briefcases were put away; the meeting—temporarily—was
at an end.

He's got an unfair advantage, Max said to himself. *How
can I run when it's not equal, him a famous TV personality
and me not? That's not right; I can't allow that.*

Jim-Jam can run, he decided, *but it won't do him any
good. He's not going to beat me because he's not going to
be alive that long.*

A week before the election, Telscan, the interplanetary public-opinion sampling agency, published its latest findings. Reading them, Maximilian Fischer felt more gloomy than ever.

"Look at this," he said to his cousin Leon Lait, the lawyer whom he had recently made Attorney General. He tossed the report to him.

His own showing of course was negligible. In the election, Briskin would easily, and most definitely, win.

"Why is that?" Lait asked. Like Max, he was a large, paunchy man who for years now had held a stand-by job; he was not used to physical activity of any sort and his new position was proving difficult for him. However, out of family loyalty to Max, he remained. "Is that because he's got all those TV stations?" he asked, sipping from his can of beer.

Max said cuttingly, "Naw, it's because his navel glows in the dark. Of course it's because of his TV stations, you jerk—he's got them pounding away night and day, creatin' an *image*." He paused, moodily. "He's a clown. It's that red wig; it's fine for a newscaster, but not for a President." Too morose to speak, he lapsed into silence.

And worse was to follow.

At 9:00 P.M. that night, Jim-Jam Briskin began a seventy-two hour marathon TV program over all his stations, a great final drive to bring his popularity over the top and insure his victory.

In his special bedroom at the White House, Max Fischer sat with a tray of food before him, in bed, gloomily facing the TV set.

That Briskin, he thought furiously for the millionth time. "Look," he said to his cousin; the Attorney General sat in the easy chair across from him. "There's the nert now." He pointed to the TV screen.

Leon Lait, munching on his cheeseburger, said, "It's abominable."

"You know where he's broadcasting from? Way out in deep space, out past Pluto. At their furthest-out transmitter, which your FBI guys will never in a million years manage to get to."

"They will," Leon assured him. "I told them they *have* to get him—the President, my cousin, personally says so."

"But they won't get him for a while," Max said. "Leon, you're just too damn slow. I'll tell you something. I got a ship of the line out there, the *Dwight D. Eisenhower*. It's

191

all ready to lay an egg on them, you know, a big bang, just as soon as I pass on the word."—

"Right, Max."

"And I hate to," Max said.

The telecast had begun to pick up momentum already. Here came the Spotlights, and sauntering out onto the stage pretty Peggy Jones, wearing a glittery bare-shoulder gown, her hair radiant. *Now we get a top-flight striptease,* Max realized, *by a real fine-looking girl.* Even he sat up and took notice. Well, maybe not a true striptease, but certainly the opposition, Briskin and his staff, had sex working for them, here. Across the room his cousin the Attorney General had stopped munching his cheeseburger; the noise came to a halt, then picked up slowly once more.

On the screen, Peggy sang:

> It's Jim-Jam, for whom I am,
> America's best-loved guy.
> It's Jim-Jam, the best one that am,
> The candidate for you and I.

"Oh, god," Max groaned. And yet, the way she delivered it, with every part of her slim, long body . . . it was okay. "I guess I got to inform the *Dwight D. Eisenhower* to go ahead," he said, watching.

"If you say so, Max," Leon said. "I assure you, I'll rule that you acted legally; don't worry none about that."

"Gimme the red phone," Max said. "That's the armored connection that only the Commander-in-Chief uses for top-secret instructions. Not bad, huh?" He accepted the phone from the Attorney General. "I'm calling General Tompkins and he'll relay the order to the ship. Too bad, Briskin," he added, with one last look at the screen. "But it's your own fault; you didn't have to do what you did, opposing me and all."

The girl in the silvery dress had gone, now, and Jim-Jam Briskin had appeared in her place. Momentarily, Max lowered the phone to watch.

"Hi, beloved comrades," Briskin said, raising his hands for silence; the canned applause—Max knew that no audience existed in that remote spot—lowered, then rose again. Briskin grinned amiably, waiting for it to die.

"It's a fake," Max grunted. "Fake audience. They're smart, him and his staff. His rating's already way up."

"Right, Max," the Attorney General agreed. "I noticed that."

"Comrades," Jim Briskin was saying soberly on the TV screen, "as you may know, originally President Maximilian Fischer and I got along very well."

His hand on the red phone, Max thought to himself that what Jim-Jam said was true.

"Where we broke," Briskin continued, "was over the issue of force—of the use of naked, raw power. To Max Fischer, the office of President is merely a machine, an instrument, which he can use as an extension of his own desires, to fulfill his own needs. I honestly believe that in many respects his aims are good; he is trying to carry out Unicephalon's fine policies. But as to the means. That's a different matter."

Max said, "Listen to him, Leon." And he thought, *No matter what he says I'm going to keep on; nobody is going to stand in my way, because it's my duty; it's the job of the office, and if you got to be President like I am you'd do it, too.*

"Even the President," Briskin was saying, "must obey the law; he doesn't stand outside it, however powerful he is." He was silent for a moment and then he said slowly, "I know that at this moment the FBI, under direct orders from Max Fischer's appointee, Leon Lait, is attempting to close down these stations, to still my voice. Here again Max Fischer is making use of power, of the police agency, for his own ends, making it an extension—"

Max picked up the red phone. At once a voice said from it, "Yes, Mr. President. This is General Tompkins' C of C."

"What's that?" Max said.

"Chief of Communications, Army 600-1000, sir. Aboard the *Dwight D. Eisenhower,* accepting relay through the transmitter at the Pluto Station."

"Oh yeah," Max said, nodding. "Listen, you fellas stand by, you understand? Be ready to receive instructions." He put his hand over the mouthpiece of the phone. "Leon," he said to his cousin, who had now finished his cheeseburger and was starting on a strawberry shake. "How can I do it? I mean, Briskin is telling the truth."

Leon said, "Give Tompkins the word." He belched, then tapped himself on the chest with the side of his fist. "Pardon me."

On the screen Jim Briskin said, "I think very possibly

193

I'm risking my life to speak to you, because this we must face; we have a President who would not mind employing murder to obtain his objectives. This is the political tactic of a tyranny, and that's what we're seeing, a tyranny coming into existence in our society, replacing the rational, disinterested rule of the homeostatic problem-solving Unicephalon 40-D which was designed, built and put into operation by some of the finest minds we have ever seen, minds dedicated to the preservation of all that's worthy in our tradition. And the transformation from this to a one-man tyranny is melancholy, to say the least."

Quietly, Max said, "Now I can't go ahead."

"Why not?" Leon said.

"Didn't you hear him? He's talking about *me*. I'm the tyrant he has reference to. Keerist." Max hung up the red phone. "I waited too long."

"I don't see that," Leon said. "Why can't you go ahead, Max?"

"It's hard for me to say it," Max said, "but—well, hell, it would prove he's right." *I know he's right anyhow,* Max thought. *But do they know it? Does the public know it? I can't let them find out about me,* he realized. *They should look up to their President, respect him. Honor him. No wonder I show up so bad in the Telscan poll. No wonder Jim Briskin decided to run against me the moment he heard I was in office. They really do know about me; they sense it, sense that Jim-Jam is speaking the truth. I'm just not Presidential caliber.*

I'm not fit, he thought, *to hold this office.*

"Listen, Leon," he said. "I'm going to give it to that Briskin anyhow and then step down. It'll be my last official act." Once more he picked up the red phone. "I'm going to order them to wipe out Briskin and then someone else can be President. Anyone the people want. Even Pat Noble or you; I don't care." He jiggled the phone. "Hey, C of C," he said loudly. "Come on, answer." To his cousin he said, "Leave me some of that shake; it's actually half mine."

"Sure, Max," Leon said loyally.

"Isn't no one there?" Max said into the phone. He waited. The phone remained dead. "Something's gone wrong," he said to Leon. "Communications have busted down. It must be those aliens again."

And then he saw the TV screen. It was blank.

"What's happening?" Max said. "What are they doing to

me? *Who's* doing it?" He looked around, frightened. "I don't get it."

Leon stoically drank the milkshake, shrugging to show that he had no answer. But his beefy face had paled.

"It's too late," Max said. "For some reason it's just too late." Slowly, he hung up the phone. "I've got enemies, Leon, more powerful than you or me. And I don't even know who they are." He sat in silence, before the dark, soundless TV screen. Waiting.

The speaker of the TV set said abruptly, "Pseudo-auto-nomic news bulletin. Stand by, please." Then again there was silence.

Jim Briskin, glancing at Ed Fineberg and Peggy, waited.

"Comrade citizens of the United States," the flat, un-modulated voice from the TV speaker said, all at once. "The interregnum is over, the situation has returned to normal." As it spoke, words appeared on the monitor screen, a ribbon of printed tape passing slowly across, be-fore the TV cameras in Washington, D.C. Unicephalon 40-D had spliced itself into the co-ax in its usual fashion; it had pre-empted the program in progress: that was its traditional right.

The voice was the synthetic verbalizing-organ of the ho-meostatic structure itself.

"The election campaign is nullified," Unicephalon 40-D said. "That is item one. The stand-by President Maxi-milian Fischer is canceled out; that is item two. Item three: we are at war with the aliens who have invaded our sys-tem. Item four: James Briskin, who has been speaking to you—"

This is it, Briskin realized.

In his earphones the impersonal, plateau-like voice con-tinued, "Item four: James Briskin, who has been speaking to you on these facilities, is hereby ordered to cease and desist, and a writ of mandamus is issued forthwith requir-ing him to show just cause why he should be free to pursue any further political activity. In the public interest we instruct him to become politically silent."

Grinning starkly at Peggy and Ed Fineberg, Briskin said, "That's it. It's over. I'm to politically shut up."

"You can fight it in the courts," Peggy said at once. "You can take it all the way up to the Supreme Court; they've set aside decisions of Unicephalon in the past." She put her hand on his shoulder, but he moved away. "Or do you want to fight it?"

"At least I'm not canceled out," Briskin said. He felt tired. "I'm glad to see that machine back in operation," he said, to reassure Peggy. "It means a return to stability. *That* we can use."

"What'll you do, Jim-Jam?" Ed asked. "Go back to Reinlander beer and Calbest Electronics and try to get your old job back?"

"No," Briskin murmured. Certainly not that. But—he could not really become politically silent; he could not do what the problem-solver said. It simply was not biologically possible for him; sooner or later he would begin to talk again, for better or worse. *And,* he thought, *I'll bet Max can't do what it says either . . . neither of us can.*

Maybe, he thought, *I'll answer the writ of mandamus; maybe I'll contest it. A counter suit . . . I'll sue Unicephalon 40-D in a court of law. Jim-Jam Briskin the plaintiff, Unicephalon 40-D the defendant.* He smiled. *I'll need a good lawyer for that. Someone quite a bit better than Max Fischer's top legal mind, cousin Leon Lait.*

Going to the closet of the small studio in which they had been broadcasting, he got his coat and began to put it on. A long trip lay ahead of them back to Earth from this remote spot, and he wanted to get started.

Peggy, following after him, said, "You're not going back on the air *at all?* Not even to finish the program?"

"No," he said.

"But Unicephalon will be cutting back out again, and what'll that leave? Just dead air. That's not right, is it, Jim? Just to walk out like this . . . I can't believe you'd do it, it's not like you."

He halted at the door of the studio. "You heard what it said. The instructions it handed out to me."

"Nobody leaves dead air going," Peggy said. "It's a vacuum, Jim, the thing nature abhors. *And if you don't fill it, someone else will.* Look, Unicephalon is going back off right now." She pointed at the TV monitor. The ribbon of words had ceased; once more the screen was dark, empty of motion and light. "It's your responsibility," Peggy said, "and you know it."

"Are we back on the air?" he asked Ed.

"Yes. It's definitely out of the circuit, at least for a while." Ed gestured toward the vacant stage on which the

196

TV cameras and lights focused. He said nothing more; he did not have to.

With his coat still on, Jim Briskin walked that way. Hands in his pockets he stepped back into the range of the cameras, smiled and said, "I think, beloved comrades, the interruption is over. For the time being, anyhow. So . . . let's continue."

The noise of canned applause—manipulated by Ed Fineberg—swelled up, and Jim Briskin raised his hands and signaled the nonexistent studio audience for silence.

"Does any of you know a good lawyer?" Jim-Jam asked caustically. "And if you do, phone us and tell us right away—before the FBI finally manages to reach us out here."

In his bedroom at the White House, as Unicephalon's message ended, Maximilian Fischer turned to his cousin Leon and said, "Well, I'm out of office."

"Yeah, Max," Leon said heavily. "I guess you are."

"And you, too," Max pointed out. "It's going to be a clean sweep; you can count on that. Canceled." He gritted his teeth. "That's sort of insulting. Couldn't it have said *retired?*"

"I guess that's just its way of expressing itself," Leon said. "Don't get upset, Max; remember your heart trouble. You still got the job of stand-by, and that's the top stand-by position there is, Stand-by President of the United States, I want to remind you. And now you've got all this worry and effort off your back; you're lucky."

"I wonder if I'm allowed to finish this meal," Max said, picking at the food in the tray before him. His appetite, now that he was retired, began almost at once to improve; he selected a chicken salad sandwich and took a big bite from it. "It's still mine," he decided, his mouth full. "I still get to live here and eat regularly—right?"

"Right," Leon agreed, his legal mind active. "That's in the contract the union signed with Congress; remember back to that? We didn't go out on strike for nothing."

"Those were the days," Max said. He finished the chicken salad sandwich and returned to the eggnog. It felt good not to have to make big decisions; he let out a long, heartfelt sigh and settled back into the pile of pillows propping him up.

But then he thought, *In some respects I sort of enjoyed making decisions. I mean, it was—* He searched for the thought. *It was different from being a stand-by or drawing unemployment. It had—*

Satisfaction, he thought. *That's what it gave me. Like I was accomplishing something.* He missed that already; he felt suddenly hollow, as if things had all at once become purposeless.

"Leon," he said, "I could have gone on as President another whole month. And enjoyed the job. You know what I mean?"

"Yeah, I guess I get your meaning," Leon mumbled.

"No, you don't," Max said.

"I'm trying, Max," his cousin said. "Honest."

With bitterness, Max said, "I shouldn't have had them go ahead and let those engineer-fellas patch up that Unicephalon; I should have buried the project, at least for a while. For maybe another six months."

"Too late to think about that now," Leon said.

Is it? Max asked himself. *You know, something could happen to Unicephalon 40-D. An accident.*

He pondered that as he ate a piece of green-apple pie with a wide slice of longhorn cheese. A number of persons whom he knew could pull off such tasks . . . and did so, now and then.

A big, nearly fatal accident, he thought. *Late some night, when everyone's asleep and it's just me and it awake here in the White House. I mean, let's face it; the aliens showed us how.*

"Look, Jim-Jam Briskin's back on the air," Leon said, gesturing at the TV set. Sure enough, there was the famous, familiar red wig, and Briskin was saying something witty and yet profound, something that made one stop to ponder. "Hey listen," Leon said. "He's poking fun at the FBI; can you imagine him doing that *now?* He's not scared of anything."

"Don't bother me," Max said. "I'm thinking." He reached over and carefully turned the sound of the TV set off.

For thoughts such as he was having he wanted no distractions.

1964

THE YEAR 1964 was a special one for the Hugo Awards, although few science fiction fans realized it at the time. It was the last year for which the Hugo would be the uncontested champion of science fiction awards.

A. E. van Vogt, on the West Coast, and Damon Knight, on the East Coast, had been working independently of each other to start a sort of science fiction writers' guild. This guild would serve as a clearing house for information on markets and the conduct of editors and publishers, a monitoring organ for contract terms and reliability of royalty payments, and other such very business-related matters of interest to writers in the field.

Almost as an afterthought, the idea of an annual literary award was added to the list.

When van Vogt and Knight learned of each other's work, they compared notes. Knight had actually moved ahead faster than van Vogt, so van Vogt quietly dropped his activities and threw his support behind Knight. The result was the Science Fiction Writers of America, and the literary award materialized as the Nebula.

The way the two series of awards have interacted, to an extent competed, more often complemented each other, will be a recurring theme in later volumes of *What If?* But in 1965 there were no Nebulas—yet—and the World Science Fiction Convention in London went placidly about its business of awarding Hugos.

This time, unlike the London convention of 1957, there was no hanky-panky over categories, no rigging the rules to protect an already moribund International Fantasy Award, no gerrymandering of procedures to guarantee a hometown winner.

There were still two awards for fiction, best novel of the year, and what was called, in 1965, best short story of the year. To repeat a familiar refrain, that really meant best-story-of-any-length-less-than-novel.

Nominated novels were *Davy* by Edgar Pangborn, *The Planet Buyer* by Cordwainer Smith, *The Wanderer* by Fritz Leiber, and *The Whole Man* by John Brunner. Again, all nominees were "*book* books." No magazine versions made the ballot, even though there had been a number of interesting works serialized in 1964. These included *Sunburst* by Phyllis Gotlieb and *Enigma from Tantalus* by John Brunner in *Amazing; The Lords of Quarmall* by Fritz Leiber and Harry Fischer, *When Idols Walked* by John Jakes, and *Seed of Eloraspon* by Manly Banister in *Fantastic; Spaceman* by Murray Leinster and *Undercurrents* by James Schmitz in *Astounding; The Star King* by Jack Vance in *Galaxy* (split with 1963); *Three Worlds to Conquer* by Poul Anderson and *Farnham's Freehold* by Robert A. Heinlein in *If;* and *The Tree of Time* by Damon Knight (split with 1963) in *F&SF.*

The British *New Worlds* ran no fewer than four serials, including *Open Prison* by James White, *Equinox* by J. G. Ballard, and *The Shores of Death* by Michael Moorcock. A companion magazine, *Science Fantasy,* ran Thomas Burnett Swann's *The Blue Monkeys* (split with 1965).

The groundswell of stylistic experimentation and attitudinal unorthodoxy known as the New Wave was shortly to break over the world of science fiction, and a few preliminary stirrings may be detected in that list of serials. The book publishers did seem to move ahead more rapidly than their *confrères* at the magazines. But for the most part, science fiction was still riding the vehicle of the Gold-Boucher-McComas innovations of the 1950s. All three editors were gone by now, but *Galaxy* under Frederik Pohl, and *F&SF* under Robert Mills, Avram Davidson, and finally the father-son team of Joseph and Edward Ferman, continued to press forward.

The *real* ferment was to come from the British magazines, *New Worlds* under Michael Moorcock and *Science Fantasy* under Kyril Bonfiglioli.

For 1964, however, the voting fans stayed with traditional matter. Their selection to receive the Hugo for best novel was Fritz Leiber's *The Wanderer,* an excellently executed book but essentially a rewrite of *When Worlds Collide,* the Wylie and Balmer opus of 30 years before.

The nominees for best short fiction were "Little Dog Gone" by Robert F. Young, "Once a Cop" by Rick Raphael, and "Soldier, Ask Not" by Gordon R. Dickson. The fact that out of three nominees one was a police yarn and one an army adventure may be significant. The winner was "Soldier, Ask Not."

But in 1964 Cele Goldsmith was still wielding her fine hand at *Amazing* and *Fantastic,* running excellent fiction by talented young writers, of whom one of the most talented was Thomas M. Disch. In fact, she was taking so many of Disch's stories—eight in 1964 alone—that it began to look embarrassing, and three of them appeared under the pseudonym "Dobbin Thorpe."

One of the "Thorpe" stories was a powerful—an unforgettable—piece called "Now Is Forever." Yet for some reason the author himself is less than enthusiastic about it. When the story appeared in *Amazing,* Terry Carr and Donald A. Wollheim were planning the first volume of their celebrated annual anthology (since fissioned into the Carr best-of-the-year and the Wollheim best-of-the-year from different publishers).

Carr asked Disch for permission to include the story, and Disch expressed reluctance. Well, it wasn't such a good story, was Terry *sure* he wanted it, wasn't there really something else around more suitable . . . ?

Carr was adamant and Disch yielded, and I must say that I was an indirect beneficiary of the incident, for I'd missed the story in *Amazing* and read it first in Carr and Wollheim's annual. I was dazzled by it.

Recently I phoned Disch to obtain the story for *What If?,* and he was *still* unconvinced of its merit. Are you *sure* you want that story? he asked me. I was very young when I wrote it, you know; it isn't really such a . . . Well, you know the line.

Specifically, Disch wanted to know when I'd read the story, and I told him in 1965. Ah-*hah!* He had me! You know, sometimes these things don't age very well. Oh, I added, I did re-read it. When? Disch wanted to know. *Yesterday,* I told him, and the story is more subtle, more complex, more effective—and as powerful and as enjoyable and as unforgettable as it was a decade and a half ago!

The man had the good sense to give in.

Now Is Forever

THOMAS M. DISCH

CHARLES ARCHOLD LIKED the façade best at twilight. On June evenings like this (was it *June?*), the sun would sink into the canyon of Maxwell Street and spotlight the sculptured group in the pediment: a full-breasted Commerce extended an allegorical cornucopia from which tumbled allegorical fruits into the outstretched hands of Industry, Labor, Transportation, Science, and Art. He was idling past (the Cadillac engine was beginning to misfire again, but where could you find a mechanic these days?), abstractedly considering the burning tip of his cigar, when he observed peripherally that Commerce had been beheaded. He stopped.

It was against the law; a defacement, an insult. Maxwell Street echoed the slam of the car door, his cry—"Police!" A swarm of pigeons rose from the feet of Industry, Labor, Transportation, Science and Art and scattered into the depopulated streets. The bank president achieved a smile of chagrin, although there was no one in sight from whom he would have had to conceal his embarrassment. Archold's good manners, like his affluent paunch, had been long in forming and were difficult to efface.

Somewhere in the acoustical maze of the streets of the financial district Archold could hear the rumble of a procession of teenage maenads approaching. Trumpets, drums, and screaming voices. Hurriedly, Archold locked his car and went up the bank steps. The bronze gates were open; the glass doors were unlocked. Drapes were drawn across the windows as they had been on the day, seven months earlier or thereabouts, when he and the three or four remaining staff members had closed the bank. In the gloom, Archold took inventory. The desks and office equipment had been piled into one corner; the carpets had been torn up from the parquet floor; the tellers' cages had been arranged into a sort of platform against the back wall. Archold flicked on a light switch. A spotlight flooded the platform with a dim blue light. He saw the drums. The bank had been converted into a dancehall.

In the sub-basement, the air-conditioner rumbled into life. Machines seemed to live a life of their own. Archold walked, nervously aware of his footsteps on the naked parquet, to the service elevator behind the jerry-built bandstand. He pressed the UP button and waited. Dead as a doornail. Well, you couldn't expect everything to work. He took the stairs up to the third floor. Passing through the still plush reception room outside his office, he noticed that there were extra couches along the walls. An expensive postermural representing the diversified holding of the New York Exchange Bank had been ripped from the wall; a gargantuan and ill-drawn pair of nudes reclined where the mural had been. Teenagers!

His office had not been broken into. A thick film of dust covered his bare desk. A spider had constructed (and long ago abandoned) a web across the entire expanse of his bookshelves. The dwarf tree that stood in a pot on the window sill (a present, two Christmases ago from his secretary) had shriveled into a skeleton where, for a time, the spider had spun other webs. An early model Reprostat (of five years ago) stood beside the desk. Archold had never dared to smash the machine, though, God knew, he had wanted to often enough.

He wondered if it would still work, hoping, of course, that it would not. He pressed the Archtype button for memo pad. A sign flashed red on the control panel: INSUFFICIENT CARBON. So, it worked. The sign flashed again, insistently. Archold dug into one of his desk drawers for a bar of carbon and fed it into the hopper at the base of the Reprostat. The machine hummed and emitted a memo pad.

Archold settled back in his own chair, raising a cloud of dust. He needed a drink or, lacking that (he drank too much, he remembered) a cigar. He'd dropped his last cigar in the street. If he were in the car, he could just touch a button, but here . . .

Of course! His office Reprostat was also set to make his own brand of cigars. He pressed the cigar Archtype button; the machine hummed and emitted one Maduro cigar, evenly burning at its tip. How could you ever be angry with the machines? It wasn't their fault the world was in a shambles; it was the fault of people that misused the machines—greedy, shortsighted people who didn't care what happened to the Economy or the Nation as long as they had Maine lobster every day and a full wine cellar and ermine stoles for a theater opening and . . .

But could you blame them? He had himself spent thirty years of his life to get exactly those things or their equivalents, for himself—and for Nora. The difference was, he thought as he savored the usual aroma of his cigar (before the Reprostats, he had never been able to afford this brand. They had cost $1.50 apiece, and he was a heavy smoker) —the difference was simply that some people (like Archold) could be trusted to have the best things in life without going haywire, while other people, the majority, in fact, could not be trusted to have things that they couldn't pay for with their own industry. It was now a case of too many cooks. Authority was disappearing; it had vanished. Morality was now going fast. Young people, he had been informed (when he still knew people who would tell him these things), didn't even bother to get married any more —and their elders, who should have set them an example, didn't bother to get divorced.

Absent-mindedly, he pressed the Reprostat button for another cigar, while the one he had been smoking lay forgotten in the dusty ashtray. He had argued with Nora that morning. They had both been feeling a little under the weather. Maybe they had been drinking again the night before—they had been drinking quite a lot lately—but he could not remember. The argument had taken a bad turn, with Nora poking fun (and her finger) at his flabby belly. He had reminded her that he got his flabby belly working all those years at the bank to provide her with the house and her clothes and all the other expensive obsolescing goodies she could not live without.

"Expensive!" she had screamed. "What's expensive any more? Not even money is expensive."

"Is that *my* fault?"

"You're fifty years old, Charlie boy, *over* fifty, and I'm

still young," (she was forty-two, to be exact), "and I don't have to keep you hanging around my neck like an albatross."

"The albatross was a symbol of guilt, my dear. Is there something you're trying to tell me?"

"I wish there was!"

He had slapped her, and she had locked herself in the bathroom. Then he had gone off for a drive, not really intending to come past the bank, but the force of habit had worked upon his absent-minded anger and brought him here.

The office door edged open.

"Mr. Archold?"

"Who—! Oh, Lester, come in. You gave me a start."

Lester Tinburley, the former janitor-in-chief of the Exchange Bank, shambled into the office, mumbling reverent how-do-you-do-sirs and nodding his head with such self-effacing cordiality that he seemed to have palsy. Like his former superior (who wore a conservative gray suit, fresh that morning from the Reprostat), Lester wore the uniform of his old position: white-and-blue striped denim overalls, faded and thin from many launderings. The black peppercorn curls of his hair had been sheared down to shadowy nubbins. Except for some new wrinkles in the brown flesh of his face (scarcely noticed by Archold), Lester appeared to be in no way different from the janitor-in-chief that the bank president had always known.

"What's happened to the old place, Lester?"

Lester nodded his head sadly. "It's these kids—you can't do a thing with them nowadays. All of them gone straight to the devil—dancing and drinking and some other things I couldn't tell you, Mr. Archold."

Archold smiled a knowing smile. "You don't have to say another word, Lester. It's all because of the way they were raised. No respect for authority—that's their problem. You can't tell them anything they don't know already."

"What's a person going to do, Mr. Archold?"

Archold had the answer even for that. "Discipline!"

Lester's palsy, as though Archold had given a cue, became more pronounced. "Well, I've done what I could to keep things up. I come back every day I can and look after things. Fix up what I can—what those kids don't smash up for their own fun. All the records are in the basement now."

"Good work. When things return to normal again, we'll have a much easier job, thanks to you. And I'll see that you get your back wages for all the time you've put in."

"Thank you, sir."

"Did you know that someone has broken the statue out in front? The one right over the door. Can't you fix it somehow, Lester? It looks just terrible."

"I'll see what I can do, sir."

"See that you do." It was a good feeling for Archold, giving orders again.

"It is sure good to have you back here, sir. After all these years . . ."

"Seven months, Lester. That's all it's been. It does seem like years."

Lester glanced away from Archold and fixed his gaze on the skeleton of the dwarf tree. "I've been keeping track with the calendars in the basement, Mr. Archold. The ones we stocked for '94. It's been two years and more. We closed April 12, 1993 . . ."

"A day I'll never forget, Lester."

". . . and this is June 30, 1995."

Archold looked puzzled. "You've gotten confused, boy. It couldn't be. It's . . . it *is* June, isn't it? That's funny. I could swear that yesterday was Oct . . . I haven't been feeling well lately."

A muffled vibration crept into the room. Lester went to the door.

"Maybe you'd best leave now, Mr. Archold. Things have changed around the old bank. Maybe you wouldn't be safe here."

"This is my office, my bank. Don't tell *me* what to do!" His voice cracked with authority like a rusted trumpet.

"It's those kids. They come here every night now. I'll show you out through the basement."

"I'll leave the way I came, Lester. I think you'd better return to your work now. And fix that statue!"

Lester's palsy underwent a sudden cure, his lips tightened. Without another word or a look back, he left Archold's office. As soon as he found himself alone, Archold pressed the Beverage, alcoholic Archtype button on the Reprostat. He gulped down the iced Scotch greedily, threw the glass into the hopper and pressed the button again.

* * *

206

At midnight Jessy Holm was going to die, but at the moment she was deliriously happy. She was the sort of person that lives entirely in the present.

Now, as every light in the old Exchange Bank was doused (except for the blue spot on the drummer), she joined with the dancing crowd in a communal sigh of delight and dug her silvered fingernails into Jude's bare arm.

"Do you love me?" she whispered.

"Crazy!" Jude replied.

"How much?"

"Kid, I'd die for you." It was true.

A blat of static sounded from the speakers set into the gilded ceiling of the banking floor. In the blue haze about the bandstand, a figure swayed before the microphone. A voice of ambiguous gender began to sing along to the hard, rocking beat of the music—only noises it first seemed; gradually, a few words emerged:

> Now, now, now, now—
> Now is forever.
> Around and around and around—
> Up and down
> And around and around—because
> Tonight is forever
> And love, lo-ove is now.

"I don't want to stop, ever," Jessy shouted above the roar of the song and the tread of the dancers.

"It's never gonna stop, baby," Jude assured her. "C'mon let's go upstairs."

The second floor lobby was already filled with couples. On the third floor they found themselves alone. Jude lit cigarettes for himself and Jessy.

"It's scary here, Jude. We're all alone."

"That's not gonna last long. It's getting near ten o'clock."

"Are you scared—about later, I mean?"

"Nothing to be scared of. It doesn't hurt—maybe for just a second, then it's all over."

"Will you hold my hand?"

Jude smiled. "Sure, baby."

A shadow stepped out of the shadows. "Young man—it's me, Lester Tinburley. I helped you fix things downstairs if you remember."

"Sure, dad, but right now I'm busy."

"I only wanted to warn you that there's another man

here—" Lester's voice diminished to a dry, inaudible whisper. "I think he's going to—" He wet his lips. "—to make some sort of trouble."

Lester pointed to the crack of light under Archold's door. "Maybe you'd better get him out of the building."

"Jude—not now!"

"I'll only be a minute, baby. This could be fun." Jude looked at Lester. "Some sort of nut, huh?"

Lester nodded and retreated back into the shadow of the reception desk.

Jude pushed open the door and looked at the man who sat behind the dusty, glass-topped desk. He was old—maybe fifty—and bleary-eyed from drinking. A pushover. Jude smiled, as the man rose unsteadily to his feet.

"Get out of here!" the old man bellowed. "This is my bank. I won't have a bunch of tramps walking about in my bank."

"Hey, Jessy!" Jude called. "C'mere and getta look of this."

"Leave this room immediately. I am the president of this bank. I . . ."

Jessy giggled. "Is he crazy, or what?"

"Jack," Jude shouted into the dark reception room, "is this guy on the level? About being bank president?"

"Yessir," Lester replied.

"Lester! Are you out there? Throw these juvenile delinquents out of my bank. This minute! Do you understand? Lester!"

"Didja hear the man, Lester? Why don't you answer the bank president?"

"He can open the vault doors. You can make him do it." Lester came to stand in the door and looked in triumph at Archold. "That's where all the money is—from the other banks too. He knows the combination. There's millions of dollars. He would never do it for me, but you can make him."

"Oh Jude—let's. It would be fun. I haven't seen money for just an age."

"We don't have the time, baby."

"So we'd die at two o'clock instead of twelve. What difference would it make? Just think—a bank vault crammed full of money! Please . . ."

Archold had retreated to the corner of his office. "You can't make me . . . I won't . . ."

Jude began to seem more interested. He had no interest

in money as such, but a contest of wills appealed to his forthright nature. "Yeah, we could toss it around like confetti—that would be something. Or build a bonfire!"

"No!" Lester gasped, then palliatively—"I'll show you where the vault is, but a fire would burn down the bank. What would the people do tomorrow night? The vault is downstairs. I've got the keys for the cage around the vault, but he'll tell you the combination."

"Lester! No!"

"Call me 'boy' like you used to, Mr. Archold. Tell me what I've got to do."

Archold grasped at the straw. "Get those two out of here. Right now, Lester."

Lester laughed. He went up to Archold's Reprostat and pressed the cigar Archtype button. He gave Jude the burning cigar. "This will make him tell you the combination." But Jude ignored Lester's advice, or seemed to. He threw away his cigarette and stuck Archold's cigar into the corner of his mouth, slightly discomposing his studied grin. Emboldened, Lester took a cigar for himself and followed this up with Scotches for himself, Jessy, and Jude. Jude sipped at his meditatively, examining Archold. When he had finished, he grabbed the bank president by the collar of his jacket and led him down the stairs to the ballroom-banking-floor.

The dancers, most of whom were shortly to die like Jude and Jessy, were desperately, giddily gay. A sixteen-year-old girl lay unconscious at the foot of the bandstand. Jude dragged Archold up the steps and into the hazy blue light. Archold noticed that Mrs. Desmond's name placard still hung on the grille of the teller's window which now formed a balustrade for the bandstand.

Jude grabbed the mike. "Stop the action. The entertainment committee has something new for all of us." The band stopped, dancers turned to look at Jude and Archold. "Ladies and gentlemen, I'd like to introduce the president of this fine bank, Mr.—what-did-you-say-your-name-was?"

"Archold," Lester volunteered from the dance floor. "Charlie Archold."

"Mr. Archold is going to open up the bank vault special for tonight's little party, and we're going to decorate the walls with good, old-fashioned dollar bills. We're going to roll in money—isn't that so, Charlie?"

Archold struggled to get loose from Jude's grip. The crowd began to laugh. "You'll pay for the damage you've done here," he moaned into the mike. "There are still laws for your kind. You can't . . ."

"Hey, Jude," a girl yelled, "lemme dance with the old fellow. You only live once and I'm going to try everything." The laughter swelled. Archold could not make out any faces in the crowd below. The laughter seemed to issue from the walls and the floors, disembodied and unreal. The band began a slow, mocking fox-trot. Archold felt himself gripped by a new set of hands. Jude let go of his collar.

"Move your feet, stupid. You can't dance standing still."

"Turn on the dizzy lights," Jessy shouted.

"You're forgetting the vaults," Lester whined at her. She took the old janitor in hand and led him up to the bandstand, where they watched Archold floundering in the arms of his tormentor.

The blue spotlight blanked out. The bank was suddenly filled with a swarm of bright red flashes, like the revolving lights mounted on police cars. That, in fact, had been their sources. Klaxons sounded—someone had triggered the bank's own alarm system. A trumpet, then the drums, took up the klaxons' theme.

"Let me lead," the girl was shouting in Archold's ear. He saw her face in a brief flash of red light, cruel and avid, strangely reminiscent of Nora—but Nora was his wife and loved him—then felt himself being pushed back, his knees crumbling, over the grille and down. The girl lying on the floor broke his fall.

There were gunshots. The police, he thought. Of course there were no police. The boys were aiming at the spinning lights.

Archold felt himself lifted by dozens of hands. Lights spun around him overhead, and there was a brief explosion when one of the marksmen made a bull's-eye. The hands that bore him aloft began to pull in different directions, revolving him, cartwheel-fashion, in time to the klaxons' deafening music, faster and faster. He felt the back of his jacket begin to rip, then a wrenching pain in his shoulder. Another explosion of light.

He fell to the floor with a shuddering pain through his whole body. He was drenched with water, lying at the door of the vault.

"Open it, dad," someone—not Jude—said.

Archold saw Lester in the forefront of the group. He

raised his arm to strike at him, but the pain stopped him. He stood up and looked at the ring of adolescent faces around him. "I won't open it. That money does not belong to me. I'm responsible to the people who left it here; it's their money. I can't . . ."

"Man, nobody is going to use that money, any more. Open it."

A girl stepped out from the crowd and crossed over to Archold. She wiped his forehead where it was bleeding. "You better do what they say," she said gently. "Almost all of them are going to kill themselves tonight, and they don't care what they do or who they hurt. Life is cheap— a couple bars of carbon and a few quarts of water—and the pieces of paper behind that door don't mean a thing. In one day you could Reprostat a million dollars."

"No. I can't. I won't do it."

"Everybody—you too, Darline—get back here. We'll make him open it up." The main body of the crowd had already retreated behind the cage that fenced in the vault. Lester, of course, had had the keys to get them into the cage. Darline shrugged and joined the rest of them.

"Now, Mr. President, either you open that door or we'll start using you for a target."

"No!" Archold rushed to the combination lock. "I'll do it," he was screaming when one of the boys shot the glass-faced regulator above the lock.

"You hit him."

"I did not."

Darline went to look. "It was a heart attack, I guess. He's dead."

They left Lester alone in the outer room of the vault with Archold's body. He stared bleakly at the corpse. "I'll do it again," he said. "Again and again."

On the floor above them, the klaxons were quietened and the music began again, sweetly at first, then faster and louder. It was nearing midnight.

Nora Archold, wife of Charles, was embarrassed by her red hair. Although it was her natural color, she suspected that people thought she dyed it. She was forty-two, after all, and so many older women decided to be redheads.

"I like it just the way it is, honey," Dewey told her. "You're being silly."

"Oh. Dewey, I'm so worried."

211

"There isn't anything to worry about. It's not as though you were leaving him—you know that."

"But it seems *wrong*."

Dewey laughed. Nora pouted, knowing that she looked becoming in a pout. He tried to kiss her, but she pushed him away and went on with her packing—one of a kind of everything she liked. The suitcase was more of a ceremonial gesture than a practical necessity; in one afternoon at the stores she could have an entire wardrobe Reprostated if she wanted to take the trouble (a kind of trouble she enjoyed taking). But she liked her old clothes—many of which were "originals." The difference between an original and a Reprostated copy was undetectable even under an electron microscope, but Nora, none the less, felt a vague mistrust of the copies—as though they were somehow transparent to other eyes and shabbier.

"We were married twenty years ago, Charlie and me. You must have been just a little kid when I was already a married woman." Nora shook her head at woman's frailty. "And I don't even know your last name." This time she let Dewey kiss her.

"Hurry up, now," he whispered. "The old boy will be back any minute."

"It's not fair to *her*," Nora complained. "She'll have to put up with all the horrible things I have all these years."

"Make up your mind. First you worry about him; now, it isn't fair for her. I'll tell you what—when I get home, I'll Reprostat another Galahad to rescue *her* from the old dragon."

Nora observed him suspiciously. "Is that your last name —Galahad?"

"Hurry up now," he commanded.

"I want you out of the house while I do it. I don't want you to see—the other one."

Dewey guffawed. "I'll bet not!" He carried the suitcase to the car and waited while Nora watched him from the picture window. She looked about the living room once more regretfully. It was a beautiful house in one of the best suburbs. For twenty years it had been a part of her, rather the greater part. She didn't have any idea where Dewey wanted to take her. She was thrilled by her own infidelity, realizing at the same time that it made no difference. As Dewey had pointed out to her, life was cheap— a couple bars of carbon and a few quarts of water.

The clock on the wall read 12:30. She had to hurry.

In the Reprostating room, she unlocked the Personal panel on the control board. It was meant only for emergencies, but it could be argued that this was an emergency. It had been Charles' idea to have his own body Archtyped by the Reprostat. His heart was bad; it could give out at any time, and a personal Archtype was better than life insurance. It was, in a way, almost immortality. Nora, naturally, had been Archtyped at the same time. That had been in October, seven months after the bank had closed, but it seemed like only yesterday. It was June already. With Dewey around, she'd be able to cut down on her drinking.

Nora pressed the button reading "Nora Archold." The sign on the control panel flashed: INSUFFICIENT PHOSPHORUS. Nora went to the kitchen, dug into the cupboard drawers for the right jar and deposited it in the hopper that had been set into the floor. The Reprostat whirred and clicked to a stop. Timidly, Nora opened the door of the materializer.

Nora Archold—herself—lay on the floor of the chamber in an insensible heap, in the same state that Nora (the older, unfaithful Nora) had been in when—that day in October—she had been Archtyped. The elder Nora dragged her freshly Reprostated double into the bedroom. She considered leaving a note that would explain what had happened—why Nora was leaving with a stranger she had met only that afternoon. But, outside the house, Dewey was honking. Tenderly, she kissed the insensible woman who lay in her own bed and left the house where she had felt, for twenty years, a prisoner.

Fair youth, beneath the trees thou canst not leave
Thy song, nor even can those trees be bare.

"Afraid?"

"No. Are you?"

"Not if you hold my hand." Jude began to embrace her again. "No, just hold my hand. We could go on like this forever, and then everything would be spoiled. We'd grow old, quarrel, stop caring for each other. I don't want that to happen. Do you think it will be the same for them as it was for us?"

"It couldn't be any different."

"It *was* beautiful," Jessy said.

"Now?" Jude asked.

"Now," she consented.

Jude helped her to sit down at the edge of the hopper, then took a seat beside her. The opening was barely big enough for their two bodies. Jessy's hand tightened around Jude's fingers: the signal. Together, they slid into the machine. There was no pain, only a cessation of consciousness. Atoms slid loose from their chemical bonds instantaneously; what had been Jude and Jessy was now only increments of elementary matter in the storage chamber of the Reprostat. From those atoms, anything could be reassembled: food, clothing, a pet canary—anything that the machine possessed an Archtype of—even another Jude and Jessy.

In the next room, Jude and Jessy slept next to each other. The sodium pentothal was beginning to wear off. Jude's arm lay across Jessy's shoulder, where the newly disintegrated Jessy had laid it before leaving them.

Jessy stirred. Jude moved his hand.

"Do you know what day it is?" she whispered.

"Hmm?"

"It's starting," she said. "This is our last day."

"It will always be that day, honey."

She began to hum a song: Now, now, now, now— Now is forever.

For ever wilt thou love, and she be fair!

At one o'clock, the last of the revelers having departed from the bank, Lester Tinburley dragged Archold's body to the Cadillac in the street outside. He found the ignition key in Archold's pocket. It was an hour's drive to the president's suburban home—or a little longer than it took to smoke one of the cigars from the Reprostat on the dashboard.

Lester Tinburley had come to work at the New York Exchange Bank in 1953, immediately upon his release from the Armed Services. He had seen Charles Archold rise from the bond window to a loan consultant's desk to the accounting office on the second floor and eventually to the presidency, a rise that paralleled Lester's own ascension through the ranks to the lieutenancy of the janitorial staff. The two men, each surrounded by the symbols of his authority, had had a common interest in the preservation of order—that is to say, bureaucracy. They had been allies in conservatism. The advent of the Reprostat, however, changed all that.

The Reprostat could be programmed to reproduce from its supply of elementary particles (some sub-atomic) any given mechanical, molecular, or atomic structure; any *thing,* in short. The Reprostat could even reprostat smaller Reprostats. As soon as such a machine became available to even a few, it would inevitably become available to anyone—and when anyone possesed a Reprostat he needed very little else. The marvelous machines could not provide Charles Archold with pleasant sensations of self-justification in the performance of his work and the exercise of his authority, but only the vanishing breed of the inner-directed required such intangible pleasures. The new order of society, as evidenced in Jude and Jessy, were content to take their pleasures where they found them—in the Reprostat. They lived in an eternal present which came very close to being an earthly paradise.

Lester Tinburley could not share either attitude perfectly. While Charles Archold's way of life was only affected adversely by the new abundance (he had been able, as a bank president, to afford most of the things he really desired) and Jessy and Jude indulged themselves in Arcady, Lester was torn between the new facts of life and his old habits. He had learned, in fifty years of menial work and mean living, to take a certain pleasure and a considerable amount of pride in the very meanness of his circumstances. He preferred beer to cognac, overalls to a silk lounging robe. Affluence had come too late in his life for him to do it justice, especially an affluence so divested of the symbols with which he (like Archold) had always associated it: power, the recognition of authority, and, above all else, money. Avarice is an absurd vice in the earthly paradise, but Lester's mind had been formed at an earlier time when it was still possible to be a miser.

Lester parked the Cadillac in the Archolds' two-car garage and wrestled the stiff body of the bank president into the house. Through the bedroom door he could see Nora Archold sprawled on the bed, sleeping or drunk. Lester shoved Archold's old body into the hopper of the Reprostat. The Personal panel on the control board had been left unlocked. Lester opened the door of the materializer. If he had been partly responsible for Archold's death earlier that evening, this was a perfect atonement. He felt no guilt.

He laid the drugged body of the bank president on the bed beside Nora's and watched them breathing lightly.

Archold would probably be a little confused in the morning, as Lester had noticed he had been in the office. But calendar time was beginning to be less and less meaningful, when one was no longer obliged to punch a time clock or meet deadlines.

"See you tomorrow," he said to his old boss. One of these days, he was convinced, Archold would open the vault *before* his heart failed him. In the meantime, he sort of enjoyed seeing his old employer dropping in at the bank every day. It was like old times.

Charles Archold liked the façade best at twilight. On June evenings like this (or was it July?), the sun would sink into the canyon of Maxwell Street and spotlight the sculptured group in the pediment: a full-breasted Commerce extended an allegorical cornucopia from which tumbled allegorical fruits into the outstretched hands of Industry, Labor, Transportation, Science, and Art. He was idling past (the Cadillac engine was definitely getting worse), abstractedly considering the burning tip of his cigar, when he observed peripherally that Commerce had been beheaded. He stopped.

1965

THE YEAR 1966 saw the first presentation of Nebula awards by the Science Fiction Writers of America and, consequently, the first opportunity for comparison between the taste of the writers and that of their audience. The novel category is most instructive in making this comparison. (And I will point out, at the risk of redundancy, that the awards presented in 1966 recognized works published in '65, regardless of the date engraved on the trophies.)

Twelve novels were nominated for the first Nebula award, including *The Genocides* by Thomas M. Disch, *Nova Express* by William S. Burroughs, *The Clone* by Theodore L. Thomas and Kate Wilhelm, *two* novels by Philip K. Dick, and others by Clifford Simak, James White, Keith Laumer, Avram Davidson, G. C. Edmondson, and Poul Anderson. The winner was *Dune,* an instant classic by Frank Herbert. We might note that all nominations were based on *book* publication—Doubleday, Berkley, Ace, Chilton, Grove Press. There were no nominations for magazine serializations, and none for productions of fan-owned specialty houses. SFWA was deadly serious about the book business.

The 1966 World Science Fiction Convention returned to Cleveland. The Hugo nominees in the novel category were . . . *And Call Me Conrad* by Roger Zelazny, *Dune* by Frank Herbert, *The Moon Is a Harsh Mistress* by Robert A. Heinlein, *Skylark DuQuesne* by Edward E. Smith and *Squares of the City* by John Brunner.

There were two winners, one of those rare cases of a dead heat in the balloting. The winners were the Zelazny novel (also published as *This Immortal*) and *Dune.*

Only Herbert's *Dune,* which won the Nebula outright and tied with the Zelazny for the Hugo, made both ballots! Otherwise, the nominee lists were completely different! And, take note, three of the five Hugo nominees specifically referred to magazine-serial versions. Another sign of the difference in orientation between the fans and the professionals.

Certainly, both winners were respectable choices, and both have held up well with the passing years. *Dune*, of course, has become the wellspring of a series of volumes as well as the center of a minor literary cult. The Zelazny book has not fared quite as well, although it certainly remains readable. Perhaps its fame would be greater had Roger Zelazny himself not gone on to surpass it with later works.

But it seems to me that the professionals missed a bet in passing over at least three truly innovative and highly memorable works: *Nova Express* by Burroughs, *Three Stigmata of Palmer Eldritch* by Dick and *The Genocides* by Disch. Why three such fine books were passed over for the actual prizes is slightly puzzling, but then there was *Dune*. How the fans could fail even to place these works on their Hugo ballot is a complete mystery.

Perhaps it was the experimental structure of the Burroughs. It was one of the author's strangely fragmented and interfolded books, and the fans, still under the lingering influence of the dying pulp tradition, tended to demand an easily followed linear plot line. Or perhaps it was the themes of the novel, for here it was clearly ahead of its time, dealing with drugs, confused states of mind, homosexuality, and other matters that might make adolescent readers uncomfortable, to say the least.

Or still again, it might have been the publisher. Science fiction readers knew who their friends were—the surviving fan-owned presses, plus such popularly oriented commercial publishers as Ace, Ballantine and other mass paperback houses, and a few of the commercial hardbound publishers.

But—Grove Press? Wasn't that some sort of oddball outfit that skirted the bizarre borderland between *avant-garde,* experimental, capital-el Literature and pornography?

As for Philip K. Dick's *Three Stigmata of Palmer Eldritch,* there was again the thematic difficulty. America and much of the western world were headed toward the strange psychedelic episode of the late 1960s. The Beatles had already arrived, but they were still in their "I Wanna Hold Your Hand" period, far, far from Pepperland.

(One notes, also, that while Phil Dick has been nominated for the Hugo and Nebula awards more than a dozen times, he has *won* only once: the Hugo for his novel *The Man in the High Castle,* which was published back in 1962.)

Palmer Eldritch is one of the most powerful and convincing novels of reality-twisting ever published—and it seems likely that the voters in 1966 weren't ready to deal with it.

What about Disch's *The Genocides?* Too literary? Too depressing? It is a novel in which aliens take over the earth and turn it into a giant plantation, treating Man and His Mightiest Works as a farmer would treat an insect pest in a newly cleared lima bean patch. Strong stuff.

In the shorter lengths, there were any number of fine exercises published in 1965. The Hugo for short fiction went to Harlan Ellison for " 'Repent, Harlequin!' said the Ticktockman," a deserving, funny and powerful story originally published in *Galaxy.* Other Hugo nominees included Philip Jose Farmer, Poul Anderson, Fritz Leiber, and (for "The Doors of His Face, the Lamps of His Mouth") Roger Zelazny.

The Nebula structure, breaking out novella, novelette and short story, produced a total of *four* winners for short fiction. For novella, there was a tie between Zelazny's two-part serial "He Who Shapes" and Brian Aldiss's "The Saliva Tree." The winning novelette was Zelazny's "The Doors of His Face, the Lamps of His Mouth." And the winning short story was Ellison's "Ticktockman" once again.

With a single exception, every nominated work of short fiction had been published in an American science fiction magazine. Both the fans and the professionals were sticking to their traditional sources of supply. *Amazing, Analog, If, Worlds of Tomorrow, F&SF* . . . You didn't see anything from *Playboy* or the other slicks. And as for original anthologies, Fred Pohl's *Star* series had already died, and Damon Knight's *Orbit* series not yet begun—although the latter was about to do so, with immense impact on the rolls of award-winners in the later 1960s and 1970s.

The "Story That Should Have Won the Hugo" that I have selected is one that didn't even make the Hugo (or Nebula) ballot when it was published in 1965. I think there were two reasons for this. First, its author, Barrington J. Bayley, was then at the beginning of a career in which he has never been prolific, in which he has never

219

socialized heavily with fans or professionals, in which he has never become a major "name" writer. He has also never won a Hugo or Nebula award, although he was mentioned, along with some dozens of others, for a novelette published in 1972.

Further, his story, "All the King's Men," appeared in *New Worlds,* a magazine that had two strikes against it from the outset, as far as placing fiction before the eyes of award voters. Strike one: it was published in England, and most of the voters were American. Strike two: *New Worlds* was (not unjustly) regarded as a source of arty lit'ry experimentation, and despite an occasional bow in the latter direction (i.e., every time Samuel R. Delany wins an award) the science fiction reader—and writer—generally prefers straight storytelling with an emphasis on action and adventure.

In the mid- and late 1960s, largely under the influence of Michael Moorcock, *New Worlds* broke ground in the direction of altered literary forms, altered thematic orientation and general innovation in the realm of fiction. The magazine featured an array of stories that were dazzling both in the sense of glorious illumination and in that of disorienting the reader. Featured writers included Aldiss, Disch, J. G. Ballard, Pamela Zoline, Norman Spinrad, John Sladek and others. They were guilty of the expected excesses of the consciously experimental but they also achieved startling and innovative things.

"All the King's Men" has slowly and quietly developed a following in the years since it was published in *New Worlds.* It has been anthologized twice by Moorcock and once by Judith Merril, and each time it reaches a new circle of readers it and its author gain a new group of admirers.

Read it now and let its quiet, understated elegance affect you. And think about it again tomorrow, and next week, and a month from now. It's the kind of story that grows in your subconscious.

All the King's Men

BARRINGTON J. BAYLEY

I SAW SORN'S bier, an electrically driven train decorated like a fanfare, as it left the North Sea Bridge and passed over the green meadows of Yorkshire. Painted along its flank was the name HOLATH HOLAN SORN, and it motored swiftly with brave authority. From where we stood in the observation room of the King's Summer Palace, we could hear the hollow humming of its passage.

"You will not find things easy without Holath Holan Sorn," I said, and turned. The King of All Britain was directing his mosaic eyes toward the train. "Things were never easy," he replied. But he knew as well as I that the loss of Sorn might mean the loss of a kingdom.

The King turned from the window, his purple cloak flowing about his seven-foot frame. I felt sorry for him: how would he rule an alien race, with its alien psychology, now that Sorn was dead? He had come to depend entirely upon that man who could translate one set of references into another as easily as he crossed the street. No doubt there were other men with perhaps half of Sorn's abilities, but who else could gain the King's trust? Among all humans, none but Sorn could be the delegate of the Invader King.

"Smith," he said, addressing me, "tomorrow we consign twelve tooling factories to a new armament project. I wish you to supervise."

I acknowledged, wondering what this signified. No one could deny that the alien's reign had been peaceful, even prosperous, and he had rarely mentioned military matters, although I knew there was open enmity between him and the King of Brazil. Either this enmity was about to become active, I decided, or else the King forecast a civil uprising.

Which in itself was not unlikely.

Below us, the bier was held up by a junction hitch. Stationary, it supplemented its dignity by sounding its klaxon loudly and continuously. The King returned his gaze to it, and though I couldn't read his unearthly face I suppose he watched it regretfully, if he can feel regret. Of the others in the room, probably the two aliens also watched with regret, but certainly no one else did. Of the four humans, three were probably glad he was dead, though they may have been a little unsure about it.

That left myself. I was more aware of events than any of them, but I just didn't know what I felt. Sometimes I felt on the King's side and sometimes on the other side. I just didn't have any definite loyalties.

Having witnessed the arrival of the bier from the continent, where Sorn had met his death, we had achieved the purpose of the visit to the Summer Palace, and accordingly the King, with his entourage of six (two fellow beings, four humans including myself) left for London.

We arrived at Buckingham Palace shortly before sunset. Wordlessly the King dismissed us all, and with a lonely swirl of his cloak made his way to what was in a makeshift manner called the throne-room. Actually it did have a throne: but it also had several other kinds of strange equipment, things like pools, apparatus with what psychologists called threshold associations. The whole chamber was an aid to the incomprehensible, insectile mentality of the King, designed, I suspected, to help him in the almost impossible task of understanding a human society. While he had Sorn at his elbow there had been little need to worry, and the inadequacy of the chamber mattered so little that he seldom used it. Now, I thought, the King of All Britain would spend a large part of his time meditating in solitude on that enigmatic throne.

I had the rest of the evening to myself. But I hadn't gone far from the palace when, as I might have guessed, Hotch placed his big bulk square across my path.

"Not quite so fast," he said, neither pleasantly nor unpleasantly.

I stopped—what else could I have done?—but I didn't answer. "All right," Hotch said, "let's have it straight. I want nobody on both sides."

"What do you mean?" I asked, as if I didn't already know.

"Sorn's dead, right? And you're likely to replace him. Right?"

"Wrong," I told him wearily. "Nobody replaces Sorn. He was the one irreplaceable human being."

His eyes dropped in pensive annoyance. He paused. "Maybe, but you'll be the closest to the King's rule. Is that so?"

I shrugged.

"It has to be so," he decided. "So which way is it going to be, Smith? If you're going to be another traitor like Sorn, let's hear it from the start. Otherwise be a man and come in with us."

It sounded strange to hear Sorn called a traitor. Technically, I suppose he was—but he was also a man of genius, the rarest of statesmen. And even now only the 0.5 percent of the population roused by Hotch's superpatriotism would think of him as anything else. Britain had lived in a plentiful sort of calm under the King. The fact of being governed by an alien conqueror was not resented, even though he had enthroned himself by force. With his three ships, his two thousand warriors, he had achieved a near-bloodless occupation, for he had won his victory by the sheer possession of superior weapons, without having to resort much to their usage. The same could be said of the simultaneous invasion of Brazil and South Africa: Brazil by fellow creatures of the King, South Africa by a different species. Subsequent troubles in these two areas had been greater, but then they lacked the phlegmatic British attitude, and more important, they lacked Holath Holan Sorn.

I sighed. "Honestly, I don't know. Some human governments have been a lot worse."

"But they've been human. And we owed a lot to Sorn, though personally I loathed his guts. Now that he's gone—what? The King will make a mess of things. How do we know he really cares?"

"I think he does. Not the same way a man would care, but he does."

"Hah! Anyhow, this is our chance. While he doesn't know what he's doing. What about it? Britain hasn't known another conqueror in a thousand years."

I couldn't tell him. I didn't know. Eventually he stomped off in disgust.

I didn't enjoy myself that evening. I thought too much about Sorn, about the King, and about what Hotch had said. How could I be sure the King cared for England? He was so grave and gently ponderous, but did that indicate anything? His appearance could simply be part of his foreignness and nothing at all to do with his feelings. In fact if the scientists were right about him, he had no feelings at all.

But what purpose had he?

I stopped by Trafalgar Square to see the Green Fountains. The hand of the invader on Britain was present in light, subtle ways, such as the Green Fountains. For although Britain remained Britain, with the character of Britain, the King and his men had delicately placed their alien character upon it; not in law, or the drastic changes of a conqueror, but in such things as decoration.

The Green Fountains were foreign, unimaginable and unBritish. High curtains of thin fluid curled into fantastic designs, creating new concepts of space by sheer ingenuity of form. Thereby they achieved what centuries of Terran artists had only hinted at.

And yet they *were* British, too. If Britons had been prompted to conceive and construct such things, this was the way they would have done it. They carried the British stamp, although so alien.

When I considered the King's rule, the same anomaly emerged. A strange rule, by a stranger, yet imposed so easily.

This was the mystery of the King's government: the way he had adopted Britain, in essence, while having no comprehension of that essence.

But let me make it clear that for all this, the invader's rule did not *operate* easily. It jarred, oscillated, went out of phase, and eventually, without Sorn, ended in disaster. It was only in this other, peculiar way, that it harmonized so pleasingly.

It was like this: when the King and his men tried to behave functionally and get things done, it was terrible. It didn't fit. But when they simply added themselves to All

Britain, and lay quiescently like touches of color, it had the effect I describe.

I had always thought Sorn responsible for this. But could Sorn mold the King also? For I detected in the King that same English passivity and acceptance; not just his own enigmatic detachment, but something apart from that, something acquired. Yet how could he be something which he didn't understand?

Sorn is dead, I thought, Sorn is dead.

Already, across one side of the square, were erected huge, precise stone symbols: HOLATH HOLAN SORN DIED 5.8.2034. They were like a mathematical formula. Much of the King's speech, when I thought of it, had the same quality.

Sorn was dead, and the weight of his power which had steadied the nation would be abruptly removed. He had been the operator, bridging the gap between alien minds. Without him, the King was incompetent.

A dazzling blue and gold air freighter appeared over the square and slanted down toward the palace. Everyone stopped to look, for it was one of the extraterrestrial machines, rarely seen since the invasion. No doubt it carried reinforcements for the palace defenses.

Next morning I motored to Surrey to visit the first of the ten factories the King had mentioned.

The managers were waiting for me. I was led to a prepared suite of offices where I listened sleepily to a lecture on the layout and scope of the factory. I wasn't very interested; one of the King's kinsmen (referred to as the King's men) would arrive shortly with full details of the proposed conversation, and the managers would have to go through it all again. I was only here as a representative, so to speak. The real job would be carried out by the alien.

We all wandered around the works for a few hours before I got thoroughly bored and returned to my office. A visitor was waiting.

Hotch.

"What do you want now?" I asked. "I thought I'd got rid of you."

He grinned. "I found out what's going on." He waved his arms to indicate the factory.

"What of it?"

"Well, wouldn't you say the King's policy is . . . ill-advised?"

"You know as well as I do that the King's policy is cer-

225

tain to be laughably clumsy." I motioned him to a seat. "What exactly do you mean? I'm afraid I don't know the purpose of this myself."

I was apologetic about the last statement, and Hotch laughed. "It's easy enough to guess. Don't you know what they're building in Glasgow? *Ships*—warships of the King's personal design."

"Brazil," I murmured.

"Sure. The King chooses this delicate moment to launch a transatlantic war. Old Rex is such a blockhead he almost votes himself out of power."

"How?"

"Why, he gives us the weapons to fight him with. He's organizing an armed native force which *I* will turn against him."

"You jump ahead of yourself. To go by the plans I have, no extraterrestrial weapons will be used."

Hotch looked more sober. "That's where you come in. We can't risk another contest with the King's men using ordinary arms. It would kill millions and devastate the country. Because it won't be the skirmish-and-capitulate of last time. This time we'll be in earnest. So I want you to soften things up for us. Persuade the King to hand over more than he intends: help us to chuck him out easily. Give us new weapons and you'll save a lot of carnage."

I saw his stratagem at once. "Quit that! Don't try to lay blood responsibility on my shoulders. That's a dirty trick."

"For a dirty man—and that's what you are, Smith, if you continue to stand by, too apathetic even to think about it. Anyhow, the responsibility's already laid, whatever you say. It depends on you."

"No."

"You won't help?"

"That's right."

Hotch sighed, and stared at the carpet for some seconds. Then he stared through the glass panels and down onto the floor of the workshops. "Then what will you do? Betray me?"

"No."

Sighing again, he told me: "One day, Smith, you'll fade away through sheer lack of interest."

"I'm interested," I said. "I just don't seem to have the kind of mind that can make a decision. I can't find any place to lay blame, or anyone to turn against."

"Not even for Britain," he commented sadly. "Your Britain as well as mine. That's all I'm working for, Smith, our country."

His brashness momentarily dormant, he was moodily meditative. "Smith, I'll admit I don't understand what it's all about. What does the King want? What has he gained by coming down here?"

"Nothing. He descended on us and took on a load of troubles without profit. It's a mystery. Hence my uncertainty." I averted my eyes. "During the time I have been in contact with the King he has impressed me as being utterly, almost transcendentally unselfish. So unselfish, so abstracted, that he's like a—just a blank!"

"That's only how you see it. Maybe you read it into him. The psychos say he's no emotion, and selfishness is a kind of emotion."

"Is it? Well, that's just what I mean. But he seems—humane, for all that. Considerate, though it's difficult for him."

He wasn't much impressed. "Yeah. Remember that whatever substitutes for emotion in him might have some of its outward effects. And remember, he's not the only outworlder on this planet. He doesn't seem so considerate toward Brazil."

Hotch rose and prepared to leave. "If you survive the rebellion, I'll string you up as a traitor."

"All right!" I answered, suddenly irritable. "I know."

But when Hotch did get moving, I was surprised at the power he had gained for himself in the community. He knew exactly how to accentuate the irritating qualities of the invader, and he did it mercilessly.

Some of the incidents seemed ridiculous, such as when alien officials began to organize the war effort with complete disregard for some of the things the nation took to be necessities—entertainment, leisure and so on. The contents of art galleries and museums were burned to make way for weapons shops. Cinemas were converted into automatic factories, and all television transmissions ceased. Don't get the idea that the King and his men are all tyrannical automata. They just didn't see any reason for not throwing away priceless paintings, and never thought to look for one.

Affairs might have progressed more satisfactorily if the setup had been less democratic. Aware of his poor understanding, the King had appointed a sort of double government. The first, from which issued the prime directive, consisted of his own men in key positions throughout the land, though actually their power had peculiar limitations. The second government was a human representation of the aboriginal populace, which in larger matters was still obliged to gain the King's spoken permission.

The King used to listen very intently to the petitions and pseudo-emotional barrages which this absurd body placed before him—for they were by no means cooperative—and the meetings nearly always ended in bewilderment. During Sorn's day it would have been different: he could have got rid of them in five minutes.

Those men caused chaos, and cost the country many lives in the Brazilian war which shortly followed. After Hotch gained control over them, they were openly the King's enemies. He didn't know it, of course, and now that it's all finished I often wish I had warned him.

I remember the time they came to him and demanded a national working week of twenty-five hours. This was just after the King's men had innocently tried to institute a sixty hour working week, and had necessarily been restrained.

The petitioners knew how impossible it was; they were just trying to make trouble.

The King received them amid the sparse trappings of his Court. A few of his aides were about, and a few human advisers. And I, of course, was close at hand.

He listened to the petition in silence, his jewel eyes glinting softly in the subdued light. When it was over he paused. Then he lifted his head and asked for help.

"Advise me," he said to everyone present.

But the hostile influences in the hall were so great that everyone who might have helped him shrugged his shoulders. That was the way things were. I said nothing.

"If the proposal is carried out," the King told the ministers, "current programs will not go through."

He tried to reject the idea, but they amazingly refused to let it be rejected. They threatened and intimidated, and one gentleman began to talk hypocritically about the will and welfare of the people. Naturally there was no response: the King was not equipped. He surveyed the hall again. "He who can solve this problem, come forward."

There was a lethargic, apathetic suspension. The aliens were immobile, like hard brilliant statues, observing these dangerous events as if with the asceticism of stone. Then there was more shrugging of shoulders.

It speaks for the leniency of the extraterrestrials that this could happen at all. Among human royalty, such insolence would bring immediate repercussions. But the mood was contagious, because I didn't volunteer either. Hotch's machinations had a potential, unspoken element of terrorism.

Whether the King realized that advice was being deliberately withheld, I don't know. He called my name and strode to the back of the hall.

I followed his authoritatively gyrating cloak, reluctantly, like a dreading schoolboy. When I reached him, he said: "Smith, it is knowledge common to us both that my thinkings and human thinkings are processes apart. Not even Sorn could have both minds; but he could translate." He paused for a moment, and then continued with a couple of sentences of the mixed-up talk he had used on Sorn, together with some of the accompanying queer honks and noises. I couldn't follow it. He seemed to realize his mistake, though, for he soon emerged into fairly sensible speech again, like this: *"Honk.* Environs matrix wordy. Int apara; is trying like light to; apara see blind, from total outside is not even potential . . . if you were king, Smith, what would you do?"

"Well," I said, "people have been angered by the impositions made on them recently, and now they're trying to swing the pendulum the other way. Maybe I would compromise and cut the week by about ten hours."

The King drew a sheaf of documents from a voluminous sash pocket and spread them out. One of them had a chart on it, and lists of figures. Producing a small machine with complex surfaces, he made what appeared to be a computation.

I wished I could find some meaning in those cold jewel eyes. "That would interfere with my armament program," he said. "We must become strong, or the King of Brazil will lay Britain waste."

"But surely it's important not to foster a discontented populace?"

"Important! So often I have heard that word, and cannot understand it. Sometimes it appears to me, Smith, that human psychology is hilly country, while mine is a plain. My throne-room contains hints, that some things you see

229

as high, and others as low and flat, and the high is more powerful. But for me to travel this country is impossible."

Smart. And it made some sense to me, too, because the King's character often seemed to be composed of absences. He had no sense of crisis, for example. I realized how great his effort must have been to work this out.

"And 'importance,'" he continued. "Some mountain top?"

He almost had it. "A big mountain," I said.

For a few seconds I began to get excited and thought that perhaps he was on his way to a semantic breakthrough. Then I saw where I was wrong. Knowing intellectually that a situation is difficult, and *why* it is difficult, is not much use when it comes to operating in that situation. If the King had fifty million minds laid out in diagram, with all their interconnections (and this is perfectly possible) he would still be no better able to operate. It is far too complex to grasp all at once with the intellect; to be competent in an environment, one must live in it, must be homogeneous with it. The King does not in the proper sense do the former, and is not the latter.

He spent a little while in the throne-room, peering through thresholds, no doubt, gazing at pools and wondering about the mountainous. Then he returned and offered the petitioners a concession of ten minutes off the working week. This was the greatest check he thought he could allow on his big industrial drive.

They argued angrily about it, until things grew out of hand and the King ordered me to dismiss them. I had to have it done forcibly. Any one of the alien courtiers could have managed it single-handed by mere show of the weapons on his person, but instead I called in a twenty-man human bodyguard, thinking that to be ejected by their own countrymen might reduce their sense of solidarity.

All the humans of the court exuded uneasiness. But they needn't have worried. To judge by the King and his men, nothing might have happened. They held their positions with that same crystalline intelligence which they had carried through ten years of occupation. I was beginning to learn that this static appearance did not wholly result from unintelligibility, but that they actually maintained a constant internal state irrespective of external conditions. Because of this, they were unaware that the scene that had just been enacted comprised a minor climax. Living in a

230

planar mentality, the very idea of climax was not apparent to them.

After the petitioners had gone, the King took me to his private chambers behind the courtroom. "Now is the time for consolidation," he said. "Without Sorn, the governing factions become separated, and the country disintegrates. I must find contact with the indigenous British. Therefore I will strike a closer liaison with you, Smith, my servant. You will follow me around."

He meant that I was to replace Sorn, as well as I could. Making it an official appointment was probably his way of appealing for help.

He had hardly picked the right man for the job, but that was typical of the casual way he operated. Of course, it made my personal position much worse, since I began to feel bad about letting him down. I was caught at the nexus of two opposing forces: even my inaction meant that somebody would profit. Altogether, not a convenient post for a neutral passenger.

Anyway, since the situation had arisen, I decided to be brash and ask some real questions.

"All right," I said, "but for whose sake is this war being fought—Britain's, or yours?"

As soon as the words were out of my mouth I felt a little frightened. In the phantasmal human-alien relationship, such earthy examinations were out of place. But the King accepted it.

"I am British," he answered, "and Britain is mine. Ever since I came, our actions are inseparable."

Some factions of the British public would have disagreed with this, but I supposed he meant it in a different way. Perhaps in a way connected with the enigmatically compelling characters and aphorisms that had been erected about the country, like mathematics developed in words instead of numbers. I often suspected that the King had sought to gain power through semantics alone.

Because I was emotionally adrift, I was reckless enough to argue the case. "Well," I said, "without you there would be no war. The Brazilians would never fight without compulsion from their own King, either. I'm not trying to secede from your authority, but resolve my opinion that you and the King of Brazil are using human nations as instruments . . . in a private quarrel."

For some while he thought about it, placing his hands together. He answered: "When the events of which I and the King of Brazil are a part, moved into this region, I descended onto Britain, and he onto Brazil. By the fundamental working of things, I took on the nature of Britain, and Britain in reciprocation became incorporated in the workings of those events. And likewise with the King of Brazil, and with Brazil. These natures, and those events, are not for the time being separables, but included in each other. Therefore it is to defend Britain that I strive, because Britain is harnessed to my section of those outside happenings, and because I am British."

When I had finally sorted out that chunk of pedantry, his claims to nationality sounded like baloney. Then I took into account the slightly supra-sensible evidence of his British character. After a little reflection I realized that he had gone halfway toward giving me an explanation of it.

"What kind of happenings," I wondered, "can they be?"

The King can't smile, and he can't sound wistful, and it's hard for him to convey anything except pure information. But what he said next sounded like the nearest thing to wistfulness he could manage.

"They are very far from your mind," he said, "and from your style of living. They are connected with the colliding galaxies in Cygnus. More than that would be very difficult to tell you. . . ."

There was a pause. I began to see that the King's concern was with something very vast and strange indeed. England was only a detail . . .

"And those outsiders who took over South Africa. What's their part in this?"

"No direct connections. Events merely chanced to blow this way."

Oddly, the way he said it made me think of how neat the triple invasion had been. In no instance had the borders of neighboring states been violated, and the unmolested nations had in turn regarded the conquests as internal matters. Events had happened in discreet units, not in an interpenetrating mess as they usually do. The reactions of the entire Terrestrial civilization had displayed an unearthly flavor. Maybe the incompatibility of alien psychology was not entirely mental. Perhaps in the King's native place not only minds but also events took a different form from those of Earth. What is mentality, anyway, but a complex event? I could imagine a sort of transplanting of natural laws, these three kings, with all their power, bringing with

232

them residual influences of the workings of their own worlds. . . .

It sounded like certain astrological ideas I had once heard, of how on each world everything is different, each world has its own basic identity, and everything on that world partakes of that identity. But it's only astrology.

As the time for war drew nearer, Hotch became more daring. Already he had made himself leader of the unions and fostered general discontent, as well as organizing an underground which, in some ways, had more control over Britain than the King himself had. But he had a particular ambition, and in furtherance of this he appeared one day at Buckingham Palace.

Quite simply, he intended to do what I had refused to do for him.

He bowed low before the King, ignoring me, and launched into his petition.

"The people of Britain have a long tradition of reliability and capability in war," he proclaimed. "They cannot be treated like children. Unless they are given fighting powers equal to those of the extraterrestrials—for I do not suppose that your own troops will be poorly armed—their morale will relapse and they will be defeated. You will be the psychological murderer of Britain."

When he had finished, he cast a defiant glance at me, then puffed out his barrel chest and waited for a reply.

He had good reason to be afraid. One word from me, and he was finished. I admired his audacity.

I was also astounded at the outrageous way he had made the request, and I was at a loss to know what to do.

I sank onto the throne steps and slipped into a reverie. If I kept silent and showed loyalty to my country I would bring about the downfall of the King.

If I spoke in loyalty to the King, I would bring about the downfall of Hotch.

And really, I couldn't find any loyalty anywhere. I was utterly adrift, as if I didn't exist on the surface of the planet at all. I was like a compass needle which failed to answer the magnetic field.

"Psychological murderer of Britain," I repeated to myself. I was puzzled at the emotional evocation in that phrase. How could a human administer emotion to the King? But of course, it wasn't really an emotion at all. In the King's eyes the destruction of Britain was to be avoided, and it was this that Hotch was playing on.

Emerging from my drowsy thoughts, I saw Hotch leave. The King had not given an answer. He beckoned to me.

He spoke a few words to me, but I was noncommittal. Then I waited outside the throne-room, while he spent an hour inside.

He obviously trusted Hotch. When he came out, he called together his full council of eight aliens, four humans and myself, and issued directives for the modification of the war. I say of the war, and not of preparations for the war, because plans were now sufficiently advanced for the general outlines of the conflict to be set down on paper. The way the aliens handled a war made it hardly like fighting at all, but like an engineering work or a business project. Everything was decided beforehand; the final outcome was almost incidental.

And so several factories were retooled to produce the new weapons, the military hierarchy readjusted to give humans a greater part, and the focus of the main battle shifted five hundred miles further west. Also, the extrapolated duration of the war was shortened by six months.

Hotch had won. All Britain's industries worked magnificently for three months. They worked for Hotch as they had never worked, even for Sorn.

I felt weary. A child could have seen through Hotch's trick, but the King had been taken in. What went on in his head, after all? What guided him? Did he really care —for anything?

I wondered what Sorn would have thought. But then, I had never known what went on in Sorn's head, either.

The fleet assembled at Plymouth and sailed west into a sunny, choppy Atlantic. The alien-designed ships, which humans called swan-boats, were marshaled into several divisions. They rode high above the water on tripod legs, and bobbed lightly up and down.

Aerial fighting was forbidden by treaty, but there was one aircraft in the fleet, a wonderful blue and gold noncombatant machine where reposed the King, a few personal servants and myself. We drifted a few hundred feet above the pale green water-ships, matching our speed with theirs.

That speed was slow. I wondered why we had not fitted ourselves out with those steel leviathans of human make, fast battleships and destroyers, which could have traversed the ocean in a few days whereas our journey required most of a month. It's true the graceful swarm looked attractive in the sunlight, but I don't think that was the reason. Or maybe it was a facet of it.

The Brazilians were more conventional in their combat aesthetics. They had steamed slowly out of the Gulf of Mexico to meet us at a location which, paradoxically, had been predetermined without collusion. We were greeted by massive gray warships, heavy with guns. Few innovations appeared to have been introduced into the native ship-building, though I did see one long corvette-shape lifted clean out of the water on multiple hydroplanes.

Fighting began in a casual, restrained manner when the belligerents were about two miles apart. There was not much outward enthusiasm for some hours. Our own ships ranged in size from the very small to the daintily monstrous, and wallowed prettily throughout the enemy fleet, discharging flashes of brilliant light. Our more advanced weapons weren't used much, probably because they would have given us an unfair advantage over the Brazilian natives, who had not had the benefit of Hotch's schemings.

Inside me I felt a dull sickness. All the King's men were gathered here in the Atlantic; this was the obvious time for Hotch's rebellion.

But it would not happen immediately. Hotch was astute enough to realize that even when he was rid of the King he might still have to contend with Brazil, and he wanted to test his future enemy's strength.

The unemphatic activity on the surface of the ocean continued, while one aircraft floated in the air above. The King watched, sometimes from the balcony, sometimes by means of a huge jumble of screens down inside, which showed an impossible montage of the scene viewed from innumerable angles, most of which had no tactical usefulness that I could see. Some were from locations at sea-level, some only gave images of rigging, and there was even one situated a few feet below the surface.

I followed the King around, remembering his warning of the devastation which would ensue from Britain's defeat. "But what will happen if we win?" I asked him.

"Do not be concerned," he told me. "Current events are in the present time, and will be completed with the cessation of the war."

"But something must happen afterward."

"Subsequent events are not these events." A monstrous swinging pattern, made of bits and pieces of hulls and gunfire, built up mysteriously in the chaos of the screens, and dissolved again. The King turned to go outside.

When he returned, the pattern had begun again, with modifications. I continued: "If you believe that, why do you talk about Britain's welfare?"

He applied himself to watching the screens, still showing no deviation from his norm, in a situation which to a normal man would have been crisis. "All Britain is mine," he said after his normal pause. "Therefore I make arrangements for its protection. That is comprehensible to us both, I think."

He swiveled his head toward me. "Why do you inquire in this way, Smith? These questions are not the way to knowledge."

Having been rebuked thus—if a being with a personality like atonal music can be said to rebuke—I too went outside, and peered below. The interpenetrated array seemed suddenly like male and female. Our own more neatly shaped ships moved lightly, while the weighty, pounding Brazilians were more demonstratively aggressive, and even had long gun turrets for symbolism. Some slower part of my mind commented that the female is alleged to be the submissive, receptive part, which our fleet was not; but I dismissed that.

After two hours the outcome still looked indefinite to my mind. But Hotch decided he had seen enough. He acted.

A vessel which hitherto had kept to the outskirts of the battle and taken little part, abruptly opened up its decks and lifted a series of rocket ramps. Three minutes later, the missiles had disappeared into the sky and I guessed what warheads they carried.

Everything fitted neatly: it was a natural decision on Hotch's part. In such a short time he had not been able to develop transatlantic rockets, and he might never again be this close to the cities of Brazil. I could see him adding it all up in his mind.

Any kind of aeronautics was outlawed, and the Brazilians became enraged. They used their guns with a fury such as I hope never to see again. And I was surprised at how damaging a momentum a few thousand tons of fast-moving steel can acquire. Our own boys were a bit ragged

236

in their defense at first, because they were busy butchering the King's men.

With the new weapons, most of this latter was over in twenty minutes. I went inside, because by now weapons were being directed at the aircraft, and the energies were approaching the limits of its defensive capacity.

The hundred viewpoints adopted by the viewing screens had converted the battle-scene into a flurry too quick for my eyes to follow. The King asked my advice.

My most immediate suggestion was already in effect. Slowly, because the defense screens were draining power, we ascended into the stratosphere. The rest of what I had to say look longer, and was more difficult, but I told it all.

The King made no comment on my confession, but studied the sea. I withdrew into the background, feeling uncomfortable.

The arrangement of vision screens was obsolete now that the battle-plan had been disrupted. Subsidiaries were set up to show the struggle in a simpler form. By the time we came to rest in the upper air, Hotch had rallied his navy and was holding his own in a suddenly bitter engagement.

The King ordered other screens to be focused on Brazil. He still did not look at me.

After he had watched developments for a short time, he decided to meditate in solitude, as was his habit. I don't know whether it was carelessness or simple ignorance, but without a pause he opened the door and stepped onto the outside balcony.

Fortunately, the door opened and closed like a shutter; the air replenishers worked very swiftly, and the air density was seriously low for less than a second. Even so, it was very unpleasant.

Emerging from the experience, I saw the King standing pensively outside in the partial vacuum of the upper air. I swore with surprise: it was hot out there, and even the sunlight shining through the filtered windows was more than I could tolerate.

When he returned, he was considerate enough to use another door.

By this time the monitor screens had detected the squadrons of bombers rising in retaliation from Brazil's devastated cities. The etiquette of the old war was abandoned, and there was no doubt that they too carried the nuclear weapons illegally employed by Hotch.

The King observed: "When those bombers reach their delivery area in a few hours time, most of Britain's fighting power will still be a month away in the Western Atlantic. Perhaps the islands should be warned to prepare what defenses they have." His gem eyes lifted. "What do you say, Smith?"

"Of course they must be warned!" I replied quickly. "There is still an air defense—Hotch has kept the old skills alive. But he may not have expected such quick reprisals, and early interception is essential."

"I see. This man Hotch seems a skillful organizer, Smith, and would be needed in London." With interest, he watched the drive and ferocity of the action on the seascape. "Which is his ship?"

I pointed out the large swan-boat on which I believed Hotch to be present. Too suddenly for our arrival to be anticipated, we dropped from the sky. The servants of the King conducted a lightning raid which made a captive of Hotch with 30 percent casualties.

We had been absent from the stratosphere for two minutes and forty-five seconds.

Hotch himself wasn't impressed. He accused me of bad timing. "You may be right," I said, and told him the story.

If he was surprised he didn't show it. He raised his eyebrows, but that was all. No matter how grave the situation may be, Hotch wouldn't let it show.

"It's a native war from now on," he acclaimed. "There's not an alien left in either fleet."

"You mean the Brazilians rebelled too?"

"I wish they would! The green bosses hopped it and left them to it."

The King offered to put Hotch down at Buckingham Palace, the center of all the official machinery. Hotch greeted the suggestion with scorn.

"That stuff's no good to me," he said. "Put me down at my headquarters in Balham. That's the only chance of getting our fighter planes in the air."

This we did. The pilots had already set the aircraft in silent motion through the stratosphere, and within an hour we slanted downward and flashed the remaining five hundred miles to England.

London was peaceful as we hovered above it three hours in advance of the raiders. Only Hotch's impatient energy indicated the air of urgency it would shortly assume.

But what happened on Earth after that, I don't know. We went into space, so I have only a casual interest.

It's like this: the King showed me space.

To see it with the bare eyes is enough, but on the King's set of multi- and null-viewpoint vision screens it really gets hammered in. And what gets knocked into you is this: nothing matters. Nothing is big enough to matter. It's as simple as that.

However big a thing is, it just isn't big enough. For when you see the size of totality—I begin to understand now why the King, who has seen it all the time, is as he is.

And nothing is important. There is only a stratified universe, with some things more powerful than others. That's what makes us think they are important—they're more powerful, but that's all. And the most powerful is no more significant than the least.

You may wonder, then, why the King bothers with such trivial affairs as Britain. That's easy.

When I was a young man, I thought a lot of myself. I thought myself valuable, if only to myself. And once, I began to wonder just how much it would take for me to sacrifice my life, whether if it came to it I would sacrifice for a less intelligent, less worthwhile life than my own. But now I see the sacrifice for what it is: simply one insignificance for another insignificance. It's an easy trade. So the King, who has ranged over a dozen galaxies, has lost his war, his army, and risks even his own life, for Britain's sake. It's all too tiny even to hesitate over. He did what he could: how could he do anything else?

Like the King, I am quickly becoming incapable of judgment. But before it goes altogether, I will say this of you, Hotch: It was a low trick you played on the King. A low, dirty trick to play on a good man.

239

46